The Execution of Bannière.

Drawn and etched by E. Van Muyden.

OLYMPE DE CLÈVES. II. *Frontispiece.*

OLYMPE DE CLÈVES ❧ ❧ ❧ A ROMANCE OF THE COURT OF LOUIS XV. ❧ ❧ BY ALEXANDRE DUMAS ❧ VOLUME TWO ❧

Fredonia Books
Amsterdam. The Netherlands

Olympe de Clèves:
A Romance of the Court of Luis XV (Volume Two)

by
Alexandre Dumas

ISBN: 1-58963-316-4

Reprinted from the 1893 edition

Fredonia Books
Amsterdam, The Netherlands
http://www.fredoniabooks.com

In order to make original editions of historical works available to scholars at an economical price, this facsimile of the original edition of 1893 is reproduced from the best available copy and has been digitally enhanced to improve legibility, but the text remains unaltered to retain historical authenticity.

CONTENTS.

————•————

CONTENTS.

OLYMPE DE CLÈVES.

I.

MONSIEUR DE FRÉJUS' VALET-DE-CHAMBRE.

MONSIEUR DE RICHELIEU had given his word to the king, and did not propose to break it. He went therefore the next day to call upon Monsieur le Cardinal de Fleury, in the capacity of an ambassador returning from his mission.

Monsieur le Cardinal de Fleury, ex-bishop of Fréjus, deserves a few descriptive strokes of our pen, if for no other purpose than to enable the reader to understand the part which he is to play in this narrative.

He was, at the date in question, a scheming, blasé, old churchman, as Beaumarchais called him later; an aged man, with a young man's passion for intrigue, a mind fertile in paltry schemes, which he had studied up at his leisure during the reign of Louis XIV. under cover of the skirts of Père La Chaise and Madame de Maintenon.

He knew the court thoroughly, and he was sure of the king; several attempts which had been made to oust him had turned to the confusion of his enemies, and yet he had not appeared to exult in his triumph in the least.

On the contrary, at each new demonstration of his power, he seemed to become even more humble than before.

On three critical occasions, when his influence had seemed to be trembling in the balance, the young king had demanded, with tears and shrieks of anger, the return of his old master, who had accustomed him to playthings and bonbons, and the utmost liberty in everything which did not tend to alienate him from himself.

Thus Fleury possessed the secret which enables men to take the measure of all those with whom they have to deal, — a secret of marvellous efficacy to one who aims at real power; the talent of hiding behind a throne, and pulling hidden wires which move the arms and tongue of the automaton who struts about with the high-sounding title of king.

At this moment it was Fleury's aim to get rid of Monsieur le Duc de Bourbon, First Minister, whose appointment to that office after the regent's death had been made at the suggestion of the cardinal himself.

Scandalous tongues whispered that Fleury aspired to hold the reins of government himself; people devoid of susceptibility declared that Monsieur le Duc deserved the cardinal's hostility on account of his manner of life, which perpetuated the memories of the regency, under a king whose character thus far seemed to be essentially moral and reformative.

The fact is that Monsieur de Bourbon, or rather Madame de Prie, longed to overthrow the cardinal, who was not in sympathy with the queen, and that the cardinal was looking for weak points in the armor of the minister, and testing it in all the joints at all times.

From the conversation between the Duc de Richelieu

and Madame de Prie we know what Monsieur le Duc's vulnerable spots were; and perhaps it is to be wondered at that there was not more real sympathy between those whose moral qualities were so well matched.

But the reader who should make up his mind in this matter without considering Monsieur de Richelieu would incur great risk of going astray. That gentleman had not returned from Vienna to hold himself aloof from all these court intrigues of which our sojourn in the provinces has kept us in ignorance thus far, but in which we are now about to plunge up to the waist.

The duke made his appearance at the cardinal's apartments.

Fleury, carrying simplicity to such a point that it became parade, spent most of his time at Issy, at the convent of his friends the Sulpicians, and assisted them to the utmost of his power in persecuting the Jansenists of France.

He had studied theology most thoroughly before passing to transcendental politics.

Accompanied by his confessor, the Abbé de Polet, and Barjac, his valet-de-chambre, each of whom possessed great influence over him, he went back and forth to Issy with an affectation of great modesty, — the modesty of a priest who had become cardinal, and hoped to become Pope!

The courtier mob was always very assiduous in calling upon him at Issy, when he, cardinal, governor of the king, and master of France, vouchsafed to allow the doors of that hermitage to be opened, — doors at which every one must humbly knock, and which were better guarded than those of the Louvre.

There Monsieur Hercule de Fleury secretly formed a court of his own, the primary purpose of which was to

aid him in his ambitious designs, and raise him to that
height of power which he secretly coveted.

Affecting good fellowship with the sons of the " roués "
of the regency, who dared not, in the presence of the
king's former preceptor, sit at the table where their
fathers, boon companions of the regent, had celebrated
their nightly orgies, the bishop had, properly speaking,
no declared enemy.

I except the military class, who had been clever
enough to see through him; but it was a rare faculty at
that time.

The cast of the old preceptor's mind was entirely
unique; it was so constituted as to prevent him from ever
lifting the veil even from what he wished to expose to
view.

People with a specialty always think they have solved
the problem of universality. To excel in one thing is to
offend the whole race of envious men, and to arouse more
hard feeling than perfection in all directions.

Thus the common herd of courtiers had as much vener-
ation for and confidence in Monsieur de Fleury, as the
old prelate could possibly ask for. Although his ambition was carefully concealed in his own bosom, heavily
veiled, if one may so speak, yet a class of people so clear-
sighted as those who always infest the antechambers of a
new court were able to divine how high a position he
might occupy if he chose; he seemed to despise it, and
he was generally thought the more of at court for despis-
ing it.

The bishop, clever diplomatist that he was, availed
himself with admirable tact of the partial favors which
were calculated to pave his way to the possession of the
absolute power which he coveted.

Mazarin, that pupil of Richelieu, who replaced Louis

XIII. in the bed of Anne of Austria, and built up for himself a degree of power which the cardinal his predecessor had tried in vain to acquire,— Mazarin and Richelieu seemed to Fleury to be mere pygmies, compared with the figure which he himself hoped to make, with the aid of the favorable opportunities which seemed to be in store for him.

This man of humble origin, raised to his present elevation by the merest chance, had been offered a peerage in the new promotion, and had refused it with contempt.

He had neither the power nor the inclination to ascend the uncertain rounds of the ladder of power too quickly. He preferred a slower but less perilous progress. The rounds upon which everything seemed to make it advisable for him to rest his weight were too weak in his eyes, and would have given way under him.

To prepare day after day some petty intrigue for the morrow; to work one week so as to score a point the following week, if the whim seized him; to search throughout a whole month the means of scoring a point the following month, if his inspiration did not fail him, — such was his life, such his incessant occupation, since his interests had connected him with the court. Louis XV., great-grandson of Louis XIV., who might say, like his ancestor, "I am the State!" could not say that he belonged to France, or even that he belonged to himself; he was Fleury's, and Fleury had raised himself to power on his own account, and to forward his own fortunes.

Thus it was that Fleury was jealous of everybody, especially of the queen,— the first object of the king's idolatry, when the lessons of his preceptor ceased, and his playthings became indifferent to him.

The queen appreciated the situation; she returned Fleury's hatred, and undertook to counterbalance his influence with the Duc de Bourbon and Madame de Prie, her sponsors when her alliance with the kingdom of France was entered into.

Richelieu, the night before his visit to Issy, by accepting the queen's cold reception without a struggle, had managed his cards so as to facilitate a close alliance with the cardinal. We will follow him as he goes to Issy to carry out the details of his game.

Fleury was expecting him. This hermit, this man of simple habits, knew what took place at court better than the lieutenant of police.

Richelieu, fully informed as to his habits, prepared on the journey to accommodate himself to them. He had reason to congratulate himself that he had done so, for in the reception-room he encountered Barjac.

This Barjac was a singular sort of man; grown old in the service of the cardinal, whose fortunes he had helped to build and to support, Barjac had acquired by thirty years of fidelity and devotion such an ascendancy over his master that the latter yielded to him not only the material direction of his life, but a good part of the spiritual as well.

Barjac owed his master's confidence and his own influence to very great tact combined with a strong admixture of outspokenness; he really loved and admired the cardinal,— a fact which was in itself no mean proof of his good disposition; and as he was sincerely devoted to the cardinal's interests, he was excused for paying some little attention to his own.

A political valet he was; he said *we* in speaking of business matters, just as he used to say *our plate* and *our estate* in speaking of Monsieur de Fréjus' private affairs.

To be on the right side of Barjac was an essential requisite in dealing with His Grandeur, who very frequently, when his own table was full, would send the most distinquished courtiers to Barjac's quarters, with these words, —

"There is no more room here; go and dine with Barjac."

In the remark of Cardinal Richelieu, "Messieurs, I claim to serve the king," and Fleury's, "Messieurs, go and dine with Barjac," is included the whole history of France from 1620 to 1720, a century of decrepitude and servility.

But this omnipotent Barjac was nobody's fool, nor was he easily led by burning incense at his feet; many a courtier had burned his fingers in the attempt. Barjac was very clever in pouring the hot coals upon those who waved the vessel unskilfully.

One day a certain duke and peer, coming to dine with him, had saluted and embraced him, and shown him a thousand familiar attentions at table, as from equal to equal. Barjac rose, took a napkin in each hand, and waited upon the great man, saying, —

"Monsieur, since you forget yourself thus with Barjac, it is doubly important that poor Barjac should not forget the respect due to you."

Such an antagonist was not easy to subdue.

Richelieu entered the reception-room.

"Ah, Barjac, good morning!" said he; "how are you?"

"Monsieur le Duc!" cried Barjac, with an assumed expression of open-mouthed astonishment.

"Home from a long distance, Barjac! Ah! you are growing stout, my friend."

"Do you think so, Monsieur le Duc?"

"That's the result of not bothering one's brain with politics!"

Barjac smiled significantly.

" Monseigneur has had a pleasant journey ? " said he.

" Excellent! Is Monsieur de Fréjus visible ? "

" He was not expecting you, but he will be very glad to see you."

" You will do me a great service, my dear Barjac, if you can arrange it so that I may see him alone."

" One moment, please," said Barjac; " we have a lot of people this morning, all on last week's business. It 's the remains of that wretched Spanish affair, of which you know something."

" Yes," said Richelieu; " her Catholic Majesty absolutely will not listen to reason."

" After all," said Barjac, " we must admit that we wounded her cruelly in sending back the Infante. Put yourself in her place, Monsieur le Duc! Suppose you had children established in a foreign land, and they should be unceremoniously sent back to you, like lost merchandise ? "

" You are right, it will last forever."

" Only on the part of the Queen of Spain; for the king — "

" Oh! his Catholic Majesty Philippe V. bears no malice; indeed he hardly has any reason to do so now. But tell me, dear Barjac, will Monsieur le Cardinal keep me waiting long ? "

Barjac, the valet Barjac, whose petty eminence never availed to put him at ease in the presence of noble blood, which always subdued his pretensions, was delighted with the duke's lapses into familiarity, and made off at once to announce him to the cardinal.

The duke was immediately ushered into the presence.

As he appeared upon the theshold, a stern-featured old man, of fine carriage, who was seated beside Fleury, rose, bowed with much gravity, and left the room, not without recognizing the formal, self-important salute of Monsieur de Richelieu.

This old man was second only to Monsieur de Fleury in power; we ought rather to say that he shared his power.

It was Père Polet, his confessor, the implacable persecutor of the Jansenists, who needed only Louis XIV. and an opportunity, to banish the heresies of Messieurs Arnauld and Nicolle from French soil.

The duke remained alone with the cardinal.

II.

MONSIEUR DE FRÉJUS, PRECEPTOR OF KING LOUIS XV.

THE cardinal was advanced in years, but still vigorous. To an unctuous and persuasive amiability he added a sort of pulpit eloquence which at certain times and on certain subjects gave to these private interviews the solemnity which his absolute lack of genius made impossible on great occasions.

He had the calm, piercing gaze of the priest, accustomed to look beneath the spoken thought and to search the conscience.

In what one said to him he listened only to what one did not say. He paid little attention to the form of speech, and rarely failed to divine what lay behind it.

Monsieur de Fleury, Abbé at first, then Bishop of Fréjus, then Cardinal, — a man of moderate parts, and who nevertheless occupied for a long time the loftiest position in Europe, absolute in his apparent humility, — Monsieur de Fleury, we say, followed out the traditions of the last reign in his policy for twenty years. You would have said that Louis XIV. was away for a while, and Père Le Tellier was filling the vacancy.

Fleury began by greeting Richelieu with much courtesy; and the ambassador, as may be imagined, was not behindhand with him. With his unfailing tact, he had divined, from Monsieur de Fleury's manner of saluting him and from his expression, that he might be of good courage.

The cardinal complimented him in fitting terms upon the success of his mission to the emperor.

"Monseigneur," replied Richelieu, "my task was an easy one, for I had your suggestions to guide me."

"That makes no difference," said Fleury; "it was difficult for one so young as you to convince those Germans, whose brains work slowly from their cradles."

Richelieu smiled.

"Monseigneur," he replied, "appearances have misled you. I am no longer young."

"So they say," said Monsieur de Fréjus, smiling in his turn. "Can it be true?"

"Oh, in one word, Monseigneur, I can make you understand why I no longer need to be young."

"Say that word, Monsieur le Duc."

"I have become ambitious."

"Good! That ought to happen sooner or later to the grand-nephew of the great cardinal."

"Well, Monseigneur, it has happened."

"Does your ambition tend toward a military or a diplomatic career?"

"Either, as his Majesty may choose."

As he said these words, the duke bowed in a way to make clear to Fleury that although he put a false address on the letter he was mailing, he desired that it should reach the person for whom it was intended.

Fleury gave him a friendly little nod, which implied that he perfectly understood him.

"You are in favor with the king, Monsieur le Duc?" asked he.

"I hope so, Monsieur. I arrived home only day before yesterday, and I have bothered nobody for two years."

"How did you find the king?"

"Delightful."

"Is he not?"

"And his manners truly royal, upon my word —
Only —"

"Only what, pray?" demanded Monsieur de Fréjus.

"Well, if I must say it, the king is bored to distraction."

"What's that you say?"

"Official information, Monseigneur; for it was the
king in person who instructed me to convey it to
you."

"The king is bored?"

"Yes, bored to death."

"It isn't possible!"

"It is really so, Monseigneur."

"He told you so himself?"

"Last evening, in so many words."

"Where was it?"

"At the queen's card-party, which I attended, as duty
demanded."

The last six words interrupted a grimace upon the
cardinal's lips, where the first five had caused it to
appear.

"Oh! indeed, this news is of the last importance!"
said the cardinal, happy to be fairly drawn into the conversation by Richelieu's delicate tact. "Let us look
into this, Monsieur le Duc, if you have a moment to
give me."

"All my life, Monsieur."

"Well, then, let us avail ourselves of it to talk a
little."

He rang, and Barjac appeared.

"Turn everybody away, Barjac," said he; "I am
tired, and shall not see anybody else to-day."

Barjac smiled at Richelieu and went out.

"I cannot get over what you just told me!" cried Monsieur de Fréjus; "and if it were not you — "

"You know that I do not lie any more."

"Not any more, — never?"

"No, Monseigneur, never!"

"Oh, Duke!"

"Upon my honor! Except at Vienna, to the Spaniards; even then it was but two or three times."

"For the good of the service?"

"I had absolution for it."

"Extraordinary man! you are still the same?"

"Oh, no, Monseigneur; I have already told you that I am so changed that I can't recognize myself now."

"I mean that you must still be attended to before any one else."

"That's not my fault, Monseigneur."

"Whose is it then, pray?"

"It is the fault of the people who are kind enough to make me out of more importance than I really am."

"For instance, I intended to speak to you about the king only, and have ended by speaking about nobody but yourself."

"A wretched subject, Monseigneur."

"Don't laugh. You say that you really procured absolution, do you?"

"Yes, Monseigneur, for I am very devout."

"Ah, Duke!" said the old fellow, shaking his head, "I seem still to hear in my ears the buzzing of certain reports from Vienna which are rather inconsistent with all these miracles of conversion."

"I know what you mean, unless I am much mistaken," rejoined Richelieu.

"Yes, a certain episode — "

"Of sorcery?"

"Precisely so."

"Pray, Monseigneur, do me, a poor foreigner, the honor to tell me how the story was told here; then I will myself give you the true version."

"Oh, it's quite short. It was said that you and the Abbé de Sinzendorf went to make some experiments in natural magic."

"Where, Monseigneur?"

"In an out-of-the-way spot, near Vienna,— a stone-quarry, I believe, — and that there, the magician having shown you too much or too little of the devil, you had a quarrel with him, as a sequel to which the poor devil (I mean the magician of course) was found dead, — let us not mince words, — murdered."

"All this is the exact truth, Monseigneur, except that just one word should be stricken out — "

"The word 'murdered,' is it not?"

"If you please."

"Neither you nor Monsieur de Sinzendorf, then — "

"Neither Monsieur de Sinzendorf nor myself murdered the magician."

"He died, however?"

"It is true that he played us that scurvy trick; but this is how the thing came about."

"Let's hear it."

"Monsieur de Sinzendorf and myself both had our horoscopes cast."

"You admit it?"

"Yes, Monseigneur, and there was the sin."

Monsieur de Fleury signified his approval as a theologian by a nod of the head.

"The sorcerer began by telling us a few truths and many lies. He posted us on certain court secrets, un-known in diplomatic circles."

"Aha! he was a sorcerer of good family, then?"

"Then he offered to procure for each of us what would please us most."

"You asked him, I suppose, that you might always be a favorite with the ladies ? "

"*Mon Dieu!* No, Monseigneur, that's just the difficulty. I was fatuous enough to think that that request was unnecessary."

"Indeed! "

"I asked for the key to the heart of princes."

"Oh, yes, I see, I see; your ambitious ideas were to the fore."

"They began to germinate about that time, Monseigneur."

"Well, did he supply you with that key ? "

"Monseigneur, the business was just coming to a close, when an unexpected event interfered with our plans. Monsieur de Sinzendorf, caring little for the key to the heart of princes, since he claimed to possess it already, asked for the key to the female heart."

"The sorcerer could thus content both, without disobliging either."

"The drama begins at this point, Monseigneur. Scarcely had he let fall those careless words than the sorcerer replied that, for certain people, the key to the hearts of women was a useless piece of furniture, since women have no hearts."

"Oho! " exclaimed Monsieur de Fleury.

"That was a slight exaggeration; so thought Monsieur de Sinzendorf, who caught the ball on the bound, and denounced the sorcerer's statement as a slander."

"Pshaw! "

"It was but natural, Monseigneur. Monsieur de Sinzendorf was at that moment deeply attached to a lady upon whose affection he believed he could rely."

"*Vanitas vanitatum,*" muttered Monsieur de Fleury.

"Whether the sorcerer had heard of this passion, or really divined it by his art, he retorted: 'Monsieur, Madame ——, whom you love, is the worst example you could select to support your opinion of women.'"

"Oho!" said Fleury, "there was no button on that foil."

"No, and it cut Monsieur de Sinzendorf to the quick, an angry flush rose to his temples.

"'Villain!' he cried, 'you lie!'

"'Monsieur,' the sorcerer replied calmly, 'one ought never to give the lie to anybody, still less to a sorcerer,—especially one ought never to insult a man whom one has disturbed for one's own purposes.'"

"A very sensitive sorcerer that."

"That is just the thought that came to my mind, Monseigneur. His sensitiveness surprised me. It seemed to me that I could see something more under all this than Monsieur de Sinzendorf believed himself to have seen. The spot was ill-chosen, as you said, Monseigneur. We were in the midst of the quarries, a league from Vienna, and in the night-time, without other light than that cast by a sickly moon. The sorcerer seemed a man accustomed to solitude, and quite ready to take advantage of it. I made a sign to Monsieur de Sinzendorf to keep quiet, but it was too late. He had steam up, and I could not stop him. He defied the sorcerer to prove anything discreditable to Madame ——."

"And what said the sorcerer then?" asked Monsieur de Fleury.

"Ah, Monseigneur, the sorcerer's evil genius urged him on. He talked and talked nearly half an hour, and in that space he told Monsieur de Sinzendorf, who shrivelled up and flushed and turned white as he heard,—told him things which made me laugh and tremble at the same time."

"What sort of a man was he, in Heaven's name?"

"He was an unfortunate man, Monseigneur; he drove Monsieur de Sinzendorf to desperation, and he undertook to chastise him; seeing which, the accursed sorcerer drew from some hiding-place among the rocks a short, thick sword, and received Monsieur de Sinzendorf's attack so roughly that the game bade fair to become disastrous for my companion."

"What sort of a man was the abbé?" asked Monsieur de Fleury.

"The abbé was a well-taught and well-set-up man, but he had a dangerous opponent to deal with. He was attacked by the sorcerer with such vigor that I thought it was high time for me to become an actor in the drama instead of a simple spectator. My purpose was to save Monsieur de Sinzendorf's life; a false step would have been the end of him; he was completely overmatched. He slipped back and fell; the sorcerer leaped upon him to make an end of him."

"Why, was it the devil himself?"

"His Satanic Majesty *in propria persona*, Monseigneur. I thought so all the time; and the proof — "

"Ah! you have a proof?"

"Yes, Monseigneur, the proof is that he received from me a sword-thrust which entered over the right nipple and came out below the left shoulder, and that not one drop of blood issued from either wound."

"Indeed! but you see that he did receive a thrust of your sword, Duke."

"Yes, and two from Monsieur de Sinzendorf, who was put at his ease again by my succor. We were acting legitimately in self-defence, and my conscience does not reproach me in the least."

"At all events, you slew the devil; that's the thing that stands out most prominently in all this."

"Monseigneur knows the proverb: 'Better to kill the devil than that the devil — '"

"'Should kill you.' Poor sorcerer! what a pity that he had two madmen like you to deal with! If I had been there in your place, the sorcerer would not have insulted me, nor I the sorcerer. I should have learned all that you learned, and many things besides: such is the reward of patience."

"Oh, Monseigneur, although we were a little hasty, I agree, still the poor devil had had time to tell us a quantity of fine things."

"I believe you; but let us return, I beg, to your conversion."

"It dates from that time, Monseigneur. Being guilty of having almost slain a man for reasons that were far from satisfactory, I broke off all relations with women, with curiosity, and with anger, which are the three principal stumbling-blocks in life."

"But what did the sorcerer tell you?"

"Well, Monseigneur, he pointed out to me an infallible method of making myself the object of the favor of kings."

"Did he require you to swear secrecy?"

"Monseigneur, I certainly could give no lessons on the subject to you, whom the king fairly idolizes; so let me retain for my own use such flowers as I pluck along the road."

"If you are determined to be reticent, keep your plan of operations to yourself; but pray put it in execution at once, Monsieur le Duc. The king is bored, you say; win his favor, then, by diverting his mind."

"That is precisely what I have in view, Monseigneur; it is also the reason of my visit to Issy."

"To Issy, Monsieur le Duc," cried the cardinal, who thought that Richelieu was surrendering too soon, and who preferred that the negotiations should be a little more spun out. "You say that you came to Issy to divert the king? Ah, Monsieur le Duc, what do you expect to find here to report to the king, unless it is weariness and ennui far greater than his own?"

"But you fail to comprehend my meaning, Monseigneur," said the duke. "I never intended to vex with worldly matters the pious retirement in which you live; God forbid! Further than that, my ideas are not worldly."

The cardinal fixed his penetrating glance upon the duke, as if to ask him what sort of ideas he could have, other than those which he was expected to have.

But the duke had studied his part carefully.

"Monseigneur," he continued, "I have done much thinking since I saw how depressed the king is, and my mind has been busy inventing means of diverting him; it is with regard to those means that I desire to ask your advice."

"Ah, that is something like!" cried Fleury. "Go on, Monsieur le Duc, go on! You are a clever fellow, and in the matter of agreeable diversions I think that your opinion must be of the greatest weight. The king turned in the right direction when he turned to you."

Richelieu smiled modestly, like a preacher whom one praises before the sermon.

"Monseigneur," he said, "I have very accurate knowledge of the sentiment which all the kings of Europe have conceived for our young king. It is not mere friendship; it is a sort of paternal feeling, with even

more affection than that word implies. It is what one
might call a combination of love and interest."

"What is he coming at?" the cardinal asked himself,
resting his elbows upon the table, and seeking to detect
the orator's secret thoughts.

"You have learned," continued Richelieu, "that his
Majesty is universally called the 'Child of Europe'?"

"I have been told so," replied Fleury; "but I don't
quite see — "

"Where I am coming out? I am out now, Monseigneur. With such an expert logician as yourself, I
thought that I ought not to neglect the precaution of an
exordium. I have to suggest to you a course of travel
for the king."

"Travel!" cried Fleury.

"Receptions without end, illuminations everywhere,
acclamations of the people, banquets, processions, sea-
voyages, will form a source of entertainment which can
be made to last for six months, if desired."

"Have the king travel for six months!" repeated the
bewildered prelate; "why, you can't mean it, Monsieur
le Duc! It is n't possible that you advise me in sober
earnest to part from the king for six months!"

"You would not part from the king, Monseigneur,
because you would go too."

"I accompany the king!" continued Fleury, moving
about uneasily upon his chair. "I live amid continual
bustle and confusion! I travel a thousand leagues!
Ah, Monsieur le Duc, were you really speaking
seriously?"

"With the utmost seriousness of which I am capable,
Monseigneur."

"What! kill the king for the sake of amusing him!
and kill me too!"

"Oh, Monseigneur, one can travel so comfortably these days; and then what a keystone for a powerful alliance! It would be to build a bridge from France to each of the kingdoms now separated from her by hostile feeling."

The cardinal shook his head with the discouraged expression which the cleverest diplomats cannot dissemble, when their dupe, instead of putting his foot in the trap they have set, slips away and forces them to new combinations.

Richelieu, while apparently disappointed by the small success of his first proposition, was inwardly enjoying the old man's cruel discomfiture.

"Your idea, Monsieur le Duc, may be a most excellent one," the cardinal replied; "but unfortunately it is impracticable."

"Let us give up all hope of diverting the king from his ennui," said Richelieu, struggling with a sigh of enormous proportions.

"You, with your inventive powers, have been able to think of no expedient but that?" queried the cardinal.

"Alas! no, Monseigneur."

"Allow me to suggest to you that if, when you were of the king's age, your father had compelled you to travel with your preceptor, you would not have considered the prospect especially agreeable."

"Oh!" cried Richelieu, "no, indeed, Monseigneur; but what a difference there is between the king and myself! I was born with every evil instinct, and soon acquired all the vices. The king on the other hand has a depth of religious feeling and faith and an abundance of moral principle which fairly amaze me."

"True," said Fleury.

"I was a perverse subject," continued Richelieu; "the

king is a saint. To educate a gentleman is to improve him; to educate a king is to ruin him."

"True, true, and very well put!" cried Fleury, waxing enthusiastic over the maxim which he had so often exposed as his own guide; "but after all, because a king is a king, need he die of ennui?"

"This ennui, Monseigneur, is one of the attributes of royalty."

"Oh, Duke! Duke!"

"Then, Monseigneur, let the king attend to public affairs himself; let him consult with his ministers and manage the finances; let him — let him go to war, and he will not be troubled with ennui."

"You go from one extremity to the other, Duke," said the cardinal, in some alarm. "Divert the king by setting Europe afire, forsooth! and yet you say that you are sobering down!"

"I don't know, then," said Richelieu, sanctimoniously; "but I confess that, having proposed travel, work, and war — "

"Let us think whether there is not something else."

"Most willingly."

"What is there, for instance, in the way of interesting avocations?"

"There is floriculture," said Richelieu; "but the king is rather tired of beanstalks."

The cardinal flushed slightly, but the duke's perfect good faith was so apparent that he could not be angry.

"There is gaming too," said Richelieu.

"That is not a fit amusement for a holy man, Duke; especially is it ill-suited to a king. When the king plays and wins, the nobles lose; when he plays and loses, the people have to pay."

"The chase?"

"Oh, the king hunts too much now."

"Do you know this is decidedly perplexing; war, travel, work, play, all out of the question. Oh, I forgot one thing which was excessively diverting to Louis XIV., but which his great-grandson has never been suspected of."

"What's that, pray?"

"Buildings, Monseigneur."

"The subject has never been in the king's mind, Duke."

"His Majesty, only eighteen years old, has exhausted all means of amusement! What can we do? His great-grandfather did n't arrive at that wretched state until he was sixty."

With that Richelieu became silent.

Fleury, after watching him a few moments, mildly ventured a few words.

"I am," said he, "the most wretched adviser that the poor prince could have. Being a priest, and advanced in years, I have no right to awaken in him the love of sin."

"Not even the sin of love," said Richelieu, laughing with well-considered freedom.

Fleury looked fixedly at him, and seemed disconcerted by his perfect self-possession.

"A terrible sin that!" said he, in a voice that was hardly audible.

"Which there is no cause to fear that Louis XV. will commit," added Richelieu. "The king's love is his wife."

Fleury had nothing to say to this.

"In fact," continued the duke, "how is it that the king, being so deeply in love, suffers from ennui? There's a problem for you. The king is mad with love for the queen, and yet ennui has fastened upon him. The king is a model husband, and still he is bored to death! An incomprehensible state of things truly! You, Monseigneur, who know all the king's secret thoughts — "

The cardinal sighed very noisily.

"What's the matter?" Richelieu asked him.

Again he sighed.

"*Mon Dieu!* Monseigneur, you terrify me; can it be that the king and queen — "

"Ah, Duke!"

"What, this apparent affection! Oh, it is not possible! Last night only, the king gazed at his wife with eyes that shone like diamonds."

"Duke, I don't know whether the Viennese sorcerer revealed all other secrets to you, but this one he seems to have omitted."

"I come down from my high horse, Monseigneur."

"Listen, Duke; up to a certain point the king is excusable. He was born with an exacting disposition; he is indeed the true descendant of his great-grandfather."

"And the queen is a straight-laced German, is she not?"

"Alas! in that fact lies the cause of my despair!"

"*Mon Dieu!* Monseigneur, but we must straighten out this complication. By so doing we shall assure the repose of the whole world, as well as the welfare of our masters."

"Yes, Duke, yes, we certainly must; for if the king is once really bored and weary, where may he not turn for distraction? It is horrible to think of!"

"You say, Monseigneur, that the king is endowed with a very vigorous and ardent temperament?"

"Fiery, Monsieur le Duc."

"I have always heard that such temperaments needed

to be either subdued or weakened. To subdue them is often impossible, but to weaken them is more practicable. Are not certain means employed to that end, particularly in the religious orders?"

"You refer to those processes which are called *minuantes*, Monsieur le Duc; *minuantes* comes from the Latin word *diminuere*. In the cloisters we call them *minutions*, and the Carthusians are required to submit to them once a year."

"Well, Monseigneur, we might consider — Violent exercise, tennis for instance, swimming, and strict diet."

"Monsieur le Duc, we have agreed, and let us not forget it, that the king is bored, and that we desire to divert him."

"Yes, Monseigneur, it is essential to find something to distract the king's mind from himself."

"I know it well, Monsieur le Duc."

"It is quite true that those things I mentioned would not amuse him. The *minutions* are remedies, and not diversions; let us pass them by."

"I have one scruple, Monsieur le Duc, — you, like a worthy gentleman, will appreciate it: the king's person is sacred, is it not?"

"Inviolable."

"It seems to me, then, that it would be an invasion of that inviolability to bleed the king and to deprive him of food. The process is — "

"Monkish and surgical, true; some ministerial process would be much better."

"You would not resort to it, Monsieur le Duc?"

"I would prefer, I admit, to give all my own blood to the king, and die of hunger myself, to enable him to eat as appetite demands and act according to his natural disposition."

"You see, Duke, we come back to where we started from."

Once more Richelieu's mouth was closed.

"Just now," said Fleury, "a thought came into my head, apropos of that scruple of mine; he who says scruple creates at once a case of conscience. Here is one which presented itself to my mind."

"I am here to listen to you, Monseigneur, and I am listening with all my ears."

"Let us admit that the king, who is the master, — for after all he is the master, — let us admit, I say, that he does as he chooses — "

"We must admit it, Monseigneur."

"That it then becomes our duty — "

"To bow before him, Monseigneur."

"Even if he does wrong?"

"To pity him in that event, and not imitate him," said Richelieu, piously.

"Admirably said, Duke. Now give ear to my case of conscience. Suppose, for instance, that while hunting the king's horse should bolt with him, and be on the point of jumping with him into a ditch twenty feet deep, but that there was on the way another smaller ditch, only three or four feet deep at most — "

"Monseigneur, I would hamstring the horse, so that he would drop the king in the little ditch."

"Would you not? Follow my reasoning, Monsieur le Duc, follow me closely, I beg. However little danger there may be that his ardent nature will lead him into the abyss of sin, yet who can say that even by trivial errors he will not compromise the honor of his name and the welfare of the State?"

"Perfectly reasoned, Monseigneur."

"What shall we do then? Might we not reconcile

ourselves to selecting for the king the ditch into which his fall would be attended with least risk to his honor and that of the State ? "

Richelieu pretended to hesitate over this last suggestion, as if he had not perfectly understood it.

" I will explain," continued Fleury, annoyed at having to enter upon details which he would have been glad to abstain from giving, — " I will explain the king's natural inclination for certain forms of pleasure. He will plunge into them blindly; you know his Majesty almost as well as I do, and you cannot have the least doubt of that; the king, I say, will naturally plunge in over head and ears. Ought we not, is it not our sacred bounden duty, to guide this inclination ? "

" Very good, very good! I begin to understand, Monseigneur," cried Richelieu.

" How can we do that," rejoined the minister, " unless we seem to favor it ? "

Scarcely had the cardinal allowed that imprudent word to fall from his lips than Richelieu, who had been awaiting his opportunity for half an hour, pounced upon it like the hawk upon the partridge. " What! favor, favor the king's debauchery ! " he cried, leaping to his feet. " Oh, Monseigneur, what a word for you to use ! "

" No, no, I don't mean that, Duke. *Mon Dieu !* no, I don't mean that! Who said anything about debauchery, in the first place ? "

" I was amazed to hear you, Monseigneur; for, after all, the king's virtue must be due to you alone, since his temperament would lead him in a diametrically opposite direction."

" Of course, of course; meanwhile he is on the point of losing it."

" You think so ? "

"Everything confirms it; he is gradually drawing away from the queen."

"Oh, no, impossible, Monseigneur! They say that the queen is in a condition — "

"That proves absolutely nothing," said the cardinal, with somewhat less regard to propriety than a Bishop of Fréjus should have shown, but without the unctuous gusto with which Cardinal Dubois, successor of Fénelon in the Archbishopric of Cambrai, would have said it. "The queen may give a dauphin to France, and yet not be beloved by her husband. In a word, I think that the king has so many leisure hours on his hands that he has plenty of time to ruin himself by ruining his reputation, as we both agreed just now. I recur to my former opinion. The question is not between good and evil, but between degrees of evil; not to keep the king virtuous, for he seems to have firmly resolved to cease to be so, but to restrict his backsliding as far as we can."

Richelieu raised his eyes heavenward.

"How soon, Duke, do you suppose we shall learn that the poor queen is deserted; how soon will the king declare that his love has gone abroad?"

"Impossible, impossible, Monseigneur, with the principles which your Eminence has instilled in him."

"Ah, Duke, there is danger everywhere; it encompasses us on all sides. There is Mademoiselle de Charolais, who slips verses into the king's pocket with her own hand; there is Madame de Toulouse, who allows the king to make love to her at Rambouillet, there are all the ladies, in short, who seem to say to the king when he passes, 'Look, Sire, your female subjects are at your service, as absolutely as their husbands and brothers.'"

"He will succumb at last, Monseigneur, in spite of all you have done, and all I am ready to do."

"What a terrible responsibility, Monsieur le Duc, for us who have watched the growth of this tendency, who have obligingly borne with it, who have not known how to keep it within bounds, and who will be devoured by it!"

"Oh, what to do! what to do!"

"Oh, weak and timorous conscience!" cried the cardinal. "Oh, how lukewarm and wavering on the side of what is good are you men of the sword, how you fear to use the knife boldly upon the part that is diseased, so that the healthy part may be saved! We poor churchmen, walking beside all the passions without daring to look at them, tremble before public opinion, which calls upon us to be upright and holy, as if we were not mere mortals. We have only one resource, — the councils of the Church; only one unobstructed faculty, — the sight; and when we call men of action to our aid, they fail us, doing more to subvert good morals than we dare to do in the way of repairing wrong."

"Why, Monsieur le Cardinal," cried Richelieu, "I am all ready to assist you, and came here for no other purpose; only of course you do not expect from me the knowledge and experience of a genius like yourself. It has required seventy winters, Monsieur le Cardinal, to bring to full maturity that patriarchal wisdom which will raise you some day to the proud eminence of omnipotent arbiter of the destinies of Europe. I am a young man myself; I have naught left but good intentions, with little power to suggest, on account of the deplorable life I have led. I have cured myself of sin by fleeing from it, and I see it everywhere. I am still ignorant in that I have not yet learned to see the cure for poison in the poison itself. Teach me, enlighten me, and employ me; I am ready to serve you faithfully, that's all."

"Agree to this, Duke," said the cardinal, in milder tones, "that nothing will moderate the king's impetuosity except a pretence of yielding to it."

"True; and yet a pretence, Monseigneur."

"Agree that I do not feel sufficiently in touch with the world to proclaim these theories; I lay that duty upon you. Agree that the married man who has some peccadillo to reproach himself with is the more eager to demonstrate his affection for his wife."

"It is so said, and I believe it, Monseigneur. That is the effect it would produce on me if I had a wife."

"What! if you had a wife? One would say, Monsieur le Duc, that you really forget that you are married."

"Oh! I am so little married, Monseigneur!"

"But we are not talking about you."

"No, indeed, but of the king."

"Very well, give the king a mistress and he will be on the best of terms with the queen, according to your system."

"Expounded by you, Monseigneur."

"As I was saying, then; very well, let the king have a mistress."

"Yes; but a mistress means public scandal!" cried Richelieu; "and then, too, you make no allowance for jealousy, which will shorten the days of that poor Polish princess."

"Do you think it impossible, then, that the king's backsliding should be concealed from the public?"

"It would be difficult."

"Duke, the queen herself would understand, we would make her understand, that it is the only means of saving him. Must I tell you everything? Well, then, I think that the queen would not be sorry."

"Oh, Monseigneur, oh!"

"I have my reasons for thinking so. The queen is the most phlegmatic creature that ever was."

"Everything will be easy to arrange, then."

"And we shall have assured comparative tranquillity for some time."

"Let us consider, Monseigneur, whether it is worth the trouble."

"Oh, yes, Duke; oh, yes!"

"Has your Eminence already lifted a corner of the curtain which conceals the future?"

"No, I confess that I have not."

"But will not the king cast his eye upon the first comer?"

"I am a novice in such matters, Duke; if I had the honor to be called Richelieu, I should not put such questions to a poor priest."

"Listen then, Monseigneur; I also recoil before the responsibility, myself."

"The best way, Duke, is to prepare our subjects. Whenever you have employed agents in carrying out your missions, you were responsible for them, were you not?"

"Why, yes, Monseigneur."

"What means did you adopt to avoid unpleasant results?"

"I was careful in the choice of agents."

"Exactly! Now I have nothing more to say to you. Make yourself the king's friend, or make up your mind to let that place in Louis XV.'s life which I am giving up go begging for an occupant. Take care that it does n't fall into the hands of one of our enemies. Imagine the result of a combination having at its head either the legitimated offspring of the late king or foreigners like the Spaniards. Distrust the influence of the Northern powers; King Stanislas guides his daughter's policy.   I

say no more to you on this point; for, unless I greatly
err, you are not on the very best of good terms with the
queen."

"All that your Eminence has said bears the stamp of
transcendent genius, Monseigneur. And so in case you
should hear of the king's diversions, you would have no
ill-will against me ? "

"By no means, for your acts will be guided by the best
interests of the realm."

"In the event of your becoming first minister,
whether through Monsieur le Duc's disgust, or the
influence of some new idea upon the king, I may be
assured that you will not frown upon me ? "

"If ever — which I do not think, because I do not
wish it — I should become first minister as you suggest,
Monsieur le Duc, with obligations to nobody, and out of
danger from the designs of the queen, I should hasten
to witness my gratitude to you."

"We must be prepared for everything, Monseigneur:
the king is at this moment under pressure from Monsieur le Duc. This combination which *we* have thought
out, you and I, will release the king, and perhaps be the
cause of Monsieur le Duc's downfall; hence, for me, a
powerful hostility — "

"Monsieur le Duc, nobody's hostility counts for anything against such a man as you, when he adds to dignities of birth and position the greatest dignities in the gift
of the State. 'Do me a favor to-day,' says the Italian
proverb, 'and I will do three for you to-morrow.'"

"By the mere fact of rendering a service to your
Eminence I am more than paid for what I do," the
cunning courtier made haste to say.

The cardinal blushed again and rose. Richelieu had
already prepared his farewell speech.

"Monseigneur," said he, "times are hard, and the king receives benefits coldly. Will you promise to ask him for me when I desire anything?"

"You shall make the bargain yourself, Duke."

As he spoke, the cardinal held out his hand to Monsieur le Richelieu.

"Either he or Madame de Prie will have a fall," thought the duke; "but that's their affair."

"One other word," said the cardinal, placing his hand on the duke's arm; "I rely upon your refined sensibility and perfect taste to see that the king's surroundings are befitting his station."

"Don't say that, Monseigneur; I have received the honor of your confidence, and that is enough for me. From this moment you have but to stretch your hand in any direction whatsoever, and you will see me take that direction."

"Monsieur le Duc, you overwhelm me," said the prelate, escorting Richelieu to the door with more affection than ceremony.

Barjac was waiting for the duke with eyes that shone with delight. It is certain that he had thoroughly learned the valet's accomplishment of listening at keyholes.

"Well, Monseigneur," said he, "are you content?"

"You should not put that question to me, Barjac, but to your master."

With a meaning smile the two diplomatists parted.

"Really," said Richelieu in his carriage, "this one will pay me better, and I shall have much less bother.

"There is only one difficulty now," he mused; "the question of fact is settled, and the question of *persons* remains. Bachelier and I must have a talk about that."

III.

A PRIVATE TRANSACTION.

Now that we have followed Mademoiselle de Charolais and Madame de Prie to the Hôtel de Richelieu, and Monsieur de Richelieu himself to the queen's card-party and to Monsieur de Fréjus at Issy, it seems to me to be quite time to leave that moral and religious gentleman to lay his wires with Bachelier, the king's valet-de-chambre, and to return for a while to Madame de Mailly, whose acquaintance we made when we entered her boudoir with Bannière, and on whom we turned our backs again almost before she had opened her lips.

We have told the whole story of that marriage which had been followed in due time by Monsieur de Mailly's journey to Lyons.

We have tried to draw Madame de Mailly's portrait, — a portrait which has been handed down to us in all its details by the *chronique scandaleuse* of the time.

We have seen that her hair was brown, and her complexion fair, that her teeth were dazzlingly white, and her eyes shaded by thick black eyebrows. We have told of the incomparable charm of her personality, but we forgot to speak of her foot, which was the prettiest, neatest little foot at court, or of her perfect taste in dress, in which she so excelled other women that all Europe took the fashion from her for a period of ten years.

At the risk of repeating what we have said before, we say that she was clever, unselfish, and kind-hearted, that she belonged to the very highest social caste, and that she knew all the ways of the court and all the workings of the human heart. That is to say, Mademoiselle de Nesle estimated the man whom she had espoused at his true value, good qualities and faults.

She knew perfectly well that his affection for her had no other basis than selfishness and convenience; but she hoped, trusting in her merit and knowing her own worth, to change his sentiment, or lack of sentiment, into veritable love.

Some women have the virtue of patience, and they are the wiser; they know that their happiness is only a question of time, and that sooner or later they will meet with due appreciation.

Unhappily for Madame de Mailly, the count was living at a period when a man of spirit needed a mistress of agreeable qualities rather than a wife of the greatest intrinsic worth. His own spouse appeared to him melancholy, thoughtful, and sensitive. Moreover, she was very self-contained, a great stickler for ceremony, and had but little property. Thus he had no reason for conciliating his wife's family, and little reason to keep terms with her.

Once married, he noticed one thing which he had never suspected; it was that he must needs play the adoring husband instead of allowing himself to be adored by her. Many men are at the feet of their mistresses, although they demand that their wives should kneel before them. Mailly was much bored to find that he had to pay court in his own house as he did at Versailles.

He sighed for the ups and downs, the extravagance and the mystery of a bachelor's life; he soon wearied of all that his wife chose to show him of her heart or her intellect. He cut the leaves and thought he had read the book; but it remained completely closed to him, he had scarcely mastered the preface.

At that point ennui claimed him for its own; and when ennui lays hold of a newly married man, its grasp is not easily broken. It clung fast to him, and he took to absenting himself from home more and more as an antidote; his absences gradually became of longer duration as well as more frequent. Finally, one morning he took a very decided course, as we have narrated. He entered a post-chaise, and went off in search of Olympe, whom he had loved to distraction ever since he had given her up.

We know the rest.

But there are some things which we do not yet know, — the silent grief of the countess, for example; the profound disgust with which she viewed the life to which this marriage had condemned her; and, when this disgust had taken possession of her, the utter indifference which she displayed in dealing with that divinity to which those who sacrifice most to it are perhaps the least devoted, and which is called public opinion.

Madame de Mailly was young, without being too young; she was fascinating rather than beautiful; she knew enough not to be bored when she really wanted to be entertained, and had sufficient strength of mind to live independently; she was prudent enough in her expenditures not to be compelled, thanks to the means which might have seemed so meagre to another, to appeal to her family or her husband.

Mailly had gone away without bidding her adieu; he had returned without advising her of the fact; a whole month had passed since he had been seen at the hotel.

These facts were sufficient to arouse the interest at least, if not the jealousy, of a young wife.

Madame de Mailly desired to know what her husband was doing, and she found out. The knowledge served to increase her contempt, her indifference, and her longing for liberty.

Matters had reached this point when Bannière's famous visit took place, when Madame de Mailly would have learned the whole truth, had she not already known it.

During the evening of that day, as well as the whole of the next day and the day following that, Madame de Mailly, who had already pondered deeply upon her position, pondered even more deeply. The result of her deliberations was a well-considered determination to put an end to a condition of things which many women, women of spirit too, would have accepted, nay more, would have striven to bring about.

But Madame de Mailly had something better than high spirit; it would be better to say that she had that and something besides. She had a sensitive heart, and with that encumbrance it was difficult for her to submit for long to such a situation.

She reflected that Monsieur de Mailly would return to his home some day or other, and she waited for him to return, as indeed he did, at last. He came to see a fine horse which had been in the stables for three days awaiting his inspection.

The count went at once to the stables, had the horse taken out and put through his paces, examined him, was content with him, and purchased him.

Having made this acquisition, he started for the gate with the evident intention of going away again.

He was already passing through, when he heard little steps hurrying along behind him as if trying to overtake him.

He turned about, and found that they were the little

steps of his wife's maid, whom we have seen treat the
dragoon so cordially.

She came from the countess to beg Monsieur de
Mailly not to leave the hotel without calling upon her.

Although such an invitation seemed strange to the
count, he made no demur about complying with it at
once: he was a man who knew how to take life easily,
like Monsieur de Grammont, to whom Hamilton remarked with breathless excitement: "Monsieur le
Comte, I think that you forgot something at London."
"True, Monsieur, I forgot to marry your sister, and I
am going back expressly to remedy the omission," he
replied. So Monsieur de Mailly replied to the soubrette:

"Say to Madame la Comtesse that I was just about
to ask the favor which she is kind enough to grant."

And he followed her.

She had hardly repeated this reply to her mistress,
when Monsieur de Mailly, who was directly behind her,
appeared upon the threshold.

"Good morning, Madame," said he, approaching the
countess, and kissing her hand with perfect freedom
from embarrassment.

"Good morning, Monsieur," replied the countess,
with a gravity of demeanor which the count took for
the sulks.

Then he looked around and saw that the maid, in obedience to a sign from her mistress, had left them alone.

"You sent for me, Madame?" said he.

"Yes, Monsieur; I begged you to be kind enough to
do me the favor to come to my apartments."

"I am here and at your service, Madame."

"Oh, never fear, Monsieur; I will not take much of
your time."

"Aha," thought Mailly; "she is going to ask me for
money."

As that was the thing which it cost him the least to give, he assumed a most gracious expression.

The countess did not unbend in the slightest degree.

"Monsieur," said she, after a moment's pause, fixing a determined gaze upon the count, "it's something more than a month since I saw you last."

"Indeed! do you think it's as long as that, Madame?" exclaimed Mailly, as if astounded.

"I am sure of it, Monsieur."

"Then I beg a thousand million pardons, Madame, for my long absence; but really you have no conception how an officer's time is taken up by these interminable provincial inspections."

"I know it, and do not undertake to reproach you. God forbid!"

The count bowed as if content with the assurance.

"But," continued Madame de Mailly, "the fact remains that you have stayed away from the house, as I said, a little more than a month."

"And I," retorted Mailly, "had the honor to reply that the inspections — "

"Take up much of an officer's time; yes, Monsieur, I heard you perfectly; but that is an additional reason, you see, why I should inquire how much longer you propose to remain away from the hotel."

All this was said with the well-bred calmness which is found only in a certain class; and although Mailly certainly belonged to that class, it embarrassed him slightly to reply to that question.

"Why, Madame," said he, "that depends on circumstances; if I go away again, I think I may remain sometime away, provided of course that I do not remain here. But why do you ask that, pray?"

"Because I did not marry you to remain alone all

the time, and because solitude wearies me," replied the young countess, concisely.

" Ah, Madame, if the discussion is to turn upon that point," rejoined De Mailly, " permit me to say that I cannot undertake to amuse you and do my duty as a military officer at the same time."

The discussion was becoming serious, and the count, as may be seen, was preparing to make harsh retorts to the harsh expression which began to gleam in his young wife's eyes.

" It seems to me, Monsieur," the countess replied, " that our marriage contract did not provide that you should marry me for the purpose of serving the king."

" I married you, Madame," was De Mailly's reply, " in order to maintain my hold upon and magnify the post which I have at court; if there is any profit in it, as we are equally interested, you will receive your moiety of the profits."

" I don't know whether there may be profit for me in the future, Monsieur, but what I do know is that there is ennui in the past; I don't know whether there is present advancement for you, but there surely is amusement."

" Amusement! How so? What do you mean, Madame?" demanded the count, amazed at her calm and determined tone.

" You were at the Comédie day before yesterday," the countess replied; " you were amused then, or at least you seemed to be very much so."

" At the Comédie, Madame, it is very possible; at the Comédie, you know, people do exhibit that appearance of amusement."

" I can well believe, Monsieur, that you were there on the king's service; but at all events you were not with me."

"Upon my word, Madame, one would say that you were doing me the honor of trying to quarrel with me."

"And one would not go astray, Monsieur le Comte! I am, indeed, trying to quarrel with you," said the young woman, placidly and with perfect self-possession.

"Oh, I hope, Countess, that you will not expose us both to the ridicule which jealousy on your part would excite."

"There's nothing ridiculous about it, Count, and this is how I argue: you married me, and I am yours; you ought therefore, in fair dealing, to be mine. I have n't you and you have me, — loss for me and gain for you."

"Explain yourself, Madame."

"That's easily done. You have a mistress! I have no lover. You look out for your own amusement, while I am dying with ennui. To sum up, pleasure for Monsieur le Comte, desertion for Madame la Comtesse."

"I.— I have a mistress!" cried Mailly, angry as men always are when they are in the wrong; "I, a mistress! I! The proof, Madame; I demand the proof!"

"Oh, nothing more simple, Monsieur. A man came here day before yesterday to weep, and to ask me for his mistress whom you had stolen from him."

"A man! what man?"

"How do I know! A soldier of your regiment."

"I have no idea what you mean, Countess," rejoined Mailly, blushing; "I am not in the habit of associating with vivandières."

"This is no vivandière, Monsieur," replied the countess, coolly; "it's an actress."

"Some strolling player from the provinces!"

"No strolling player from the provinces either, but a very lovely and distinguished-looking young woman, who made her first appearance at the Comédie-Française

day before yesterday, and whose début was announced
on the bills under the name of Mademoiselle Olympe."

"That's another good one!" sneered the count;
"the Mailly dragoons have actresses of the Comédie-
Française for mistresses! Nonsense! Fables!"

"*Dame!* you understand, Monsieur le Comte, that
I have not worn myself out collecting gossip; the fact is
proved to my satisfaction, and as there is no need that it
should be proved to anybody else, why, that's enough."

"Proved," cried the count, — "proved that I have a
mistress?"

"Pray be sensible!" replied Madame de Mailly;
"own up, Monsieur! You injure yourself to no possible purpose by denying it."

Mailly, whose self-esteem was deeply wounded, straightened up.

"Even if I had a mistress, Madame, and an actress
at that, would that be any reason for a woman of spirit
like you to make a scene from jealousy?"

"In the first place, Monsieur," the countess retorted,
still with unruffled composure, "I am making no scene;
I am not in the least jealous. I lose you — what would
you have? I complain, and — "

"And?"

"And I make my own plans."

"Ah! you make your own plans?" said Mailly, sar-
castically. "Come, what sort of plans have you made,
if I may ask?"

"It is undeniable," said the countess, as if speaking
to herself, "that men are selfish to the point of bar-
barism. Here you are scolding me and mocking me.
And why? Because my vision is clear and just."

"The clearness of your vision has nothing to do with
it," returned Mailly.

"Why is it then, pray?"

"It's because it is the worst of form to set spies on one's husband."

"I have done absolutely nothing of the sort, Monsieur, and I flatter myself upon one thing, especially since the beginning of our conversation."

"What is that, may I ask?"

"That I know what is good form as well as you do. And since you have undertaken to give me a lesson, Monsieur le Comte, I venture to beg you to accept one."

"A lesson, — I?"

"Yes, Monsieur, why not?"

"I am ready for the lesson, Madame."

"I am young, and I have my good points; you don't see them, — so much the worse for both of us. But I will leave you to be a dupe by yourself; either take me back seriously and absolutely, or give me back my liberty."

"Do you mean this seriously?" exclaimed Mailly, exasperated by the imperturbable coolness and logical reasoning of the countess.

"You cannot doubt it, Monsieur, from my manner of speaking."

"What! you propose a rupture?"

"Frankly, yes."

"To me, — to your husband!"

"To be sure. I would not propose it to my husband, if my husband loved me."

"Forgive me, Madame; you are young and inexperienced, although you have developed extraordinary decision of character. I cannot then, knowing life as I do, allow you to take such a suicidal step."

"I do not understand you, Monsieur. In what way would it be suicidal?"

"The free man, Madame, enjoys, by virtue of his freedom, all the pleasures of life."

"And the woman, too, Monsieur."

"And it is for that reason that you desire to be free?"

"Precisely."

"I admire you."

"And do you accept?"

"Why —"

"Why, what?"

"Have you made any preparations?"

"For what?"

"To fill your husband's place?"

"You give me no account of your actions, Monsieur; permit me to take the same course."

"And yet, Madame —"

"However, Monsieur, I don't see why we should prolong the discussion on that point. Do you wish me to explain?"

"I should be much pleased, I confess."

"Very well; you know, Monsieur, that thus far I have done absolutely nothing toward filling your place. If I had taken any steps, you understand, my demand would be for separation alone, or else I would demand nothing at all, whereas I now ask with equal eagerness for separation or reunion, as you choose."

Mailly began to reflect.

The countess gazed inquiringly at him.

"Upon my word, that's the male species all over!" said she: "recoiling always before what is certain, they accuse women of being capricious, and are themselves a thousand times more so than women, or than the clouds, or the waves of the sea!"

"Listen, Madame! this is a serious matter."

"What is a serious matter?"

"This that you propose to me."

"In what particular, I pray to know? Are we not already completely asunder? Is it not a month and some days, if my reckoning is right, since I saw you? Let us say that it is only a month. One month out of twelve since our marriage. Tell me, what will you lose by being separated outright? Nothing. While I, on the other hand, shall gain a great deal. Do this for me, Monsieur, and it will be a kindness which I will not forget."

"I should be curious to know, Madame, what you will gain by this separation; tell me, I beg you, like a good creature."

"I shall gain in this, Monsieur, that I shall not be always waiting for the day or the night, as I have done for a year. I shall gain in not tiring myself by making toilettes for a husband who never sees them. I shall gain in being esteemed by you, as a man esteems every object the possession of which is contested for by another. In short, I shall regain my true value, which my lord and master does not know, blinded as he is by the mere fact of proprietorship."

"But which others, not so blind, do know, I take it?"

"No, Monsieur, not yet."

"But they will know in time?"

"Oh, it may be so."

"Madame!"

"But I venture to ask you this," retorted the countess, proudly: "suppose it should be so, by what right, pray, would you cast it in my teeth?"

"Madame, I do not say that, and I have no reproaches to offer; God forbid! I simply repeat that your firm bearing, after a year of married life, fills me with admiration; indeed I did not know you, and now that I do know you —"

" Well, what then ? "

" I confess that you frighten me."

" Very good! " said the countess; " I prefer that rather than to have you pity me, — still another reason for you to accept, if I frighten you."

" Be good enough to formulate your proposition, Countess," said Mailly, driven to desperation by this unpleasant persistence.

" Here it is, Monsieur."

" I am listening," said the count, with his mind made up to try to inspire terror in his turn, by an appearance of stern determination.

" It is very simple, Monsieur: we will separate as friends, without scandal, without apparent rupture, — you to have entire liberty to do as you please, and I to enjoy the same prerogative. Is that clear ? "

" Perfectly, Madame, but whither does it lead ? "

" The result will be for you, that you will never have to hear again what you are hearing to-day, for I will never say another word to you about it, if you consent to what I ask. That in itself is something; so it seems to me. Does n't it seem so to you ? "

" What notary will draw up the contract ? " asked the count, ironically.

" It is all drawn up, Monsieur, and we have no need of a notary for that," rejoined the countess calmly, drawing a folded paper from her bosom. " I have myself prepared, rough-drafted, and copied, as they say, the little contract for our mutual happiness."

" Under what guaranty ? " the count sneeringly inquired.

" Under the guaranty of your word as a gentleman, Monsieur, and mine as a woman nobly born."

" Read on, notary," said the count, jokingly.

Madame de Mailly read: —

" Between the undersigned :
" Louis Alexandre, Comte de Mailly, and Louise-Julie de Nesle, Comtesse de Mailly,
" The following agreement has been entered into : "

" And you drew that up all alone, Madame ? " exclaimed the count.
" All alone, Monsieur."
" It's marvellous! "
" I resume," said the countess; and she resumed: —

" The Comte, with the consent of the Comtesse, resumes his absolute and entire freedom of action, confiscated by the marriage.
" The Comtesse, in like manner, with her husband's consent, resumes her entire freedom of action.
" In virtue whereof, both bind themselves upon their honor to offer no obstacle or hindrance of any sort to the execution of this contract, entered into on both sides under the sanction of their respective promises.
" Done in duplicate at Paris, Hôtel de Nesle, this — "

" You have left the date blank, Madame ? " asked the count.
" *Dame!* you understand, Monsieur, that I did so because I had no idea when I should have the honor of seeing you."
" And there is no need to antedate the contract, Countess ? "
" On your part, perhaps, Monsieur, not on mine."
" Then we will sign — "
" Under date of to-day, if you please."
" Very well."
' You will sign, then ? "
' Madame," said the count. " I have reflected that

with such a disposition as yours you would make me very unhappy. I am not the man to enjoy a continual struggle in my household; you would vanquish me. I prefer to surrender with the honors of war."

"I have done well, Count, in that case?"

"You have indeed, Madame; and if I sign —"

"If you sign —"

"It will be from selfish motives."

"As in love; selfishness for two," said the countess, sweetly.

The shaft buried itself in the count's self-esteem, and inflicted a deep wound.

He seized the pen which the countess held out to him, and wrote his signature hastily at the foot of the instrument.

"It is your turn, Madame, " said he.

The countess pointed out to him that she had signed in advance; and he blushed.

The contract was drawn in duplicate. The countess handed him one copy, and retained the other. Then she offered him her hand.

For a moment the count was tempted to refuse to take it, and to leave the room in a rage.

But pride came to his aid; he stopped, took the countess's hand, and deposited a most gracious kiss upon it.

"Well, Madame," said he, "now you are satisfied, I trust."

"As you will be to-morrow, Monsieur le Comte."

"Do not abuse your freedom, I implore you."

"Count, no conditions outside of the bargain as signed; full and entire freedom of action."

"Full and entire freedom, so be it."

The count bowed low in recognition of his wife's courtesy, and went out without turning again.

The countess pressed to her heart the sheet which gave her her freedom.

Then she rang for her maid, and made her toilette.

She supped that evening at Rambouillet, with Monsieur le Comte de Toulouse, who was giving theatricals for the king.

IV.

RAMBOUILLET.

RAMBOUILLET, a magnificent abode, embellished by all that art and wealth could procure, belonged to Monsieur le Comte de Toulouse, one of the legitimized sons of the late King Louis XIV. and Madame de Montespan.

No court could be at once more refined and more brilliant.

The Comtesse de Toulouse wielded the sceptre there, with that gracious majesty of which the tradition was already beginning to fade away.

The young King Louis XV. went there to breathe the fresh air, and enjoy the untrammelled liberty of the place, for they treated him there like a spoiled child. There again he could breathe the noble memories of royalty, which were perpetuated at Rambouillet, like the dregs of the generous wines of which Horace tells us, whose intoxicating odor was preserved even in the empty amphora.

The Comtesse de Toulouse had been beloved by Louis XV. Beautiful and coquettish, albeit perfectly sincere, for she loved her husband, she had won the heart of the king. Under her tuition the young prince had studied and learned the courteous demeanor which he succeeded in maintaining exteriorly, to his court at least, up to the very last moments of a life wasted by vulgar debauchery, but which, though gangrenous at the core, remained polished on the surface.

The useful training in refinement of bearing and manners which women impart has an influence which never ceases to act upon the mind and morals. The maladies which attack a constitution thus strengthened, may doubtless change the character for the worse, but can never destroy it.

Louis XV., young though he was, and completely under the influence of Cardinal de Fleury, understood that a love affair with the Comtesse de Toulouse would cause great scandal with no compensating pleasure. So he soon abandoned the thought of that poetic creature in any other capacity than as one for whom he always retained profound respect and esteem, and a sentiment which was something more than friendship but was not love.

It is true that love, notwithstanding his bandage, had flown away very slowly, and with his head turned back, and that he was ready to return at the first sign.

We have said that Louis was in the habit of going frequently to this beautiful château of Rambouillet. He hunted there, drove and walked, and amused himself with the ladies.

The society which he found there retained none of the peculiar flavor of the regency.

Living in comparative retirement on their own estates, with none of the frantic and noisy rage exhibited by Madame la Duchesse du Maine at Sceaux, the Grand Admiral of France and Madame la Comtesse de Toulouse were completely engrossed by the king, sacrificing their former fancies of the rights of the legitimized progeny to the living reality of the great principle of legitimate descent.

Thus politics was absolutely tabooed. At Rambouillet they talked of literature and sacrificed to the arts, as

they used to say at that time. They loved and sang the
praises of beauty, wit, intellect, and warlike prowess. It
was the court of the true descendant of Louis XIV.
On the façade of the château might well have been
graven the device of the great king, *Nec pluribus
impar*. Nothing was lacking except the Jesuits and
heart-blasting ambition, and it was a fortunate lack.

Thus the young king, upon arriving at Rambouillet,
felt that everything which might annoy him was kept
carefully out of sight, that the flowers exhaled a sweeter
perfume for him, that he was in the bosom of his real
family, and that side by side with the affection due to
blood-relationship dwelt the respect which illegitimacy
always feels for the prince whose right is incontestable.

Louis XV. brought to Rambouillet all the wild ten-
dencies of his youth, all the ardor of his temperament,
and his whole heart, if indeed he had such an organ.

On this particular occasion his Majesty had been
specially bidden and was expected at Rambouillet. The
Comte de Toulouse had assembled the best of company
to do honor to the *fleur-de-lis*.

They were to try to amuse the king, who for several
days past had given symptoms of incomprehensible
melancholy, and whom the crotchety, ill-conditioned
spirits at court were outspoken in declaring to be beyond
the possibility of being amused.

Some attributed this melancholy to his recent illness,
while others sought unknown causes for his extraordinary depression. The leading courtiers alone knew the
real causes, and they did not know how to put an end
to it.

The road to Rambouillet was thronged all day with
carriages emblazoned with coats-of-arms, all tightly closed
because of the cold, which began to be very sharp;

horsemen bearing orders, or rare and unseasonable deli-
cacies, purchased at Paris, the home of early fruits; or
musicians in hired cabs, making the trip in high spirits,
like true artists, and hoping to requite themselves for
the slender repasts and the fatigues of the journey with
the royal hospitality of the château of Rambouillet.

The plan was for the king to hunt in the forest during
the day, and to return at six o'clock to supper at the
château; then there was to be a play, — a short one, however, — so that the ladies might have some opportunity to
talk or play cards before retiring.

As may be seen, the programme met every require-
ment of pleasure and fitness.

The king arrived at eleven o'clock in the morning,
having himself chosen the hour of departure from Versailles. The princes, two ambassadors, and his intimate
friends were present at the ceremony of removing his
boots.

Louis, so we are informed by Sergens, hunted all day
long without apparent interest. He ate scarcely anything
when the halt was made for lunch, and allowed the stag
to be killed without showing any desire to be in at the
death. At just five o'clock he returned to the château.

Rumors as to the events of the day were already circu-
lating among the courtiers. They knew of the king's
lack of interest, and the royal absent-mindedness had
caused an air of gloom to settle down upon the apartments of the Comtesse de Toulouse.

Every one sought to model his expression upon that of
the young master, — like the courtiers and familiars of
Alexander the Great, who carried their heads on one side
in imitation of him.

When the king walked through the gallery on his way
to the salon, it was observed that his beautiful bright

eyes were bent upon the men rather than upon the ladies. He seemed to be looking for somebody who was not there.

At the table he sighed several times.

The Comtesse de Toulouse was seated beside the king at table; she enjoyed the privileges of an elder sister.

His excessive melancholy, which neither the journey down, nor the chase, nor the different diversions which had been resorted to in the hope of amusing him, had availed to overcome, — his evident internal suffering, disquieted the countess.

Availing herself of her privilege as a relative and dear friend, Madame de Toulouse leaned over to her royal guest.

" Sire," she said.

Louis seemed to emerge from a profound reverie at the word. He looked at her.

" Sire," she said, " your Majesty is bored at Rambouillet ? "

" Madame, I am a little bored everywhere except here, I assure you."

" Did your Majesty have poor sport in the forest ? "

" I don't even know whether I was in the forest," said the king.

These words were overheard, and aroused a lively sense of alarm among those present. This king, who was so pale, and ate so little, and was so absent-minded as all that, must surely still be ill.

To what could his condition of health be ascribed, now that the regent was dead ? During his lifetime they could always fall back on calumny, and that was a comfort.

The king must not be questioned. Madame de Toulouse was on thorns, waiting for him to speak.

He did not speak, however.

After the banquet he passed into the theatre, where a little opera was performed.

As he took his place in an easy-chair, Monsieur de Richelieu appeared.

On the instant the king's brow cleared; his glance was riveted upon the duke, and he made a little friendly sign which summoned him to his side.

We may imagine how speedily this sign was responded to by the noble courtier, who, to tell the truth, rather expected it.

The opera began.

Nothing could be more bewitching than the little hall under those conditions.

A hundred or more young ladies of glorious beauty and illustrious rank; a hundred men glittering with orders and decorations; war, politics, finance, from ministers to intendants; cardinals, archbishops, and bishops, — such were the embellishments of that apartment.

Richelieu was in an ecstasy of enthusiasm; the king began to listen to the music.

"Now we will see," said the duke to himself, "which one of these hundred women whom I hold in my hand the king will look at."

He began to watch the king and the women alternately.

Suddenly the king leaned toward Pecquigny.

"Duke," said he, "when one plays certain rôles, can one play certain others also?"

"Yes, Sire, certainly," replied the Captain of the Guards, without understanding the drift of the question; "certain others, and still others."

It was essential always to make some reply to the king when he asked a question, even though the reply should be a horrible exaggeration or a downright lie. Louis, since his childhood, had had the habit of asking questions and never waiting for the answer.

Thus it mattered little what the answer was, provided there was one.

This time, contrary to his custom, he waited.

Pecquigny was astounded, and feared he had made a fool of himself.

" Ah! so," said the king; " and then, when one acts a speaking part, one may sing also? "

" Yes, Sire," replied Pecquigny.

This time the reply was guided by the tone of the question.

Monsieur de Richelieu listened attentively to questions and replies.

" Why in the deuce did he ask Pecquigny that? " he asked himself in some perplexity.

It will be remembered that Richelieu arrived from Vienna on the very evening that Olympe made her début at the Comédie-Française, and was, therefore, not present thereat, and did not know the consequences of that début to which the king alluded. Pecquigny, after the two questions which had been put to him, was equally at a loss to fathom the king's meaning.

" We must wait until he explains himself," thought the Captain of the Guards.

The first and second acts came to an end.

" Who sings in this opera? " asked Louis.

The names of the performers were repeated to him.

" What! " said he, " are those all? no other actors or actresses ? "

A ray of light entered the brain of the Captain of the Guards.

" Aha ! " he said, " good ! I see now."

" Would your Majesty have liked something different? " said Richelieu.

The king made no reply.

Pecquigny broke the silence.

"I will wager," said he, "that your Majesty was expecting to see other faces on that stage."

"I? Why do you say that to me, Duke?" said Louis.

"Because your Majesty does n't seem to enjoy the opera particularly."

"I detest music," was the king's reply.

Then, after a moment's silence, he asked, blushing deeply, —

"Does that girl sing whom we heard the other day?"

It was very clear that the king had needed to make a mighty effort to reach the point of making that inquiry.

"What girl?" asked Richelieu, quickly picking up the question.

"Mademoiselle Olympe, an actress," replied Pecquigny. "No, Sire."

"Who is this Olympe?" the duke's eyes inquired of Pecquigny.

"A perfect marvel of beauty, my dear fellow," replied the Captain of the Guards.

"A girl whom I saw in 'Britannicus' the other day," added the king. "A fine actress."

"Aha! so he has noticed somebody!" thought Richelieu; "it 's a good thing to be warned."

"He must be in love," said Pecquigny to himself; "it 's a good thing that he has betrayed himself. I will remember that."

The king took no further interest in the performance; he talked with Madame de Toulouse until the curtain fell, and never once applauded.

"He is bored to death. and no mistake." Richelieu

reflected. "What a pity not to have at hand the remedy he longs for!"

Drawing his tablets he wrote, without allowing any-one to suspect what he was doing, —

"Mademoiselle Olympe of the Comédie-Française."

Then he ran his eyes slowly along the dazzling circle of lovely women, upon whom, notwithstanding their superb toilets and their personal charms, the king's eyes had not once rested.

"It's an extraordinary thing!" he muttered; "why, at his age, I would have loved every one of those women."

When his reflections had reached that point, he was conscious of a luminous something which exerted a power-ful attraction upon him, and drew his eyes to the king's left. He saw there, at the end of the row of ladies, a face, pale with all its rouge, with a crown of lovely hair, and two great black eyes, dilated in a feverish gaze.

Those eyes seemed to be turned incessantly, fanati-cally, so to speak, in his direction. Richelieu was a handsome fellow, and much sought after; many a time he had surprised these mute but none the less expres-sive challenges, sometimes offered openly and sometimes delivered from behind a fan.

He had no doubt therefore that these glances were meant for him; and he proceeded to examine the owner of the eyes with more attention.

The face, of a strange type of beauty, largely due to its expression, affected Richelieu strongly, and gave him, on the instant, the wish to know more of the woman whose eyes he had thus attracted.

But she was quite unknown to him; in two years and more of absence from the court, the hunter had lost many tracks.

He went up to Pecquigny, and, while the king was trying to persuade Madame de Toulouse, who was in despair, that he was enjoying himself extremely, —

"Duke," said he.

"What?" said Pecquigny, coming out of his musing-fit with a bound.

Richelieu looked at him in wonder. Musing was not one of Pecquigny's habits.

"Duke," he continued, "who is that dark woman?"

"Where is she? there are many dark women here. The king does n't like them."

Pecquigny was replying to his own thought, and not to Richelieu.

Richelieu smiled.

"I'm not talking about the king," said he; "I asked you the name of that dark woman there at the left, at the end of the gallery and next to the stage, with a silver-gray dress, few diamonds, and much style."

"Oh!" said the Captain of the Guards, "that's nobody."

"What! nobody?"

"No, it's De Mailly's wife."

"Bah! one of the De Nesles?"

"Yes, my boy; and there are four more just like her. Do you know anybody who wants to invest?"

"Do you see how she stares at me?"

"At you?"

"Just look!"

"By Jove! that's so;" and Pecquigny leaned forward to see better. "Are you taken with her?"

"I have always liked women whom everybody else likes or who like everybody."

"You like them all, then?"

"That's about so."

" Look out, the king is listening ! "

In fact, while lending one ear to the Comtesse de
Toulouse, the young king had opened the other to the
conversation of the two courtiers; and our respect for
truth compels us to say that the ear which was opened
the wider was not that devoted to listening to Madame
de Toulouse.

The conversation was rather light in tone; and the
king, being, as we have said, a novice in the art of love,
was deeply interested in it.

The dukes paused in their conversation.

" What was that you said, Monsieur de Richelieu ? "
the king inquired.

" I, Sire ? "

" Yes, something about women whom everybody likes
or who like everybody."

" Your Majesty has very sharp ears."

" That is not an answer to my question, Duke."

" Pecquigny, Sire, who deserves hanging for it, was
slandering the fair sex to me."

" And you ? "

" Oh! I ? Faith, I was letting him go on."

The play came to an end; the king rose and offered his
arm to Madame de Toulouse. He would have preferred
to remain where he was, and continue the conversation.

He went into the ball-room, however, and danced a
minuet with Madame de Toulouse.

Richelieu seized the opportunity to approach Madame
de Mailly, and see what would become of the eyes which
had been so persistently fixed upon him.

To his unbounded astonishment he saw that the direction of their gaze did not change as he changed his
position; instead of being fixed upon him, they were
fixed upon the king.

It was the king at whom the young woman was and had been staring so intently.

Richelieu, who saw a thousand interesting possibilities in that discovery, was careful not to disturb her. He was almost as well content to have Madame de Mailly look thus at the king as at himself.

He took up his position behind a large chair, and took his turn at gazing fixedly at the fair student of royalty.

He saw her swallow deep draughts of that amorous poison which goes from the eyes to the heart. He saw her turn her head as often as Louis turned his, and frown darkly whenever Madame de Toulouse smiled at any remark of the king.

Madame de Mailly was jealous, as well as in love.

Alone and unobserved amid the throng, unnoticed because it was her object to see rather than to be seen, she had no suspicion that within ten feet of her a piercing eye was reading her every thought at the bottom of her soul.

She thought with every muscle of her face, poor girl! as she felt with every fibre of her heart.

What were the thoughts with which the countess's brain was busy? Is it hard to tell and to prove that we are right?

No. Since Monsieur de Richelieu could read them upon her features, we will do the same for ourselves. Free as air, drawing her breath with a sense of keen delight, feeling herself bound by no earthly bond, she was tasting the bliss of filling her whole being with novel sensations, and was eagerly absorbing new impressions with a mind which nothing hitherto had been able to satisfy.

For the first time since her childhood, she was living

in a world of fancy. Set free by her husband, she had the supreme happiness, unknown to all faint-hearted persons or those made of common clay, of refusing herself a pleasure at the very moment when she had accorded it to herself. She had cast her eager gaze into the assemblage, to select there at her leisure an ideal being whom she could love; for her heart was overflowing with love, and no one in the world made even a pretence of loving her.

"All these men here," she was saying to herself, "are mine. Insolent princes! scornful Alcibiades, who will not so much as cast a disdainful eye upon the poor deserted girl!—you are mine, and I may love you if I choose. In my heart of hearts I can mould you according to my desires. I can pursue you with my wishes and my hopes. Possession will never cost my pride less, or bring me more solid enjoyment.

"What do I say? Illustrious nobles and princes? Why, I may love the king, if I please. The king is the fairest and proudest and most adorable of all the great men at court; very well! there is nothing to prevent my appropriating him to myself.

"Nor is there anything to prevent my saying to him, as I say to myself, that his eyes have the brilliancy of diamonds and the languorous expression of love; that his features are noble and his figure charming; that he cannot make a movement or take a step without spreading pleasure around him.

"Who then can prevent my loving the king? I have the right to do it, all signed in my desk. It cost me more than I shall get for it."

Richelieu, notwithstanding his skill in reading female faces, had not divined such thoughts as these; especially had he not divined that the Comtesse de Mailly, floating on a sea of fascinating illusions, was really very far astray in her reckoning, and that her rupture with Monsieur de Mailly had been placed at a very high rate of interest.

V.

MUST IT BE?

AFTER the minuet which Louis walked through,— outwardly smiling, it is true, but very evidently without the least thought of the dance or his partner,— he returned to Pecquigny, who was wandering about in perplexity as complete as Richelieu's after his discovery.

As he saw the king coming toward him, he stopped.

"Pecquigny!" said Louis.

"Sire!"

They stood looking at each other,— the king at Pecquigny, Pecquigny at the king.

For a moment neither spoke.

The king evidently would have been glad that Pecquigny should guess what he had to say to him, but he did not; so the king was compelled to speak for himself.

"Pecquigny," he said at last, "what did you say was the name of the girl who played 'Junie'?"

"What an infernal fool I am!" muttered Pecquigny to himself. He added aloud with his most charming smile,—

"Olympe, Sire."

"Oh, yes; I can't seem to remember the devilish name."

"There's no doubt about it," thought Pecquigny; "he's over head and ears in love."

He expected further questions, but the king asked no more.

Pecquigny, seeing that Louis seemed to have nothing more to say, resumed his conversation with himself at the point where he had dropped it; but he addressed himself with more respect, and employed the conditional mood.

"Pecquigny, my boy," said he, "if you are not an unmitigated ass, within three days you will have rendered a great service to your master."

As the king, either not wishing or not daring to say more, moved away from him, he continued his promenade.

"Yes," said he, pursuing his monologue, "I must do it; but Olympe is the object of Mailly's adoration, and if I march against that fortress, the Mailly battery will be trained upon me. What shall I do? Send a herald to Mailly to declare war upon him? What better herald could I find than myself? Since the king is in love, really in love, there can be no hesitation, and Mailly must be led to the sacrifice. I must be about it."

He raised his head and met Richelieu's look, still on the watch.

"Aha! the duke doubtless suspects something," he thought; "he is as sly as Satan; he means to outstrip me."

He approached the king, who awaited his coming with much interest. He thought, no doubt, that Pecquigny was going to speak to him of Olympe, but he was mistaken.

"Sire," said he, "what are your Majesty's orders for the night?"

"Orders! What orders?"

"Why, for the guard, Sire."

"Send away my light horse, and keep only the Swiss here."

Such was the king's custom at Rambouillet, as Pecquigny knew perfectly well.

"Ah! the Swiss?" said he. "Your Majesty retains the Swiss?"

"Why do you ask?"

"Because I am not very well, Sire."

"You?"

"Yes, Sire."

"I think you are somewhat flushed." Pecquigny bowed.

"One moment, Duke; it isn't the small-pox that you have, is it?"

And the king, who was always in dread of the small-pox, fell back a step or two.

"No, Sire," replied Pecquigny, "I've had it."

The king came close to him again.

"And you were saying —"

"I was about to say, Sire, that if your Majesty did not keep the household troops here, I would beg your Majesty to give me leave of absence, and put up with the lieutenant of the Swiss for this one night."

"Very well, Duke," said the king, with a smile; "go."

"How kind you are, Sire! many thanks. The king will find me a better servant to-morrow than I have been this evening, I am sure."

"Oh, I trust you for that!" said the king. "Go, my dear Duke, go."

Pecquigny bowed.

"Take care of yourself, Duke," cried the king; "I don't want you to be ill."

"Oh, the king is too kind!" said Pecquigny, with beaming face.

He called for his people, jumped into his carriage, and gave orders to be driven to Paris.

The king followed him to the door with his eyes, as one follows a gleam of hope.

When the Captain of the Guards had disappeared, he resumed his walk about the salon.

It was very cold outside, and the frost had drawn a thousand fantastic silvery designs upon the window-panes.

Madame de Toulouse, like a good hostess, did not lose sight of the king; she saw his embarrassment and his deathly ennui.

She came to his side, and said, —

" Sire, I have an idea."

" Oh, have you, Countess ? " he cried; " it should be a brilliant idea, coming from you."

" I think it is.   Listen, Sire ! "

" I am listening with all my ears."

" In the first place, take my hand."

" Oh, that I will do most willingly ! "

" And try to speak so that no one can hear us."

" Oho, Countess, I like the beginning immensely ! "

" It 's a mystery."

" A mystery to be shared with you, Countess; oh, as many as you please !   Come, what are you going to tell me ? "

" Something which I have already told you, Sire."

" You could not repeat yourself too often, Countess, especially for me, who am never weary of listening to you."

" Sire, you are bored to distraction."

" Alas, Countess," said the king, bestowing upon her such a glance as Cherubino was to bestow upon Alma-viva's wife sixty years later, " whose fault is it ? "

A reproachful glance it was, and almost mournful, — a glance which from the eyes of Louis XIV. would have been the ruin of La Vallière.

Madame de Toulouse simply smiled; she knew those looks of old.

"To amuse one's guests is a bounden duty," she said gayly; "to amuse one's king is an honor."

"Very well!" said Louis. "I put myself in your hands, Countess; for Heaven's sake, amuse me."

"Then you must do — "

"What?"

"What I tell you."

"Blindly."

"Well, then, go to bed, Sire."

The king looked at her.

"What do you see so intensely diverting in that, Countess?" he asked.

"Well, then, pretend to go to bed."

"And what then?"

"Why, then everybody will go away, or follow your example."

"Well?"

"Then a certain number of choice spirits will come to your apartment, and we will try to amuse ourselves."

"Oh, yes," said the king; "and we will put out the lights."

"What for?" asked Madame de Toulouse.

"Why, so that no one will know that we are all wide awake," replied the king, innocently.

"Oh, if that's what you mean," said the countess, "I agree."

The king pressed her hand, as pleased as a child.

"One moment," said she; "we have not finished yet."

"What remains for us to do, pray?"

"We must prepare the list of those who are not to go to sleep."

"Oh, Countess, how can we make a list here before everybody ? "

"Yes, they would guess what we are doing. You are quite right."

"How can we do it, then ? "

"Oh, another idea ! "

"Tell me."

"We will walk around among the different groups; your Majesty will give me your hand."

"Of course, Countess, of course ! "

"I will stop your Majesty before all those whom I think likely to afford amusement; and if your Majesty agrees that they should remain, you have only to say 'Yes' to me at each halt."

"Good, very good; let us begin."

"All right; we will begin."

"But you will never be able to remember them all ! "

"I not remember, Sire ? " replied Madame de Toulouse, maliciously. "It's easy to see that your Majesty's memory is not of the best, to say such a thing to me."

The king pressed her hand affectionately.

"But then, Sire," she added hurriedly, to change the subject, "I should be very badly off, you must agree, if I had not memory enough to retain seven or eight names."

"No more than that ? " cried the king.

"Ah, Sire, if you invite more than that number you must be very careful, or there will be very little amusement."

"You are always right, Countess."

Like an impatient child, he dragged Madame de Toulouse off among her guests.

The very first person they encountered was Mademoiselle de Charolais.

The princess was laughing with all her heart, for a

great laugher was she. The motion of laughing shook her lovely white shoulders, and showed her teeth, which shone whiter still by contrast with her lips, which were moist and red like the coral as it comes from the sea.

Madame de Toulouse smiled as she looked at the king.

"If this person is not diverting," said she, "she is at least highly diverted."

"Yes," said the king.

"Registered," replied the countess.

They passed on and met Monsieur de Toulouse, who had no suspicion of the danger which threatened him.

The countess brought the king face to face with her husband with a most significant smile.

But the king said not a word.

The countess insisted.

"Indeed," exclaimed the king; "it wasn't necessary to tell me to choose, Countess, if you propose to do the choosing yourself."

"Sire, if I insist upon making this particular selection, you can charge it to yourself."

"Why so ?"

"It is entirely your fault."

"How ?"

"Because you said something just now which is the cause of Monsieur de Toulouse's good fortune."

"Oho ! what did I say, Countess, I pray to know ? How quickly I will take it back !"

"You said that we would put out the lights."

"I certainly did say that."

"In the darkness I cannot dispense with my husband's presence."

"So, Countess, you mean to reproach me for not bringing the queen here. I am very sorry," he continued, shaking his head; "we would have made a fine conjugal party, — a most amusing thing."

It was the first time that the king had joked upon that subject.

Madame de Toulouse looked at him in amazement, and shook her head in turn.

"No, Countess," continued the king, "we didn't arrange this well, you see. Those whom I should choose might not suit you, while those whom you would choose might not be to my taste. It is much better — "

"Speak, Sire! "

"Much better to let chance decide."

"But we can't make them draw lots for the privilege, Sire; too many would cry out against the result, and too few would be satisfied."

"You had your idea, Countess; now it's my turn to have one."

"I have no doubt that the king's idea will be a thousand times better than mine."

"Good or bad, I will tell you what it is. You will present to me the gentlemen and ladies whom we both select; I will put a question to them, and they will be admitted or left out according to their reply."

"Very good, admirable, Sire! "

"Very well, then, let us agree on the details. I will go up to each person in turn, and say, 'Faut-il?' (must it be?)"

"That is not compromising."

"No; but you will see, Countess, how many will say 'No,' — you will see."

"What answer must they make to be admitted ? "

" 'Yes.' "

"So that the one who says 'Yes' will be admitted ? "

"Exactly."

"Take care, Sire, you are taking a great risk."

"Why so, Countess?"

"Because nobody will dare to say 'No' to your Majesty."

"Do you think so?"

"I am sure of it."

"Very well! you will see: I have a way."

"Oh, Sire, explain it to me, I beg."

"To those whom I wish to make say 'No,' I will put the question in a crabbed kind of way."

"Good!"

"While to those whom I want to say 'Yes,' on the other hand, I will say 'Faut-il?' with a seductive expression, that will surely take them in. Lastly, to those as to whom I am indifferent —"

"Sire, so far as your Majesty is concerned, it will be as if there were none of that class here."

"How so?"

"Because I will not stop your Majesty before any such."

Louis smiled.

"First of all," said the countess, "two parts must be assigned, without regard to the lot: one to me —"

"Agreed with all my heart."

"And the other —"

"And the other?"

"To Monsieur de Toulouse."

"Signed 'Louis,' Countess."

"But how about poor Mademoiselle de Charolais, who has already passed the ordeal once?"

"She must take her chances with the rest, Countess; now to work!"

"All ready."

The king and the countess thereupon approached Mademoiselle de Charolais.

VI.

THE MAGNETIC CURRENTS.

THE princess was talking with her mother and Monsieur le Duc de Bourbon, and was laughing incessantly as she talked.

The king stopped before her; it was the second time within ten minutes.

"Faut-il ?" he asked with a strangely mysterious expression.

"No," replied the teasing princess without hesitation, thinking that she detected in the question a threat on the king's part.

The king began to laugh with cruel glee; the countess herself could not keep a sober face.

"What have I done, pray?" asked the princess, in surprise; "is it a wager?"

"Silence!" said the king, putting a finger to his lips; and he passed on, leaving her in dire perplexity.

"At least tell me if I have won?" cried Mademoiselle, running after Louis, who was already at some distance.

"That depends," he replied

The princess stopped; everybody had turned in her direction, and she set about describing the episode to the whole assemblage. In a moment every one knew all about it, and every one thought from the king's actions that Mademoiselle de Charolais had won a bet.

Thereupon, as she was the sister of the first minister, as she was powerful, and beautiful besides, every one thought himself or herself wonderfully sharp in following her example, and replying " No " to the king's " Faut-il ? "

The king roared with laughter, and everybody else laughed with him. He drew the countess along with him in his hilarity as well as in his course through the salon. The rage for saying " No " spread from one to another, and his Majesty received none but negative responses.

At last he came to Richelieu.

That most artful of courtiers, realizing that there must be something beneath all this mummery, ran away from the king and the countess in joke, and hid behind the chair on which Madame de Mailly was sitting.

Louis followed close upon his heels, but was compelled, in common courtesy, to stop before Madame de Mailly, who rose, in much trouble, as he approached.

Madame de Toulouse's hand stopped him so that he stood face to face with the countess. His first feeling was a sort of surprise, almost a shock.

Without warning he had come directly within the circuit of the electric current which had been directed upon him all the evening from the battery of those black eyes which formed Madame de Mailly's principal attraction.

He meant to say " Faut-il ? " roughly, for the sensation which he experienced as he stood before her was not a pleasant one.

There is discomfort in anything that is too acute, even though it be pleasure.

But fascinated and subdued by the fire which shot from the countess's eyes, he involuntarily softened his gesture and his voice. His look changed from ardent to timid; his voice took on a tender, almost imploring intonation.

"Faut-il?" he asked in the tone in which he might have asked, "Do you love me?"

The Comtesse de Mailly, deeply impressed in her turn by the wave of sympathetic emotion which flowed out upon her from the king's whole being, turned pale, put her hand to her heart, and replied, —

"Yes."

And it seemed as if her reply had been, —

"Love me."

All this took place more quickly than light can travel.

After Madame de Mailly, there remained only the Duc de Richelieu to whom the king had not propounded his question.

Sheltered but not hidden behind the chair, he rose at the sound of this short but pointed dialogue.

He understood everything, from the tones of the two voices and the touching significance of the tell-tale pantomime.

" Yes," he said to the king even before the question was put to him. "Yes, Sire, yes, yes, yes!"

The courtier saw that the surest way to pay his court was to say just what Madame de Mailly had said.

"There," said the king, leading Madame de Toulouse to a seat; "what did I tell you? You see, Countess, that out of a hundred people, by the most provoking bad luck, we are reduced to five, three of whom did not even choose. What can we do with five people, I ask you? Nothing."

"With five," said Madame de Toulouse, "we can play at puss-in-the-corner or blindman's-buff."

"But then," said the king, "in the last game, we should be certain never to make a mistake. We know one another too well."

"Then you give it up, Sire?"

"Faith — "

The king was on the point of saying "Yes," when suddenly, turning about as if drawn by an invisble chain, he found the patient, persistent, unwearying gaze of Madame de Mailly fixed upon him.

"Faith! no, I don't give it up; the unforeseen is the best sport in the world."

"Very well! but we must enjoin upon Monsieur de Richelieu and Madame de Mailly to be very entertaining; otherwise your Majesty is likely to be even more bored in your own apartments than at the Opera."

"I bored!" he repeated. "Oh, no, I don't think I shall be bored."

And he continued to look in the direction in which his eyes were drawn by that fascinating gaze.

He said, after a moment's thought, —

"Tell Monsieur de Toulouse, Countess; tell that lady also. I — "

"You, Sire?"

"I have a word to say to Monsieur de Richelieu."

Richelieu was staring at the king as intently as Madame de Mailly, and hastened to him at his first gesture.

"I have won, Sire, have I not?" said he.

"Faith! yes."

"May I ask the king," Richelieu added, bowing, "what the stake was?"

"Duke, we are soon going to try to enjoy ourselves without witnesses."

"Where, Sire?"

"In my apartments. Knock at my door when everybody has gone to bed."

Richelieu almost blushed with delight.

As for Madame de Mailly, the color fled from her

cheeks, and she was near fainting, when the Comtesse de Toulouse announced the good news to her.

"I imagine," mused Richelieu, taking his leave like the others, but without being, as the others were, deceived by this pretended retirement, — "I imagine that the night which is just beginning will assist me much in solving my problem."

Instead of entering his carriage, he took shelter in a little cabinet where Madame de Toulouse had already hidden Madame de Mailly.

Richelieu had never in his life addressed a word to Mademoiselle de Nesle, nor had he ever taken particular notice of that lady before the evening the events of which we are relating.

"If I were the old Richelieu," said he to himself, "this young lady should ask the king to intercede with me for her to-morrow. But what an ass I am! It's too late for me to enter the lists, and I have but one resource."

Having thus reflected, he at once and without preface accosted Madame de Mailly.

"Madame," said he, "never again perhaps shall I have an opportunity to say to you something which you will be very sorry to hear."

"What can it be, Monsieur le Duc?" asked the countess, somewhat uneasily.

"Madame, for two hours I have been looking at you."

"Well, Monsieur?"

"For one hour — "

Richelieu almost said, "I have been in love with you." But he controlled himself in time, and finished his sentence.

"For one hour I have been sure that you are in love."

"I!" cried the countess.

"Madly, Madame."

"And with whom, *mon Dieu?*" cried she, trying to hide her embarrassment with a laugh.

"Oh! Madame, that is a pleasure which I prefer to leave to you when you shall yourself tell him."

Madame de Mailly, half alarmed, half indignant, was about to insist upon an explanation, when the countess, entering suddenly with her husband, announced that the king wished to see his guests.

Madame de Mailly therefore had to bear with her anxiety as best she might.

All lights were out in the château. The carriages had taken back to Paris all those guests who had no apartments set aside for them, and the privileged ones were already in bed. Nothing could be heard in the freezing courtyard and under the porches but the closing of the last carriage-doors, and the measured steps of the Swiss Guards on their beats.

Madame de Toulouse guided the conspirators by a secret stairway to the entrance of his Majesty's suite.

Profound silence reigned in the château and its appurtenances, save for the occasional howling of a dog in the kennels, replying to the howls of some kennel-mate lost in the forest, the noise of gunstocks falling upon the flags, and the shrill whistling of a cold wind through the tree-tops.

At this moment the soft footfalls of Madame de Toulouse and Madame de Mailly were heard upon the carpet; and the king, in high glee over the frolic, came to meet them at the door of his salon.

The two ladies were followed by Monsieur le Comte de Toulouse and Monsieur le Duc de Richelieu.

The king laughingly told them that he had sent for two violins, and had ordered a lunch, which awaited their attacks, upon red plates covered with superb napkins of Dutch flowered damask.

The king escorted the four elect into his salon, and ordered that all the doors should be closed,— an order which was carried out upon the instant.

"And now," said he, "since we are here to enjoy ourselves. let's set about it."

VII.

BLINDMAN'S-BUFF.

Of the five persons thus brought together by the caprice of chance, only one appreciated Madame de Mailly at her real value.

Monsieur le Duc de Richelieu found himself fairly launched as one of the king's most intimate circle, and about to witness a scene which his astute intellect, having in view a well-defined secret purpose, would surely turn to the best use that could be made of it.

The Comte and Comtesse de Toulouse endured with some annoyance the king's whim, which made them participants in a clandestine pleasure-party with a person almost unknown at court, with no connections there, and in no way distinguished above the ordinary nobility.

Madame de Mailly, frightened and bewildered, a prey to the twofold torment of her thoughts and of the possibilities which those thoughts revealed to her, still excited by her rupture with her husband, found herself upon strange ground, breathing an unfamiliar atmosphere, like a transplanted shrub hovering between life and death.

The king knew nothing of all these conflicting emotions; his only thought was that he was going to escape the wearisome etiquette which ordinarily attended his retirement for the night, to enjoy two or three hours of fooling, and to vex a lot of people who would hear about the strange freak on the morrow.

Richelieu observed that when the ladies arrived he gallantly took the hand of Madame de Toulouse, and paid scarcely any heed to poor Madame de Mailly.

Beside his Majesty, there stood, straight and solid as an oak, a man in the prime of life, with a frank, open countenance, refined in its very coarseness. He was clad in green velvet, and occupied a middle position between the greatest dignitaries and the most humble servitors of the court.

He was the favorite valet-de-chambre of the King of France. Bachelier he was called by Louis, Monsieur Bachelier by the courtiers. A person of great influence within doors was Bachelier, but he thought little and worried little about external politics. He was the happy mortal who had the king under his charge from his retiring to his rising inclusive, and who enjoyed the privilege — so coveted by all, and which he would not have surrendered for the world — of sleeping in the royal apartment.

While the Comte de Toulouse was talking with the king, and the two ladies were talking together, Richelieu, always with an eye to the main chance, exchanged a few words with this omnipotent bed-chamber minister, who never made advances to anybody, but in whom the whole court centred, and to whom everybody bent the knee.

" Well, we are in for a little pleasure-party, it seems," said the duke, with a gracious smile to the valet, who saluted the heir of the great cardinal with an answering smile, as condescending as it was haughty.

" It seems, Monsieur le Duc, that we are going to make a night of it. So much the worse for the king ! for his Majesty will surely be ill to-morrow."

" Really ! His Majesty's health is not robust, then, Monsieur Bachelier ? "

"Quite the contrary, Monsieur le Duc; but he will probably get over-excited; then he will sleep badly, and our day to-morrow will show the effects of it."

Monsieur Bachelier said "our day," for he quite justifiably looked upon his Majesty's day as his own.

Richelieu smiled, — he knew Monsieur Bachelier of old.

"Do you think, then, my dear Bachelier, that his Majesty will retain memories of the night?"

"Most assuredly I do."

"Madame de Toulouse still occupies his thoughts?"

"Oh, no, that's all over."

"Will it be Madame de Mailly, then?" asked Richelieu, eagerly.

"Not yet, Monsieur le Duc; but it's a great pity that it should not be."

"Why so, if I may ask?"

"Just look at her, — examine her carefully. But pardon me, Monsieur le Duc, I am not encroaching on your preserves, I trust!"

"Not in the least, my dear Bachelier. Monsieur de Mailly is neither relative nor friend of mine, so you may speak with perfect freedom. I even request you to do so, as it concerns our common interests."

Monsieur Bachelier felt peculiarly flattered by the duke's phrase, in which he thus coupled himself with his Majesty's first valet-de-chambre.

"Just see what a creature that is, Monsieur le Duc! Look at her hands and her arms! and her neck and her hair and her eyes, how beautiful they all are! See how her blood speaks out in the graceful sweep of her figure; and what lovely teeth!"

"She is a little thin," said Richelieu.

"Too much spirit, Monsieur le Duc, — too much

spirit, take my word for it. I hardly know the woman,"
added Bachelier, in much the same tone in which he
might have said, "I don't know that mare." "I have
been looking at her all the evening.   There's fire in her
blood, Monsieur, — wild fire."

"But the king has no eye for the ladies."

"He sees them all the same," replied Bachelier.

"He is bashful."

"Yes, his Majesty will never lisp a word of love to
any one."

"Who will begin, then, or rather make him begin?
Respect will prevent them all from speaking first."

"There's a pair of eyes which would not be long in
expressing themselves, once the heart was engaged," said
Bachelier, smiling; "those eyes would speak very
plainly, and would most certainly make themselves
understood."

Bachelier heaved a sigh.

"Bachelier," said Richelieu, "when can I say a few
words in your ear in private?"

The valet caught the duke's eye, and for the moment
neither sought to conceal his thoughts from the other.
Their mutual understanding was complete.

"When you choose, Monseigneur."

"When are you at leisure?"

"The king will return to Paris during the day
to-morrow."

"By carriage?"

"Yes, Monsieur le Duc."

"And you?"

"I go in the saddle with the household."

"I shall be in the saddle too. Stay behind, and let
the household go on ahead, and we will have a little
talk."

"At your service, Monsieur le Duc."

"Bachelier!" called the king.

And he ordered him to prepare a card-table.

But before long the game seemed a very tedious and insipid amusement to these personages, who indulged in it every day in public.

They sat down to supper with increased animation.

It was an entertaining diversion for them to be very careful about making a noise, to make sure that the corks were not drawn with an explosion, and to pitch their voices so that they would be indistinguishable from the moaning of the wind without.

When the repast was concluded, the Duc de Richelieu, who had assumed the leadership of the party by virtue of his great experience, proposed that they play some more noisy games.

They were all tired with keeping silence so long.

So they started on a game of blindman's-buff, a form of amusement fertile in surprises and opportunities for mad antics.

In the vast apartment tenanted by the king, the blind man was cast adrift among a hilarious crew. Monsieur le Comte de Toulouse was the first to try his hand. The lot had decided it, and Monsieur the Grand Admiral was unlucky.

The king began to show great animation. He grew excited over the little shrieks of the women, — shrieks which were uttered in a tone that expressed much more emotion than fear. He was especially amused by the warnings which the crafty Bachelier kept whispering to him every moment: "Sire, they'll hear you in the château."

At last Monsieur de Toulouse caught the king, who was a willing victim, and guessed his identity correctly.

It was a curious spectacle.

Monsieur de Richelieu was well aware how absurd it would be if the king should catch him, and so he avoided him with the utmost care. On the other hand there was the fear of allowing the prince to wear the bandage too long.

The ladies, deeply interested in the game, ran hither and thither, taking shelter behind chairs and tables.

Louis, with ears alert and arms extended, paying little heed to the traditional cry of "Casse-cou!" followed the waves of perfume, and the silken rustle of the dresses, and the sound of satin slippers upon the carpet.

One little scream would turn him in one direction, and another head him back again; he would rush off madly toward the quarter where somebody was in collision with a piece of furniture, and the next moment make for a hand-clapping in the opposite corner.

His Majesty devoted his attention particularly to following the ladies, whose hurried steps he could detect, as well as their loud breathing, and the soft ejaculations which they let fall at every step.

The Comtesse de Toulouse, small and plump, yet light as air, leaped from shelter to shelter; her smooth white bosom rose and fell quickly beneath the velvet knots of her corsage.

Madame de Mailly, taller and more shapely, slender and straight as Diana, stretched out her lovely arms, while her eyes sparkled with joy and excitement.

The king was running after Madame de Toulouse; Madame de Mailly, seeing that the princess was the object of his attack, thought she should have time to cross the salon behind the king.

But when half-way across, Louis heard her; she was

betrayed by the rustling of her dress, which was worked
with silver-wire. The king darted toward her, wheeling
about upon his high heels; and he had only to extend
his arms to enclose the palpitating countess within them
as in a trap.

Louis' hands rested upon her shoulders, which were
not so fully rounded out as those of Madame de Toulouse;
the restless fingers of the young monarch touched lightly
the satin of her dress, which was, contrary to the fashion
at court, cut very high in the neck, instead of stopping
half-way between the waist and shoulders.

The countess was modest or coquettish to that extent, —
modest, said her partisans; coquettish, said her foes.

The king, finding dress-material under his hands
where, had it been Madame de Toulouse, he would have
encountered the natural covering only, cried out, —

"It is not Madame la Comtesse de Toulouse!"

This cry escaped him, in spite of himself; it declared
at once the physical superiority of the Grand Admiral's
spouse, and the difference which the king had noticed
between the two.

To be sure, Louis, instead of exclaiming, "It is not
Madame la Comtesse de Toulouse!" might have said,
"It is Madame la Comtesse de Mailly!"

But to explain himself thus explicitly would have been
equivalent to saying that he recognized Madame de
Mailly by the prudery or the coquetry of her high-
necked dress.

To the mind of that poor creature the king's remark
had so much significance that it tore from her a sigh of
vast proportions, —almost a cry, almost tears,— and led
her to reply, as if involuntarily,—

"Alas! no, Sire, it is not Madame la Comtesse de
Toulouse!"

" The King darted towards her."

Drawn and etched by E. Van Muyden.

OLYMPE DE CLÈVES, II. 86.

Louis liked quick wit, and appreciated it; he had it himself.

He realized the force of the blow he had dealt; his hands slid from the shoulders of the countess to her hands, which were moist and cold and trembling.

Richelieu watched him closely.

"There was an affront," he said to himself, "which Madame de Mailly may turn to very great advantage, if she chooses."

He was not mistaken.

Madame de Mailly took the bandage from the king's eyes, and bound it, still warm, upon her icy brow. All her blood had flowed back to her heart.

The game was renewed.

The king, anxious to repair his error, threw himself in front of the countess, in a determined effort to force her to catch him.

She clasped him in her arms, and pressed him so close that the color left her cheeks, and she nearly swooned with pleasure.

"Ah!" she whispered; "it is the king."

She added, for her own ear alone, —

"Who could it be, if it were not he?"

Richelieu and Bachelier exchanged a swift glance.

The king was flushed and breathing hard; his eyes shone like stars.

"Enough!" said he, with throbbing pulses.

"Oh, yes, enough!" stammered Madame de Mailly.

VIII.

DUKE AND VALET-DE-CHAMBRE.

STRONG emotions naturally demand an opportunity for repose.   Over-excitement, as Bachelier said, is the elder sister of prostration.

The tendency to dreamy reverie of our two friends who were thus brought into sympathetic connection with each other, put an end to the festivities.

No other game was suggested.

After some attempts at conversation, in which Richelieu was absent-minded, the king sleepy, the Comte and Comtesse de Toulouse uninterested, and Louise de Nesle extremely nervous, the king made a sign to Bachelier, who appeared at the door of the cabinet, candlestick in hand.

He handed the candlestick to the king, from whose hands Monsieur le Comte de Toulouse received it with a low reverence ; and this sudden return to serious matters — that is to say, to the formal court etiquette — at once restored the company to that respectful attention which is entirely inconsistent with reverie.

The king was left alone long before the hour which he had himself named for the conclusion of the diversions of the night.

The next day Richelieu was very careful not to forget his appointment with Bachelier.

While the king was on his way to Paris in a carriage with the Captain of his Swiss Guards and the Comtesse de Toulouse; while Madame de Mailly, who took her departure at the same time without a single significant glance or even a paltry word of leave-taking from the king, was having a lonely journey in the fine carriage in which she returned to Paris, Richelieu overtook my lord Bachelier on a fine jennet, about two hundred paces behind the cortege.

At this time people could still remember the trips which the late king used to make to Fontainebleau with his entire household, when some thirty carriages or more, forming a line half a league in length, would wind along the roads and through the patches of forest, fringed with a double file of musketeers or light-horse, laughing, drumming, and whistling in a fashion to frighten away all the jays and magpies in the province.

When the superb parade of prancing horses, gleaming weapons, and magnificent equipages woke the echoes of some village, the peasants would appear at the doors or the wretched little windows of their huts, gaping with wondering admiration, and laughing with pleasure to see so many splendid seigneurs.

And if some whipper-in or stable-boy remained behind because he was hungry or thirsty, or to adjust a girth or punch a hole in a strap, the whole village, taking courage when they saw only one at a time, would pounce upon the laggard like ants upon carrion.

Then questions would come thick and fast, followed by offers of milk and sour wine and brown bread.

" How is the king ? "

" Which is the king ? "

" Who is the lady in the king's carriage ? "

" Who was the man with the blue ribbon, riding at his Majesty's carriage door ? "

The servant, bursting with importance, would condescend to talk with the peasants, tell them the news of the day, say "us," and at last make off at a gallop upon his sluggish horse, leaving his auditors in amazed admiration, as he was lost to sight in the dust.

In his youthful days, when he was adored by his subjects, Louis XV. aroused emotion of another sort; it was idolatry rather than curiosity.

Wherever he passed, he saw only arms extended, women weeping, and men praying with their eyes wet with tears.

Some dreamed of kissing the king's boot; others would have given their lives to kiss his hand; and there were many, who, like the worshippers of Juggernaut, would have asked no sweeter boon than to be crushed beneath the gilded wheels of his chariot.

Richelieu and Bachelier, remaining behind, began their conversation like men who knew the value of time and of a clear understanding.

"Well," said Richelieu, "did you see yesterday — did you see how nearly right you were?"

Bachelier reflected. He did not care to have been too nearly right with so great a nobleman as Monsieur de Richelieu certainly was, in position if not in name.

"Right in what particular, Monsieur le Duc?" he asked humbly.

"Why, in your prediction!"

"Did I predict something?"

"Don't you remember what you said to me?"

"On what subject?"

"*Apropos* of the king and Madame de Mailly."

"Well?"

"The king took Madame de Mailly's measure."

"And Madame de Mailly took the king's."

Bachelier began to laugh, and Richelieu laughed with him.

For the moment the duke was paying court to the valet.

"What will be the end of all that, do you think, my dear Bachelier?"

"Of all that?"

"Yes; of what took place yesterday, I mean."

"Nothing, Monsieur le Duc."

"What! nothing?"

"No."

"Go to! You say that the king is very excitable; you claim that Louise de Mailly is of the ardent temperament characteristic of the De Nesle women, and yet you say now that these two inflammable natures when brought in juxtaposition will not sigh for each other!"

"Very good, Monsieur le Duc; but the king wavers."

"Wavers?"

"Yes."

"Between whom? On what subject?"

"The king thinks of the queen; he is troubled with remorse. Since he left Versailles, he has thought much about Versailles. Since the queen turned her back on him, he has regretted her; her image haunts him. Believe me, Monsieur le Duc, I have seen the king shiver and shake sometimes, from seven o'clock in the evening, just from thinking that at ten he was to go to the queen's apartments; and at least ten times, as I was carrying his sword thither, I have heard his Majesty's heart beat beneath the lace of his waistcoat."

"With love, do you mean?"

"Physical love, if you please, Monsieur le Duc, but, at all events, love of the utmost vehemence. This sort of passion is very hard to forget. I would swear that the queen, cold as she is to her husband, — I would swear, I say, that the queen, who is so harsh to this fine young man, will, whenever she may choose, take precedence of all these capricious figures which are flitting around him."

Richelieu ignored the poetical flight of his companion.

"Will she ever choose, Bachelier?" he asked.

"Never."

"You are sure of it?"

"Morally and physically sure, Monsieur le Duc."

Bachelier emphasized the two adverbs, like a man who knows the value of every letter of the alphabet.

"Very well; since you are morally and physically sure of the queen's indifference," said Richelieu, repeating the valet's words, "let us set out from that point, my friend. The king is wavering, you say?"

"Yes; he is in love with a shadow."

"Whose name is — "

"Ah, Monseigneur, right here my embarrassment begins. The other evening the shadow's name was Olympe; it was a lovely actress whom he had seen act, a girl who inspires love of the heart and of the senses at the same time."

"Pshaw! an actress! and I knew nothing of it!"

"That is not surprising."

"Why?"

"Because she is just from the provinces, and you from Vienna."

"True. Let us return to Olympe, dear Monsieur Bachelier. What sort of a creature is she?"

"She 's a damsel who has an ankle as slender as a kid's; great eyes, open and closed at the same time, which makes them languishing and deadly; hands like a baby's; the arm of a Cleopatra; the neck of Holbein's Anne Boleyn; and, so far as could be seen, Mademoiselle de Charolais' bust."

"Well, well! why, she must be the goddess Venus in person, my dear Bachelier. And you say that the king — "

"The king has dreamed about her, Monseigneur. I don't know whose she is."

"*Pardieu!* she is the king's, if the king wants her."

"They say no."

"She is well guarded, is she?"

"Better than that; she guards herself."

"Nonsense! nonsense! Tell me, Bachelier, are you sure that the king is in love with her?"

"If I were sure of it, Monsieur le Duc, I would have tried before this to cure his disappointment, but I am afraid of drawing the cover blank. You who have hunted with the king, Monsieur le Duc," continued Bachelier, with a smile, "know how ill-humored that makes him."

"Very well, Bachelier, go on; you are a great philosopher, my friend."

Bachelier bowed; it was evident that his own opinion of himself coincided with that expressed by Richelieu.

"I have said," he continued, "that I thought the other evening that the king's head, if not his heart, was full of this Olympe; so I did n't lose sight of him while he was awake, to see if he would speak of her; and I listened while he was asleep to see if he would dream of her. He said nothing, awake or asleep; on the contrary, I heard him ask for an invitation to Rambouillet. He had received a rebuff from the queen. Every time that an idea enters his head, he goes to do penance at her Majesty's feet; he asks nothing more than to be a worthy husband *à la mode de* Rue Saint-Martin. Poor king! The queen herself will be the one to blame if he becomes a husband *à la mode de* Versailles."

"You are a clever fellow, Bachelier, and I am no longer despondent concerning the king."

"Monsieur le Duc is too kind."

"Go on."

"Well! as he asked three times this morning if the queen had sent him no message, it's clear that his thoughts were busy with somebody during the night. Was it Olympe?　Was it Madame de Toulouse?　Was it Louise de Mailly?"

Worthy Bachelier suppressed the "Mademoiselle" or the "Madame" with a freedom which bore witness to his power.

"Well?"

"My reply to my own question," he added, seeing Richelieu's perplexity, "is this: It was not Olympe, because he has not seen her again; it was not Madame de Toulouse, because he has no hopes in that quarter."

"It was Madame de Mailly, then, Bachelier?"

"Yes and no, Monsieur le Duc."

"Wait a moment," said the duke, "and I will tell you a circumstance which may perhaps assist you."

Richelieu told him what he had observed at the time of the blindman's-buff.

"I think," said he, "that sympathetic communication was established between them for a moment."

"Madame de Mailly, Monseigneur, has her moments of weakness, like every good Frenchwoman in presence of her king; but, after all, she has moral principle, and a husband —"

"A husband, my dear Bachelier, a husband who neglects her."

"Aha!"

"Who abandons her, and she is proud."

"But it is essential, I think I have already told you,

that she be not proud, if she wishes that the king — It will even be necessary that she should be — "

"That's the difficulty. However, I will admit that I don't think that's the only difficulty."

"Tell me what you mean, Monseigneur."

"Suppose the king to be in love, deeply in love, with Louise de Mailly, — or with Olympe, if you choose."

Bachelier smiled.

"That smile I can understand," said Richelieu, looking amiably at the valet, who seemed to see his own reflection in the duke's eyes. "It means, if I mistake not, that the king will be in love only with such ones as you choose."

"Monseigneur, I did not say that."

"But you *do* it, my dear Bachelier; and that is much better."

"Monseigneur, it is most absolutely necessary that it should be so; otherwise, as you know yourself, the utmost confusion would ensue."

"You dabble in politics, then."

"For our own interests, yes. Lebel and I have joined forces. The king belongs to us, who have taken care of him, reared him, and taught him. He belongs to us more than to anybody else."

"Monsieur de Fréjus makes much the same claim."

"Monsieur de Fréjus has the king when he is dressed in his kingly robes. We have him in his bedroom, in his bed and in his bath. That is why we think that we have him more than all the rest of the world. We have the young man; let them have the king."

"You are quite right. I say again then, Bachelier, that you will not share the possession of the king, since he is yours, with any save those whom you judge to be of the right sort and worthy so to share him."

" Yes, Monseigneur."

" Do you think well of Olympe ? "

" I desire to speak frankly to you, Monseigneur."

" By all means, especially as I mean to be perfectly frank myself. If it is profitable to share the king with you, I desire to make it profitable for you to share him with me."

" Ah, very good! "

" I know that you have everything you want, that you are not inordinately ambitious, that you care but little for dignities, but that you do like fine estates and good honest louis d'or."

" That 's no more than natural, Monseigneur; I have not enough gentle blood to avoid being laughed at, if I chose to wear a blue ribbon or become a peer of the realm. But if I have money and land, my son and my daughter will be able to purchase whatever their ambition shall counsel them to acquire, at some future day."

" Bachelier, I will go on with what I was saying. You know the small entailed estate of Fronsac, do you not ? "

" The one which produces an income of sixteen thousand livres, Monseigneur, and is watered by two rivers ? "

" Yes, Bachelier: do you think well of it ? "

" I should have a perfect passion for it, were it not a dukedom with a peerage attached."

" Being entailed, it loses its privileges; it remains a rentable property, made much more valuable by the fact that it has no justice-tax or road-tax to pay, but becomes a simple seigniory."

" I understand."

" It is a most suitable appanage for a worthy servant of the king, who has obtained his patent of nobility and dreams of the possibility, for the third generation, of a baronial if not a ducal crest upon the porch of the Château."

"True, Monseigneur."

"Bachelier, if I furnish the king with a mistress of my selection, you shall purchase Fronsac, and I will give you the deed in return for a hand-shake."

"Monseigneur, that is doing business like the great man that you are."

"You accept?"

"One objection. As to furnishing the king with a mistress, I do not want it to be a woman to meddle with politics."

"What do you mean by that?"

"I mean this, and you will agree with me, that if we put the king under political guardianship, the guardian will domineer over us all."

"That's a difficulty."

"Do you know Madame de Mailly well? for I see that it is she whom you have in mind for his Majesty."

"She or another; I don't limit myself to her by any means. After what you have said I must make serious investigation."

"Understand me, Monsieur le Duc. The cardinal desires to guide the State; the King of Poland desires to guide the queen; the queen would be very glad to guide the king. The king, perhaps, would not like any too well to be guided by his mistress. What would be the result of this conflict of ambitions? War, inevitably, — war, of which all the disasters would fall upon the king, that is to say, upon us. Now, I am growing old, and have begun to get fat. My *embonpoint* becomes me, they say, and I don't care to lose it. That is why I want peace in the establishment, at any price."

"Oh, yes," said Richelieu; "what you say is emi-
nently sensible, my dear Bachelier."

"If the queen becomes jealous, and the mistress undertakes to play the part of a second queen, there will be
war, and the mistress will be sent away, for the queen
will have a dauphin as a counterpoise to the bastards. If
the mistress turns out to be the stronger, the queen, who
is much beloved here, will be humiliated; and from the
hatred of the Parisians will come stones against my windows, and the glass in your carriage. Exile, the Bastille,—
who knows? The domain of Fronsac, Monseigneur,
will produce no more good wine for you or for me. Let
us avoid such grave possibilities by giving to the king a
mistress whose masters we shall be."

"Oh, Bachelier! Bachelier! what a wise head you
carry on your shoulders! Verily, King Solomon would
be unworthy to be your valet-de-chambre."

"Self-interest, Monseigneur, is a philosophical tract
which fixes the tariff upon all the emotions, and accurately measures all the faults. I had already fixed my
choice upon this actress, who would have amused the
king as Monsieur was amused in the old days by La
Raisin, that lovely girl of humble origin."

"Yes, but look out that an actress does not get control of the king; that would never do."

"At certain hours it might happen, Monseigneur."

"But that is not enough, Bachelier; what we must
have is a passion that will engross him all the time.
Otherwise, and you have not thought of this, the king
will have three or four different favorites all at once,
thrust upon him by chance or curiosity, or love of show.
And then there will need to be as many Bacheliers as
there are favorites."

"Ah, Monseigneur, there spoke the true diplomatist.

It is easy to see why you are an ambassador, and I only a valet-de-chambre. Most certainly every one must remain at his post, and I propose to remain at mine."

"Only one favorite, only one, Bachelier; that's my advice."

"Then it must be a very reliable favorite."

"Let us find one who is in love with the king; then we shall be sure of her."

"In love with the king, Monsieur le Duc! What ideas you do have! Alas! La Vallières aren't born every day."

"Pshaw! it's only a question of choosing a brunette instead of a blonde, that's all. The former will last longer. So you have nothing against Madame de Mailly?"

"Absolutely nothing, when you have proved to me that she will not meddle with politics."

"I will prove that to your satisfaction, if she will permit me."

"I warn you that I shall be very exacting, Monseigneur; I am playing for too high a stake."

"How so? I am in for half of it."

"No, Monseigneur, you have interests opposed to mine. To you intrigue is the essential, — that is to say, war under another name. On every battlefield you win an office or a decoration; from one mistress you get one thing, from another something else; while I get nothing but blows."

"Bachelier, I will prove to you that I am coursing the same hare as you."

"If you do that, Monseigneur, I will say, 'Agreed!'"

"But first, upon your honor, have you made no promises in any other direction?"

"Not seriously, no."

"But jokingly ? "

"Ah! that 's another matter."

"Come, be frank, Bachelier, be frank ! "

Bachelier stopped his horse for a moment, and Richelieu did the same.

Bachelier looked about him, and Richelieu scanned the horizon in all directions.

"Monseigneur," said the valet, "somebody spoke to me last evening."

"When was that? I did n't leave your side," said Richelieu, with a degree of animation which denoted the importance of the revelation.

"Last evening, before you joined me."

"Oh, yes! Come, be frank, Bachelier, for God's sake ! "

"I will, Monseigneur; I will be frank with you."

"Well, who was it then, my dear Bachelier ? "

"Monsieur de Pecquigny."

"In Olympe's behalf ? "

"Yes, Monseigneur."

"And you said — "

"That I would think it over, Monseigneur."

The duke knitted his brows.

"After all," said he, "my dear Bachelier, you must see that my reasoning is sound, and that an actress — "

"Monseigneur, an actress will keep her fingers out of politics: you see I always come back to that point; it is my *Delenda Carthago*."

Richelieu realized the valet's tenacity of purpose, which held firm as a vice.

"Oh!" said he, "your Olympe may last a month ! "

"So be it, Monseigneur; then we will find some one else who will last another month."

Richelieu's mouth was closed again.

"You don't deceive me, Monseigneur, as to your real intention, which is to give the king a female politician for a mistress. Why fight shy with me when I am playing all my cards on the table with you, and am going straight ahead? Why play the game out with a man who has only to say 'yes' or 'no,' to overturn your card-house, which you have built with so much labor but on such an insecure foundation? Once more I say, the king shall never have, with my consent, and I will never give my support to, a mistress who will talk politics with him. When that comes about, Monseigneur, you may be certain that I shall be no more; and believe me, Monseigneur, I am firm of foot and dry of eye, and my nails are hard, and I have promised myself to live so long that it will be necessary to kill me to be rid of me."

"Bachelier," said the duke, after some moments of reflection, "I give you my word as a gentleman, that I will do nothing without you."

"Useless to take any oaths, Monseigneur; but I defy you to do anything without me."

"You don't understand me," rejoined Richelieu, vexed by the man's arrogance, but restraining his annoyance; "I promise you that I will keep you informed of whatever I do."

"And I, Monseigneur," said Bachelier, in a pacified tone, "promise you that I will keep you thoroughly posted. In any event you could not take a hundred steps without me, before you would acknowledge the truth of what I say. Any woman whom you might give to the king to govern the State for him, would govern you more than anybody else. Be careful then. If she is in love, she will submit to the yoke, for it is a light one. If she is cold and selfish, she will either use you

or ruin you. Beware! A simple-minded creature, living
from one day to another, unable to get along without
you and me, will not bother her head with Monsieur de
Fleury, nor the Duc de Bourbon, nor Jansenists, nor
Austrians; she will do for the king what the Queen of
Spain does for Philippe V. That is enough, God knows!
Europe is inclined to think it's too much."

"Bachelier, you have more wit in your portmanteau
than I have in my ambassadorial palace."

"An hour ago, Monseigneur, I feared I should find
it unavailing. But, see, they are beginning to look
back. We have been seen talking together, and there
will be comment upon it. You and I, one at the top
and the other at the foot of the ladder, will be the most
talked-about men at court. Come, let us separate; it
would be wiser."

"I have your promise?"

"Conditionally."

"I accept the condition, Bachelier."

"Then the promise will be kept, Monseigneur."

Whereupon Bachelier and the duke parted.

IX.

THE LOVE OF THE SHADOW.

THE gentle reader may perhaps remember that Pecquigny, feigning indisposition, had requested permission to leave Rambouillet just as his Majesty Louis XV. was passing from the little theatre to the salon; and it will also be remembered that the king had graciously accorded that permission.

Pecquigny thereupon had returned post-haste to Paris; he left the king at ten o'clock, and at quarter-past twelve was at the Hôtel de Nesle.

It can easily be understood that after what had taken place in the morning, the Hôtel de Nesle was not the most likely spot on earth at which to find Monsieur de Mailly, and, as a matter of fact, he was not there.

Pecquigny was so persistent in questioning a valet-de-chambre, who knew him to be one of his master's close friends, that the man said to him in an undertone, —

"Monsieur le Duc desires to see Monsieur le Comte at once?"

"I am so anxious to see him," said Pecquigny, "that I will give twenty-five louis to the one who will tell me where I can find him."

"Monsieur le Duc takes away all the merit of doing him a service for nothing," said the valet.

"Were you going to tell me where he is?" asked Pecquigny.

"Certainly."

"Well, then, tell me, my friend, and imagine that I give you the twenty-five louis for something else."

"Done. Monsieur le Comte is at his little place on Rue Grange-Batelière."

"Good!"

"Do you know it?"

"Yes. It's all right, my friend, that's all I wanted to know."

Pecquigny went around by way of the Pont Neuf, as the wickets of the Louvre were closed at midnight.

Mailly was, in fact, as his valet said, at his secret establishment.

Somewhat bewildered at first by the scene with the countess, he had ordered a saddle to be put upon the horse he had tried an hour before, and which had been taken back to the stables.

Leaping lightly upon his back, he had gone for a ride in the Cours-la-Reine.

At first he was, as we have said, bewildered by the blow which the countess had struck; but youth, experience with the gentle sex, and hope for the future speedily console a man for wounded pride.

Nevertheless the count was taken aback for a moment, during which he experienced sensations he had never felt before.

In fact, this most unlooked for revelation of his wife's character had caused him a certain feeling of disappointment which he could not account for satisfactorily.

Soon, however, he began to realize one thing; and that was that if he allowed gloomy thoughts connected with the Hôtel de Nesle to take the upper hand in his mind, they would eventually overpower his cheerful thoughts of the little house on Rue Grange-Batelière.

The outcome of his reflections was a resolution to

fight Louise de Mailly with Olympe de Clèves, since he had the last-named weapon at hand.

So he became once more the true nobleman of 1726, — that is to say, the heir of the regency, — cast aside his disagreeable thoughts, shook his ear, as the saying was, and about eight o'clock in the evening rushed off to visit Olympe, upon whom he had decided to rest all his hopes of earthly happiness.

Men are strangely constructed; they are forever quoting horrible examples to others, but never take warning themselves. The difficulty is that each one thinks that he is made of different clay from other men, — clay of a superior quality, which is made perfect, in his own case, by taking advantage of all the defects in other poor mortals.

To have a fickle wife and an imperious mistress is thus a double misfortune. Mailly was not a fool, all things considered. Nevertheless he imagined that the faults of his wife's character were due to his having given her too much freedom, while Olympe's defects sprang from being held under too severe restraint.

He had left Paris to go in search of her. Chance willed that he should find her at a moment when, in her desperation, she would have welcomed any expedient that promised relief. She had no need to offer herself to him, but she responded to his offer. Mailly had recaptured her, and had her now. What more could he desire?

Is it not true that for some men that which they possess is of vastly more value than the possessions of all the world? Happy, a hundred times happy, is the man who has sufficient pride to enrich his life, and increase an hundred-fold the worth of that which he possesses! Such a man feels the lack of nothing; his children are as lovely as those of the owl in the fable, —

lovely just because they are his; his copper dishes are silver, his silver gold, and his gold precious stones.

When such a man looks in a mirror, all his ugliness turns to beauty in his eyes, and such beauty as he has becomes surpassing loveliness.

Mailly, luckily for himself, was of such a temperament; he needed the appearance of misfortune to bring into play as an antidote all the cheerfulness of his imagination.

He betook himself, then, as we have said, to Olympe, who, carefully secluded, as much by her own choice as the count's, had not left the establishment on Rue Grange-Batelière, — except to make her second appearance, which was as successful as the first. Olympe was beginning to reflect seriously upon the propriety of taking measures to shake off the fierce ennui which was consuming her.

Alas! one cannot breathe the free air of heaven without feeling the loss of it; one cannot with impunity change from one lover to another, as the traveller changes his abiding-place; one cannot make comparisons without reflecting. Comparison is the bitter foe of contentment.

When Mailly reached Olympe's side, he found her lost in thought; ennui was in possession.

The count, whose mind was full of the conjugal scene of the morning, had also before his eyes his wife's disdainful features, contracted by that internal anger which is so much the more pitiless within, because it is denied external expression. The pallor of restrained emotion always disfigures a woman more or less; it deprives her eyes of the brilliancy which they should have, and imparts to them a flame which is not pleasant to contemplate.

The countess's hands were trembling, and her voice pitched in a strange key; she was less a wife than a bitter foe.

But when his eyes fell upon his mistress, calm and tranquil and glorious in her beauty, which seemed almost gentle in comparison, he said to himself, —

"It 's best so; I gain by the change."

He went up to her and took her hand.

"Dear Olympe," said he, "how lovely you are ! "

Olympe rose, looked in a mirror, and said as she resumed her seat, —

"Ennui improves one's looks, then."

"Are you bored, Olympe ? " said De Mailly, hoping that her ennui was due to his having left her alone.

"I am always bored," she replied.

"Oh, well," said Mailly, "I have some news for you which will interest you and divert you, unless you are very hard to please."

"What is the news ? " asked Olympe.

"Well, my dear, I have to inform you that your two appearances have made a great commotion in the city, and at court too."

"Really ? " said Olympe; "you are very good."

"It seems that the king himself is more delighted than you can imagine."

Olympe shrugged her shoulders.

"I know well enough," continued De Mailly, "that the king's opinion matters little to you."

Olympe smiled.

"A woman of your worth is as good as any queen; however, in your capacity of actress, it is flattering to your talent — "

"I have no talent," Olympe interrupted.

"You have no talent ? "

"I am wrong. I should say that I have lost what talent I had."

"How about beauty, then?"

"Beauty is a thing which has no perfume unless it is diffused."

"Oho!" exclaimed De Mailly, with a forced laugh. "Permit me to tell you, dear Olympe, that such maxims grate on my ears."

"Why so?"

"Because, dearest, I am like a miser, guarding his treasure."

"A sleeping treasure."

"Yes, but sleeping for its proprietor, dear Olympe."

"A man is not the proprietor of a woman," said Olympe, shaking her head.

"Oho!"

"Unless she be a Georgian, like Mademoiselle Aïssé, or the proprietor be a Monsieur de Féréolles."

"Olympe!"

"Unless, instead of calling himself proprietor, he calls himself jailer."

Mailly felt a cold shiver run through his veins.

"What!" said he, "do you really mean to speak thus to me, my dear?"

"I don't seem to be speaking to anybody else," retorted Olympe.

"Pray, what have I done to you?"

"You? Nothing."

"Come, Olympe, have you not loved me?"

"Formerly very dearly, yes."

"Does it give you no pleasure to receive my visits now?"

"I don't say that it does not."

"I implored you," he said, taking courage from this

very slight admission, " to come and live in my little house here, because it was not decent for such a woman as you to be living in lodgings in the city like any actress."

" Am I not an actress ? "

" You are a young lady of quality."

" I am a young lady of the theatre."

" Is not your name Mademoiselle Olympe de Clèves ? "

"If you were free, Monsieur de Mailly, would you marry Mademoiselle Olympe de Clèves ? "

The count was staggered.

" Really," said he, " you will make me think that you are seeking a quarrel with me."

" On what subject, Monsieur le Comte ? "

" You recriminate, and sigh, and shrug your shoulders."

" True."

" And when I ask you for the cause of all these signals of distress, you reply, 'Ennui.' "

" True again."

" Do you wish for liberty, then ? "

" Am I asking for anything ? "

" Are you no longer content with my love ? "

" Count, don't question me, I beg you."

" Why not, for Heaven's sake ? "

" Because questions weary me."

" But after all, Madame, you did not consent to come with me because you were forced to do so."

" Here ? "

" No; down there at Lyons. When I sought you out, you said nothing to me to make me suspect all this suffering which you complain of to-day; you made no conditions precedent to coming with me."

" It is true, I did not."

" I promised that you should appear at the Comédie, and I have kept my promise."

" Have I made any complaints ? "

" No, but you are not happy living in this house."

" Did I conceal my disinclination to come here ? "

" What is it that annoys you ? "

" Hold, Monsieur le Comte ! " said Olympe ; " we shall never understand each other."

" But do you love me ? "

" I have much affection for you ; you are a very worthy gentleman."

With these words Olympe sighed deeply.

Mailly frowned as he heard the sigh, and appeared to decide upon his course.

" It is especially disheartening to me to have you treat me so ungraciously, Olympe, as I have just given myself absolute freedom."

Olympe looked keenly at him.

" Were you not free ? " said she.

" Not altogether."

Olympe's eyes were still upon him.

" I was married," said he.

" Is your wife dead ? " cried Olympe, in alarm.

" Better than that: she has made me sign a deed of separation."

" What for, pray ? "

" Because I made her too unhappy."

" If you must say such things, Monsieur le Comte, pray say them so that I can't hear you."

" Why should I not say them to you ? "

" What ! your wife leaves you because she is too unhappy with you ? "

" Too unhappy because of my love for you, Olympe."

" Oh, don't boast of this sacrifice to me ! "

" I boast of nothing ; I simply tell you the fact."

" Poor woman ! "

"Do you pity the countess?"

"Of course; it would be much better for you to leave me, I assure you, and restore peace to Madame de Mailly's heart."

"Are you mad, Olympe, to ask me to leave you?"

"You have left your wife. Why should you not leave your mistress?"

"Impossible! Olympe, I love you more than I have ever loved. I can find reason enough for it in your spirit, and your goodness to me. But it is one reason more for not consenting to suffer the loss of so priceless a treasure. No, not at any price will I leave you free to love another."

"Take care what you say! You have left me once already."

"I thought I had explained to you the cause of that separation. My people wished to marry me, and succeeded in doing so; their object was to perpetuate the family name, and in that they have failed. Ah! if instead of meeting you on the stage, I had only met you in the society in which your birth entitles you to shine!"

"Come, come, Count, be careful what you say, or I shall begin to think that I make you talk like a coward."

"I don't understand you, Olympe."

"You left me, Count, because you had had enough of me; you took me back again because you had had too much of your wife."

"Put it so if you please, but love is like a new building which settles down until it finds its proper level; when that is once found, it is all right, and the building lasts forever."

"Oh! but that's an unfortunate illustration, Count."

"Why?"

"My love has not yet found its level."

" So that — "

" So that I am bored to death."

" Still ? "

" All the time."

" But, after all, what cause is there for your ennui ? "

" Suppose it were nothing but uncertainty as to my real position ? "

" What do you mean ? "

" I mean just that.   Am I free or a prisoner ?   May I go out, or must I stay in the house ? "

" Olympe, you are free! you know it very well. Only — "

" Only — "

" Only it would be a bitter thing to me to see you plunge into dissipation, to see men around you who would make you listen to them.   Olympe, jealousy is not familiar to my mind."

" You pride yourself on not being jealous ? "

" One may pride one's self upon it, so long as one is not."

" And suppose one is ? "

" Then life does not seem possible without keeping watch."

" So you propose to watch me ? "

" God forbid! "

" Yet you say you are jealous."

" Yes."

" Very jealous ? "

" Insanely so."

" It 's all to no purpose, Count."

" Why so ? "

" Why, *mon Dieu !* because the very day that I fall in love with any one, I will tell you so without delaying an hour, a minute, a second."

"Yes, you have told me that already."

"Well?"

"Well, that promise is no more satisfying to me the second time than the first."

"That is why I am astonished that you keep me so closely confined, Count. You know one thing."

"What is that?"

"That when I choose to go out, out I shall go."

"Alas, that is only too true!" sighed the count, with a terrible pain at his heart.

"For that reason," continued Olympe, "I can speak to anybody under the sun without giving you cause for uneasiness."

"But you don't appreciate my situation."

"No? Explain it to me, then."

"Faith, Olympe, I know you, and I know that you will not fail to warn me when your heart is won. You will say to me, 'I love such an one.' Alas! if you tell me that, my love, it will be because I, like a fool, have given you the opportunity. Whom will you love? Probably one of my friends, some man whom I shall have brought here and introduced to you; and when you tell me that, *mon Dieu!* it will be already too late to undo the mischief. I shall have to endure a calamity which I could and should have warded off from myself; I shall be well advanced on that road when you tell me frankly, 'I have ceased to love you.'"

"Oh! the logic is unexceptionable, and no link is missing."

"You admit that?"

"But you forget —"

"What?"

"Just one thing."

"What is it?"

"You neglect to provide for the contingency of my falling in love without any object to love."

"Oh, Olympe, such loves exist only in romances, and are never met with elsewhere."

"Count, Count," said Olympe, shaking her head, "there is no more dangerous romance than a woman's imagination, my word for it!"

"You, in love without any visible object!"

"I tell you it is quite possible."

"In that case I shall not be jealous. What harm can a phantom do me? What sort of a thing is the kiss of a shadow?"

Olympe seized De Mailly's hand, and gazed intently at him.

Then she said, in a tone which froze the blood in his heart, —

"Unhappy man! you know nothing about that which you affect to despise. The love of which you promise not to be jealous, is the most cruel, the most dangerous of all loves. She who loves a phantom, she who loves the shadow of a shade, she who listens to the voice of the wind, she who gazes at the setting sun, she who salutes the star as it rises, she who bathes in the rays of the moon, — she is lost beyond recall to the mortal who calls himself her lover. If she loves a nothing, it is because she has ceased to love something."

As she saw the terror depicted on the count's face at these words which fell from her lips with such cruel distinctness, she continued, —

"Oh, do not desire (it is I who say it) that your mistress should make you jealous of a shadow. Jealous of the vast universe, jealous of God himself, is he who cannot be jealous of any mortal. A man slays his enemy, and exchanges sword-thrusts with his rival: but the shadow which is beloved of your mistress is an invisible foe, an intangible rival, an incessant, pitiless, unspeakable sorrow which bites and chafes and kills! Count, do not let me suffer from ennui; Count, do not, at any price, let my heart become an empty void! The shadow will find its way in, Count; and now you know what the love of the shadow is."

As she ceased speaking, Olympe, bursting with all that she had not said, uttered a stifled moan, and rose to go to her room; but long before she reached the door, she turned deadly pale, closed her eyes, and fell senseless upon the floor.

The count gazed at her as she lay, with more terror than anxiety, more anguish than love.

His expression grew more and more sombre.

"Upon my soul!" he muttered, "I am in bad luck to-day. Is it I who love too much, or does she not love me enough?"

He went to Olympe and took her in his arms, still unconscious, and carried her into her bedroom.

He had just laid her on the bed, when our old acquaintance, Claire, rushed into the room, crying to the count that one of his friends had forced the courtyard door and was making ready, if the outer door of the house was not opened, to do the same by that.

"And has this good friend condescended to tell his name?" said the count, frowning darkly.

"It is Monsieur de Pecquigny, just from Rambouillet, and he declares that he must speak to you."

"The Captain of the Guards!" cried Mailly; "it must be on the king's service. Claire, look to your mistress; I will go and receive Monsieur de Pecquigny."

With this he hurriedly left the room, closing the door carefully behind him.

X.

THE KING'S SERVICE.

THE danger was not so pressing as the femme-de-chambre had made it appear.

Pecquigny had forced the first door, it is true, but had not yet made his way into the reception-room.

He was in the courtyard astride a horse all covered with foam. A servant, also on horseback, stood a few feet from him.

The two, master and man, were directly within the rays of a huge lantern which lighted the courtyard; in the dim light the white foam with which the horses were covered, and the steam rising from their flanks could be plainly seen.

Mailly appeared at the door.

" Is it you, Duke ? " he asked.

" Is it you, Count ? " replied the duke, matching one question with another.

" Pray, what has happened ? " asked Mailly, walking quickly toward the horseman.

" Ah! many things, Mailly, many things. But do you know that your people refuse to let me in ? "

" I cannot find fault with them for obeying my orders to the letter, Duke; you know that here I am in my secret establishment ? "

" Yes, and you keep it well locked and barred."

" Quite true."

"I had found that out; but if you keep this house closed so tightly, where do you suppose I can have a talk with you?"

"Have you something important to say to me?"

"*Pardieu!* do you suppose that otherwise I would come and rout you out at midnight?"

"Duke, I don't want you to take me for a surly knave who turns his friends away from his door; dismount, come in, and try to make yourself comfortable."

"How about some supper?"

"What! you have had no supper?"

"No, faith!"

"Whence do you come?"

"From Rambouillet, in a straight line, and I'm hungry."

"So much the better!"

"That's a pleasant hearing; explain it."

"That's easily done. It appears that the news cannot be so terrible as I feared at first. Come in, come in, my dear Pecquigny; and if you are hungry, why, you shall have some supper."

He led the duke into the house; the two horses were taken to the stable, and Pecquigny's servant was turned over to the valet-de-chambre.

Mailly escorted his nocturnal visitor into the *salle-à-manger* on the ground-floor, after he had whispered a few words into the ear of his valet.

"A fine fire, but little to eat," said Mailly; "but what would you have? We were not expecting so illustrious a guest. Come, make yourself at home."

Without waiting for a second invitation, Pecquigny proceeded to make himself at home in a huge easy-chair.

"So you come from Rambouillet?" asked Mailly.

"I arrived from there ten minutes ago."

"How is the king?"

"Too well, Count. You have dismissed your people, have you not?"

"I have only one valet-de-chambre here, the one you saw; he is busy, I think, doing the honors of the pantry to yours."

"Doors closed, are they?"

"Surely. You must have something to say to me."

"Of the utmost importance."

"Speak, then."

"It is this. By the way, how is your wife?"

"Very well."

"What the devil was it I heard at Rambouillet?"

"What! was my wife talked about at Rambouillet?"

"They did n't speak of her alone."

"What did they say? I pray to know."

"They say that you have boasted of having left her."

"I have not a very clear idea whether it was I who left her, or she who dismissed me. However, there has been a deed of separation."

"Of what date?"

"This morning."

"And signed?"

"And signed."

"It turns out better than I hoped. There has not yet been time to do anything toward executing the contract."

"In what connection is that remark pertinent?"

"You will take back your wife."

"Take her back?"

"Yes; but we will talk of all that later."

"What! what are you talking about, Pecquigny?"

"That's a minor point. I was wrong; I ought not to have touched upon it. By emphasizing matters of detail too much, my dear Count, one is apt to obscure the main subject."

"Come, come, let us talk common-sense, if it's possible."

"Oh, I am most serious. Only, you understand that under present circumstances — "

"What circumstances ? "

"Those in which we are placed. This report that you had left the countess — "

"Ah! "

"Don't imagine that I mean to offend you; *pardieu!* no; but, my dear fellow, the countess — "

"Well, what of her ? "

"Is virtue itself."

"I am sure of that, Pecquigny."

"Then why leave her ? "

"She has a bad disposition."

"What has that to do with it ? "

"Indeed it has everything to do with it; it is altogether unbearable to me."

"Apparently, since you have not borne with it."

"It is hateful! "

"Look here, my dear fellow, don't say so many unpleasant things."

"I ? "

"It will be more prudent."

"What! more prudent not to speak as I think about my wife ? "

"Yes; it may turn up to embarrass you some day when you are compelled to return to her."

"I don't understand you."

"My meaning is very clear, however. I recommend you to be more reserved; if you don't follow my advice, you and I will be likely to have trouble later. But in the first place, can we be perfectly sure that there is no woman about who can hear what we say ? "

" Yes, a thousand times, yes; you may be certain of it."

" The trouble is that what I have to say is not by any means easy to say."

" You alarm me.   Does the king know anything ? "

" About your wife ? "

" About my wife or my mistress either."

" Tell me about your mistress; are you fond of her ? "

" To be sure I am."

" Very fond ? "

" Passionately."

" The devil ! that 's a great pity."

" What ! a great pity ! a great pity that I love my mistress ? "

" Indeed it is; it would be more proper to love your wife."

" That may be; but it 's just because of my love for my mistress that I do not love my wife."

" Is this mistress of whom you are so fond — "

" Olympe de Clèves, yes."

" Olympe de Clèves ! Poor fellow ! You love her passionately, you say ? "

" To distraction."

" Aha ! "

Pecquigny rubbed his chin in perplexity.

" Oh, well, so much the better ! " he cried suddenly; " the sacrifice will be the more meritorious."

" Sacrifice of what ? "

" Of your mistress Olympe."

" To my wife ? "

" Oh ! who is talking about your wife ? "

"To whom do you propose that I should sacrifice Olympe, pray, if not to my wife?"

"Come, come, Count," said Pecquigny, "we must come to the point."

"Most certainly we must."

"Very well! Of course, my dear fellow, you are not in ignorance of the fact that Mademoiselle Olympe de Clèves played ' Junie ' the other evening?"

"*Pardieu!* I know it well enough; it was I who brought her back to Paris from Lyons, and was responsible for her début."

"Oh! I think I helped a little in that."

"In what?"

"In arranging for her début."

"Very true. But pray go on. I am on the rack — "

"Well, Olympe acted so charmingly, and is herself so beautiful, that some one fell in love with her over head and ears."

"Some one?"

"Yes."

"What do I care? Unless — " The count looked at Pecquigny. "Unless it should happen to be you?"

"Oh! oh!"

"Listen, Pecquigny! I hasten to tell you this, because you are one of my best friends, and on that account I am anxious not to cause you the least pain. I love Olympe; that word ought to be sufficient. The adverbs with which I might encumber the word would add nothing to the depth of my love; they might rather belittle it, and as I love her, I will not give her up to you."

"My friend, if only myself were in question, you would do well; but — "

"Whom are you talking about, then?" rejoined Mailly, alarmed by Pecquigny's portentous gravity.

"Of some one, my good friend, whom it is not customary to resist in this fair realm of France. I refer,
my dear fellow, to the Most Christian King."

"Louis XV. ?"

"His Majesty in person."

Monsieur de Mailly turned as white as a ghost.

"The king in love with Olympe!" he exclaimed,
raising his head and gazing at Pecquigny like a man just
waking from a dream.

"It would seem that our illustrious master is so far
gone that he cannot eat or drink. A king who does n't
eat or drink, my friend, has n't long to live. I do not
suppose that you will allow your love for your mistress
to make you a regicide."

"Listen, Pecquigny!" said the count. "If you are
perpetrating one of the jokes that are so popular at
court; if you were sent here to annoy me; if Monsieur
de Maurepas, who has charge of the police, is paying
you for it; if the Jesuits have got possession of you, —
why, then it 's all right, and I forgive you; but if you
imagine that I am likely to give up Olympe, even to
the king, my dear fellow, why, then you are wrong, and
I do not forgive you."

"Very fine, very fine! There 's no necessity of load-
ing your eyes up with powder and ball, like pistols, as if
we were going to shoot each other with angry looks.
Be calm! it 's a serious matter."

"No, it 's very simple. The king loves Olympe, you
say? Very good! the king shall not have her. I have
Olympe, and I propose to keep her."

"Pshaw!"

"Besides, it is not true."

"What is it that 's not true?"

"The king is not in love with my mistress."

" But I tell you that he is."

" He! a devotee! a prince pickled in sanctity! a model for husbands! Why, it's impossible! "

" Oho! so you speak ill of the king! *Lèse-majesté!* Beware! "

" It would be a fine thing, would it not, to see me, after I had won a charming creature, a model — "

" Ah, she is indeed a charming creature! Ah, yes, she is a model! You see that the king has not made a mistake. And is Olympe really as charming as you say ? "

" Much more charming than I can say."

" You overwhelm me with joy ! "

" Are you mad ? "

" When you understand me, you will see whether I am behind the seven wise men of Greece in wisdom. So you say then, my dear Mailly, that — "

" She is a very model."

" Upon my honor, you delight my soul. In that case the thing is done."

" What thing ? "

" Let me unfold my plan to you."

" You can flatter yourself that you are unfolding things that are very disagreeable to me to hear."

" Dear Count, these disagreeable things are such as cannot escape an honest gentleman, and as an honest gentleman cannot escape. Lugeac, for instance, who had his nose cut off, found it a disagreeable experience; so, too, with Chardin, who was disinherited by his father-in-law, the farmer-general; and then there's your wife, who was fortunate enough to get rid of you, and will be obliged to take you back again, — that's exceedingly disagreeable for her."

" Come, do you want me to laugh or get angry ? Are you joking or are you ridiculing me ? "

"Both; but one after the other. Laugh first; you will lose your temper afterward."

"Enough of this, Pecquigny; cut it short!"

"Oh, no, it is not for me to cut it short to suit you or even to suit myself. I have begun, and I must go on to the end."

"Go on, then; but be quick!"

"I resume the exposition of my plan. Suppose, in the first place, that you are ambitious — "

"Not in the least degree!"

"Let us alone, then! Do you, who are always jumping into fire, like a Basque, mean to tell me that you don't care for decorations and duchies?"

"What has Olympe in common with a duchy, or how can Olympe procure me a decoration?"

"I'm coming to that! I'm coming to that! The king, being in love with this Olympe, and finding her a model, a true model, as you say yourself — Now don't deceive us about that, for just see what a position you would put me in!"

"Look here, Pecquigny! do you know that an idea has come to me while you have been twisting your plan up instead of unfolding it?"

"An idea to you, too! Two ideas! Well, well, this is superb! Speak, my dear Mailly, speak, and see how I will listen!"

"My idea is this; I will not shuffle around the truth as you do. Pecquigny, you were sent here by my wife."

"By your wife?"

"Pecquigny, you are my wife's lover!"

"I! I!"

"Pecquigny, you have explained to me, without suspecting what you were doing, the quarrel my wife insisted on picking with me. You have shown me why she thinks it necessary that I should return to her. My treaty with her was only signed this morning. Whatever propositions you please for the future, Pecquigny, but not a step backward, — *mordieu*, no! "

" You're mad; your eyes are coming out of your head, my dear fellow! "

" I don't joke with my own name, Duke, do you hear that? "

" What! You poor fool, who spoke of your name? Who is thinking about your wife, and future propositions, and steps backward? I don't even know your wife; I care less than nothing about your separation, which I never heard of until to-day. "

" I believe that, since it dates only from two o'clock. "

" Mailly, upon my honor, the countess is not involved in this matter, except secondarily. "

" But you demanded that I should be reconciled with her, only a moment ago. "

" For your own good, my dear man, so that you might not be left alone after your rupture with poor Olympe. Solitude is a fatal thing for such vivid imaginations as yours, and in such a case one's wife is better than nobody at all. "

" Don't imagine, Duke, that I will let you say another word without a word from me. "

" What word from you, Count? "

" Duke, I don't mean to threaten you, — we are both too honorable gentlemen and too loyal friends to lose our heads in dealing with each other; but you must swear to me, Duke — "

" What shall I swear? "

" That you do not know my wife, as you say. "

"My dear Mailly, the word of a duke for it! I swear to you, by the unsullied honor of my family, my blood, and my race, that I have never seen your wife but three times, — the day of your marriage, when I was your witness, the day of her presentation at court, and to-day at Rambouillet."

"Ah! so Louise was at Rambouillet?"

"Yes; I saw her there, but did not even speak to her. By the way, that reminds me of another little circumstance."

"What was it?"

"Concerning your wife."

"What was it?"

"What concern is it of yours?"

"That depends on what it is."

"Well, suppose it were a very peculiar circumstance?"

"Well, it's no concern of mine, as you say, since we are separated. However, it is proper that a husband — "

"Oh, yes, it is, indeed, very proper. Well, then! do you maintain that the husband — "

"My wife is free."

"Yes; but is she free for one purpose or for all purposes, inclusively or exclusively?"

"I should prefer to say exclusively."

"Exclusively for a duke and peer, for instance, if he be twice duke and twice peer?"

"Pecquigny!"

"Well, man, if it displeases you to have your wife look too much at somebody else, and to have somebody else look too much at her, why, it's high time — "

"High time for what?"

"To put yourself between your wife and the person at whom she is looking."

The count passed his hand over his face.

"Oh, no," said he, "that's a weak argument. I have a mistress. I know Louise; she may indulge in a little ogling here and there, but that's all."

"So you believe in your wife, do you?"

"I do."

"Good! My friend, your faith is your salvation."

He added beneath his breath, —

"If Olympe is a model, Mailly is another. What a couple, and what a shame to tear them apart!"

"I have your word, then," continued Mailly, "and I may be sure that your visit here really concerns Olympe?"

"You may depend on it; now for my plan once more!"

"My dear friend, don't go into details; it would be time thrown away."

"Why so?"

"Because it would have no effect."

"Oh, the idea that I could form an impracticable plan!"

"It's true nevertheless that you have. I have lost my wife's love, or rather it is sleeping and will awake when God pleases."

"Or the devil."

"Have it so, Duke; but as for Olympe, I say again that I propose to cling to her: she is mine, and nothing shall take her from me."

"Mere words! *Verba volant*, as Père Porée used to say."

"You know, my dear Duke, that there are words which are called words of honor, or words as true as the Holy Gospel!"

"Don't get excited, and especially don't run wild about the Gospel! You waste your time."

"How so? Am I not the master of my mistress, in heaven's name?"

"Well, no."

"That's a strange thing, I should say."

"Strange or not, it's about so."

"To whom does my mistress belong then, if you please?"

"*Pardieu!* to the king, just as Paris does. When the king chooses to lay a tax upon the city, I don't think he comes to consult you, or the city either, for that matter."

"Very true; but — "

"There is no *but*. Mademoiselle Olympe is an actress, and belongs to the Comédie; the Comédie belongs to the king, for the actors belong to the king's troupe."

"Oh, you're joking!"

"I joking! 'Pon honor, I'm a thousand leagues from it."

"Very well! just tell the king to come and take Olympe away from me, and we shall see what we shall see."

Pecquigny shrugged his shoulders.

"The king is very likely to put himself out of the way to come here, is he not?"

"Pecquigny, you are a precious friend. I appreciate all your delicacy; you see the danger which threatens me, and are anxious to save me from it."

"How?"

"You know that there is a conspiracy against poor Olympe, and you are giving me notice of it without seeming to do so."

"A conspiracy!"

"That's all right, don't deny it; it is noble of you, and I am very grateful. This very night I will set out with her for my little estate in Normandy. You know it is near Courbe-Épine, which belongs to Madame de Prie."

"It is my turn to thank you for forewarning me. You may be sure that Mademoiselle Olympe will not go to Normandy."

"The devil!" said Mailly, in utter amazement. "Pray, why will she not go?"

"Because I will prevent her."

"You?"

"Myself. You understand, my dear Count, I have no wish to kill the king with disappointment, and then go and take my place beside Jacques Clément and Ravaillac."

"This is very fine, upon my word!"

"If it were your wife, my dear Mailly, I don't say that I would authorize you, but I would advise you, to hide her; for in such case it would be a theft on his Majesty's part, although there is a precedent in the case of Louis XIV. and Madame de Montespan. But a mistress — "

"Duke!"

"Yes, I mean it."

"You! My friend!"

"Your friend when off duty; but in this matter, my dear fellow, I am on the king's business."

"You conspire to rob me of the woman I love."

"Pshaw! a mere actress!"

"But if the king wants her, why should not I want her as well as he?"

"The king, my dear, is the king."

"Do you mean to drive me to desperation?

"If I should see you in desperation over this, it would make me laugh."

"You have gone altogether too far, Duke, and I think it's high time to have done with it."

Pecquigny rose.

"I thought you a man of spirit," said he.

"Yes, and without heart."

"Here for an hour I have been twisting and turning and lying, and laying traps, and springing mines — "

"And all for what end?"

"Why, you know very well."

"To spirit Olympe away, yes."

"*Dame!* if the king orders me to do it, it is less difficult than to carry a bastion."

"Pecquigny, in the bastions you have stormed you found Spaniards or Germans."

"While by Olympe's side I shall find you; is that what you mean?"

"Yes."

"My dear fellow, that will be a source of grief to me; but I shall swallow my grief, and having swallowed it, I shall carry the bastion. You know my theory about disagreeable occurrences."

"Listen, Pecquigny, one last word."

"Go on."

"Suppose Olympe loves me!"

"You talk nothing but nonsense, you have degenerated since our interview began. All that I have heard from you is a farrago of horrible platitudes. Suppose Olympe loves you, you say? Well, *pardieu!* suppose she does love you. What does that matter?"

"You ask, what does that matter?"

"To be sure; I return to my comparison. Do the taxes love the king? Yet they are the king's. If Mademoiselle Olympe does not love the king, will she be likely to tell his Majesty that she hates him?"

"Yes, she will indeed."

"Well, my dear fellow, that would be a vulgar piece of folly, and I believe her incapable of it. She will never say that to the king, because she has a sense of propriety, and the king deserves to be loved. He's a charming fellow, is the king! If you had only seen him this evening! He is much handsomer than you, and much younger too; and then he is king, which counts for something. A woman who would not love the king! For shame! A woman! Look here, man, your arguments are all against common-sense! This passion of the king's for an actress will not last forever. *Mordieu!* if you are so wild over this Olympe, you can take her back again!"

"Oh, that's a shameful thing to say to me!"

"You have acted a thousand times worse than I have talked. Let us sum up."

"It is all summed up. I refuse."

"Very good. Let me pass then; I propose to go and speak to the lady herself."

Mailly threw himself in front of the duke, to bar his way.

"Speak of these infamous things to Olympe!" he cried. "Never, Duke, never!"

"If I don't speak to her to-day, I shall to-morrow; that's all."

"Never, under my roof!"

"If not under your roof, it will be elsewhere, — at the Comédie, for instance."

"I will kill you first."

"If you kill me, Mailly, I shall bequeath to some friend this plan of mine which you refuse to consent to. My friend will follow it up, and you will be compelled to kill him also, to prevent him from speaking to your Olympe."

"Then I will kill her."

"Pshaw! from nonsense you pass to downright absurdity. You will be like the Roman Virginius, a gentleman who killed his daughter. Very fine that! but Virginius killed his daughter, not his mistress; and then Appius Claudius was a wicked decemvir, a fiendish tyrant, while Louis XV. is a fascinating monarch."

"What matters it to me?"

"Faith, it does matter to you, and you shall see how. The king will think you mad after so many murders, and will have you shut up in the Bastille, and there you will rot, writing sonnets on the wall in praise of your mistress. Consider if you wouldn't better draw in your horns. There, I have sketched the position in few words. Now listen."

"Good God! I have listened far too much already."

"The king is in love with a woman. What do you say to that?"

"Nothing; it's all the same to me."

"That woman is your neighbor's wife. What do you say to that?"

"Why — "

"You have nothing to say, have you? Better still, if it were the wife of your friend Pecquigny, for example, you would laugh about it as gayly as a lot of flies playing in the sun. Come, admit these two points, for heaven's sake! "

"Very good; but the woman whom the king loves is my mistress, not your wife."

"Well! do you expect to prevent other people from laughing?"

"No; but I have no inclination to laugh myself."

"What does that matter? Those other people will lend a hand to the king, as it is natural for good Frenchmen to do. The king has a natural fascination, and in default of that fascination, which is irresistible, there is the Bastille, — Bastille for Olympe if she is stubborn; Bastille for Mailly if he rebels against his Majesty; Bastille to the right, Bastille to the left, Bastille everywhere. My good friend, I have talked too much; my throat is scorched. During this long interview you have n't so much as offered me a bit of refreshment, except in the shape of a sword-thrust."

"Oh, pardon me, my dear Duke."

"Yes, I understand, it is hard; but even the satisfaction of administering a sword-thrust may lead to the Bastille. Always the Bastille! A devilish pleasant prospect! Look here! it used to be said that the Pyramids were the highest structure in the world. I swear to you that it is false, for they can't be seen ten leagues away, while that infernal Bastille can be seen everywhere. It is entitled to be called the loftiest structure in the world."

Mailly was plunged in deep despondency.

"Oh, all my beautiful dreams!" he muttered; "all vanished, lost!"

"Nonsense! Have you never noticed that when one dream is ended, another one almost always begins, when one is a good sleeper? Come, have you made up your mind?"

"To leave Olympe? Never!"

"To let me broach the subject to her?"

"Never, never!"

"Very well, my friend. We are enemies now, without abandoning that loyalty of conduct which is inseparable from enmities between Frenchmen. I ought to say one thing to you, however — "

'Say it, and say it again and again, you will never move me by one hair's breadth."

" Yes, I see that, and so I will add but one thing."

" What is it ? "

" It is this, — that since this is a woman's affair, strategy is indispensable, and I am too much your friend not to make use of whatever is indispensable. Instead of using force I will use the wiles of the serpent. Be suspicious of everything, — doors, windows, and trap-doors; I shall employ whatever means comes to hand, and if you don't want to be made a fool of, if you don't want to play Cassandra with Olympe while I am making her play Isabelle, be on your guard! Once more, my dear Mailly, be on your guard! I, Pecquigny, your friend, your true friend, and your foe at the same time, bid you beware ! "

With these words the captain took his leave without having so much as put his lips to the glass which Monsieur de Mailly had filled when Pecquigny reproached him for letting him die of thirst.

XI.

THE SHADOW WAS A BODY.

IT was late, or rather it was very early, when his Majesty Louis XV.'s Captain of the Guards took his departure from the secret establishment of Monsieur de Mailly.

Six o'clock was striking in the neighboring church-tower; the first rays of dawn were beginning to appear, ushering in one of those gray autumn days which begin in mist and end in fog. A sharp, piercing air gave promise of a fine midday. It was during that midday that the king with his entire household was to return from Rambouillet.

Daylight was beginning to peer in at the windows of the dining-room when Mailly roused himself from the stupor in which Pecquigny's scheme had plunged him.

The fire was out, and the servants were either dozing in their chairs or in bed.

Mailly shook his head as if to drive away the clouds which the duke had thrown over his faculties, and went upstairs to Olympe's apartment.

He expected to find her in bed and asleep; but she was sitting upon her sofa, with her feet stretched out toward a fire that was hardly a spark, while the dying candles were sputtering in the rich candelabra.

Olympe was not asleep, and her eyes were wide open.

This was another blow for Mailly.

He looked closely at her, and was struck with the change in her face.

"Already up?" he said.

Olympe, who had not stirred at the noise the Count made in entering, slowly turned her head.

"Not yet in bed, you should say."

"You have not been in bed?"

"No."

"Why not?" cried Mailly. "*Mon Dieu!* Olympe, are you ill?"

"No, I am not ill."

"Then why did n't you go to bed?"

"I did not go to bed because you did not order me to," said she.

"Order you?" echoed Mailly.

"Yes, I was afraid of displeasing you; are you not my protector?"

Mailly's arms fell powerless at his sides, and his head fell forward on his chest.

"Oh!" he groaned, "cruel, cruel woman that you are, have you not done enough to convince me that you look upon me as a tyrant?"

Olympe made no reply.

"But you can't love me any more, Olympe," he cried, in tones which witnessed the sincerity of his passion. "Oh, I do love you *so* dearly!"

"Henri," said she, "you pay no heed to the wound in my heart, which is still open; be careful of it, I beg you."

"What wound?"

Olympe smiled bitterly.

"Oh!" cried Mailly, as if struck for the first time by the thought; "I tremble to believe that I understand you."

"I told you not to probe it, Count."

" You have preserved your love — for — "

" Don't say another word."

" You still love this Bannière ? "

" Count, don't say that, so long as I don't say it."

" On the contrary, let us say it, Olympe. You love that fellow, that actor, that soldier ? "

" What matters it whether I love him or love him not, since he no longer loves me ? "

Mailly was on the point of crying, " But he does still love you; he is in Paris, he is seeking you," when it came home to him that of all his rivals he was the most formidable, and that he must allow Olympe to believe that he was far from her.

" Olympe, " said he, " without you life seems impossible to me; without you there is no hope for me on earth. Oh, Olympe, do not take away your love, for it would be equivalent to taking away my life! "

" Yes, I believe that you love me."

" Well, then, if you believe that I love you, Olympe, for God's sake, tell me that you love me, — not only that you love me, but that you prefer me to all the world, and that you will suffer no homage from any other than myself. Oh, I do need to have you tell me that, and be gentle with me ! My life, yes, my very life is hanging by that one thread."

" To make you happy without being happy myself, — is that what you ask ? Strictly speaking, it is possible, I suppose."

" If it is possible, do it for me."

" Selfish love ! "

" Like all loves."

" Count, " said Olympe, " I will force myself to make you happy."

" But listen! that is not all."

" What else is there?   Tell me."

" It may be that obstacles will be interposed to prevent your carrying out your kind intentions toward me, dearest."

" What kind of obstacles? "

" Suppose that a power higher than mine seeks to dispute my right to you? "

" To dispute your right to me? "

" Yes."

" With force? "

" With force, — that is to say, against my will."

" And against my will too? "

" As for that, I am unable to say, Olympe."

" Who, then, would dare to ask a woman for the love which she cannot give him? "

" How do I know? "

" The man who would do that would be the lowest of mankind."

" Or the highest."

Olympe gazed earnestly at Mailly.

" Aha! " she exclaimed.

" Do you understand? "

" Perhaps."

" So much the better, if you do, and can spare me the grievous necessity of going into details."

" I played ' Britannicus ' the other day, did I not? "

" You are on the right track, Olympe."

" And a certain person thought me fair? "

" That 's it."

" And that person is more powerful than you? "

" More powerful than I; you are quite right."

" That person — is it the king? "

" It is the king."

Olympe shrugged her shoulders.

"Well, Count," said she, "what matters it to you?"

"Olympe, it is the torture of my life. The king is handsome, amiable, and young."

"The king, being young, will give his sanction to no violence. It would need a Nero to poison Britannicus and take Junie away by force."

"Yes, but suppose that Junie loves Nero?"

"Suppose that Junie loves Nero, if you please, but do not imagine that Olympe loves Louis XV."

"But if they should employ — "

"What?"

"Fear."

"Fear?"

"Suppose they should threaten you with the Bastille?"

"Count, in my present situation, nothing would be more sweet to me than absolute captivity, except absolute independence."

"Olympe, don't blame me any more for keeping you close, and hiding you from all eyes. You see now that I was right, and yet from this moment you are free."

"So they want to take me away from you?"

"That announcement has been made to me."

"Is there anything in my power which will set your mind at rest?"

"One assurance."

"Name it."

"Your word that you will never yield to fear."

"What you ask is altogether too easy."

"Then you will not yield — "

"To aught but love."

"There, you see you say in advance that you will eventually love the king."

"I do not say and do not think that I shall ever love the king."

"Oh, yes, you will love him, I tell you."

"You see, yourself, that all my oaths are of no avail, and give you no sort of security; so let yourself go with the tide."

Mailly threw himself at her feet.

"My love," he cried, "my only treasure, I am going to look at you for a long while, — I am going to accustom myself to the thought that you have been mine, that you have been mine alone, and I shall end by believing that you will always be mine."

"Ah, how we fall back into our illusions, Count!"

"Olympe, you are cruel!"

"No, I am outspoken. You know that I fainted yesterday?"

"Alas! yes."

"Well, as I recovered from my swoon, it seemed as if I had left one world and entered another. The world which I left was the world of illusions; that which I entered was the world of realities. What am I? where am I going? Why all this delicacy? I have already changed masters once; perhaps I shall change again. I am a treasure, and treasures sometimes are stolen."

"Olympe! Olympe!"

"And, don't you see, perhaps this is a means."

"A means?"

"Yes, a means of loving you. If the king steals me from you, why — why — I am sure that he will no sooner have stolen me than I shall find that I love you dearly."

"Olympe, you tear my heart!"

"I?"

"Yes, you are one of those terrible women who always love the lovers whom they have lost."

"Do you think that?" she said with a start.

" Yes, I do."

" Then keep me away from just one man."

" Bannière ? "

" Yes."

" Do you love him ? "

" Yes."

" But you told me at Lyons that you loved him no longer."

" I thought I did not."

" Unhappy woman ! "

" Unhappy, indeed; for I love him still."

" You love an actor ! "

" I am an actress."

" You love a gambler ! "

" He gambled to win money for me."

" You love a man who betrayed you ! "

Olympe's face grew dark, and her lips were tightly closed.

" And for whom ? " continued Mailly; " for an unworthy rival."

" Hold, Monsieur," said Olympe, " forbear to speak of that, I beg you, and we shall get along much better."

" Why so ? "

" Because the more I think of it, the more I am inclined to believe that there was some treachery in that whole business."

" Of course there was; but Monsieur Bannière was the traitor."

" He swore to me in that prison that he was innocent."

" Bah! a man of his sort always will swear to anything."

" Bannière was an honorable man, Count."

" Olympe ! Olympe ! "

" You see that I was right when I said to you, ' Do not speak of Bannière.' "

"What does it matter if we speak of him, so long as you are thinking of him ? "

"I can govern my words, Count; but I have not learned how to control my thoughts."

" And your thoughts ? "

" Go back, in spite of me, to that cell where he grovelled at my feet, saying, 'I am innocent, Olympe; I am innocent, and I will prove it to you.' "

" Did he prove it ? "

" No; but suppose he should ? "

" Well, if he should prove it, what would happen ? Tell me."

" King Louis XV. would not be the man for you to fear, Count."

" It would be Bannière ? "

" Yes."

" Oh, you are right, Olympe; let us talk of something else."

" I am always right."

" Then guide me, command me.   What shall we do ? "

" What shall we do ? "

" Yes; tell me."

" Well, Count, let us have breakfast, as we were so foolish as to go without supper last night; then, taking life as I find it, I think I will go to sleep, after breakfast, having been silly enough not to sleep last night."

Mailly took Olympe in his arms.

" Very well," said he; " so be it ! Let us live from day to day; and when you see how much you are to me, my Olympe ! why, then you will have pity on me, and will strive to preserve your love and yourself for me."

" I will do my best," she replied.

At two o'clock in the afternoon Mailly was still asleep, and dreaming that Olympe's heart was his, and his alone.

The dream was too lovely to last very long

His valet knocked at his door and awakened him.

"What is it now?" asked Mailly; "why do you dis-turb me?"

"Monsieur le Duc de Richelieu absolutely insists upon speaking with Monsieur le Comte," said the valet.

"The Duc de Richelieu! on what subject?"

"The king's service, he says."

"Oh, the devil!" said Mailly, leaping out of bed; "say that I will be with him at once."

XII.

DE MAILLY IS JEALOUS OF HIS WIFE.

MONSIEUR LE DUC DE RICHELIEU was, in fact, waiting to see the count, as the valet had said.

The greeting between them was courteous upon both sides, as became polished gentlemen. Mailly was not the man to allow himself to be so put out by his interview with Pecquigny as to receive with discourtesy the frankest and most affable nobleman of the age.

They embraced each other, as the custom was.

"Can you spare me a half-hour of your time, my dear Count?" said the duke, after these preliminaries were satisfactorily concluded.

"Well, Duke, you know that here — "

"Yes, this is the abode of pleasure and not of business, I know."

"You come on business, then, do you?"

"Yes, and most urgent business too."

"But you see — "

"That you are with your mistress?"

"Precisely."

"*Mon Dieu!* I am terribly sorry to disturb you."

"But after all, Duke — "

"Well?"

"If it is absolutely essential?"

"It is absolutely essential."

"In that case I am at your service. Where do you prefer that an interview should take place?"

" If I can have my choice, I should like very much to take a walk somewhere."

" We have the garden."

" That will suit me admirably."

" This way, then."

Mailly led his visitor through the dining-room where he had received Pecquigny, and they descended a flight of steps, bordered with superb flowers sheltered under glass, into the garden, which was left desolate and bare by the first frosts; and yet one could still imagine, even in these first days of winter, what it had been, and what it would be again with the return of the balmy days of May.

It was a long rectangle, with a row of tall sycamores near the wall, from whose branches the frost had already begun to hang its sharp stalactites.

" Now, Monsieur le Duc, we are quite as secluded as you seem to wish that we should be. Speak then; I am ready to listen. It would seem that you come as an official messenger ? "

" 'Pon my soul! I am something of that sort, my dear Count; so allow me to congratulate you on your perspicacity."

The two men gravely saluted each other.

" Do you know that you have a delightful little place here, Count ? "

" Coming from you, Monsieur le Duc, the praise is doubly flattering."

" It must be a lovely bird who is worthy of such a lovely cage."

" Duke! "

" However, if rumor does not exaggerate, it appears that your mistress is the pearl of pearls. In what waters did you plunge to secure such a treasure ? "

"The devil!" thought Mailly; "has he got his eye on Olympe too?"

He smiled as he said,—

"You spoke of an official message, Duke; are you changing your residence?"

"What do you mean?"

"After being accredited to the great house of Austria, are you now intrusted with a mission to the little house on Rue Grange-Batelière?"

"Why, your guessing is marvellously accurate, my dear Count! this is your day, upon my word!"

"Yes," said Mailly to himself,—"yes, he is going to ask me for Olympe too."

He began to brace himself for another struggle.

"Monsieur le Duc," said he, aloud, "my penetration goes even deeper than you suppose."

"Indeed!" said Richelieu.

"For I have not only detected in you an ambassador, but I have divined the object of your embassy."

"Do you mean it?"

"Yes; but I warn you of one thing."

"What is that?"

"That I am ill-disposed toward your mission."

"Oho!" said the duke, in surprise.

"Yes, I was approached on this subject very recently; and the interview was as disagreeable to me as anything could well be, I assure you."

"You have been approached?"

"Yes, and very frankly and forcibly too."

"Would it be indiscreet to ask by whom, Count?"

"No, faith! especially since by my way of receiving him—"

"Well?"

"I cured him of any desire to come again."

"Still you don't tell me the name of this officious meddler."

"Oh! he is a friend of mine."

"Pecquigny, perhaps?" said the duke, at a venture.

"The same!" cried Mailly; "how did you know that?"

"Pecquigny! Deuce take him!" muttered the duke; "the damned courtier got the start of me." He added aloud: "And you refused to listen to him?"

"On the contrary, I heard him to the end. It was then that, having no further room for doubt, I dismissed him in a way to let him see that it would be most unpleasant for me to have him return."

"But perhaps, my dear Count," said Richelieu, in his most insinuating tone, "he did not present all the arguments in their most favorable light?"

"Oh, indeed! with all your eloquence, Monsieur le Duc, I doubt whether you could surpass Pecquigny; he was far ahead of Demosthenes."

"Let us talk it over, I beg, Monsieur le Comte," said Richelieu; "and, in order that we may do so satisfactorily, pray do not confound my suggestions with Pecquigny's. I am your friend."

"Pecquigny began with precisely the same assurance. You alarm me, Monsieur le Duc; for it is to his friendship that I attribute his remarkable eloquence."

"Eloquent as he was, I hope to say some things to you that he forgot."

"You may try."

"First of all, let us clear up one matter."

"Go on, and clear it up, Duke."

"It is a good thing to know where we start from, isn't it?"

"To be sure."

"In the first place, it is almost certain that you have left Madame de Mailly, have you not?"

"What! is it already known?"

"It is public property."

"Upon my word, she has lost no time."

"She or you?"

"She."

"It matters little; in any event, the thing was done extraordinarily well."

"That is known too!" cried Mailly, not yet recovered from his astonishment.

"Believe me, my dear Count, if I had not known it, I should not have shown myself here."

"Oh, yes, of course," said Mailly.

"Why of course?" asked Richelieu.

"You are laying out your plan of attack."

"What do you mean?" Mailly shook his head with a very knowing look. "I don't understand," said Richelieu.

"I understand, if you don't," said Mailly.

"Does it mean that the rupture with Madame de Mailly is a serious one?"

"It means that I give you *carte blanche*, Monsieur le Duc; henceforth Madame de Mailly and I are strangers."

"You have a way of saying that, my dear Count —"

"In what way did I say it, pray?"

"In a way to make me think that you regret the fact."

"I do not regret it, — no, Duke; and yet she has some excellent qualities."

"She is charming!"

"Oh, don't praise her too highly to me, I beg you."

"Why not?"

"Because, after all is said and done. I am her husband."

"Well, because you're her husband, does it follow that you ought to be insensible to the worth of a most lovable wife?"

"Did I not say to you a moment ago, Monsieur le Duc, that she had some excellent qualities?"

"Which did not prevent you, however, from giving her her liberty. But, *dame!* I can imagine that."

"What! you can imagine it?"

"To be sure, when one has a mistress like yours!"

"Damnation!" thought Mailly; "here he comes back to Olympe!"

"Well, upon my word!" said he, "can it be that you have already found time to make the acquaintance of my wife and my mistress, although you only returned from Vienna three or four days ago?"

"Of your wife, yes; of your mistress, no; but yesterday, in a very good place, I heard it said that she was a lovely creature."

"At Rambouillet?"

"Nowhere else; how did you know?"

"Did I not tell you that I have had a visit from Pecquigny?"

"True; in fact, it was he who said it."

"To whom?"

"To the king, I believe."

Mailly stamped upon the ground.

"Aha!" said Richelieu, "I infer that common report does not exaggerate?"

"As to whom?"

"As to Mademoiselle Olympe, of course. Is not that the name of your mistress? They say that she is beautiful."

"Very beautiful!"

"And instinct with grace."

"She is a perfect fairy."

"And talented withal."

"She is an artist of the first rank."

"And she loves you?"

"What the devil is there remarkable about that?"

"Nothing, *morbleu!* you are a charming cavalier, and I but asked you a simple question."

"Does it interest you, then, whether Olympe does or does not love me?"

"Tremendously."

"Well, then, Duke, she does love me."

"And how about yourself, — do you love her?"

"It is an absurd thing to say, Duke, I know; but — but — I worship her, that's the truth."

"So that nothing could separate you from her?"

"Nothing."

"No future prospect, howsoever brilliant it might be, could prevail upon you to give her up?"

"Not only could nothing induce me to give her up, but if any one should undertake to steal her from me — "

"What would you do?"

"*Dame!* I would kill him who should undertake the commission for another, were he my best friend, were he my brother, were it yourself, Duke!"

"Your hand!" said Richelieu, holding out his own.

"My hand, do you say?"

"You make me the happiest man on earth."

"By telling you that I love my mistress, and that my mistress loves me; that I would refuse to give her up to you, yes, to the king himself?"

"How fortunate that is!" cried the duke.

"Why is it fortunate, pray? You are keeping me on the rack, my dear Duke."

" Why, because it removes all my conscientious scruples. "

" You had scruples, then ? "

" Indeed I did, my dear Count; you understand, as you just said yourself, a husband is always a husband, unless he has ceased to be one — as you have — in which event — why — "

" Well ? "

" Why, one may venture to speak to him about his wife. "

" What! do you want to speak about my wife ? "

" To be sure, as I came for no other purpose; that is what embarrasses me. "

" *Pardieu!* Duke, " rejoined Mailly, " I would be very glad to know which of us is the more embarrassed of the two. "

" Clearly I am, " said the duke; " the proof of it is that here have I been beating about the bush for an hour without knowing where to begin. "

" Do you wish me to help you ? "

" *Pardieu!* that would be more than kind, my dear Count ! "

" Oh, it 's very easy; you saw Madame de Mailly yesterday at Rambouillet, and found her to your liking. You know that I have a mistress, and you wanted, like a good fellow, to make sure that I had no wife. "

" Faith, that 's about it. But who the devil told you ? "

" I have my sources of information; now go on. "

" Really, my dear Count, no one is so clever as you: yes, I have designs upon Madame de Mailly; yes, she is the person whom I must have, and I do not despair of convincing you — "

" Ah, this is too much ! " cried Mailly, laughing uproariously, but with a violence which proved that his

heart was not in his merriment: " you come here and ask
my permission to take my wife from me! "

"Would you prefer, my dear Count, that I should
come like a villain, or one of these vile imitators of the
regency, and steal her from you without so much as a
'by your leave,' in the shadow of your separation still
only half known?   Fie! fie! that would be terribly
vulgar!   Would you like me to explain to you, Count,
why most of my missions have been successful?   It is
because, since there must always be two parties to a
negotiation, I always try not to surprise my adversary;
I win his good-will by my straightforwardness, and then
vanquish him by my logic."

" All this means," cried the count, " that you expect
to convince me that it is right for me to leave Madame
de Mailly to you?"

" I certainly count upon it."

"Do you mean it?"

"Except for that I most assuredly would not have
intruded upon you."

"Good, very good!" cried Mailly, somewhat brightened up by the turn affairs had taken; "prove it, prove
it, my dear Duke, and if you convince me of it, I shall
consider you, whom I know to have been thus far uncon-
quered, unconquerable."

" To begin with, you no longer care for your wife, do
you?"

" I admit it; she has a fearful disposition."

" For you."

" Ah! but you see it was for myself that I took her,
my dear Duke."

" Now you are speaking ill of Madame de Mailly."

" Why should you want me to speak well of her?"

" Count, be serious, I beg of you," said the duke.   "I

swear to you that it 's worth while; and since Pecquigny
has spoken to you, you ought to realize the situation."

"Let us come to details, Duke."

"Well, then, I think it essential that you should not
seem to take notice of what is going on. A sacrifice
which one is bound to make is not compromising in the
eyes of the world; and besides there are two reasons why
you should make it: first, the king's will which one cannot resist —"

"That 's just the way Pecquigny talked."

"Oh, the corrupter!   Secondly, the best reason of all
which your good angel himself could furnish."

"What is that?"

"Incompatibility, my dear Duke, — incompatibility of
temper."

"I beg your pardon."

"I said incompatibility.   Don't you see what a lucky
chance it was that this separation should come just at the
very moment when we had need of it?"

"What separation?"

"Why, between you and your wife."

Mailly looked at the duke.

"Upon my soul," said he, "I fail to see what our
separation has to do with this business."

"Very well, Count, did I not say to you that Pecquigny did not present all the arguments?   What! do
you mean to tell me that it is anything short of miracu-
lous that you and your wife on the very same day, without premeditation or scandal, should have signed that
little document, which makes you safe from ridicule and
her from the charge of infidelity?"

"Upon my honor, Duke," cried Mailly, "I still fail to
understand you."

"You alarm me; pray let me explain then."

"Oh, I shall be exceedingly obliged to you, for you and Pecquigny between you will drive me out of my wits."

"Well, then, what would the world have said if this fortunate separation had not preceded the step which I am now taking? — 'Monsieur de Mailly is an ambitious fellow.'"

"Ambitious?"

"'Madame de Mailly sacrifices her husband, who is only a count, to the king because he is king.'"

"To the king!" cried Mailly, losing color.

"Why, yes, to the king of course."

"What! my wife?"

"Well?"

"The king is after her?"

"Most assuredly."

"And you?"

"What about me?"

"You come in the king's behalf?"

"In whose behalf do you suppose I come, in heaven's name? I am an ambassador of France, and France — is the king. The deuce take me, my dear Count, but when one's name is Richelieu, one attends to nobody's business but the king's or one's own."

Mailly was speechless, stupefied; an unfamiliar prospect, of which he had never dreamed, opened out before him. Wholly absorbed by thoughts of his mistress, he had believed until that moment that it was she who was the object of the duke's mission.

"The king in love with my wife!" he muttered at last, recovering from his stupefaction.

"Well, well!" cried Richelieu, "one would say that you were falling from the clouds. Here I have been singing the same song in ten different keys for half an hour."

"Oh, Duke! Duke!" muttered Mailly, "is this really true?"

"Why, haven't you been listening to me, for God's sake?"

"My wife! the king loves my wife!"

Richelieu nodded his head affirmatively.

"Why, it can't be so!" suddenly exclaimed Mailly.

"Why not, pray?"

"Because this very morning Pecquigny told me just the reverse. You are inventing this, Duke."

"Inventing it! God forbid!"

"Yes, inventing it."

"For what purpose, pray?"

"For the purpose of taking my wife from me."

"Come, come, Count!" retorted Richelieu; "what sort of infernal nonsense is that? Is this the way they talk at Paris since I went away? Invent! I invent anything! Did you make such a charge as that? My dear Count, you are wandering."

"Oh, Pecquigny! Pecquigny!"

"Well, tell me what he told you."

"He told me that it was Olympe, my mistress, whom the king was after."

"Do you mean it?"

Richelieu laughed heartily.

"That amuses you, Duke, does it?" said Mailly, all ready to lose his temper.

"Indeed it does."

"May I ask why?"

"Because it is excruciatingly funny. But, after all, suppose it were so?"

"The king in love with two women?"

"He is quite capable of it, Count."

"I implore you not to joke thus."

"But it may well be that he will take both of them from you, my poor Count."

"Ah! Duke, you must, in fairness, agree with me that it's an intolerable position for me."

"Upon my word, it is an extraordinary state of things."

"Olympe, whom I love so dearly! "

"Well, let your wife go, then."

"Madame de Mailly, who bears my name! "

"Then let your mistress go."

"Duke, I am a lost man; all Paris will make sport of me: here you are beginning already."

"God forbid, my dear Count; on the contrary, I bring you my deepest sympathy and friendship."

"Advise me, then."

"Oh, pshaw! now you are laughing at me."

"How so?"

"Does one advise people in your condition, — people who are in love and selfish?"

"You came here for some purpose, Duke."

"*Dame!* I thought I had already told you often enough why I came."

"Tell me once more."

"Very well; I came to offer you a means of escaping ridicule."

"Give it to me quickly."

"I came to say to you: 'Your wife is sought by the king: you never loved your wife; your wife no longer loves you. Make haste.' "

"I am to make haste?"

"Yes."

"To do what?"

"Why, to imitate Monsieur de Montespan, who throughout his life was feared by the king, hoodwinked by his wife, and esteemed by everybody."

"Duke! Duke! that is a downright infamous proposition!"

"Are you mad, my dear fellow? Why, it's supreme good-fortune, on the other hand; it is what is called drawing a cover, or holding the enemy for ransom."

"I should be glad, Duke, to see things from your standpoint."

"I will prove what I say. If you hesitate, the king will begin by attacking you in a weak spot, just as they do in laying siege to a town. He will take away your mistress first, and everybody will approve, on the score of morality."

"You say that everybody will approve?"

"Faith, yes; for everybody loves to laugh, do they not? The king, weary of your mistress, passes on to your wife; he steals her away also, and finds that operation the more easy, because allowing herself to be stolen she plays you a twofold trick. The result of it all is that you find yourself beaten by your mistress and your wife both, and all the world looks on at the spectacle; for there will be no spectator who will not long to witness the second act, after he has seen the first."

"Hold, Duke, this is frightful!"

"But true! Have your wits about you, on the other hand. Assume a sarcastic smile. Make your choice; reject the chaff, and select the good grain; in the tempest which threatens to overwhelm everything, cast an anchor to windward. Emerge from it a duke and peer, a knight in the royal orders; obtain a promise of a lucrative government, or the government itself, if possible, and see how everybody will laugh with you instead of laughing *at* you."

"Impossible! Impossible!"

"You are losing your senses! Do you love your mistress?"

"I am mad with love of her!"

"Do you love your wife?"

"I know not."

"Oh, the devil! faltering and turning back already! Weak, feeble creature that you are! Have you or have you not abandoned your wife?"

"Almost."

"Well, then, your abandoned wife will have her revenge."

"Perhaps."

"She will have her revenge, I tell you. Why, in God's name, do you suppose that any exception will be made in your favor? If she doesn't take her revenge with the king, she will with somebody else, and then good-by to the duchy, good-by to the peerage, good-by to the decoration, good-by to the government; you will have been a cuckold for nothing! Upon my soul, my dear Count, I cannot comprehend how a man of spirit, having such a lovely mistress as you have, and embarrassed by his wife as you are by yours, can help thanking heaven for sending him an opportunity for freedom."

"But freedom in such a case is rank dishonor!"

"Fine words, fine words! Suppose your wife loves the king, Monsieur; then prevent this dishonor, if you can!"

"Suppose my wife loves the king?"

"Why should she not? Is this Louis XV. young or old, ugly or handsome, king or shepherd? Is not the king worth more than you and I and all the rest?"

"Oh, Pecquigny again!" muttered the count.

"This which you don't choose to do with the advantage all on your side, you will be forced to submit to. Then you'll see, you'll see!"

"Duke, this is enough to drive a man mad!"

"No, Monsieur, it is a simple matter of protecting yourself. If you were reasonable, your choice would not be long in doubt."

Mailly buried his face in his hands.

Richelieu gazed pityingly at him, as the haughty victor gazes at his enemy at his feet.

"I came," said he, "to tell you a piece of good news, and to keep you informed as to what is going on; you take the thing altogether wrong, so let's talk no more about it."

"Do you know that all this you are saying to me is insulting?" cried Mailly, raising his head.

"Take care," said Richelieu, "lest you provoke me so far that I resent it. I am his Majesty's ambassador, and must maintain the honor of the crown."

"Like Pecquigny still again!" shouted the poor fellow; "like Pecquigny!"

He rested his head against the marble pedestal of a statue.

The duke evidently had led him to the point where he wished to lead him; for he took advantage of the unhappy count's momentary prostration to turn upon his heel and disappear.

XIII.

MAILLY IS AGITATED.

IT is easier to imagine than to describe Mailly's suffering after Richelieu's departure.

Lover and husband, he saw mistress and wife equally threatened. The wife is never of any value to the faithless husband until he sees that other eyes have distinguished her; but at that moment the wife represents to him property, name, honor, everything.

At that moment what a priceless treasure is that same wife, and how brilliantly shines all that had been disdained, how reasons for loving return with reasons for hating!

In an instant Monsieur de Mailly flew from one extreme to the other. He saw in his fancy his wife, whom he had left alone and desperate, — he saw her flattered and courted, enveloped in clouds of incense. He felt a sharp pang at his heart.

"Abandon my wife!" he said to himself; "abandon my property to him who has no claim to aught but my life! Never!"

Then he checked himself.

"But," he thought, "these artisans of intrigue and corruption have themselves told me that the king is kind, that he will not want to take away his all from an unhappy gentleman. Of the two objects which he covets he will go without one, so as to leave something for Monsieur de Mailly. A very model of continence

and virtue is the king! A veritable Scipio or
Alexander!"

Happy Mailly, go to! The king will take from you
only your wife or your mistress. It is for you to choose
the one which it pleases you to allow him to take, —
your wife if you choose, your mistress if you choose.
What noble generosity! After all, why should you
have a wife and a mistress at one and the same time?
It is a surplusage at which morality rebels.

And then the king, reared by Monsieur de Fleury, is
so moral! There is no patriarch in France but his
Majesty. The king alone can maintain a harem in
France, if he please. You have a mistress who loves
you, and a wife whom you think you ought to love.
No, no! the king will prove to you that it is too much;
he will prove it, perhaps by the Bastille, perhaps by
Vincennes, or by some other means equally agreeable.

He will prove it by sending the Captains of the
Guards to you, armed with long swords.

He will prove it by sending you his cleverest diplomatists arrayed in their armor of protocols and subtleties.

He will prove it by exile.

He will prove it as David proved it to Uriah for
Bathsheba.

He has not only the example of Louis XIV. in his
favor, but of King David too.

In the first affair against Spaniards or Austrians, you
will be assigned a place so well chosen that a furnace
will open beneath your feet, as happened to Monsieur
de Beaufort before Candia.

Or perhaps you will be killed by a Spanish chasseur
fighting manfully, face to face, and braving the ordinary
chances of war.

Or you may receive a ball in the loins from one of

your own grenadiers, — a deplorable piece of awkwardness which will bring tears to the eyes of sensitive folk, who read the gazettes.

Mailly! Mailly! it 's a serious crisis!

It is especially serious because it demonstrates the possession of unruly passions by this young prince whom all France, with one accord, calls the " well beloved."

" Poor France!   What will happen when she knows him better! His own wife, my wife, and my mistress! Marie Leczinska, Madame la Comtesse de Mailly, and Olympe de Clèves, all for a young man in his teens! Serious, indeed, it is ! "

Yes, Mailly, it is a serious matter; and what will it be when he is thirty years old, and when he is sixty ?

How many people at such a time have closed their eyes, as the Duc de Richelieu suggested, — prudent people, clever in handling themselves, and whose affairs have not ceased to run smoothly under the twofold impulsion of those two excellent motors, a beautiful wife and a beautiful mistress!

Ah! they are the shrewd fellows!

" It is certain that if I do not adopt that course, as the Duc de Richelieu, himself the cleverest of the clever, says; if I choose to despise my wife, to laugh at her and the king, to make a faction for myself among the sour old courtiers who snarl at virtue; if 1 wish to recast myself, and carry myself back to the last century, or rather to the years of Madame la Marquise de Maintenon, to be called Montausier, Navailles, Montespan, and to be blessed in the almanacs printed in Holland, — it is certain that if I carry the spirit of resistance to the point of undergoing exile, of presenting remonstrances to the king, and of asking justice at the hands of the queen, the *rôle* becomes superb.

" With a little tact, — and I have that quality, God be praised ! — I can insult his Majesty with my broadside, conspire with Marie Leczinska against my wife, and arrange for a triumphal procession to the Bastille, escorted by all the unhappy and deceived husbands in the country, who will make of me their Cæsar or their Pompey.

" Then will come rehabilitation after exile, and a shower of dignities pouring upon my head after the Bastille, or at least a reputation that will cast into the shade all the conquerors of this overrated age.

" There 's another course open to me. No outcry, no scandal; a legal separation, which will be much more fitting for a man of delicate sensibility than this little rough draft of a divorce, which Louise and I entered into between ourselves; disinheritance of any so-called legitimate children who might be born; and all this arranged secretly and in due form. Thus I assure myself a life of tranquillity and full of honors. No one will laugh at the king, to whose will I shall have bowed. No one will laugh at me, for I shall have made my name respected. My wife will be no longer my wife; they will rechristen her, and call her the ' Well beloved of the well beloved.'

" What could be better than that ?

" But no, no, never shall it be said that a French gentleman, when he has given his name to a woman, allowed himself to be forced to deny her. I, Comte de Mailly, have a wife by my own will, by the law civil and law canonical. King Louis XV. shall not take my wife from me; no, I do not choose that it shall be so!

" But Olympe, my mistress, — ah! that is another matter, unhappily. I have a mistress, but she is mine by no law, civil or canonical; and yet it is a right made sacred by custom. There has been no instance among the nobility for a hundred years, of a man doing without a mistress.

"Yes; but if there is no instance of a man doing without a mistress, it is equally true that there is no instance of a woman doing without — "

At this point Mailly interrupted the flow of his own thoughts.

"What was I about to say?" he cried; "I am condemning myself out of my own mouth. Yes, that is unprecedented; but I — I, Comte de Mailly, will prevent it nevertheless. Let me also play at arbitrary conduct, since these other people are trying to monopolize it."

Thereupon Mailly, trembling with excitement and pale as a ghost, went into the house to get his sword; and without waking Olympe, who was sleeping soundly and peacefully, he was off at lightning speed for the Hôtel de Nesle.

Louise had returned comfortably in her carriage with the king's suite, lying back among her cushions, and alone with her thoughts.

She was in ecstasies over her memories of the preceding night. Filled with hope for the future, she had not ceased, after leaving Rambouillet, to pursue the pleasant dream which nascent love, free from restraint, always brings to vigorous youth.

It was not that the countess's thoughts had really carried her so far as Richelieu had gone. No. Being by nature modest and reserved, though open to such impulses as a well-placed passion might impart, Louise had not allowed her thoughts to wander among chimeras; she was confident that she had it in her to take advantage of any opportunities that circumstances might bring to pass.

She had resumed control of her hotel, as if Monsieur

de Mailly were not expected to return. In her eyes the whole past — the marriage, the nuptial blessing, administered in the presence of the families of Mailly and of Nesle — was an insignificant line of demarcation between the preceding and the following year, — nothing more.

The Comte de Mailly was no longer a factor in her calculations. The dreams of the present hour had driven her husband from her mind.

She had no bitter feeling, no feeling of enmity or hatred against him. If the count should present himself before her, she could call him her friend without reproaching her lips or her thought with falsehood.

As for the heart, we say nothing about that organ, as the heart counted for little in the relations between Monsieur le Comte de Mailly, Mademoiselle de Nesle's husband and Olympe de Clèves' lover, and Madame la Comtesse de Mailly, smitten with Louis XV.

Suddenly the count's presence was announced to her by the same maid whom we have seen smile at Bannière. Monsieur de Mailly had arrived at the hotel in hot haste.

She rose, astonished beyond measure, and looking through the window saw that he was indeed ascending the steps of the portico, apparently in great agitation.

A moment later he entered her room.

Louise uttered an exclamation of surprise.

"You!" said she.

"Yes, Madame, it is I."

The maid opened her eyes to their fullest extent, and there was even more curiosity expressed in them than in those of her mistress.

Monsieur de Mailly noticed her eyes in a mirror.

"Be good enough to dismiss Mademoiselle," said he.

The maid left the room, with her mind made up to

listen at the door. The count followed her with his
eyes until the door closed behind her.

Then he turned to his wife.

"Well, Monsieur le Comte," said she, "what is the
matter, and to what am I indebted for the unexpected
pleasure of seeing you?"

"To a very serious reason, Madame."

"Oh, *mon Dieu!* you frighten me!"

Mailly smiled bitterly; he thought that a bitter smile
could not in any event do him any harm.

"Be seated, pray!" continued the countess; "am I
sufficiently fortunate, Monsieur, to find myself, since
yesterday, of some consequence to you?"

"You have become — indispensable to me."

This time it was Madame de Mailly's turn to smile.

"How can that be, *bon Dieu!* Tell me, I beg you."

"You have no suspicion of what brings me here?"

"Not the least; and so I am overflowing with
curiosity."

"Madame, do you know what people are saying?"

"Where?"

"Everywhere."

"Tell me what people are saying everywhere; I am
listening, Monsieur."

"Well, they say that the king— Ah! you are blushing already!"

"Monsieur, if you continue to stare at me in that
fashion, I shall not only blush, but shall lose my color
too. So I entreat you, Monsieur, to lay aside these
lieutenant of police airs, and go on. What do they say
of the king?"

"They say that the king — that the king —"

"Well, go on."

"That the king has cast his eyes upon a certain lady

with a view of passing with her such time as he does not pass with the queen."

"Aha! they say that, do they?" replied Madame de Mailly, much disturbed.

"Ah, you told the truth!" cried the count; "see how pale you are now, Madame!"

Louise rose.

"Monsieur," said she, "I have no clear idea what the object may be of this wretched comedy which you are performing for my benefit; but be good enough, before you carry it any further, to understand that it is not at all to my taste."

"Oh, Madame," said Mailly, "I beg you to accept a *rôle* in it."

"By no means, Monsieur. I am not in the habit of replying to things which I do not understand."

"Never fear, I will make myself understood. I will not be long. Those interested are desirous to know whether the person whom the king has chosen will accept his homage; and as you are acquainted with her, I am charged to ask your opinion."

"A deplorable business for a worthy gentleman, Monsieur, I should say. I am surprised, knowing you as I do, that you accepted it."

"Don't get excited, Madame, pray; you judge me too quickly. If I accepted the commission, be sure that I had my reasons for it."

"What were they, Monsieur?"

"I know the person too."

"Then do your errand yourself."

"Yes, I know her. You — you yourself are the one."

"I!" cried Louise; "it is I whom the king is after?"

She uttered these few words with such imprudent eagerness that Mailly, if he had been less blind than he was, would have attributed her emotion to something besides anger.

" Yourself, Madame," he repeated.

For a few moments she was buried in deep thought.

" The thing is impossible," she said at last.

" Be good enough to believe that I have it on the best authority."

" Oh! whose ? "

" It makes little difference. That is not what you want to know; you would like perhaps to be enlightened further."

" I don't understand you now."

" A husband who speaks out is always incomprehensible."

" But, Monsieur, you forget that you are not my husband ! "

" A mere joke, Madame."

" What do you mean by a mere joke ? How about our agreement ? "

" Our agreement — our agreement," stammered Mailly, in much embarrassment; " oh, Madame, yesterday I played a game which it does n't suit me to play to-day."

" I must beg you to go on with what you have to say, in the hope that among all your words I may find one or two to give me some satisfaction."

" I have but little more to say. The king has his eye on you, Madame, so they say; and I presume that that is the explanation of all this sulking, and all the high and mighty airs which you have been inflicting on me for some time past."

" You charge me with sulking and with putting on airs ? "

" Oh! of course you will deny it; such perfidious conduct is worth an attempt at an excuse, I suppose."

" Monsieur le Comte, you forget that you are speaking to a woman."

" I am not speaking to 'a woman,' but to my wife, which is a very different matter."

" Ah! but you did n't think of that yesterday."

" Agreed; but I think of it to-day, when there is a probability of my being made a laughing-stock by you. Yesterday my mind was occupied only with my unhappiness — "

" A subtle distinction, that! "

" A distinction which satisfies my argument; I make such use of it as I can. Come, Madame, if you are willing to receive the king's addresses, be so good as to tell me so."

" I could answer your question, Monsieur."

" That is all that I ask, Madame."

" I should be as discreet as you are foolish."

" Ah! you deny that the king — "

" I deny absolutely nothing, Monsieur; the king does as he pleases. Go and ask him, and he will answer you."

" A fine thing to do, that would be ! "

" Do you think so ? "

" Oh, you, who became free yesterday, beware! You presume altogether too much upon your freedom to-day."

" I, who became free yesterday, am to-day such as I choose to be to-morrow, and such as I shall always be. You are yourself responsible for this condition of things; you must take the consequences."

" Take the consequences, when they lead to dishonor ? "

" Oh, Monsieur, we have not reached that point."

" Madame, let us go no farther toward it. I appeal to your probity; will it respond to the appeal ? "

" Always! But, look out! a woman's probity finds expression in frankness."

"I accept the terms. Are you pleased with the king?"

"Greatly, Monsieur."

"There's frankness for you," cried the count, with a forced smile.

"You asked for just that, and I promised that you should have it."

"And you will be equally frank to the end?"

"To the end."

"I resume my investigations."

"Be careful!"

"Always the bird of ill omen. I am not weary of you, Louise."

"So much the better, blind man!"

"If the king should offer you his homage, what have you determined to do?"

"Monsieur, for pity's sake, don't force me to reply to such impertinent questions."

"You forget that I am a self-constituted ambassador, and that I have accepted your stipulation of perfect frankness."

"You insist, then?"

"I insist."

"Very well! Monsieur, I am free; I received an indirect dismissal from my husband, who took unto himself a mistress almost before I had had time to call him my husband. I am young, and am told that I am fair; I have a heart and eyes which belong to me, and since I am free, I shall avail myself of my heart and eyes."

"You will love another?"

"If I choose to, yes."

Exasperated by his powerlessness to deal with this extraordinary woman, who revealed her inmost thoughts to him so proudly, Mailly allowed his indignation to carry him to the point of threatening.

"Madame," he cried, with an angry gesture, "you had best beware yourself!"

"Count," said she, coldly, "your extravagance will put me wholly in the right, if I am not now."

Mailly was vanquished, and his outburst of temper was checked on his lips.

"I see," he resumed, after a moment's hesitation which enabled him to recover his wits, — "I see what reply I shall have to make. Madame, you love the king."

"True."

"Will you do me the honor to tell me since when it has been true, lest I learn it from the mouths of others? You must understand, Madame, that for me to learn it from others would be deplorable for us both."

"Monsieur," said the countess, with the same unruffled demeanor which had characterized her throughout the interview "I ceased to love my husband day before yesterday, and yesterday I began to love the king."

A flame of rage and despair — of jealousy, in short — blazed in the count's eyes.

Suddenly he seemed to grow calmer.

"Assure me that you are not joking," said he, in tones of the utmost mildness and melancholy. "I am sadly in need of that assurance, Louise."

He folded his arms upon his heaving chest.

"Monsieur, my heart is torn to be compelled to give you that assurance; it is no subject for joking, for sorrow entered my heart with that love."

"But shame and misery await you at the end of this passion which you dare to avow. Reflect seriously, Madame, I beg you."

"I have reflected."

"Then I will myself prevent you from rushing to your own destruction."

"I believe, Monsieur le Comte, that in so doing you would render me a valuable service; and yet you can see how far my frankness goes with you, — I honestly do not dare to ask you to assist me."

"Why not?"

"Because — must I confess it? — I believe I should curse your good offices."

"Marble heart!" muttered Mailly to himself. "In vain do I rend my soul in search of a soft and loving heart! Patience, patience! I was born to suffer; in all France there are no two women like Mesdemoiselles de Nesle and de Clèves, and it must needs be that I must lose them both."

With that his ideas became calmer, if not less painful; he bent before the countess's immovable will, and contented himself with saying, —

"Luckily, Madame, I am still your master, and in our respective positions a private agreement is binding upon neither of the contracting parties."

"You are in error, Monsieur le Comte; for if I have determined to listen to other men than you, I will make good use of this agreement which gives me my freedom. It may be void in the eye of the law, but it will carry the case against you before the tribunal of public opinion, the only one from which I have anything to fear. And now, if you have nothing else to say to me — "

With a queenly gesture she pointed to the door.

Mailly, completely crushed, bowed and left the room.

XIV.

SERPENT NUMBER ONE.

MAILLY could find no comfort in being continually driven to dreary monologues; and yet, judging from what we have seen, the monologue contained less that was disagreeable for him than the dialogue.

After his scene with Louise, her despotic manner, and above all the imperial majesty with which she had shown him the door, the count, repulsed by his wife, had said to himself that she certainly must possess some qualities that were hidden from the eyes of a husband; but since he, being her husband, could not detect them, he would, if he must, put out the eyes of all the rest of the world, so that there might not exist a man who could see what he could not.

Threats, entreaties, brute force, persuasion, — he had reviewed them all in his brain in the process of arranging a plan of campaign. Having determined upon his plan, which was the work of a quarter of an hour, passed by him in walking back and forth from one end to the other of the terrace on the bank of the river, Mailly's legs quite naturally bore him from the Hôtel de Nesle to the little house on Rue Grange-Batelière, from Louise de Mailly to Olympe de Clèves.

A poor wretch must look for consolation somewhere, especially when the author of his misfortunes gives him the right to console himself.

After all he had heard from his wife, Mailly certainly was not so culpable in paying a visit to his mistress as he had been the night before.   His conscience derived a vast amount of satisfaction from that thought.   A clear conscience is such an excellent thing!

Mailly, then, arrived at his little house in the best of all possible frames of mind to be comforted.   He went quickly upstairs, like a man who was in haste to exchange unpleasant thoughts for pleasant ones.   But half-way up he was stopped by his valet-de-chambre.

" Pardon, Monsieur! " said he.

" What do you want with me ? "

" You are going to Madame's apartments ? "

" To be sure I am. "

" But Madame — "

" Well, Madame — "

" Is not alone. "

Mailly was beginning to expect surprises at every turn, yet at this intelligence he stopped in bewilderment.   Then he reflected that where Olympe was at home he was equally so, and motioning the servant aside, he entered the room.

The Duc de Pecquigny was sitting by Olympe's side, as gracious and smiling as you please.

Mailly frowned darkly, as befits a man who is on the point of becoming jealous.

He did not abandon his purpose of entering, however.

The duke was eager to show him some civility, and offered him a chair.   Mailly sat down.

This air of familiarity which Pecquigny seemed to have assumed toward Olympe in so short a time, amazed Mailly to the last degree.   He looked upon himself as a man attacked by robbers on the highway, who receives a blow on the head from a club, just as he is preparing to defend himself. Was he awake or dreaming? Was it really the light of day that he saw, or was it the reflection of the thousand fantastically shaped candles which the imagination, when once excited, forthwith sets alight in the brain of a passionate man?

By the light of day or of the aforesaid candles, whichever it was, Mailly saw the duke clad in the latest fashion and with extreme elegance; nothing finer than the point-lace in his sleeves could be imagined; he was playing carelessly with the hilt of a sword which might have been made for a child born to sit upon the throne of the world: that single sword-hilt was worth as much as all the swords in the universe.

Opposite the duke Olympe was sitting, or reclining, upon an ottoman. She was listening tranquilly, with her sweetest smile and with her great watchful eyes, to all that the duke was assuming the right to say to her.

Such was the picture.

Mailly outside the door, upon the threshold, and in the room heard a few fragmentary phrases, like these, —

"Oh! never mind public opinion, Mademoiselle, but do what will make you happy."

"Beware of the absurdities of virtue; they are the worst of all, because there is no cure for them."

"Do you know that so-called reserve is often another name for incapacity?"

Such were the words which struck Mailly's ear as he was entering Olympe's room in a state of intense excitement.

The corrupter, as we have said, was sitting comfortably in his easy-chair, with a placidity which was not disturbed in the least by Mailly's arrival.

"Duke!" cried the count.

It was only one word, but that one word expressed all sorts of reproaches and all sorts of warnings.

Pecquigny made no other reply than to extend to the count the ends of his fingers, which were hidden in his lace cuffs.

Then the conversation went on just as if Mailly had not appeared to interrupt it.

"Duke," Olympe replied, "I have already told you that I was not born to be happy."

It was a blow fit to fell a bull in a slaughter-house.

Mailly received it full in the face, but kept his head erect.

"That is not kind to those who love you, Olympe," he said with a forced laugh.

"You are quite right, my dear fellow," said Pecquigny, "and I am just giving Mademoiselle a little lecture on that subject."

"Thanks, Duke! so I see," rejoined Mailly.

"But in spite of my arguments, Mademoiselle is obdurate," continued Pecquigny.

"Oh," said Olympe, "that does n't mean anything! Monsieur le Duc, instead of attacking me with those commonplaces which almost always make an impression on idle women, has laid himself out to call things by their right names."

A film came over Mailly's eyes.

"Yes, and great names, too," said Olympe, smiling, touched as she was at Mailly's sudden pallor.

"And your reply?" he asked in a shaking voice.

"My reply was," said Olympe, "that when I love, I shall love."

Mailly did not know whether that was a compliment or an insult. Like all men in a false position, he preferrea angry reproaches to argument, and brutality to the victory which peaceable discussion brings.

"I am sorry to see," he said, with an insulting sneer, "that Monsieur le Duc comes to my own house to steal my property."

"Count," Pecquigny retorted, "we have had an explanation on this subject. I had the honor at that time to tell you all that I mean to do, and I give you my word now that I shall do it; that is settled. It will take something more than your death-dealing eye, your clinched fists, and your faltering insults to turn me from my duty."

"Your duty!"

"*Parbleu!* my dearest Count, is it not a duty to prevent this fair damsel from being bored as you bore her?"

"Duke!"

"Oh, lose your temper, if you please! *Mordieu!* what do I care for that?"

Olympe remained silent.

"Madame deigned to receive me because I have the honor to be Captain of his Majesty's Guards," resumed Pecquigny, "and every door at which I knock must needs open before me and my staff of office. Madame received me because I am a worthy gentleman of spotless reputation, and because I bear a name which is never left standing in the street, do you hear, Comte de Mailly?"

"What does that mean?" cried the count, in a boiling rage.

"La, la!" continued Pecquigny, "I promised to make war upon you, and I am carrying out my promise; whether it angers you or not, you will see siege laid to your castle. I have succeeded in making my way into

the place you are defending, thanks to my individual
influence. Make a sortie, if you choose; try to dislodge
me, — it is your privilege."

"I will do it, too, eh, Olympe?"

"How do you mean, Monsieur le Comte?" said the
young woman. "Monsieur le Duc has said nothing to
me which he ought not to say."

"You hear, Mailly?"

"I did not comprehend a word of what Monsieur de
Pecquigny said to me."

"If you had heard more, Olympe — "

"But I did not hear more."

"Pray, let me explain to you, you ogre!" continued
the Captain of the Guards, laughing heartily; "you will
see that the scheme I have concocted is perfect, and I
defy you, with all your strategic skill, to resist it
successfully."

"Go on!"

"In the first place I desire to express my regrets to
Mademoiselle. It is my right."

"Your right?"

"My dear fellow, in my capacity of gentleman of the
chamber, I have my *entrée*."

"In my house?"

"Is it his house, Mademoiselle?" said Pecquigny
calmly, turning to Olympe.

She said nothing.

"You are not on your own premises here, my dear
fellow. Mademoiselle belongs to the Comédie troupe; she
has superb talents, which have made me her idolater. I
come, knock at her door, and she receives me; I describe
my feelings to her, and she listens to me: what have
you to say to that?"

"Nothing; but these phrases — "

"You have said them to a hundred women perhaps, — to everybody except your own wife."

Mailly blushed to the roots of his hair.

"Come, Count, be reasonable; you leave this charming creature to die of ennui, I come and console her; you imprison her, I introduce myself into her cell and make myself agreeable to her; you adopt the theory of compression, while I raise the banner of expansion; jealous you are, or pretend to be. I admit, if you choose, the first hypothesis. Madame is your slave; I propose to break the chains which bind her, and to prove that up to this time you have been only a horribly selfish jailer."

"Yes; and your horrible schemes — "

"What! who spoke of them? But, listen! you have some influence: you were able to bring Mademoiselle to Paris, and by your friends at court to obtain the order for her appearance at the Comédie, where she displayed marvellous talent; and now that the whole court has tasted the delicious draught, you close the fountain, hide it away, and you actually wish to deprive us of the pleasure of listening to that fascinating organ of speech with which Olympe sings rather than speaks Racine's lines. You steal from us that touching beauty which made a Titus of Nero. You deprive us of that Pandora's box, full of cleverness and spirit, and fill its place with your interminable sulkiness. Come, come, Mailly, bow to the inevitable: I will open the doors, and let your lovely nightingale fly away."

"Listen to me," said Mailly, while the captain was practising seductive grimaces and superb movements of the head and shoulders before the mirror, and Olympe, much amused, was laughing to herself, — "listen to me, Duke, you who are the bravest of the brave courtiers of France."

"Listen! I have done nothing else since you came, and I have not yet heard anything that paid for the trouble of listening."

"Listen to this, then: this woman is my property!"

"You are in error, Count; Mademoiselle Olympe is catalogued."

"Catalogued! what do you mean?"

"She belongs to the public, great and small."

"Duke, if you take her away from me —"

"What will happen, you idiot?" said Pecquigny, rising. "Just amuse this mistress of yours, and I 'll take my oath that she will not listen to me any more."

"Oh, Count," cried Olympe, seizing Mailly's hands, "you have done all that you could for me; and yet —"

"And yet?" repeated Mailly, with an expression of keenest anguish.

"And yet you weary her," the duke interrupted. "She loves acting, and you deprive her of it. When she can act so as to bring tears to the eyes of other people, why do you force her to cry her own eyes out in solitude?"

"Ah, Olympe!"

"I tell you she is bored to death. That very fact will put her in my hands, in spite of you and before your eyes. I will play no tricks, I will not be a disloyal foe. I will go to her, I will show her the reverse of her life with you; and, my word for it, she will leave you."

"Have some consideration for true love, libertine! atheist!" cried Mailly.

"Do you call your love true love?" was the duke's retort. "Go to! Your love is an easy-going affair, made up of all the petty meannesses with which you embellish life. You fancy that I will respect that! You expect me to pay any regard to this little abode of hypocrisy, in which you hide from your creditors, your wife, and your mistresses! You expect me to take my pay in your languishing glances, your sighs, and your jeremiads, when I know that you have just come from a minister with whom you are carrying on an intrigue, and a lady of the court with whom — "

" I did not come from either place you mention. "

" It 's much worse, then, for you come from your wife. "

Olympe cast a keen glance at Mailly, who stood as if transfixed by a sword-thrust.

" Let us have an end of this, " said she, wearily.

" Olympe, " he replied, " you don't know my purpose in going there. "

" Oho! my friend, " sneered Pecquigny, " you went to take your oath to her that you did not come from Olympe, just as you would be glad to prove to Olympe that you have not just come from the countess. "

" Monsieur le Duc, " said the Count suddenly, straightening up, " you have passed the limit; you are meddling with my affairs in the most impertinent fashion. "

" Fine words those! "

" To be followed by deeds. "

" Good! a sword-thrust in your own house! What charming manners! "

" Don't insult me, then. "

" Then don't try to breathe through your bronchial tubes and your gills at the same time. "

" Duke, we will discuss this matter more fully below. "

" Well! when I have killed you, or you have stretched a Captain of the King's Guards out on the snow, you will be no nearer proving that you have not at one time a mistress who is a grievance to your wife, and a wife who is a grievance to your mistress. *Cordieu!* my friend, make your choice; don't monopolize everything. Is it your mistress that you prefer? take her then, but carry her away so far that we shall never see her again.   Is it your wife? then throw the doors of your secret establishment open wide to us.   The assault is impending; what do you propose to do?"

Olympe cast another glance at Mailly.

"Olympe! Olympe!" he cried despairingly, detecting a something that terrified him in the expression of her eyes.

"Monsieur le Duc is right," said she, coldly; "the time has come for you to make your choice."

"Do you love some one, then?" cried Mailly; "was this recent explanation and reconciliation a mere lie?"

He relied upon these words to weary the duke or pique him; but he was dealing with a rough adversary, and a clever hand at paradox.

"What!" he said, without the least embarrassment, "are n't you ashamed of yourself?"

"Why ashamed?"

"You say you have recently had an explanation with her?"

"Certainly."

"And that you were fully reconciled?"

"I thought so."

"And have n't you sense enough to see that if you fall out again in the afternoon with the woman who forgave you in the morning, you are a lost man?"

Olympe smiled in a way to show that, in her judgment, Pecquigny was entitled to the honors of victory.

The count's haggard eyes wandered aimlessly around; this logic was quite beyond his powers.

"Olympe! Olympe!" he cried, turning to his mistress with clasped hands, "I have nothing left in the wide world but your love, Olympe!"

"A great effort!" muttered Pecquigny.

"I have nothing left in the world save my trust in your probity and fidelity!"

Pecquigny did not dare to interfere any further, lest he should offend her for whom he had been fighting for the last hour, with the hope of winning her over to his side.

"Olympe," continued Mailly, "whatever sacrifice is necessary I will make; but tell me, I implore you, that you will not allow yourself to be corrupted, — tell me that I shall never have to suffer the mortal agony of knowing that you have yielded to the evil demon who desires to abase you as he has abased me."

"Count," said she, "I shall never love him who gives me only half of his life. Give me the whole."

"Ah!" said Pecquigny; "what do you say to that?"

"So be it!" muttered Mailly, gloomily; "I shall not get the worst of it. Yours only, Olympe, yours only! And now, send away this man, who is well aware that I cannot kill him."

Olympe walked up to Pecquigny, who awaited her with a smile on his face.

"Monsieur le Duc, my lord and master has spoken," said she; "do not make him wretched. He does for me all that he can, almost more than he can."

"No," said Pecquigny, "no! I will not stir from this spot until he has restored you to the world. You are not his, you are ours!"

"What do you want, demon, in the name of God?" cried Mailly, foaming with rage.

"I will bring Mademoiselle two new parts. I desire her to study them."

"No."

"Oh! she will say yes."

"Olympe, say what your wishes are."

"I prefer studying new rôles to dying of ennui. There is no harm in studying them."

"You see, Count; she talks like a book. Let her have her way; she will appreciate you more when she has seen a few others."

"Coward!"

"You make me smile. Look at him, Olympe: he is the youngest and handsomest and bravest of us all; but he is not content with those advantages, and must needs add hypocrisy. Play openly with us, put your cards on the table, and we will give a good account of ourselves. Here are your rôles, Olympe; will you play them?"

She looked at Mailly.

"Yes," said he. "If she should say to-morrow, 'I have been false to you,' and it is for her happiness, I will say to her, 'You have done well.'"

"Ah!" said Pecquigny, "I am beaten, Count; you need go no farther." And he bowed to the ground.

"*Cordieu!* Olympe," he continued, "there's a man who does love you." And he bowed again.

"Look!" he added; "study 'La Fausse Agnès.' It is a delightful part; and as you positively must make a hit in it, I put myself at your service for whatever you lack."

Then, as he saw that Mailly was fuming, he went on:

"Be calm, my dear Count, be calm; after what you just said you may sleep in peace. Olympe is sacred so far as I am concerned. It is understood, of course, that you will not force her into political or religious infidelity; if you do, I shall resume my rights. You doubt me? On the faith of a duke! it is settled."

He bowed once more with the charming ease characteristic of the fine gentlemen of that day, gracefully kissed

Olympe's hand, and left the count in a state of utter bewilderment, with a promise to return the next day.

"I am lost!" thought Mailly. "I love my mistress better than my wife's honor. Beside Pecquigny, Richelieu is a mere bungler and makes me laugh."

XV.

WHAT IS PERMITTED BY THE CANONS OF THE CHURCH, AND WHAT IS FORBIDDEN BY THEM.

To return to Monsieur le Duc de Richelieu, who seemed to the count a less dangerous adversary than Pecquigny, it is plain that he could not stop half-way. Having loyally given the husband warning, — that is to say, having declared war,— it only remained for him to commence hostilities. Thus we see that similar tactics were adopted on both sides.

Richelieu had warned the husband, Pecquigny the lover. Immediately after his interview with Mailly, the former took his way to Monsieur de Fréjus at Issy. Barjac was expecting him.

These great men of the antechamber had an unerring intuition which one seeks in vain among the prophets of modern times. A mutual smile at the moment of meeting revealed to each — to duke and valet alike — that the occasion was well chosen, and Richelieu was ushered into the presence of the cardinal.

That prelate, very moderate and regular in the matter of bodily refreshment, had just finished his dinner, which seemed to have had an exhilarating effect upon his brain. Richelieu, detecting this favorable symptom, hastened to place the conversation on a level with the minister's expectations.

" Monseigneur," he said, " I have done as you desired."

"How desired, dear Monsieur de Richelieu?" said the Bishop.

"We had a little talk the other day, you remember."

"Oh, yes; pardon me!"

"A talk about trifles which, nevertheless, had a serious side."

"Oho! so you took our talk seriously, Duke, did you?"

"Yes, Monseigneur, and I was much impressed by it."

"Indeed!"

"So much so that I set to work as soon as I left you." The bishop unbent somewhat.

"Tell us about it," said he.

"I had in view, as you always have, Monseigneur, the prosperity and tranquillity of the realm."

"Of course; for such should be the wish and aim of every good Frenchman, and Monsieur de Richelieu is among the very best."

"And yet, Monseigneur — "

"Well — "

"I have some scruples."

"Ah!" said the bishop, fearing defection on Richelieu's part, "you have scruples, you! — scruples which bring you to a standstill?"

"*Dame!* it is as I tell you, Monseigneur; I became very faint-hearted while I was away."

"Scruples! when I thought — "

"One moment, Monseigneur, and I will explain. Vienna wrought a great change in my morals."

"So I see; but what is it that you fear? Have all these women lost their attraction for you since you reached Paris?"

"It's not that, Monseigneur."

"You have seen the queen, then, and hesitate on her account?"

"It's not that either, Monseigneur, because I imagine that my contemplated action would have done even more for her Majesty's happiness than for the king's."

"Then, Monsieur, I can conceive of no possible scruple on the part of a diplomatist, who is at once a military man and a courtier."

"But, Monseigneur," said Richelieu, delighted to have alarmed Monsieur de Fréjus a little, "your Grandeur does not seem to understand me at all. My scruples that I speak of were all on your account."

"Nonsense! what were they, pray?"

"I am trying to make up my mind how to begin."

"Why, what are you afraid of?"

"Your devout ears, Monseigneur."

"The surgeon, my dear Duke, ought to be able to cure wounds; and am I not doubly a surgeon, — a surgeon in religion and in politics?"

"Well said, Monseigneur. I will begin; and first of all, this is the main fact. I have seen everybody and everything at court."

"And your conclusions?"

"My conclusion is that the king does not seem to be in a mood — "

"For what?"

"For — anything, Monseigneur."

"Do you think so?"

"I am sure of it."

"But — "

"But what, Monseigneur?"

"Who is the cause of his disinclination?"

"Ah, Monseigneur, that's a hard question to answer: if a king of the age of ours were in the mood for anything, he would not probably be very scrupulous in the choice of his instrument."

"You alarm me."

" I should be very glad, Monseigneur, to hear your ideas on this subject. What would be your Grandeur's preference ? "

" *Dame!* that is rather for you to tell me."

" I will try to do so, then," said Richelieu.

" Go on, pray ! " said Monsieur de Fréjus, as he settled himself comfortably in a huge chair, enjoying in advance, thanks to his good digestion, the secret pleasures of a scandalous little intrigue conducted by the Duc de Richelieu.

" Here is my list," began the duke, drawing a paper from his pocket.

" Oho ! "

" In the first place, we have Madame de Toulouse."

" No, no! " cried the cardinal, hastily; " to take a woman of her position would be to create discord at once in the very bosom of the royal family. Really, Duke, did you think seriously of Madame de Toulouse ? "

" I thought seriously of everybody whom the king seemed to like, Monseigneur; and the king — "

" Has always taken much pleasure in kissing the shapely hands and looking at the fair white shoulders of Madame de Toulouse, you would say ? "

" That 's about it."

" But there is a husband."

" Oh! are there such things as husbands, where the king is concerned ? "

" Impossible ! impossible ! " exclaimed Fleury, with much vehemence.

" I was very doubtful about it myself, Monseigneur, for political reasons."

" And, after all," continued the cardinal, " if we are to give ourselves a master, it ought at least to be one of our own choosing, and Madame la Comtesse de Toulouse would make choice of herself altogether too readily."

"Monseigneur, you are entirely right. Let us pass to number two."

"Very well."

"Mademoiselle de Charolais?"

The prelate looked at Richelieu with a smile.

"So you are giving up your own, Monsieur le Duc; that's very noble of you!"

"I, Monseigneur! why, it's in the king's service, you know!"

"Very good; may I speak frankly?"

"By all means, Monseigneur."

"But upon this person in particular, I mean?"

"Would you like me to assist you, Monseigneur?"

"I should be so much the more pleased to have you, because you can speak by the book, Duke."

"Very well; Monseigneur, I admit that Mademoiselle de Charolais is beginning to be a little *passée*."

"Is she not? Yet she is still very agreeable."

"To be sure, to be sure! It's fine blood."

"A little too rich."

"Too fertile, you mean, do you not?"

"Yes, just that. It seems, as you probably know, as if no woman on earth had ever received from above in such bountiful supply the gift which the Lord denied of old to Sara, the wife of Abraham. Do you know what I heard about her a week or so since?"

"When I have the honor of hearing it, Monseigneur, from the lips of your Grandeur, I shall appreciate it the more."

"Well, just come a little nearer, Duke."

Monsieur de Richelieu drew his chair up beside that in which his Eminence was sitting.

" Here I am, Monseigneur."

" Mademoiselle de Charolais has a house of her own, you know, and that house has a Swiss porter. Oh! but before I come to the house — She has a custom."

" What 's that, Monseigneur ? "

" *Dame !* every year she presents a son or a daughter to him whom her heart has chosen to console her for having remained — Mademoiselle de Charolais."

Richelieu laughed appreciatively.

" You tell it wonderfully well, Monseigneur."

" Well, Duke, when that time comes around, all Mademoiselle's friends, to whom it is an open secret, pretend to think that she is simply indisposed. She keeps her bed a fortnight and her room a month, and that 's the end of it. These occasions are commonly called ' Mademoiselle de Charolais' paroxysms.' "

" Very good."

" You know what 's coming, do you not ? "

" Monseigneur, I have been at Vienna two years."

" Well, this year she had a new Swiss porter, a great, hulking fellow, who arrived suddenly from Berne during the month preceding the paroxysm, and to whom the traditions of the place had not been imparted."

" So that — "

" So that, while Mademoiselle was still in bed, and her friends were beginning to leave their cards upon her, the Swiss replied smilingly to the first caller, showing thirty-two huge teeth, —

" ' Montsire, Matemoiselle is ferry well, und der shild alzo.' "

Richelieu roared with laughter, and the priest followed his example. Both gave full vent to their amusement.

The ice being thus fairly broken, the interview could continue without circumlocution.

"Well?" said Richelieu, at last.

"Erase number two, my dear Duke, in the interests of — "

"The king?"

"I did not say that. In the interests of the public treasury, which ought not to be subjected to such a burden."

"Number three, Mademoiselle de Clermont."

"Mademoiselle de Charolais' sister! Should we not have much to fear from Monsieur le Duc's influence?"

"I think not, Monseigneur."

"You have not looked closely at Mademoiselle de Clermont, have you?"

"Why, yes, Monseigneur."

"She is pretty, that's true."

"Very pretty, in fact. And then I think she has no Swiss porter."

"But it seems that she has a false leg."

"Oho! Monseigneur, are you sure of that?" said Richelieu, mischievously.

Fleury blushed.

"They say so," he replied.

"Yes; but how do they know?"

"My dear Duke, everything is known."

"Let us pass her, then, although she is really a charming creature, and we ought to give her a chance to prove that story a slander, before putting her aside."

"A female politician, Duke, a female politician!"

"That's an unanswerable reason. Number four, Madame de Nesle."

"Madame de Nesle?"

"You seem startled, Monseigneur."

"I should think so, indeed; a woman thirty-nine years old. — on her own admission, too!"

"But she is extremely handsome, and they say that the king — "

"You don't know, apropos of what you were about to say — "

"I was at Vienna, Monseigneur."

"The king, on his return from Fontainebleau, where Madame de Nesle, they say, had been a guest at his supper-table, said — "

"What did he say?"

"It was to Pecquigny that he said it."

"What was it, for heaven's sake, Monseigneur?"

"Faith, Duke, there are canons which forbid a bishop from telling what the king said to Pecquigny."

"Indeed!" said Richelieu. "Let us pass to number five, then, — Madame Paulmier."

"What! Paulmier the innkeeper?"

"The same, Monseigneur; a plump little gossip, and pretty withal! — Venus at thirty painted by Rubens."

"Yes, indeed; a marvellous arm and hand and figure!"

"Her ankle, too! Golden hair falling to her hips!"

"Dainty little feet."

"Lustrous, speaking eyes."

"Skin as soft as satin."

"Ah, Monseigneur, you know Madame Paulmier very well, it seems."

"Alas! yes."

"Well, is she a female politician?"

"No; but all the pages, all the light-horse, all the musketeers, all the Swiss, and all the students are in love with her. She is a woman who receives more notes in one day than I receive letters in a week."

"Whence you conclude — "

"Oh, it's very simple! I conclude that if the king aspires to Madame Paulmier, he will take her himself, and we shall not be under the necessity of giving her to him."

"Number six, — Mademoiselle Olympe de Clèves."

"The actress?"

"Herself. What have you to say to her, Monseigneur?"

"Duke!"

"She is to Madame Paulmier what real beauty is to mere attractiveness."

"Yes, she is very well."

"You know her?"

"Of course."

"She has talent."

"Yes, considerable; sincerity particularly."

"You have seen her act?"

"I have heard about her."

"It's a pity that you have n't seen her yourself; you would admit that you could conceive of nothing lovelier."

"As far as mere beauty goes, that is true. When this girl takes a step, they say that she seems to tread upon the fibres of your heart, and makes them quiver like the strings of a harpsichord."

"Well, well, Monseigneur, I see that somebody has described her to you very fully."

"Candidly, Duke, I have seen her act."

"Fie, Monseigneur! but what did you think of her?"

"Oh, she is superb. Further than that, I have made inquiries."

"With what result?"

"The girl is unexceptionable. Barjac has talked with a certain lady's-maid named Claire."

"So! and — "

"And this maid made him play the part of one of the heroes of mythology."

" Pray go on, Monseigneur."

" Do you know the fable of Actæon ? "

" Has Pecquigny been changed into a stag ? "

" No ; but Barjac, before — "

" Ah, very good! Actæon hid in the prompter's box, did he ? "

" Better than that, Duke ; otherwise the fable would have been but imperfectly reproduced. You know that in Actæon's experience there was something about a — "

" A bath ? Oh, Monsieur Barjac ! " exclaimed Richelieu.

" There 's my source of information, Duke."

" Go on, Monseigneur."

" The canons forbid churchmen to misuse living paintings."

" Oh, Barjac ! But you must know how happy the king would be, loving such a pearl among women."

" Duke, that is not what is called loving."

" The canons forbid, Monseigneur."

" Such a love is called a pastime."

" What then ? "

" Why, what his Majesty needs is a real, veritable love, a downright passion, Duke, understand ; it matters little whether it proceeds from the head or the senses, or even from the heart if you please, provided that we remain at its source with the key to regulate the supply, to open or close the gates."

" We shall be there, Monseigneur."

" No."

" And then the king has noticed this damsel."

" Another argument against her, — the Pecquigny faction."

" But Monsieur Pecquigny will become great only when we wish to use him : the Fleury faction."

"Consider, Duke! An actress? No, never! Why," said he, with great seriousness, "the king ought not to descend from his elevation. An actress at Versailles or at the Louvre? No, it's not to be thought of. Let us leave the actresses to the sluggish kings of England to fill the gaps between their duchesses. Let us refined, civilized people not expose gentlemen to the degrading associations of the wings, or run the risk of changing the royal apartment into an appurtenance of the theatre."

"However, Monseigneur—"

"Louis XV., you see, sleeps in the bed of Louis XIV.; let us be careful not to forget that circumstance."

"You have destroyed all my convictions, Monseigneur," said Richelieu, coldly; "therefore I bow to your superior wisdom."

"Let us pass on, as you yourself said just now."

"Number seven, then."

"Who is number seven on your list?"

"Madame la Comtesse de Mailly."

"Oho!" ejaculated his Eminence.

"Startled again?" said Richelieu.

"The quality is all right this time, Duke; but—"

"Expound your 'but,' Monseigneur, I beg you."

"There is a husband."

"*Pardieu!* I am well aware of it."

"There's a family too."

"I see that you prefer to consider the rest of the family; so be it. I had begun with the eldest of the daughters; but since you insist, here goes for the others. Number eight, Pauline-Félicité de Nesle, still at a convent."

"She is ugly."

"That's one reason why I did not mention her. But I ought to tell you one thing."

" What is it ? "

" Pauline is very clever."

" I know it."

" You know what is going on inside the walls of convents ? "

" A bishop! "

" Oh, to be sure! "

" I could tell you also that she is ambitious, and that her ambition is of the most worldly description."

" I know that, too, Monseigneur."

" What, Duke! do you know what is going on inside the walls of convents ? "

" Oh, I used to know her abbess, Monseigneur."

" Oh, to be sure, say I in my turn."

" However, Pauline is too clever and too worldly for us."

" She is too ugly."

" Number nine, Monseigneur: Diane-Adélaide, the third sister."

" Almost a baby."

" Then I will not speak of Hortense-Félicité, number ten, the fourth sister."

" No, Duke."

" Nor of Marie-Anne, the fifth sister, a beautiful girl, whom they say the Marquis de la Tournelle is already making love to."

" Duke, if she already has a suitor, we will leave Marie-Anne de Nesle, the fifth sister, out of our calculations, and not give her to the king. We can get rid of husbands, but not of lovers."

" Monseigneur, I am edified beyond measure. But my list of numbers is exhausted, and we have come to no decision."

" It may be, Duke, that we passed too hastily over number seven."

"Madame de Mailly, Louise-Julie?"

"Wife of Louis-Alexandre de Mailly, the lover of Mademoiselle Olympe de Clèves."

"It is a great pleasure to talk with you, Monseigneur; there never was a memory equal to yours."

"That is true, Duke; they tell me sometimes that I resemble your great uncle the cardinal somewhat in that respect."

"Monseigneur," retorted Richelieu, dryly, "as to that I am unable to judge; I never saw my uncle, and I do see you."

This double-edged reserve might have been meant for a bit of delicate flattery.

Fleury took it in that light, and was delighted with it.

"Shall we return to Madame de Mailly then?" said the duke.

"Experimentally."

"Oh, of course; I have no definite plan, Monseigneur."

"Duke, she is very thin."

"What do you call thin, Monseigneur?" asked Richelieu, unconcernedly.

"I call thin, my dear Duke, the woman who when you first approach her — "

"Go on, go on, Monseigneur."

"I do not wound you?"

"Not at all, not at all. Go on."

"Well, then," the cardinal continued, "the woman who when one sees her face to face — "

"The canons, Monseigneur, the canons!"

"Alas, yes!"

"Well, Monseigneur, I will reply to you."

"Oh, I think that Madame de Mailly carries off full dress better than any woman in France."

"That is something."

"Indeed it is."

"In the eyes of a flirtatious young king."

"True!"

"The ability to dress well, Monseigneur, is always a promise of better things."

"The dress is fine foliage, but how about the tree itself?"

"There, there, Monseigneur, with a woman like her of whom we are speaking, we must not go beneath the bark."

"I agree! I agree!"

"The loveliest hands!"

"Indeed her fingers are as tapering and shapely as those of Aurora herself."

"A pearly, transparent skin, beneath which flows generous crimson blood."

"A dilated eye, as honest and fearless as the young roe's."

"A foot—"

"Let us not leave the head, Duke."

"Moist, rosy lips!"

"Yes, and veritable pearls for teeth."

"A little black mustache which makes her always seem to be smiling at the corners of her mouth."

"And which is, like her eyebrows, as black as ebony."

"Have you noticed the way her hair grows?"

"On the back of her neck, you mean?"

"Yes."

"And the waves on her forehead?"

"There are seven of them."

"As the rules of beauty demand."

"The forehead itself is superb."

"It makes no pretensions."

"No, it is the forehead of a lovely woman, not of a woman of genius."

"Ah, that's an important point!"

"Monseigneur, do you know one thing?"

"Say it."

"You said that she was thin."

"I mean that her chest is that of a young girl."

"Monseigneur, one would say that you had never noticed her arms."

"Ah! are her arms fine?"

"They are not only fine, Monseigneur, but plump."

"Oh, Duke!"

"Don't be incredulous! Look for yourself! What the devil! if you would only do as Saint-Thomas did, Monseigneur! He put his hand in our Lord's side, and surely you might well put yours under the sleeve — "

"Duke, Duke, the canons!"

And the bishop began to laugh a truly Rabelaisian laugh.

"I insist upon this point, Monseigneur; do you know why?"

"I shall know if you tell me."

"Because a plump arm on a young woman is an infallible diagnostic."

"Of what?"

"Of health and the future."

"Of the future? Brachiomancy, eh? Did your Viennese sorcerer teach you that?"

"No, Monseigneur, I am not talking about the future in a moral but in a physical aspect. A woman whose arms are plump when she is young and thin, as most young women are, cannot fail to become a very beautiful woman as she grows older."

"What a depth of physiological insight, Duke!"

"It's as I say, Monseigneur."

"So that you have not the least uneasiness as to the physical future of Louise de Mailly?"

"Monseigneur, do you know anything about her ankles?"

"I have heard of them; but common report — "

"Monseigneur, she has an ankle the like of which I never saw. Now, you know, Monseigneur, that the finest ankles in the world are in Paris, and that I always lived in Paris until they sent me to Vienna. But let us leave the subject of physique, Monseigneur, if you please, as we are substantially agreed thereon."

"Yes, Duke, we agree that Louise de Mailly will some day become a very beautiful woman."

"Very good, Monseigneur; now let us speak of what there is within that shapely head."

"Very little, perhaps."

"I beg your pardon, there is much wit."

"Oh, the devil! hidden wit!"

"You said 'the devil!' Monseigneur; in the mouth of a bishop, that is a fearful oath!"

"True; I ought to have called on the duke instead of the devil: that would have been only right. She has mental powers that are hidden, then?"

"Yes."

"That's the very worst variety, do you know."

"Very considerable powers, too, which are hidden only from those to whom she does not wish to show them."

"That is very ominous!"

"No."

"But pardon me, Duke, the clever woman will govern the king, now that nothing else but cleverness is needed to govern him."

"You 're rather hard on Monsieur le Duc in what you say, Monseigneur."

Fleury began to laugh.

"The very worst thing for us, Duke,— you said so yourself, — is cleverness."

"Pardon me, Monseigneur; in speaking of that quality, I forgot her heart."

"She has a heart, has she ? "

"Yes, and a heart which the king has invaded."

"Do you think that she loves the king ? "

"Monseigneur, I fear she does. The result of that state of things would be to give us the security which we seek. Madame de Mailly in love with the king would never encroach upon our preserves."

"Very good, my dear Duke; but, after all, is one ever sure of these things ? May not a woman's disposition change when she thinks she has a firm hold upon a man, and that man a king ? "

"No, Monseigneur, not so long as she loves."

"But is she likely to love very long ? "

"This particular one is, I think."

"By what diagnostics do you figure that out, Monsieur prophet ? " asked Fleury, banteringly.

"She is ardent and thoughtful at the same time."

"Which signifies what to your mind ? "

"That she will find the king a fine fellow and worth keeping, and that she will do whatever is necessary in order to keep him."

"Explain yourself a little more fully."

"It 's like this. By leaving her husband, she creates a scandal; she is not a woman to be afraid of scandal, nor on the other hand is she a woman to rush from one affair to another. She will do once for all what her heart and head tell her to do. Her brain works quickly,

I warn you, and her heart is very talkative; but once the head and heart have expressed themselves in fit terms, they will be dumb forever. Now, a woman, in order to make up her mind to impose silence upon her senses or upon an honest passion, must have so many good reasons that she can never get them all together; she prefers to surrender. That is why Madame de Mailly will always surrender in her affair with the king."

"Will she endure his selfishness?"

"Cheerfully."

"And poverty?"

"Why poverty? Monseigneur, did you speak your thoughts then?"

"I say this. Madame de Mailly will be abandoned by her husband, will she not, Duke? Her family will have nothing more to do with her, and the king will not be generous."

"The king not generous!" cried Richelieu.

"I did not say, 'The king *is not* generous,' Monsieur; I said *will not be*."

"So, so, Monseigneur! Pray, what makes you think that?" asked Richelieu, with great interest.

"In the first place, Duke, my instinct; in the second place, my necessities,— I should say the necessities of France."

"The necessities of France will require the king to be a miser!" cried Richelieu, again.

"Monsieur le Duc, don't look at this upside down. I say to you, in all sincerity, I am old, the king is young, and gives great promise of a vast number of sins to be committed hereafter; sooner or later he will plunge into the abyss of reckless extravagance, as his ancestor Louis XIV. did."

"Well, Monseigneur."

"Well, Monsieur, France will be ruined. Now, I do not propose that that shall come to pass in my day. It is inevitable, without doubt, but not for me. I have ten years or so yet to live, and while I live I will manage the resources of the state with strict economy; another, my successor, may take the perilous leap, not I!"

"The leap! Why, you horrify me, Monseigneur! Is it so near as that?"

"It is altogether too near; makeshifts are beginning to be necessary: I am not young enough to be forever imagining new and productive ones. When you are minister, you, who are so fertile in expedients, can bring order out of chaos."

"Oh, Monseigneur!"

"I don't conceal my thoughts, as you see. I am all for myself until I die; that will not be very long."

"Oh, what a mass of exaggerations!"

"Not one word, Duke."

"Monseigneur, you exaggerate the expenses."

"You will see."

"You exaggerate the danger."

"Burn your fingers, if you choose; it will not be for lack of warning from me."

"After all, do you propose to prevent the king from being a young man?"

"Good God, no! There! you see that after swearing by the devil I return to God; that's a good sign. No, I will not prevent the king from being young; on the contrary, don't you see I supply him with two sources of strength where other young men have but one, and I do it at the cost of great effort."

"Two sources of strength?"

"Yes, youth and power, — two magnificent torches, made of beautiful hard wax, moulded by that great man, your grand-uncle, and hoarded up by the clever Mazarin; two torches which King Louis XIV. burned so fiercely, at the same time and at both ends, that, by my faith, they are pretty well reduced."

" True! "

" You see that it is necessary that they should last the present king, my pupil, to the end of his days, which will be long in the land, I trust."

" Let us hope so."

" I take the responsibility upon myself, therefore. I allow the king to draw upon one of these sources of supply at one time, never upon both. He has youth, which costs nothing; let him use that for the present, and then we will see."

" But a young king is an extravagant king."

" By no means! A young king is a charming lover, whom all the women try to attract. He consents to love them and to let them adore him. He gives a sprat to catch a herring."

" Upon my soul, Monseigneur, what edifying morality! Do you know that I have crimps in my regiment who practise that system, and the soldiers call them *grugeurs*."

" I can well believe it; your soldiers are soldiers, and the crimps are only sergeants, or at most humble quarter-masters. Make colonels of them, and they will become of some importance; make them marshals, and you will speak respectfully of them; princes of the blood, and you will admire them; kings, and all their acts will be perfectly proper."

" Oh, Monseigneur, why proper? "

" Because, Monsieur le Duc," said Fleury, sternly, " a king's mistress has not a pearl which does not cost that king's subjects ten thousand loaves of bread."

Richelieu bowed.

"My policy does n't seem to you befitting an honest gentleman, perhaps ? "

"Monseigneur, I have nothing more to say."

"Believe me, Duke," added the shrewd old fellow, " I never consent that my friends' interests shall suffer."

"Madame de Mailly is accepted, then, on condition that she takes a vow of poverty ? "

"Yes."

"And obedience ? "

"Yes; I waive the rest."

"Those are hard conditions, Monseigneur."

"Do you suppose that I would give to a mistress what I refuse the queen ? "

"Perhaps the king will compel you."

"Ah," cried the old man, with a degree of animation which disclosed his whole scheme to Richelieu, "that is what I expect! Let the king but force my hand, and then, when my real authority is unveiled, we will see! "

"Good!" said Richelieu, "I understand you."

"Besides," Fleury hastened to add, "did you not tell me that the countess had ceased to love her husband ? "

"She has left him."

"And that she loves the king ? "

"That is supposition."

"Supposition! You said positively that she is ardent and thoughtful, that she has a little mustache and black eyebrows."

"Those facts are undeniable."

"In that case she cannot help loving the king."

"We must investigate."

"That 's for you to do."

"I will do my best to obey you."

Fleury restrained an impatient exclamation at Richelieu's obstinacy in remaining out of sight.

"To conclude: If Madame de Mailly loves the king, it will matter little to her whether he treats her like Cleopatra or like Lucrece."

"Possibly not; but her pride?"

"We agreed that she should have none."

"Monseigneur vanquishes me."

"With your own weapons. Once for all, Duke, have you any doubts of the availability of number seven? Do you think we had best look elsewhere?"

"Oh, no, Monseigneur, let us stop where we are. A struggle with you is fatiguing in the extreme."

"Yes, because my logic is unanswerable."

"I prefer to use my wits against the fair sex."

The priest smiled.

"Duke," said he, "never forget that I am your best friend, if I may have that honor."

Richelieu bowed.

"In all this matter," said he, "I have had only one disappointment."

"*Mon Dieu!* what was that?"

"To hear it said that a King of France was going to be a miser. That has not happened since — "

"Since — the time of your uncle," said the old man, maliciously.

Richelieu would perhaps have made a sharp retort, but Fleury cut him short.

"After all, what difference is it to you," he said, "whether the king is a miser or a spendthrift?"

"Why, Monseigneur, you speak like a man who has cut loose from the world; upon my soul you do!"

"My dear friend, it is true that I have cut loose from the world, but you have all that the world has to give."

"I?"

"Yes, you, to be sure."

"*Mon Dieu!* what have I if the king turns out to be a miser?"

"A king is never a miser, Duke, when he makes a promise, or has people make promises in his name."

"Bah! Monseigneur, you 're joking."

"No, upon my honor!"

"Do you call a man rich, Monseigneur, who has nothing but promises?"

"Certainly I do."

"It may be so, if the promises are fulfilled."

"That is self-evident; but who can have such an idea as that a King of France or a Minister of the King of France would ever fail to keep his word?"

"Oh!" cried Richelieu, in an ecstasy of delight, "that is something like. So Louis XV. you say, although a sordid miser, will always keep his word?"

"Do you doubt it, Duke?"

"No, if you answer for him."

"I answer for him, body for body!"

"Monseigneur, not another word!"

"You lack only one thing, Duke, and that is memory."

"You think I lack that, Monseigneur?"

"I do. What promise was given you?"

"Oh, *pardieu!* I know, of course. I have not forgotten, no, indeed."

"That is all that is necessary, Monsieur. Adieu."

"Monseigneur, a thousand respects."

And Richelieu took his leave.

XVI.

SERPENT NUMBER TWO.

RICHELIEU, having concluded his double contract with the minister, thought that it behooved him to set to work; and without losing a moment, he set out to call upon Madame de Mailly.

He did not give himself a moment's uneasiness about the king; for had he not full powers from Monsieur de Fréjus?

As for the countess, she was sitting in her boudoir, in a state of intense exasperation over the scene with her husband, and bursting with a longing to be revenged, when the duke was announced by her maid.

At any other time Louise de Mailly would have refused to receive the duke, whose more than compromising reputation closed to him the houses of all the respectable ladies at court; but the poor countess had been living for two days in such a state of tense excitement that nothing seemed more improper to her than the conventional proprieties.

It is a terrible moment for a woman when she first hides her pallor with rouge, or her blushes with her fan; but it must be admitted that when that moment has passed, she is stronger and better armed for good or evil fortune than men.

The countess, although she had not reached that point, felt that she was already half abandoned. Her husband's desertion inspired in her a deep disgust for men; and such a feeling is conducive to superiority, using the word in the sense of putting public opinion under one's feet.

Louise felt, in her conscience as well as in her heart, that while Monsieur de Mailly was intent upon public *liaisons*, there was no reason why she should not build up a little private romance for herself; she remembered that Monsieur de Richelieu was present the preceding night at the little festivity at Rambouillet, and that he had been a witness of the king's acts and movements.

She remembered, also, that in her short *tête-à-tête* with Monsieur de Richelieu while they were waiting for the rest of the party to leave the road clear, he had read what was going on in the recesses of her heart as clearly as if she had had in her breast that window which the old philosopher sighed to see there, and which, luckily for very many people, modern philosophers have not yet succeeded in arranging.

Her first thought, when the duke was announced, was that a conversation with him might bring about an opportunity to learn what the king had said or done since that fateful occasion.

There is no woman, perhaps, who can resist curiosity of a certain sort, — that is to say, the violent itching to know what opinion is held of her by those whom she has distinguished above the common herd, and above all by that one, among those people, whom she has honored with her love.

And if the one whom she loves happens to be the king, it is plain that the curiosity would naturally become frenzy.

It has been very justly said that it is this very curiosity which causes the destruction of most women; for by making inquiries they arrive at knowledge, and knowledge is their ruin.

Madame de Mailly, so great was her desire *to know*, without taking time to remember that the night before she was still a woman of unassailed and unassailable character, at once ordered that Monsieur de Richelieu be admitted.

As to any ideas regarding the duke individually, she had formed none at all; and yet the duke at thirty was a singularly handsome man. His maturer years had more than fulfilled all the promise of his youth.

But the countess had taken no note of his personal charm. All that she had seen was the king, young and beautiful, — not Louis XV. the sovereign, but Louis, the youth of eighteen, glowing with youthful beauty.

She was aware that the duke was a fine figure of a man, and very popular with her sex, just as we know that Raphael was a great artist. His beauty and fashionable vogue were matters of public notoriety which she neither denied nor affirmed.

Consequently she had taken no precautionary measures as to light and shadow, as the ladies of that time were accustomed to do, to make their complexion count for its full value. She had neither added nor removed a single beauty spot, when the duke calmly entered her apartment in the wake of her maid.

Without the least embarrassment or affectation she smiled upon Richelieu, as he bowed low to her, and allowed the maid to leave the room without hastening or delaying her departure.

They remained alone.

Madame de Mailly was the first to break the silence, as she began to feel somewhat embarrassed under Richelieu's persistent gaze. He had his eyes fixed upon her with a sort of fascination, which, according to his ideas, was the most satisfactory sort of conversation.

"Monsieur le Duc," she finally said, "to what lucky circumstance, may I ask, am I indebted for the honor of this visit?"

"Madame," he replied with exquisite grace, "will you first pardon me for looking earnestly at you?"

Louise's cheeks flushed purple, and all the tales of the antics of the duke when he was Duc de Fronsac came to her mind.

But his eye did not shine with the suggestive expression which insults a woman, or the passion which alarms her.

"It is impossible for me," she replied, trying to smile, despite her confusion, "to prevent you from looking at me, Monsieur le Duc, or even to be angry with you for it, for you do it with the utmost frankness, and, as I believe, without any intention of affronting me."

"You may well believe it, Madame la Comtesse."

"Tell me, however, — I have already asked you, — if it is to nothing beyond your desire of looking at me that I owe the distinction of this visit?"

"Madame, it is true that at Rambouillet I had an opportunity to see you, and for a considerable time, but yet with little satisfaction, — too little, indeed, if I believe all the suggestions which have come to my mind since yesterday, and upon which I said a few words to yourself, Madame, in the cabinet."

"Well, well," she thought, "here it comes! Is it not possible in this world to pass an hour with a man but he must needs begin to make love to you? What a paltry thing a man's nature is!"

Richelieu seemed to divine her thoughts.

"Madame," he said with a smile, "I am going to say something very impertinent to you."

"Who knows?" said she, frigidly.

"But you will forgive me for it, I am sure," he continued.

"Perhaps so, Monsieur le Duc."

"I rely entirely on your good nature, Madame la Comtesse."

"Don't trust too much to it," said she, sharply; "but you have not yet begun. As it is in my power now to remember you as an extremely courteous gentleman, and most agreeable withal, pray do not give me reason to think differently of you."

"Madame," rejoined the duke, with the smile with which he had begun still upon his lips, "let me explain myself, I beg you."

"No, no, Monsieur le Duc, no! I much prefer doubt to certainty."

"But the impertinence to which I refer is pardonable, Madame, if I do not carry it too far."

"Duke, I fear not. A man of your rank should not call upon a lady with the assurance that any impertinence upon which he has determined beforehand is pardonable."

"Whatever it is, Madame, I yield to you ; otherwise our interview would never begin. Do not take anything agreeable that I may say to you now, Madame, as said in furtherance of any designs of my own, I beg. I have the misfortune — the good fortune I should say — to be aminated by a very warm sentiment toward you — "

"Duke! Monsieur le Duc!"

"Of friendship, Madame," continued Richelieu, with a courteous gesture, "the most respectful friendship imaginable."

Louise de Mailly uttered an exclamation of surprise.

"You see, Countess, that upon this footing we cannot fail to understand each other."

"Certainly, Monsieur."

"I will go on, then," said he, "and you will tell me
if my reflections since yesterday have not been just and
profitable."

"I am all attention."

"It often happens to those who have used their
powers of observation well to reflect deeply, is it not so,
Countess?"

"Why, I think so. By the same token it always
seems to me that those whose powers of just reflection
are well developed are likely to observe closely."

Richelieu bowed in acquiescence.

"Now you have used your powers of observation,"
she said.

"I observed a very curious and interesting fact,
Madame."

"Where was that, Monsieur le Duc?"

"Yesterday at Rambouillet, Madame la Comtesse."

"In connection with whom?"

"With you. The same fact, you know, which I mentioned to you in the cabinet."

"It is hard for me, Monsieur le Duc; being naturally
retiring and uncommunicative, I did not think, I
admit—"

"You did not expect to be noticed? That is impossible, Madame."

"A compliment?"

"No, better than that; an observation. To look at
your eyes and see that they are black, is nothing; to
look at your mouth and see that it is lovely, and your
smile charming beyond measure, those are mere common-
place observations. But I have done better than that,
you see; and I have my share of self-conceit too, — a
commodity which has long been familiar at court."

Madame de Mailly's heart began to beat fast. She

tried to conceal the emotion which threatened to make itself manifest beneath a forced playfulness.

"Well, well, Duke, haul me over the coals, if you will; I authorize you to do it, as I cannot help myself."

"Oho, Countess, you understand. Listen a moment! I noticed that black eyes shone as they rested upon such and such an object; that lovely speaking lips could form themselves into smiles which contained a world of meaning."

"Monsieur le Duc!"

"When the same object was in view, of course. Nothing could be a more interesting study to me. The whole evening long, I watched with keen delight the play of that adorable countenance. All night long I seemed to feel as if I held all its fibres in my hand, the beating of that heart rich in the possession of an inestimable treasure so much the more precious because you yourself knew not its worth, — that heart rich in the possession of love!"

"My heart, — mine?"

"Yes, yours; none other."

Louise pressed her hand upon her heart, as the blood fled from her cheeks.

"For pity's sake, Madame," cried Richelieu, "do not forget for one moment, I conjure you, that I began the conversation by declaring to you that nobody can be more sincerely and devotedly your friend than I have the honor to be."

"Love!" she repeated, with an attempt at sarcasm, — "love! Oh, Monsieur, no, no — "

"Madame, do not deny it."

"I assure you, Monsieur — "

"Madame, I cannot allow myself to question you, and consequently I ask you for no confession."

"You are an extraordinary visitor, Monsieur le Duc, and in truth I fail to comprehend you."

"Have I had the misfortune to offend you, Madame?"

"I must admit that you have aroused my curiosity."

"The battle is half won then, Madame. I was saying to you that I needed no avowal from you, because I am about to confide in you. The utmost that I shall require will be your acquiescence."

"Indeed! As for what you were saying about your observations —"

"They are accurate, Madame."

"No, Duke, they are all astray."

"There, there, Madame, don't force me to prove what I say."

"They are all astray, I tell you."

"Why do you give the lie to your lovely eyes and your charming smile?"

"What does a mere glance amount to? It signifies a gleam of intelligence, that's all. What is a smile? A dimple in the cheek."

"Madame, it is the language of the heart."

"You call a glance and a smile from a woman with nothing to do, the language of the heart?"

"Come, come, now, don't give the lie also to your warm and generous heart."

"Now you are casting reflections on my heart, which is as cold as a stone."

"Aha! you challenge me; just reflect, Countess, that I have an interest of my own to defend against you."

"An interest against me! What is it?"

"That which I mentioned to you just now, that toward which all the smiles and sighs at Rambouillet yesterday converged. I omit glances, since you seem to take umbrage when they are mentioned."

"Prove it to me."

"I challenge you, Madame, to deny that at this moment you are in love with somebody," cried Richelieu, energetically. "Deny that and I abjure the admiration which you have aroused; deny that and I deny your warmth of heart, your ardent gaze, your heartfelt sigh: in short, I deny *you* and have no more to say."

"But pray, Monsieur," said Louise, in a tremor of excitement, "with whom am I in love?"

"The king, Madame."

He let those two words fall like two vast mountains beneath whose bulk the resolutions and attempts at prevarication of the young woman were crushed out in an instant.

She fell back in her chair with colorless lips, pale brow, and eyes which had lost their brilliancy.

Richelieu did not stir.

"This is terrible, terrible, Monsieur le Duc," murmured Louise.

"You cannot say that I insult you, Madame la Comtesse," rejoined the duke, coldly. "There is no one on earth more worthy of your love, now that you have the right to love another than your husband."

The first blow had crushed her; the second restored her to life.

Richelieu, with marvellous tact, had given her what seemed in her eyes the advantage.

She gradually recovered herself; her cheeks resumed their color, and her eyes took on something of the old animation.

"I do not say, Monsieur le Duc, that you insult me," said she. "I say that you torture me, and that very cruelly."

"God forbid, Madame la Comtesse, that I should be

guilty of such a crime. Torture you! Oh, no! I have told you your own story; but I was sure that you were in ignorance of it yourself."

"I am still in ignorance."

"Yes, I believe it; but I am no longer so."

"Oh!"

"And I agree that it is natural in every respect; that it would indeed be most extraordinary if you should not love the king, such as he is."

"Monsieur le Duc, spare me."

"Why, Madame, what am I doing, in what capacity am I here? I have come not only out of consideration for you, but to bring you most useful assistance."

She fixed a piercing gaze upon him.

"What do you mean?" said she.

"In two words, this. Yesterday, as I was just telling you, I caught a glimpse of the noble quality of your heart: I guessed how much you were likely to suffer from all that has happened."

"What has happened?"

"I am coming to that. The king was very fond of the queen."

"Ah! is he less fond of her now?" she exclaimed eagerly.

"Look out for your eyes, Countess," interrupted the duke, with a smile; "they were very near betraying the truth. Yes, Madame, the king is a little less fond of the queen, and more than that, he is beginning to bestow his affections elsewhere."

"Indeed!"

"If he has not done so, they will make him think that he has. You know what enthusiasm he excites at court."

"Yes, yes!"

"The king's heart is quickly aroused."

"You mean that he is in love with some one, do you not, Monsieur le Duc?"

"Madame, that would very soon be the case if he should look at you very often, as he had an opportunity to do and did do yesterday."

The countess blushed.

"Oh, the king looked very little at me," she said.

"The king is absent-minded, and they seem to be seeking to make him more so. So many people are drawing his eyes this way and that, that it will hardly be possible for his Majesty to have a glance to spare for two months to come."

"Poor prince! how closely he is besieged by feigned passions, sordid lies, and sensual allurements, — so many cloaks for treason!"

"Your heart spoke there with a depth of philosophical insight of which I believed that you must be capable, Madame. I have, like you, reflected on the risk which the king incurs of being deceived, and also of the danger which threatens you."

"Danger to me!"

"Yes, beyond any question."

"I don't know what it is."

"Why, pardon me, Madame; but did we not agree a moment ago that you love the king?"

"Cruel man!" cried Louise, with tears in her eyes.

"Cruel, if you please, but strictly logical. We certainly agreed upon that fact. Now, if you love his Majesty, do you think it will be agreeable to see him making love to other women?"

"Brutal!"

"Brutal, also, if you please, but more and more logical, you see. Thus, if you love the king, and are pained to see him waste his time upon unworthy objects, do you think that you should fail to devote yourself to the task of making the king love you, — you, who have it in your power to save him and secure your own happiness at the same time?"

"Oh, Monsieur, Monsieur!" sobbed Louise, hiding her face in her hands.

"Madame, believe, I implore you, that if I did not esteem you beyond anything, I would not speak to you thus frankly. You should have no thought beyond the fixed desire to make no mistake, and a firm determination to succeed in whatever you undertake.

"With a less estimable person I either would not have put myself out at all, or would have beaten about the bush more; but to you I say, frankly and unequivocally:

"Beautiful, loving, generous creature, worthy to be loved by a fascinating prince and by a great king, do you choose to assume your proper station or abandon it to the unworthy females who have their eyes upon it?

"Reply! No tears, no childish blushing, no boarding-school hysterics! If the discussion were on the subject of making you Queen of France, I would await your reply as eagerly; but that place is taken. Only the secondary place remains, alas! but it may well become the first. Do you choose to take it?"

Bewildered, frightened, and overwhelmed, Louise rose and fell back again upon her chair time and again, in a state of feverish desperation, which finally moved even the immovable heart of Richelieu.

"Madame," said he, "I was in error; I thought that you were endowed with a stronger character. Forgive me, and forget, I beg you, all that I have said. I have but one very sincere regret in all this, and that is that I have been guilty of wounding you by addressing you in terms which you did not understand as they were intended."

The duke rose with the utmost respect, and stood before her to take his leave.

She was bathed in tears, and was trembling like a little bird that has fallen from the nest.

But at last seeing that the pitiless duke was about to leave her, she faltered, —

"Monsieur, do not triumph over a poor woman who loves, since you claim to have detected her love."

The duke bent his knee before her, and kissed the cold hand which hung down over the arm of her chair, as if he were adoring a saint.

"I am entirely at your service," said he. "Be calm, Madame; once more I say I am yours till death. Speak, pray! I am listening with all my ears."

XVII.

WHEREIN IS DISCUSSED THE POWER OF SOUND REASONING UPON A LOGICAL MIND.

RICHELIEU uttered an exclamation, the evident purpose of which was to take a long breath.

Madame de Mailly picked up her fan which had slipped gently from her hand to the chair and thence to the floor.

"I propose," said Monsieur de Richelieu, "to come to a clear understanding with your mind."

"Why not with my heart, Duke?" asked the countess.

"Because my understanding with your heart is already perfect; you have yielded to the charm, and have no need now of aught but resolution."

"Ah, Duke!"

"Pshaw! we shall not make much progress, if the first truth I utter makes you rebel. Beware, Countess, for I warn you that I have nothing but the unvarnished truth to say to you."

"I will listen."

"Are you quite sure of yourself?"

"Yes."

"Very well! now that the ice is thoroughly broken, and you know that I am a friend, you must know another thing which will tend even more to reassure you."

"What is it?"

"It is that I am an interested party."

Comtesse de Mailly.

From the Petitot Enamel.

OLYMPE DE CLÈVES, II. 222.

Madame de Mailly raised the shapely head, which the preliminaries of this fateful conversation had caused her to bow.

"An interested party?" she asked in surprise; "why, I thought you were on the best of terms with poor Monsieur de Mailly."

"Oh, how you do lose yourself, Countess! *Bon Dieu!* who is thinking of Monsieur de Mailly? Has Monsieur de Mailly any possible interest in what we are saying?"

"What do you mean then?"

"I mean, Madame, that the question to be decided is, who will govern France two months from now?"

"Monsieur le Duc —"

"What! again! Oh! I cannot forgive your hesitation, Countess. What the devil! The end is worth the means, as my great-uncle used to say, who said a good many great things, if not good things, in his lifetime. Do you choose to seek the end?"

Madame de Mailly muttered a word which was neither yes nor no; but the mere muttering of an unintelligible word under such circumstances was equivalent to giving her assent.

So at least Monsieur de Richelieu chose to understand it.

"Well, then," said he, "if you agree with my great-uncle and myself, why this wandering glance? It did seem to me that between us everything would be easy to say and easy to understand."

"Speak, then, I pray you," said Madame de Mailly, with a sigh.

"The king —"

Madame de Mailly unfolded her fan, just as a warrior in ancient days used to prepare his shield for single combat.

"The king is so young," the duke resumed, "that we are not yet quite sure whether he has a heart; the queen alone might be able to tell us. But let us be on our guard, for when the day comes that the queen will be able to solve that momentous problem, on that day, Madame, we shall be on the wrong road, and the king will no longer have a heart."

"Will he have two hearts?" inquired Madame de Mailly, smilingly.

"No, Countess; but he will have the passion of the senses, which will be much more dangerous for you and for me and for everybody — "

"For me?" said the countess, who had noticed only the phrase which concerned herself.

"Yes, indeed, Madame; for consider that what others have taught him he will know, and consequently there will be nothing left for you to teach him. You know how grateful his Majesty is toward his teachers."

"Is it so very hard, then, Duke, to love and be loved?"

"Humph!" said the duke.

The countess repeated her question.

"Oh, Countess," cried Richelieu, "what a narrow way you have of looking at the thing, what a vulgar idea of your mission you have! Fie, and you a De Nesle!"

"Teach me my lesson, then, Duke."

"Well then, Countess, understand this: that from the day —"

He hesitated, and the countess glanced up at him.

"Oh, faith!" he exclaimed, "let us call things by their names; from the day when you are the king's mistress the duties imposed upon you will be multifarious. In order to hold the king, you must appeal at once to his thoughts and his heart and his passions. It 's no small matter, Madame, upon my word, to be everything at once."

"Duke, Duke," said the countess, "I fail to comprehend."

"Be careful, Countess!"

"Upon my honor!" said Madame de Mailly, quickly, "I have no idea of being offended, indeed no; but I really do not understand."

The duke made a motion with his head which implied, —

"If you don't understand, why, you must be made to."

He said aloud, —

"Listen to what I say. It is essential that you should know, Countess, that at this moment, when you are still nothing but Monsieur de Mailly's wife, hardly separated from him — "

"Oh, separated altogether!" cried the countess.

"Very good. Well, even now you have rivals."

Louise de Mailly drew her black eyebrows together, like two clouds laden with storm wind and lightning.

"Rivals!" she muttered, less like a woman in terror than like one ready to fight for her rights.

"Good!" said the duke; "that really pleased me; you said it for all the world like Clairon. Yes, Countess, rivals!"

"Who are they?"

"First of all, the queen. Oh, don't raise your lovely lip scornfully; the queen, believe me, is not a rival to be despised."

"If you believe, Monsieur le Duc," retorted Madame de Mailly, "that the queen is so formidable an adversary, and that the king loves her so dearly, is it best for a woman of my birth and my disposition to venture upon the struggle? Beware, Duke! to enter the lists under such circumstances against a woman who has had four years' experience is to court dishonorable defeat; you are my friend, Duke, and the dishonor will rebound upon you."

"One moment! That is not all. You have, in addition to the queen, who, whatever you may say — I speak of what I know, you understand; I would not have said of Louis XIV. what I say of Louis XV. — you have, in addition to the queen, who has the great advantage of being queen, a woman more beautiful still, — a woman who has as much wit as you,— a woman (oh! this will sound severe, but no matter, you must hear it) who has a more regular beauty than yours, and who is of noble birth; but all this is nothing! an actress, that is to say, a chameleon able to assume any form she pleases; an actress, that is to say, not a beauty simply, but a combination of beauty and talent and heart and smiles and intoxicating perfumes."

"*Mon Dieu ! mon Dieu !* do you know how you alarm me!" cried Louise.

"*Pardieu !*" retorted the duke, "I intended to do just that. It is from none but generals of moderate capacity that one conceals the real strength of the enemy. I deal with you as with a Condé, a Turenne, or a Comte de Saxe."

"Do you know that such a portrait as you have drawn is a bitter satire upon my person?"

"Pshaw! now my general is coming down a peg; my Turenne is nothing more than a Villars."

"Who might this ravishing creature, this pearl of pearls, be?"

"Mademoiselle Olympe de Clèves."

"I know that name," said Madame de Mailly, pursing her lips

"I should suppose that you might know it, as she is your husband's mistress," rejoined Richelieu, smiling.

"Yes, I remember," said she.   "Let us leave her."

"No, indeed; let us not do anything of the kind; let us stop where we are."

"Very good.   So this woman is as you describe her?"

"Better, perhaps."

"Have you seen her?"

"Countess, forgive me if I do not reply directly to that question.   Before he knew you, Monsieur de Mailly had a mistress."

"Well."

"He became your husband, and after a year of married life returned to his mistress."

"Yes, you are right; she is indeed a rival to be feared. Is the king in love with her?"

"Not yet, luckily; but I am afraid that he is thinking a good deal about her, and love may well come in time."

"Do you think it will come?"

"Who knows?   Vessels make progress only in proportion to the wind that blows upon their sails."

"And is the wind blowing upon this particular vessel?"

"Very briskly."

"Who is the wind?"

"*Pardieu!* a very clever fellow! that's just what disturbs me; it's a pig-headed friend of mine, Monsieur le Duc de Pecquigny."

"Is it his wish to give her to the king?"

"Nothing else."

"And my husband?"

"Oh, the poor devil, what do you suppose?   He seems fated to suffer."

Louise smiled, despite her absorption.

"Duke," said she, drawning her eyebrows together once

more in a charming frown, "since I have stooped to
fight against an actress, would you mind telling me if
the odds are in my favor?"

"Madame," said the duke, bowing, "you are fighting
against a queen at the same time, and that makes up for
the other."

"Ah, that's true! still another chance against me, I
had forgotten that."

She added, in a bantering tone, —

"However, perhaps his Majesty will deign to take my
small stock of youth and beauty as a stopgap. That is a
glorious prospect."

"You are an adorable creature, but learn how to exert
your will; you lack but that."

"Exert my will to bring about my own dishonor, yes."

"Don't exaggerate, Countess; you have no idea how
exaggeration spoils the effect of what you say."

"Ah, Duke, but I am also — "

"Well?"

"I am inclined to rebel."

"Don't blush, Countess; when you blush, your principal beauty, the marvellous evenness of your coloring,
is the sufferer. Ah! now you understand me fully.
Fight on; the queen has her party, but it is few in numbers.
Still, she is queen, after all; she has the ambassadors,
the other powers, the Pope, and the women."

"Is that all?"

"Oh! but Olympe has vastly more than the queen."

"What has she?"

"She has Pecquigny and the *roués* and her all-
powerful beauty."

"Is she really so very lovely, then, this creature?"

"More so than one can say, Countess."

"Try to make me understand how lovely she is."

" She is yourself amplified."

Louise turned pale, and cast a swift glance upon her slender form, which did not escape Richelieu, and which satisfied him that she understood him.

" What am I to do then ? " she asked.

" Almost nothing, Madame. In the first place, let yourself go with the tide, and then set all the sail you can. That's all."

" And will you blow ? "

" With all the strength of my lungs."

" Have you some hope then ? "

" *Pardieu !* yes. You have certain advantages of your own, and they are enormous ones; you are a great lady, and you are in love."

" I am to understand that this stage girl does not love him, then ? "

" Who knows ? "

" She loves Monsieur de Mailly, perhaps ? "

" I can't say."

" Indeed she must love him; for she abandoned for him a fine youth, my word for it! who was innocent enough to come here and ask me for her."

" Indeed! " said Richelieu. " The devil! there may be something in that. What was this fine youth ? "

" Oh, a sort of madman."

" What became of him ? "

" I have no idea. You can understand that I did not set spies upon him."

" Disappeared. We will give up that idea. It would take too long; besides, it would be an expedient unworthy of us."

" You say that you doubt whether this creature loves Monsieur de Mailly."

" I do doubt it, yes."

"Then why does she live with him? Would it be from selfish devotion to her own financial interests?"

"I would swear that it is not that."

"For Heaven's sake, who is the woman?"

"A living secret, a mystery, which speaks but does not solve the riddle. She has a talisman. You know the full force of what I say, do you not?"

"What could I do against her?"

"You love the king, and love is a wise counsellor."

"That's the first point, then; let us pass to the next."

"Countess, are you vain, are you proud?"

"A little."

"Are you bent upon becoming a duchess like Madame de Fontanges, or queen like Madame de Maintenon?"

"Tell me why you ask me such questions."

"Answer them first."

"Very well, in a word: I want people to salute me with a smile, and not to turn aside to avoid the necessity of saluting me."

"Countess! Countess!"

"What is it, Monsieur le Duc; you don't treat me fairly."

"Let us not lose our tempers. You began by telling me that you had some pride."

"What then?"

"I felt bound to believe it."

"Duke, I cannot see what there was in what I had the honor to reply to you, to cause this furious manner and distorted countenance. A man like you ought to know something as to what a lady of quality should be."

"It is because I do know and have seen it with my eyes, Countess, that I am alarmed. Will you allow me to tell you a little story, Countess?"

"Pray, do; you have a reputation in that line which should make you sure of never being refused permission."

"Countess, there was one woman who never cost Louis XIV. a sou. It was not Mademoiselle de la Vallière, as you might imagine. No; Louis XIV. built Versailles for Mademoiselle de la Vallière, and pensioned Lebrun, Lenôtre, and Molière. For Mademoiselle de la Vallière he re-established tournaments and joustings, roundabouts and serenades; and it was a very good thing, for the money which the king spent went into the hands of poets and painters and artists; all of whom resemble grand seigneurs, especially in the matter of their hands, which are like sieves, every one. Now the money which dropped from the coffers of the state into the hands of these people filtered through their hands into those of the tailors, lace and ribbon dealers and bath-keepers, all of them large employers of workmen. The result was that not a sou of all this vast expenditure was wasted. No, I do not refer to Mademoiselle de la Vallière, nor to Madame de Fontanges, nor to Madame de Montespan,— all of them women for whom Louis XIV. spent much, but spent it royally; spent it as the sun spends his beams when he spreads them over the whole earth,— all of them women, I say, for whom he spent five or six hundred millions. No, I refer to Madame de Maintenon, a woman who cost him nothing, but who ruined France. Instead of deflecting ten millions, twenty millions, from the treasury, she forced upon the king a policy which cost the country a milliard of francs, and benefited not one single soul, and which resulted in a war wherein three hundred thousand men lost their lives, which benefited none but their heirs. Monsieur le Regent knew that. I tell you that Monsieur le Regent was a man of infinite cleverness; he was by no means all bad."

"You ought to know, for he sent you twice to the Bastille."

"Countess, I was not a thief; so I should do wrong to lay it up against him. Well, one day or one night, when a great lady, his best friend, was trying to talk politics with him, Monsieur le Régent cut it short with a kiss, and led her in front of a great mirror, wherein her charms were reflected.

" 'Tell me,' said he, 'if such a sweet little mouth as that has any right to sully itself by talking politics?' He closed that same mouth with another kiss, and never again did the lady who reigned over Philip's heart make an attempt to reign over France. Countess, I told you there was some good in Monsieur le Régent, and the same is true of Madame de Parabère."

"But, Duke," rejoined the countess, "I don't see at all what application you can make of this story to poor Madame de Mailly; I am not the woman to meddle in politics, I assure you."

"What!" cried the duke, "shall you be content with love-making?"

"Certainly I shall."

"You will not play the confidential adviser?"

"No, indeed."

"You will not want to review the troops, as Madame de Maintenon did?"

"It would bore me to death."

"You will not assume to make ministers?"

"Never, with a single exception, Duke."

She extended her hand to Richelieu with a charming smile.

"Are you really in earnest, Countess?" said he.

"Do you doubt it?"

"No; and yet — "

" What ? "

" Give me your word as a woman nobly born."

" On the faith of a countess ! " said she.

" Countess, your hand."

" Here it is."

" Now sleep in peace, Countess; there is only one woman suitable for the king, and you are she."

She blushed with pleasure.

He drew nearer to her with the remark, —

" Upon my honor, I am ill pleased with myself."

" Why ? "

" Because I am only a poor devil, twice duke and twice peer."

" What do you mean ? "

" That you are a woman above my deserts, Countess."

He kissed her hand with most respectful courtesy, and took leave of her, to hasten off to Monsieur de Fleury again.

Louise de Mailly, left alone, felt her strength leaving her; she was tempted to throw herself on her knees before her crucifix and weep.

Her tears suffocated her.

" Oh ! " she said, shaking her head; " no, it is useless: the time has gone by for heroic dishonor; I should pray in vain, for I shall not even be a La Vallière."

She rose and looked in a mirror at her eyes, which shone like two stars under their long black lashes.

" La Vallière," said she beneath her breath, — " bah ! a lame woman ! "

She added with the smile of a demon, —

" And a blonde ! "

XVIII.

BY ORDER OF THE KING.

THUS Mailly, with all his distrust, both as lover and as husband, which kept him at fever heat all the time, could not succeed in shutting out the enemies of the twofold treasure he was defending.

He was in the plight of those ill-fated Spanish bulls who are harassed and tormented on both sides, — on this by the picadors, and on that by the chulos, whose purpose it is to divert their attention from the blow about to be struck by the toreador.

He was scarcely out of Richelieu's hands, before he fell again into Pecquigny's, who, though the most brutally outspoken, was not really the most dangerous.

Mailly was by no means at ease with regard to him, however, although he had given the strictest orders to the servants at the house on Rue Grange-Batelière. Mademoiselle Olympe was never at home to Monsieur le Duc de Pecquigny.

Twice had he hurled himself against that obdurate door. He broke his horns against it, and swore revenge.

Revenge was hard to obtain, however, for Olympe did not appear again upon the stage. It was a difficulty which might easily have been surmounted by an order from the king; but in that case Mailly would come in her train, and he could not procure an order from the king forbidding the count to accompany Olympe to the theatre.

Besides, there is little satisfaction in discussing such matters behind the wings or even in a box. He desired to have a good long talk with her, — a talk which should last without interruption at least as long as it took Satan to lead Eve astray, — a quarter of an hour.

There was nothing for him to do, then, but to watch Mailly's goings and comings, for Olympe never went out.

Pecquigny was very badly off in one aspect, for the ordinary expedients of seducers were not open to him; he could not accomplish his designs by means of letters.

For how could he write to Olympe?

A love-letter never dishonors the man who writes it; it may bring him a rebuff, or he may have to fight a duel on account of it: nothing more. But there were few precedents for a gentleman of Pecquigny's rank writing to a woman in some other person's behalf, even though that other were the king.

The duel which would have followed such an epistle would have disgraced Pecquigny, and the king himself would have applauded instead of feeling grieved. And, worse than that, the king would not in that case receive his mistress from the hands of the offender.

Thus Pecquigny was forced to act with tiresome circumspection; and meanwhile time flew.

Time is the life-blood of negotiation, and if it flows to no purpose, death ensues.

And while Pecquigny was losing his time, Monsieur de Richelieu might carry his point, — a reflection which much disturbed Pecquigny, and afforded Mailly some little consolation.

For he had not yet given up all hope of his wife; he knew that she was virtuous, quick-tempered, and that she soon recovered her equanimity: she had threatened, but he was sure that she would come down from her high horse.

Thus, on the one hand, he trusted in his watchfulness; on the other, in the power of his name.

But the day had come when circumstances were to help Pecquigny renew his attack. It was a day when Mailly was absolutely obliged to be on duty at the inspection of three regiments of cavalry; but as the king was to review the regiments, Mailly's mind was untroubled, for he was sure that his Majesty would not be with his wife or his mistress.

His Majesty's agents, however, remained to be reckoned with, — Richelieu and Pecquigny.

Against the former he had the safeguard of Madame de Mailly's virtue.

Against Pecquigny he had the locks and bolts of the house on Rue Grange-Batelière.

But he had hardly reached the scene of the manœuvres at Satory, when Pecquigny, warned by his spies, arrived at the house.

He expected to be refused admittance, and he was.

"By order of the king," he said, laconically, to the open-mouthed Swiss.

"But — " began the honest fellow.

"By order of the king," Pecquigny said again.

The Swiss melted a little at this repetition of the phrase.

"You are the Duc de Pecquigny?" he asked.

"Gentleman of the Chamber," said the duke, "and I am the bearer of an order from the king. Do you want me to call a commissioner?"

"Oh, Monsieur le Comte will discharge me!" cried the Swiss.

"Well, what do I care, villain!" replied the duke;

"if he does discharge you, you will have kept clear of a worse fate."

"What is that, Monsieur le Duc?" faltered the trembling giant.

"The fate of going to bed in some underground dungeon, to teach you to have respect for an order from the king."

The Swiss bowed to the ground, vanquished by this logic, and threw the gate wide open; but the duke was considerate enough to leave his carriage outside.

Just as he crossed the threshold of the house-door, Olympe was leaving her bath.

She heard her women and the valets rushing around in the hall, and rang to inquire the cause of all the uproar.

Mademoiselle Claire entered the room hurriedly in dire alarm.

"What's the matter?" asked Olympe.

"Oh, Madame, what a misfortune!"

"What is it? tell me."

"An order from the king for Madame."

"An order from the king!" echoed Olympe, as the blood left her cheeks; for at that time, when princesses of the blood were not sure of their personal freedom from moment to moment, the princesses of the stage were even less so.

"Yes, and I am the bearer of it," replied Pecquigny, from the reception-room, where he had heard Olympe's exclamation of alarm.

"Who are you?" she asked.

"Monsieur le Duc de Pecquigny, Madame," said Claire, peering through the half-opened door and recognizing the intruder.

Olympe returned to her boudoir, hastily made her

toilette, gave a twist to her hair, and ordered that the
duke be admitted.

"*Mon Dieu!*" he began, "what a vast amount of
trouble one must needs take to obtain speech of you,
fair lady!"

"On the contrary, Monsieur le Duc," replied Olympe,
"it is for me to ask you why we see you so seldom."

"Oh, that is delightful," said Pecquigny; "and you
have the face to say that to me!"

"To you? why, of course."

"Am I to understand that you don't know why you
have not seen me since my last visit?"

"I do not."

"Well, I will tell you. It is because your tyrant
orders people turned from the door."

"You have been turned from the door, do you say?"

"Yes, I do say so."

"You have been so grievously insulted, Monsieur le
Duc?"

"Yes. Do you choose to avenge me?"

"I choose to be mistress in my own home," said
Olympe; "and as I have given no orders that you should
not be allowed to enter the house, you may come in
henceforth, if you please, without hindrance, and without the necessity of alleging an order from the king as a
pretext, as you did to-day, for the bare words make me
shudder."

"But I did n't invent any pretext at all, I beg you to
believe. I have an order from the king, bearing his
Majesty's signature."

"To take me to Versailles or to the For-l'Evêque?"
asked Olympe, laughingly.

"Neither, Madame; but to compel your appearance at
the Comédie."

"Do you mean it?" cried Olympe, interested and delighted beyond expression; for next to Bannière, she loved the stage better than anything else.

"Yes, I mean it."

"How does it happen? I thought that I had failed miserably, and owing to my failure had become free once more."

"No, far from it; you made a success, — a very great success, in fact. But *some one* has noticed that you have gone into voluntary eclipse. All great artists, if they absent themselves from the stage, seem to deprive us of warmth and light; and since your absence, fair Olympe, it has been very dark and very cold. The *some one* who has noticed your absence demands your presence once more, and here is an order signed by him."

Thereupon Pecquigny drew from his pocket a folded paper which he handed to the actress.

Olympe took it from him, and with a sensation of joy difficult to describe read as follows: —

"By the king's command, Messieurs his actors will play within the fortnight, upon the order of one of his Gentlemen of the Chamber, 'La Fausse Agnès' and 'Hérode et Mariamne.' The Gentleman of the Chamber who is on duty will distribute the parts, and arrange for rehearsals from this day forward."

"Am I to act in both pieces?" asked Olympe.

"Of course; do you not know both parts?"

"I know 'Mariamne;' but although I have memorized 'La Fausse Agnès,' I have never acted it."

"Would you prefer some other part?"

"No; that is a fascinating part, but it requires long, hard study."

"Oh, not long."

"You are mistaken, Monsieur le Duc; it is a delight-

ful part, as I had the honor to say to you, but it needs to
be thoroughly learned."

"*Noblesse oblige*, as you know, fair lady; I am telling
you nothing new."

"Very well," said Olympe, smiling, "I will do my
utmost to please his Majesty."

"Oh, Madame, you have already pleased the king so
much that you are absolutely sure of satisfying his
artistic sense."

"Are there such things as that in his Majesty's order,
Monsieur le Duc?" said Olympe.

"No; but they are written in your eyes."

"Do you desire that I should give my sanction to
Monsieur de Mailly's action in closing my door upon
you?"

"No, I have nothing to say to you which he ought not
to hear."

"And I have nothing to say to you except in jest."

"The deuce you say!"

"However, since you are here, do you know that he
has gone away?"

"He is at Versailles, in attendance upon the king; he
is very fortunate, don't you think?"

"He is very fortunate?"

"Why, yes."

"Of course every good Frenchman ought to esteem
himself fortunate to be by the king's side."

"Do you include the French ladies?"

"Oh, Monsieur le Duc, the French ladies are good
Frenchmen too."

"*Tudieu!* what a delightful speech, and how pleased
the king will be when he hears of it!"

"Yes; but he will not hear of it."

"Why not?"

" Who will repeat it to him ? "

" I will."

" You! and why ? "

" To give him pleasure, of course. "

" I believe Monsieur de Mailly is just coming in," said Olympe, slyly.

Pecquigny rose hastily, frowning, and laying his hand upon his sword-hilt.

But Olympe began to laugh heartily.

Pecquigny looked at her in amazement.

" There, you see that you are either doing or thinking something that you know to be wrong," said she.

" Well, I admit it. "

" Stick to the king's order; it's the safest way, believe me. "

" Yes; but the king's order is that you should do as the king orders. "

" Even here ? "

" Here especially. "

" Then bring me a second order from his Majesty to that effect," said Olympe.

" Oh ! but I will do that sooner than you think. "

" Written with his own hand. "

" And countersigned ' Pecquigny.' " "

" Beware! when that comes, I shall advise with Monsieur de Mailly. "

" Upon my word, this woman is as hard as steel. "

" Let us talk about ' La Fausse Agnès,' Monsieur le Duc. "

" What day will you act it ? "

" What will Monsieur de Mailly say if I go back to the stage ? "

" If he desires to pick a quarrel with the king, he is at

liberty to do so. When will you play 'La Fausse Agnès'?"

"Duke, there is some difficult work in that part."

"What do you refer to?"

"The mad scenes."

"Pshaw! it's pretended madness only."

"That only makes it the harder to do. The person who takes the part ought to enter into the feigned mental condition, and I never saw a madman."

"How does that happen?"

"Because I have always been afraid of them."

"Very well!" said Pecquigny, "you see one now."

"Where, pray?"

"At your feet."

"That's very true," retorted Olympe, coolly.

"Take me for your model," said Pecquigny, slightly disconcerted.

"No, your madness is too absurd. We must see some others, Monsieur le Duc."

"What! do you want to see some madmen?"

"Yes."

"Real madmen?"

"Why, of course."

"Be careful!"

"Of what?"

"Madness is catching."

"Nonsense!"

"Oh, *mon Dieu!* yes, it is contagious; it is caught from people's lips and in their eyes."

"Oh, no! I have no fear of it."

"Don't joke about it. I have heard it said that those who visit Charenton too often, or stay there for any length of time, are in great danger of losing their reason."

"Ah! the madmen are at Charenton, are they ? "

"Yes, fair lady, and they are a fearful sight to look upon, I warn you."

"I will go to Charenton."

"Are you callous to human suffering ? "

"No; I am an artist much in love with my profession, and very ambitious to succeed."

"Very well! then I will see that you have an opportunity to visit Charenton."

"Thanks."

"I will go with you, too, if you will allow me."

"As you please, Monsieur le Duc."

"You shall have your permission this evening, and to-morrow at such hour as you may name, my carriage shall be at your door."

"Thanks, I have my own."

"Will you give me a seat in it ? "

"That is not my right, Monsieur le Duc."

"How so ? "

"Because my carriages are Monsieur de Mailly's, and it is for him to authorize others to enter them, just as the king does with his own."

"But it 's on the king's service, my dear."

"Doubtless, then, Monsieur de Mailly will be very happy to demonstrate his submission to the king; ask him."

"Oh, you know that it 's impossible; he would refuse me."

"If he refuses that, he will refuse to let me act; he 's a stubborn fellow."

"Pshaw! "

"He is more than stubborn, he is immovable."

"And you think that his immovability will hold out against the king ? "

"It would hold out against all the powers of hell! "

"What are we to do then? "

"Wait a moment; the best course, if you really want me to act in 'La Fausse Agnès,' will be to leave Monsieur de Mailly in ignorance of my purpose to act."

"Do you know that's a wretched expedient for the ambassador of his Most Christian Majesty to resort to? "

"Oh, Monsieur de Richelieu is not so proud an ambassador as you, and yet he's very clever."

"What does Monsieur de Richelieu do? "

"Well, in the first place, he succeeds in what he undertakes."

The name of Richelieu, which Olympe had pronounced without the slightest ulterior purpose, had nevertheless a magical effect upon the duke.

He shuddered as he thought that perhaps Richelieu would succeed with Madame de Mailly, while he was fighting a losing battle for Olympe.

"You are right," he cried suddenly, — "you are right, Madame. Go to Charenton alone, say nothing about the king's order, do just as you please; but in any event, and to be ready for any emergency, you shall have your permission to-morrow. And I rely upon you to play 'La Fausse Agnès' in a week."

"No, in a fortnight, if you please, Monsieur le Duc," said Olympe.

"Well, a fortnight, then, if you insist. But your word."

"Here is my hand."

"You know that the king will be there."

"I rely upon his being there. Why should he command me to act if it was not to be before him? "

Pecquigny kissed the hand which Olympe held out to

him, and executed very much such an exit as Richelieu's from Madame de Mailly's presence.

He was as triumphant on his side as Richelieu was on his.

Poor Mailly!

XIX.

THE NEW CHAPLAIN AT CHARENTON.

THE same day that Pecquigny paid his visit to Olympe, armed with the king's order, and at the very hour when he was promising to obtain leave for her to visit Charenton, an interesting ceremony was taking place within the walls of that establishment.

The manager of the institution was leading from cell to cell, from room to room, and from dungeon to dungeon, a new chaplain, whom the Archbishop of Paris had just appointed to that painful post, on the recommendation of one of his friends, the principal of the Jesuit college at Avignon.

This new chaplain walked with a firm and resolute step. He held his head with much dignity, and seemed as proud of his clerical garb as one of the most brilliant officers in the army might have been of his uniform.

They visited first the refectory, the dormitories, and the parts of the institution which were most used.

From time immemorial it has been the custom for every manager of a hospital or prison to let his visitors taste the soup and other viands which the inmates live on; so they visited the kitchen, which at Charenton was furnished with a degree of magnificence which would have aroused the envy of the Prince de Soubise's scullions.

There were coppers and turnspits fit to make Apicius swoon with delight, had he returned to earth and been transported from Naples to Paris.

Moulds for pastry and moulds for cream, fish-kettles of all sizes, from that which would just hold a grated whitefish to the enormous vessel in which a whole sturgeon could be cooked.

The ravished eyes of the onlooker furnished food for a thousand fond hopes to the stomach.

The manager proudly called the new chaplain's attention to this glittering array.

"My father," said he, "you see that we can do some good cooking here."

"Yes, Monsieur," replied the new functionary, indifferently.

"Pardon, my father, but I am forever forgetting your name, and yet it seems to be familiar to my ears."

"My name is Champmeslé, Monsieur."

"Monsieur l'Abbé de Champmeslé,— that's curious: Champmeslé, it seems to me — Ah! on my soul, it's extraordinary."

"What is it that's extraordinary, pray?" demanded the abbé.

"I seem to want to smile when I hear that name. Here are our stewpans, Monsieur de Champmeslé."

"I see them."

"There are six for turkeys, eight for chickens; and this enormous one, for a whole hog, was given to the institution by the Benedictines. The medium-sized one is for two hares or two rabbits, Monsieur de Champmeslé! Ah! *mon Dieu!*"

"What is it?"

"Why, that's a stage name."

"An actor's, you mean."

"An actor's or actress's; yes, an actress's, I remember, — Monsieur Racine's mistress."

" She was my grandmother, Monsieur," said the new chaplain, with noble humility, and blushing to his ears.

Stupid as he was, the manager realized his stupidity.

" I beg your pardon, Monsieur l'Abbé," said he.

" Monsieur, I was born to suffer," rejoined the abbé.

" Ah, Monsieur l'Abbé, I had no intention of hurting you."

" Monsieur, I am doing penance."

The manager bowed, and passed on to the frying-pans and dripping-pans, and thence to the cisterns and distilleries.

" Monsieur," said Champmeslé, " this kitchen makes one long to play the madman, so as to come here and eat all these good things. But, pardon me, I see nothing but beef in the dishes now, and the soup was so weak that there can have been very little chicken in it."

" Monsieur l'Abbé, there 's a physician here, and he prescribes very light diet for the patients; when a lunatic is fed, he is stronger than before."

" Naturally, Monsieur," said Champmeslé.

" And when he is stronger, he is more dangerous."

" Ah ! "

" Monsieur l'Abbé, we are going to see some of them at once."

" Poor creatures ! Do they go to confession ? "

" Never. Confession is a thing which excites their evil passions."

" Why ? Is it because they don't understand it, Monsieur manager ? "

" Oh, Monsieur l'Abbé, there are some who understand it perfectly."

" Then why do they not confess ? "

" Because there are no confessors, Monsieur l'Abbé."

"Why, I had the impression that there was a chaplain here before I came."

"Certainly there was."

"Well?"

"He did just as you will do."

"What is that, pray?"

"He remained in his room or in the garden, — two places of sojourn infinitely more agreeable than the cells or the dungeons."

"Horror!" cried Champmeslé; "you say he was such a wretch as to hold aloof from them!"

The manager looked at Champmeslé with an expression which combined surprise with cunning.

"Bah!" said he, "would you have had him make companions of those people?"

"Why not?"

"Why, they bite."

"Suppose they do."

"And they strike."

"No doubt."

"And they kill."

"Why did he accept the post of chaplain to them?" rejoined Champmeslé, simply.

"Come, come, Monsieur," said the manager, "wait till after you have visited them."

"Let us go on."

"Since you are in that frame of mind," continued the manager, "I will abridge the ceremony. I might have taken you first to the infirmary and the dormitories."

"Useless."

"You prefer to visit the dungeons, do you not, and the cells?"

"Precisely."

The manager gave a signal to a turnkey, who lighted a lantern and walked ahead of them.

"Why, it's daylight, is n't it?" said Champmeslé.

"Not in the places where we are going, Monsieur," replied the manager, ironically.

Indeed the turnkey preceded them into a horrible vault, eight feet underground, and which received its only light through an air-hole very near the ceiling, guarded by sentries.

Each dungeon had its door of solid oak, with a lozenge-shaped aperture heavily barred, through which one gazed upon many a ghastly spectacle.

In the dense gloom of these dens Champmeslé could make out haggard, frightful spectres, — some dancing and howling, others terrified, and others as motionless and inert as corpses.

He felt a shudder run through his whole system; he was afraid.

"Well," said the manager, "what do you think of it?"

"I think," said he, "that if these poor wretches, instead of being left to rot in these pest-holes, had a little light and air and could see their fellow-men, they would be less like wild beasts and less miserable."

"That's just the way every one talks at first," said the manager.

"I shall end as I begin," said Champmeslé. "What are these people?"

"Desperate lunatics."

"Do they live in these places?"

"Oh, some of them die every day, and they are the lucky ones. When one dies, one suffers no more."

"True," said Champmeslé.

"Hallo there!" cried the manager, "Martin, come here! — Martin is a head keeper."

"Indeed!"

"A perfect Hercules!"

"Indeed!"

"Yes, a man who can kill an ox with a blow of his fist."

"What is the advantage of that? Do you kill oxen here?"

"No, it's his duty to go into the cages."

"Does his strength help him in that?"

"If one of those who are thought to be dead, or who are shamming death, — for a lunatic is a cunning fellow, — if, I say, one of them undertakes to jump at Martin, he makes an end of him at a single blow and painlessly."

"How admirably humane! He is your executioner, then?"

The manager laughed in appreciation of what he thought an agreeable bit of pleasantry on Champmeslé's part.

"Martin," said he, "go into number nine; there's a bad smell there, and he must be dead."

Martin, the Hercules aforesaid, rolled up his sleeves, entered the hole like a dog hunting a cat, and lifted up a lifeless mass.

"Dead!" said he.

"Take him away, and put in here in his place that raving madman from number seven on the stone gallery."

Martin made ready to obey.

"One moment, in pity's name!" exclaimed Champmeslé, whose soul rose in protest: "don't cast another poor wretch into that deadly cavern with such unseemly haste!"

"It's easy to see that you don't live as I do, directly over the stone gallery," said the manager: "I have an office there; it's the canteen of the institution."

"Does this fellow make much noise?"

"You shall hear him; he declaims like the maddest of madmen, roars and shakes his chains and ends up with an epileptic fit; then he breaks everything within reach, and threatens to kill everybody."

"Oh! perhaps there is some cure."

"None whatever."

"Let me see him."

"You shall see him at once; more than that, as his room is higher up, and it is light there, you can speak to him."

"I would gladly speak also with those who are down here," said Champmeslé; "but — "

"The smell is too much for you, is it not?"

"I can put up with it."

"Yes; but I can't, and I beg that you will permit me to go upstairs for a breath of air."

"Let us go!" said Champmeslé, who proposed to return, — "let us go!"

They went up to the stone gallery. It was a long rectangle bordered with stone cells, with iron bars, like those made for wild beasts.

There was a sanded court in the centre which afforded a little air and daylight to the forty or more wretched men and women who could be seen, hideous, half naked, covered with blood and filth, behind the bars.

Shrieks and sighs and unearthly laughter resounded in mournful chorus in this pleasant abode.

Champmeslé, less embarrassed by the manager, began with number one, resolved to make the whole circuit.

The manager gave the necessary explanations with an air of increasing displeasure.

At number four he looked at his watch, at number five he showed signs of uneasiness, and at number six he said to Champmeslé, —

'· Pardon me, Monsieur l'Abbé, I have an engagement; and if you are determined to see everything, we shall not get away from here till midnight."

" Just this one, I beg," said Champmeslé.

He had stopped in front of a cell occupied by a man of some fifty years, tall and thin and grizzled, his head covered with a mat of grayish-white hair, and his face with a grayish-black beard, and his eyes glowing like phosphorus beneath their shaggy eyebrows.

" That man is frightful to look at," said Champmeslé, in an undertone.

" He is one of the most savage in the whole place."

" Ah! he seems to suffer."

" He can never suffer enough."

" Why, what did the madman do?"

" He is no more mad than you are."

" Why is he here, then?"

" Ah, Monsieur l'Abbé, that's the affair of the minister and the lieutenant of police "

" Is it a secret?"

" For most people, yes; for you, no.'

" Tell it me, then."

" I am in a tremendous hurry."

" Just this one, and then you may leave me."

" It is very long."

" You can tell it quickly, and then you can tell it so well."

After this bit of flattery, which tickled immensely the self-esteem of this tiger with a buffalo's head, the manager stepped aside a short distance to avoid being overheard. Champmeslé followed him.

The manager hesitated a moment, coughed and expectorated as every man does preparatory to beginning a story; then he said, stretching his arm toward the raving madman's cell. —

" There you see, Monsieur l'Abbé, a man who is no more mad than I am."

" Who is the poor devil ? "

The manager shook his head.

" He 's no poor devil, either."

" What is he, then ? " inquired the abbé, with growing interest.

" He 's a petty Sardinian noble."

" A noble ! "

" A marquis."

" Do you know his name ? "

" No one is supposed to know it; but as manager of the institution, I do know it."

" And it is ? "

The manager lowered his voice.

" No, don't tell me what it is," said Champmeslé, on reflection. " He will tell me himself in confession."

" You will confess him ? "

" Of course."

" You will go into his cell ? "

" To-morrow."

" Why, he 's a murderer ! "

" An additional reason why I should hear him in confession," said Champmeslé, with a simplicity of manner which was the more sublime because he could not prevent an internal shudder.

" His name is Marquis della Torra," said the manager, either not remembering or not caring to remember what Champmeslé had said to him on the subject of the prisoner's name. " Do you recognize that name ? "

" No," replied Champmeslé; " it is the first time I ever heard it."

He took a step toward the cell.

" Pray, wait," said the manager, " until I finish the story."

"Yes," said Champmeslé, "perhaps I may find in what you tell me some suggestion of a means of giving comfort to the man."

"To begin with, he was a Greek!"

"Greek? You told me Sardinian."

The manager laughed.

"Oh, admirable, excellent!" he cried. "He was a Greek by profession, not by birth."

"Ah, I understand!" said Champmeslé.

"He was at the head of a band of sharpers who have infested the provinces for a long while."

"Then his place was in prison."

"In prison! and he a nobleman?"

"Very well; but Monsieur le Regent," said Champmeslé, "had the Comte de Horn broken on the wheel, and he was connected with reigning princes."

"Monsieur le Regent was an atheist who believed in nothing," said the manager, "while the present king does not desire to dishonor the nobility. That course was recommended to him by the late king."

"Let us get on, I beg," said Champmeslé; "those are not my ideas."

"Aha! so you have ideas, have you?"

"Go on, Monsieur, I beseech you."

"At last, from swindle to swindle and theft to theft, this Marquis della Torra — pardon me, I forgot to say that in his travels he was accompanied by a very pretty and attractive creature whose name was — "

"Well, her name was — "

"Ah! Help me, pray!"

"That's rather difficult, Monsieur, as I do not know of whom or of what you are speaking."

"I am speaking of a young girl."

"Indeed!"

" Who bore the name of a famous woman."

" Semiramis ? "

" No, not great in that line."

" Lucrece ? "

" No, still less in that. *Dame!* help me. The opposite of Lucrèce."

" Laïs ? "

" No, no — a Frenchwoman — Ninon ? — no. Ah ! Marion, I have it, Marion."

" Ah! Marion, indeed! You were thinking of Marion Delorme, were you not, Monsieur ? "

" Yes, Monsieur l'Abbé, just so. Have you read of her ? "

" Yes, a little."

" Well, this Marion (who, be it said parenthetically, seems to have been a lovely girl) was not so wicked as her lover; and although he kept her with him to help in his swindling, she sometimes betrayed him. Now, it chanced, one day, that the marquis had despoiled a fine young fellow whom he had enticed into a game, and, the youth being ruined, Mademoiselle Marion took pity on him, and informed the dupe that he had fallen into a nest of vultures. Thereupon he gave the marquis a hiding, and undertook to recover his money. But it was too late; a third rascal, as worthy La Fontaine says, had made off with it. I say 'worthy La Fontaine,' because that is the title ordinarily given him. I have no doubt that you cordially detest him.''

" Ah, Monsieur," said Champmeslé, blushing, " he wrote many immoral tales! But let us return to the Marquis della Tórra, Monsieur."

" Yes, let us return to him. Well, after this little episode Marion separated from the marquis, and followed the good-looking youth."

"So much the better! If he was an honest man, she may perhaps have found her salvation in that way."

"Oh, yes, her salvation indeed! You will see in a moment. After three or four days it seems that the youth had private business which did not admit of the presence of a third party, and he left Marion, sharing with her six or seven louis, which with her assistance he had succeeded in recovering. Marion, left alone, and not knowing what course to pursue, let chance guide her footsteps, and was captured by Della Torra, who was on the lookout for her: there was a quarrel, recrimination, and insulting taunts. Instead of denying everything, she avowed everything, and even boasted of it, until in a fit of temper Della Torra ran his sword through her heart."

"Oh, the abominable villain!" cried Champmeslé. "Is it such nobility as this which his Majesty Louis XV. wishes to be held in honor in his realm? How was the affair found out?"

"Oh, very simply! Marion lived long enough to tell the story. They caught the marquis with a companion of his who had assisted in the murder. He was a simple sharper, and was broken on the wheel at Lyons. Della Torra, adjudged insane, was brought here and put in double chains."

Champmeslé leaned forward to look at Della Torra, who, seeing that he was the subject of their conversation, ground his teeth and made an angry movement.

"Look at him," said the manager, "look at the poor wretch! What a villanous eye he has! On due reflection I will send him down into dungeon number nine, instead of the man in number seven. And now that I have told you what you wished to know, adieu, Monsieur l'Abbé. You know now as much as I do, — about this fellow, at least. Adieu, Monsieur l'Abbé. Will you do me the honor to dine with me?"

Without even waiting for the abbé's response the manager withdrew.

XX.

THE MAN WHO WAS MAD WITH LOVE.

CHAMPMESLÉ, left alone, once more scrutinized the Marquis della Torra, who was crouching in the corner of his dungeon, glaring out into the court with a ferocious yet crafty expression.

It seemed to him a terrible punishment to be always alone, always treated like a mad man, and continually haunted by his crime, with no one to reproach him, to be sure, but equally without means of consolation.

He made up his mind to speak of God and of hope to the forsaken, hopeless wretch, and he drew nearer the bars, thinking thus to make a good beginning in the performance of his duties as chaplain.

A keeper leaning against the wall of a neighboring cell watched him with much interest, and stood ready to defend him at need.

" My friend, " said Champmeslé to the assassin of poor Marion, " I am the chaplain of the institution.   Are you sufficiently penitent to listen attentively to the words of hope I bring you ? "

But Della Torra, instead of replying, turned his face to the wall, and maintained an obstinate silence.

Champmeslé tried to arouse the despair-laden soul, but to no purpose.

He called the keeper.

" I don't believe I can do anything with him to-day,' he said.

"No, Monsieur l'Abbé, not to-day or to-morrow," was the reply.

"Who is the man in number seven?" queried the abbé.

"Ah! he's a bird of another color. He is mad with love, Monsieur l'Abbé; a very noisy lunatic, who never ceases, day or night, to call down imprecations upon those who betrayed him."

"Really? Poor fellow!"

"It seems that he was in love with some girl named Julie; for when the archers arrested him in the vestibule of the Comédie-Française, where he was trying to force his way in, he kept saying that name over and over again with the utmost violence; so the archers said, at least."

"Is he ugly?"

"No one knows, Monsieur."

"What! no one knows?"

"No, for he has no chance to injure any one but himself. He keeps up a continual crying, however."

"What does he cry?"

"Oh, *mon Dieu!* the same things that every one does who is afflicted with the worst of all forms of madness."

"What form is that?"

"I mean those who fancy that they are not mad because they have lucid moments."

"All right!" said Champmeslé. "I will go and speak to him to see if I can't induce him to keep quiet, so that the manager will not carry out his purpose of putting him in the underground dungeons."

"Very well, Monsieur l'Abbé," replied the keeper; "I don't think you have much to fear from him."

Champmeslé thereupon approached the barred door, and saw within a young man with the top of his head

covered with long hair, and the lower part with a light
beard; he was sitting in a corner of his cell in a patch of
sunlight, and seemed happy in that, in his thoughts and
in his solitude.

His eyes were fastened upon the floor, but there was a
smile on his face; he was twisting in his fingers a wisp
of straw, the end of which he nibbled from time to time
with his fine white teeth.

Champmeslé scanned his face for a moment; it seemed
to him a noble and a touching one, and he expressed the
sensation it produced in these three words, —

"Ah, poor boy!"

The madman's eyes at once opened.   He fastened
them upon the chaplain, who looked with the emotion of
a true Christian at the pallid features of the unfortunate
fellow.

"Oh, *mon Dieu!*" cried the madman, springing with
one leap from the stool on which he was seated to the
door of his cell.

The keeper quickly fell back, and drew the abbé after
him.

"What is it, pray?" said the latter, yielding to the
keeper's grasp, but keeping his eyes upon the madman.

"He an abbé!" exclaimed the prisoner, pressing
close against the bars.

"Why, yes, I am an abbé."

"What! Is it you, Monsieur de Champmeslé?"

"How does he know me?"

"Monsieur de Champmeslé! Monsieur de Champmeslé!" cried the madman.

"My friend?"

"It is Heaven that sends you here!"

"I hope so."

"For God's sake, don't you recognize me?"

" Alas, no ! "

The madman put his hair away from his eyes.

" I am Bannière ! " said he.

" What ! the young novice of the Jesuits ? "

" Yes."

" Bannière, who played King Hérode ? "

" The same."

" And the lover of Mademoiselle de Clèves ? "

" Yes ! oh, yes ! " shrieked Bannière, with despairing gestures fearful to see. " Oh, yes ! I was her lover ! "

He wrung his hands frantically, and sobbed as if his heart would break.

" My friend," cried Champmeslé to the keeper, " open the door of this poor fellow's cell at once, I beg."

" But he will assault you, Monsieur l'Abbé."

" Oh, no, no ! Monsieur knows well that I will do nothing of the kind," exclaimed Bannière, with the most amiable expression he could command.

" Pray open the door," repeated Champmeslé.

" Yes, yes, open," Bannière said beseechingly ; " open for Monsieur l'Abbé, my friend ; and you, Monsieur l'Abbé, shall see how I love you ! "

" Yes, he will love you as my cat loves rats ; that is to say, he will eat you."

" That 's my lookout," said Champmeslé ; " open."

" You order me, Monsieur l'Abbé ? "

" Yes."

" You will declare that you have demanded that I should open his cell-door ? "

" I will so declare ; now open."

" It is my duty to obey you, and obey you I certainly will ; but be guided by me, and take my club."

He opened the door, keeping a watchful eye upon Bannière at each turn that he gave the key in the lock.

Champmeslé darted into the cell, where he was greeted by Bannière with the utmost gentleness.

"Oh!" said he, "if I were not afraid of frightening you and of soiling your clothes, oh, dear Monsieur de Champmeslé, how I would hug you!"

The good chaplain threw himself into the madman's arms; it was a sight which many curious people would have paid to see.

"Sit down upon my stool, Monsieur de Champmeslé," said Bannière, "sit down, and have no fear. Oh, let us talk, let us talk; I have so many things to tell you."

"Yes," said Champmeslé, with an affectionate smile, "let us talk, but let us talk reasonably."

"Why, can it be that you think I am not in my right mind?" said Bannière.

"Look out!" said the keeper, "his madness is coming back."

Champmeslé looked significantly at the surroundings, and then brought his eyes back to Bannière's face, with a movement of the shoulders which said as plainly as could be, "Alas! if you were in your right mind, would you be here?"

"I understand you," said the young man, sadly, "and it is very natural, for you are prejudiced against my sanity; but as you listen to me, you will see whether I am mad."

"Well, then, if you are not mad," said Champmeslé, "tell me what strange chain of circumstances has brought you to Charenton."

"Send that man away."

Champmeslé unhesitatingly made a sign to the keeper, who walked off out of hearing.

Then Bannière told his whole pitiful story, from the evening when he had taken his place and played Hérode.

He told of his flight with Olympe, after the Comte de Mailly's desertion, of their stay at Lyons, and his arrest in that city on the requisition of the Jesuits, from whose college he had deserted. Then he went on with his experiences from the time of his desertion from the dragoons to the day of his arrest in the vestibule of the Comédie-Française; and the whole tale was told so clearly and with such pathos that the abbé cried out, when he had made an end of his narrative, —

" This man is no more mad than I am! "

" That is so, is n't it, Monsieur de Champmeslé? " cried Bannière; " I 'm no lunatic, am I? "

" I would swear it! I would answer for your sanity! "

" Good! " said Bannière. " God has sent me what I have asked for ever since I have been here, — an impartial man who would listen to me and pass upon my condition. But I never dared to ask for anybody better than a stranger, and behold! God has sent me a friend. "

" Yes, indeed, my dear Bannière, a true friend. "

" But now do you tell me, " said Bannière, " how it happens that you are here and in this garb? "

" My vocation, my dear sir. "

" Oh, *mon Dieu!* yes, a vocation exactly the reverse of mine, " said poor Bannière, with a mournful smile.

" Exactly. As you took my place and my costume at the theatre, so I took your place and your costume at the convent. "

" The convent which I left? "

" The convent which you left; and I became the favorite of the reverend father principal. "

" Ah, there again, my dear friend, " said Bannière, " your experience was just the reverse of mine. "

" As I asked nothing more than to leave the stage, and as my renunciation of that profession was a great triumph for religion, I was received with open arms, carefully taught, taken into the order, and at last given this position."

"Alas! it's an unhappy position, my dear Abbé!"

"Yes, you are right; I know that it is considered the least desirable of all: no one wanted it, so that my application was successful."

"If I were not so happy to see you, I would say to you, 'You made a mistake, my dear Abbé.'"

"I have so much to atone for, my brother," said Champmeslé; "I was more than three fourths damned."

"The devil! at that rate, I must be damned altogether," said Banniére, smiling sadly.

Champmeslé smiled back at him.

"But," Banniére continued, raising his eyes to heaven, "I hope for better things from God; he has given me too much suffering on earth to continue it after my death."

"Don't complain of God, my dear brother," said Champmeslé, glad of an opportunity to preach a little.

"I have no further complaint to make of him, since I have met with you again, dear Abbé," said Banniére, gently.

"God is putting you to the proof, my son."

"A very cruel proof."

"God has his own purposes to fulfil."

"What object can God have in inflicting suffering on a poor devil like me?"

"He desires to make you forget a guilty passion."

"What passion?"

"Your passion for Olympe de Clèves."

"My passion for Olympe? You call that a guilty passion! I am to forget that! Though I were to pass for a madman all my life; though I were to be a prisoner forever, to be beaten, scourged, and tortured, as the poor wretches whose shrieks I hear are beaten, scourged, and tortured,—never, never would I renounce my love for Olympe: rather death! rather damnation!"

"There, there, my brother," said Champmeslé, "you are wandering; I shall think you are mad."

"True," said Bannière, gloomily; "but what would you, Monsieur? I love that woman so dearly that nothing under heaven can make me forget her."

"Not even God?"

"Not even herself."

"And yet, my dear Bannière, it seems to me that you owe all your misfortunes to her."

"Yes, no doubt, I do owe them to her: she betrayed me, and has forgotten me; it is possible, even, that she procured my arrest in order to be rid of me. Very well, such as she is, I bless her; such as she is, I love her with all my heart! Oh, if you, who knew her,—if you could only tell me something of her!"

"I am just from Lyons," said Champmeslé.

"Then, too," continued Bannière, with a deep sigh, as if another hope were lost to him, "you have broken with the stage."

"Oh, *mon Dieu!* yes, and yet I retain some acquaintances there, whom I cultivate, to try to lead them to God."

"You will have but ill success," said Bannière, shaking his head.

"They will not all be in love with Olympe, I hope; and then," continued Champmeslé, approaching Bannière as if to confide a secret to him, "I have my plan all laid out."

"What is it?" asked Bannière.

"I shall attack them on the side of their worldly interests, to lead them to heaven without their knowing it."

"Indeed!" said Bannière, wonderingly.

"This is what I mean to do," rejoined Champmeslé, overjoyed to be able, newly ordained as he was, to expound a theory of salvation. "I have for a friend — I venture to call him so, although he is a duke and peer — Monsieur le Duc de Pecquigny, one of the Gentlemen of the Chamber, who has full power over all actors."

"Oh, a fine acquaintance, my dear Abbé! a man who can give one leave to make one's début, who secures engagements for one, and assigns all the parts. Oh, I say again, a valuable acquaintance you have in him! Lucky man!"

"Take care," said Champmeslé, smiling, "or I shall call you mad."

"Go on, go on."

"Where was I?"

"You were talking about leading actors to God through their worldly interests."

"That's what I mean to do."

"I understand. You will see that they have good parts, and through gratitude they will become religious. Well, I confess that I don't think much of that plan, nor indeed have I much confidence in its success."

"Pray listen to me, you everlasting talker!" cried Champmeslé, taking advantage of the first halt made by Bannière's tongue, to take his turn and expound his idea. "No, that is not my plan at all; I know actors too well for that. Give them good parts, indeed! On the contrary, I will see that they get disgusted with those they have, and will make the stage a place of torture to them; and when they are weary of it, I will beg my friend the Duc de Pecquigny to give them a little pension if they will withdraw into some good religious establishment."

"Good! that is a superb idea!" cried Bannière, forgetting his own situation for the moment in his advocacy of those whom Champmeslé was persecuting in intention. "Where, in heaven's name, do you get such ideas as that, my dear Abbé? What! you would inflict such disappointment upon those in whom you take an interest! The devil take you and your patronage, say I! I should much prefer your enmity."

"Ingrate!" cried Champmeslé.

"I may think, then, may I not," continued Bannière, recurring to the hope which had not abandoned him since Champmeslé appeared on the scene, — "that you are thoroughly convinced that I am not mad? For now that I have talked with you a half-hour without once speaking of myself, you must be convinced that I am not mad, are you not?"

"I am fully convinced of it," replied Champmeslé.

"And so," Bannière went on, "with your theory of salvation, in your desire to make everybody leave the stage as you have done yourself, you prefer to see me unjustly detained here rather than to see me return to the stage?"

"Faith! I should almost dare to say yes to that!" cried Champmeslé.

"Are you speaking seriously?"

"Yes, indeed."

"Beware!" said the prisoner, with an expression and an accent which would have routed the manager and the keeper and made the famous Martin himself draw back, — "beware! Here despair dwells; and despair is a wicked counsellor, Monsieur de Champmeslé! Here behind these bars men are dying every minute in the day; so that one who knew that he must remain here forever, as I have remained here for two weeks, that one would be wise to dash out his brains at one blow against the flag-stones."

Bannière made an ominous movement.

Champmeslé threw himself upon him, and took him in his arms in an effusion of real affection.

"Your salvation, my brother!" he cried.

"Oh, don't prate to me of my salvation!" cried Bannière, wildly; "my love is my salvation!"

"But this woman deceived you, my friend; she passed from your arms to those of another!"

"Well! had she not previously passed from that other's arms to mine?"

"My brother! my brother!"

"What would you have me do?"

"I wish to tell you that these are mad hopes of yours, and that your reasoning is sophistical."

"Have it as you please, Monsieur l'Abbé, but it's as I say."

"After all," said Champmeslé, "I begin to understand why you were declared to be mad."

"And although convinced that I am ¦sane," retorted Bannière, "you will assist, by your hostility, in making me undergo here all the suffering which is intended for real madness! That would be hardly Christlike, Monsieur Champmeslé, my worthy compeer on the stage at Avignon, my successor at the Jesuit convent."

"Come, come, let us not lose our tempers!" replied the good abbé, who felt the rebuke. "Alas! I am weak, and by appealing to me thus in the name of humanity, you bring me back to thoughts more in keeping with the wicked world we live in; I feel the force of what you say."

"Indeed, if you did not," cried Bannière, "you would be harder than flint; for you must see what an amount of self-restraint I have used since you came here and I recognized you."

" How so ? "

" Pray, do you suppose that I think of anything else than my desire to get away from this place, or that I have any other prayer upon my lips ? You will help me to do it, will you not ? "

" How do you suppose I can help you in that direction, my child ? "

" Tell me this: now that I have talked reasonably with you, and replied clearly to all your questions, are you not sure that my detention here is unjust ? "

" *Dame !* it seems to me that it is."

" Well, this is all that I ask. When you leave here, go to the lieutenant of police; go to the judges who sent me here: tell them, assure them, swear to them that I am sane, that I have never been mad, and they will set me free."

" I will do so."

" When ? "

" This very day."

" Good ! "

" It is my duty, and I will perform it."

" Thanks."

" But I am greatly afraid — " He checked himself.

" Of what are you afraid ? "

" I am afraid that what I may say will make no change — "

" In what ? "

" In your situation."

" What ! a declaration made by a man of your cloth, a positive, formal declaration that he is not mad, will make no change in the situation of a man who is kept in custody on the ground that he is mad ? "

Champmeslé looked cautiously around, and then said in a low tone, —

"Are you quite sure that you are confined here because you are mad?"

"*Parbleu!* why else do you suppose it can be?"

"*Dame!* for some fault, for some crime perhaps."

"My dear Abbé," said Bannière, "I have probably committed a great number of faults; but as for crimes, I hope and believe that God never abandoned me to that extent."

"My friend, every day men commit crimes without thereby becoming great criminals. For instance, Horace slew his sister through patriotism; that was a noble crime. Orosmane's killing of Zaïre through jealousy, too, was a pardonable crime."

"I thank God, my dear Abbé, that I have never killed any one either through jealousy or patriotism. Besides, murderers are not sent to Charenton."

"There you are in error."

"How so?"

"Your neighbor, for example; look no farther away than on the other side of that partition."

"Well?"

"Your neighbor is no more mad than you are."

"What's that you say?"

"The truth; and yet I shall take very good care not to go about declaring that he's not mad."

"Why?"

"Because he's an infamous murderer, who killed a poor girl because she was guilty of an honest act."

Bannière started at this.

"What! What's that you say?" he cried; "my neighbor! my neighbor! Can it possibly be — "

" What ? "

" *Mon Dieu !* more than once it has seemed to me as if I had heard his voice before."

" Impossible."

" Why ? "

" He is not French."

" He 's a Sardinian, is he not ? "

" How did you know that ? "

" And a marquis ? "

" Yes."

" And his name ? "

" My brother, his name is a secret," said Champmeslé.

" A secret which I will tell you," cried Bannière. " His name is Marquis della Torra."

" Yes."

" And you say that he killed some one ? "

" Yes."

" Who was it ? "

" A woman."

" A woman whom he loved ? "

" He seems to have loved her, as he killed her. Murder is always done for one of two reasons, — either because one hates or because one loves."

" The woman's name ? "

" The woman's name was Marion," said Champmeslé.

" Marion ! " cried Bannière. " Is it known why he killed the poor child ? " he asked, making a powerful effort over himself.

" Because she had rescued from his claws a comely youth who went away with her, then deserted her and left her entirely unprotected; then this miserable villain fell in with the poor girl, and despatched her with a blow of his sword."

"Ah! I — I am the miserable villain!" shrieked Bannière, throwing himself upon the stone floor of his cell, and rolling wildly about in his desperation.

"What do you mean by that?" demanded Champmeslé.

"Poor Marion, poor girl!" cried Bannière; "it is I who am thy murderer. Pardon, Marion, pardon!"

Champmeslé seized Bannière in his arms.

"Calm yourself," said he; "be careful, or they will say that a fit of madness is coming upon you."

"Oh, my father! my father!" groaned Bannière, "I was wrong when I told you that I had been guilty of nothing worse than faults; I have committed a crime, — the greatest and most heinous of crimes: I am an assassin!"

"Calm yourself."

"I deserve death, my father; deliver me to the judges, hand me over to the executioner. It is I, it is I who am Marion's assassin!"

But at these words, which he shrieked in a paroxysm of grief and despair, a great noise of rattling chains was heard, accompanied by a deep growling sound.

"Who is it," cried Della Torra, beating upon the partition and the door, — "who is it who speaks of Marion? Who dares to say, 'I am Marion's assassin'?"

"I — I, villain!" roared Bannière. "My sword, my sword! bring me my sword! You escaped me once, but you shall not escape me twice."

He began to beat upon his side of the partition as Della Torra was beating upon his.

Terrified by the bursting of this unlooked-for tempest, Champmeslé called the keeper, whose attention was already engaged by the twofold outbreak of rage, and hastily left the cell, saying to himself that Bannière was

mad after all, that his madness was of the raving kind,
and that it was useless to think of restoring his reason.

While the unhappy youth in the hope of strangling
the Marquis della Torra was kicking and pounding the
partition, stricken with awful remorse, the keeper said in
Champmeslé's ear, —

"Well, what do you say now? Confess that for a
moment you thought him sane."

XXI.

BETTER NEVER THAN LATE.

WHILE the abbé made his escape, less terrified than disappointed, because he had hoped to do a charitable office for one worthy of sympathy; while Bannière, plunged in real sorrow, was lying with his head in his hands, in despair at the fearful thought that he was the cause of the death of a poor harmless creature who had been fond of him; while Della Torra, driven wild by the name of Marion, and thinking perhaps that he recognized Bannière's voice, as Bannière had recognized his, was trying to tear down the partition which separated him from his neighbor, — the grated door of the court opened to admit some visitors who exhibited to the keeper a pass signed by the minister.

There were two, — a lovely young woman in a gray dress and pink cape, and a gentleman of very distinguished bearing. Both set about inspecting the cells in rotation, as the Abbé de Champmeslé had done two hours before.

The gentleman ran hither and thither, dancing attendance upon the lady in the gray dress, heaping questions upon the manager, who was very civil and very patient, and, recognizing doubtless the rank of his interlocutor, anticipated some of his inquiries.

" Madame desires to see the mad women," the gentleman had said as they came in.

"Here they are," the manager replied, "at the left, Madame; but I have the honor to warn you that their appearance is not appetizing."

"Are they love-mad?" the lady asked, in a voice so soft and musical that one would have said she was singing.

"I think not," replied the manager.

"Oh, the devil!" said the young nobleman, "I thought you were better provided than this."

"Believe that I am more than sorry, Monsieur le Duc."

"*Dame!* arrange it as you can. You keep lunatics here, and you ought to have some of all sorts."

"But — "

"Madame has reasons for wishing to see somebody who is love-mad, and you must show her somebody."

"The king's order, — is it not, Monsieur le Duc?" the young lady said, with a smile to her companion.

"Madame," replied the manager, "my regrets are most sincere; but we have in this section only one patient, a man, who is mad with love."

"A man! Ah, perhaps that would be even better than a woman!" said the young lady. "Let us see him."

"Number seven, Madame."

"Can I go near him?" she asked; for with a stealthy glance between the sticks of her fan, she had observed the filthy condition of most of the occupants of the cells.

"He has his clothes on," replied the manager, "and if he is not handsome, he is not a revolting sight; but he is bad-tempered."

"Oh, however bad-tempered he may be, he will not bite me through the bars."

"Never mind, never mind!" said the gentleman. "Be very careful, Olympe; for if any mishap should befall you, if the slightest scratch should be inflicted upon that lovely face, I know some one who would never forgive me."

"Oh, say nothing about that some one!" said the lady; "you are already sufficiently guilty, I should think, in having come to wait for me here at the gate, and forced your company upon me, in spite of the conditions we agreed upon."

"Fair Olympe, I plead guilty, and throw myself upon your mercy."

"Shall we go near the cell?" said she; for this conversation had taken place some fifteen feet from the door of number seven.

Upon Olympe's lovely features, as she approached, could be seen the sorrowful expression which is called forth in every being endowed with a heart by the sight of the most pitiful of all the ills that flesh is heir to.

Olympe de Clèves took her stand before the cell, and in a low voice, with that sort of religious timidity which takes possession of all noble hearts in the presence of Nature's grandest aspects, whether grave or gay, —

"Is that man mad with love?" she murmured, so low that the manager could hardly hear the question.

"Yes, Madame."

Bannière's head was turned toward the wall; he was insensible to all that was going on about him.

The terrible revelation which Champmeslé had made had been the last straw in the burden which bore that nervous, delicate nature to earth.

The tremendous uproar of the explosion had been succeeded by the silence of despair. After the thunder, tears.

Bannière, with his head buried in his arms so that his ears and eyes were closed, was weeping and sobbing bitterly.

"*Mon Dieu!* I should say that he was weeping," said Olympe, putting her head nearer the door with some curiosity.

Still subject to the same impression, she let her voice fall lower and lower, the nearer she came to the unhappy madman.

"Oh, he often does that," said the keeper, who heard her remark.

"Often!" rejoined Olympe; "poor man!"

"All madmen either weep or laugh a great deal," said the manager, who had inquired of the keeper the substance of Olympe's remark, and gallantly hastened to explain.

"I have been told just the reverse," said Olympe.

"I don't know whether that is their normal condition, Madame; but it is, at all events, the condition of this particular one."

"Is he in pain, pray?"

"Madmen laugh without merriment, and weep when they are not in pain; however, I will console this fellow for you."

"Ah, do!"

The manager went up to the cell, while the two visitors fell back a little.

"Hallo there!" called the manager; "come, comrade, you must not weep so."

Bannière made no reply, but continued to weep as if he had not heard.

The manager went on, —

"Turn this way a little, won't you? Here's a beautiful lady who wants to see you."

"Oh, Monsieur!" said Olympe, in an undertone, — "Monsieur!"

But without comprehending that exclamation or the modesty which dictated it, the manager continued, —

"Come there, number seven; just look a moment at this lady who has come to see you: it's Julie, your dear little Julie."

But Bannière never stirred.

"Who is this Julie?" queried Olympe.

"Oh, I don't know," was the reply; "his mistress, I fancy."

"What makes you fancy that?"

"*Dame!* when they arrested him, he kept saying over and over, 'Let me go! I must be there before Julie changes her clothes. Julie! oh, Julie!'"

"Poor boy!"

Still Bannière remained as unmoved as a stone.

"Oh, if I only knew all the verses he recites, " said the manager, "in which that name of Julie occurs again and again!"

"Yes; but you don't know them, nor do I," Pecquigny interposed.

"No."

"The devil take the stubborn boor! Madame desires to see his face and hear his voice."

"Is he young?" asked Olympe.

"Oh, yes, Madame, not more than twenty-six or twenty-seven."

"Twenty-six or seven," echoed Olympe, sadly. "And of what station in life was he?"

"Apparently very good. The men who arrested him claim to have seen on his finger a ring worth quite a hundred pistoles."

"Did they let him keep the ring?"

"It has disappeared."

"Where was he arrested?"

"In the vestibule of the Comédie-Française, where he was trying to get in without paying."

"Was it long ago?"

"About a fortnight. It was at the time of the début of a very famous new actress, I understand."

"What do you say to that, Olympe?" said Pecquigny. "Suppose it should turn out that this fellow is mad with love of you?"

"Is my name Julie, pray?"

Turning again to the manager, for she began to take a deep interest in the poor unfortunate, —

"What is his appearance?" she asked.

"He's not very ugly," said the manager; "and if Madame wishes to see him — "

"But it is n't possible to make out his features in his present attitude," said the duke.

"Oh, never fear! I will make him change his attitude."

He turned to the keeper:

"Hallo there!" said he; "pass me the pike."

The impassive keeper, well used to that order, at once handed the manager a pike, consisting of a sharp piece of horn set in a huge pole.

"What are you going to do with that?" Olympe inquired, in some alarm.

"I'm going to stir him up," replied the manager, calmly.

"It will hurt him, Monsieur."

"I trust so, Madame; and as he feels the pain, he will look around."

"It's fearful!" exclaimed Olympe, hiding her face in her hands. "Oh! I don't want you to do it! I don't want you to!"

As she muttered these words, she tried to draw the duke away from the awful spot.

"Why," Pecquigny coolly remarked, "if it's the only way of letting you see the pig-headed brute's face, why should you refuse?"

Meanwhile the manager had used his pike.

Bannière did not move a hair.

The manager pricked him again.

Still the same silence and the same immobility.

The soul was dead in that body; nothing was living there save despair.

"*Mon Dieu!* enough, enough, in heaven's name!" exclaimed Olympe. "You see that he will not turn."

"Oh, Madame, don't be alarmed about that!" replied the manager. "I have some men here whom I could brand with a red-hot iron without interrupting their smiles."

He dug the pike viciously into poor Bannière as he spoke.

"Enough! I tell you," cried Olympe; "enough, Monsieur! I do not desire you to torture the poor wretch; if he persists in hiding his face, let him have his way. Cursed be the curiosity which should add to the agony of a poor fellow who is love-mad!"

At these words, which were the only ones Olympe had uttered in a voice loud enough to be overheard by the prisoner, he, the dead man, the insensible, raised his head, put aside his long hair, and cast around him an angry, surprised look, like that of a tiger in his cage.

When his eyes fell upon Olympe, the spark of life was rekindled in them, he leaped to his feet, and seized and shook the bars with a terrible cry, — the most terrible of all that had ever been heard in that hell.

His mouth opened as if to utter a name and remained

open, parched and dry, unable to articulate a single word of all that his surging, superabundant thought brought to his lips.

Then he fell back senseless; while Olympe, gasping for breath, taken out of herself by the rapid movement, the piercing cry, and the agony of the madman in whom she had recognized Bannière, recoiled to the centre of the court.

Bannière measured his length upon the flags, where his body lay as devoid of movement as a corpse.

"There, do you see," said the manager, triumphantly, "how I compelled him to show his face to Madame?"

"Yes; but why did he swoon?" asked the duke.

"Oh, ask lunatics for the reasons for their actions! If they give them to you, then you know that they are no longer mad; and then, too," he added, "this fellow is love-mad, and Madame is so lovely!"

"Duke, Duke!" cried Olympe, "in the name of heaven, come, come!"

And she left that abode of desolation, murmuring a heart-broken prayer, and dragging Pecquigny after her.

When she reached her home, she had to take to her bed.

All that night she was delirious.

Her excited nerves did not become tranquil until the following morning, when, having come to a decision, she ordered a cab to be called.

She entered it, and was overheard to direct the coachman to drive to the bureau of the Minister of Paris.

The Minister of Paris of that day corresponded to what we now call the Minister of the Interior.

XXII.

WHEREIN BANNIÈRE PROVES TO THE ABBÉ THAT HE IS
NOT SO MAD AS APPEARANCES WOULD INDICATE.

POOR Bannière, doubtless, also determined upon the
course he would pursue; for the next morning, at about
eleven o'clock, he was as calm and reasonable as he had
just been agitated and wild.

He had even tried to make a sort of toilette, so far as
it was possible.

Not that he had any hope of seeing Olympe again, — not
for a moment did he indulge in such an illusion as that;
but he did rely upon seeing his good friend, if not his mistress, — Champmeslé, if not Olympe.

The abbé had returned to his own lodgings deeply
moved. Having thought for a moment that his protégé
was the most sane of all the madmen at Charenton, he
began to fear that he might turn out to be the most
demented.

He passed the night musing over the strange freak of
fate which had brought Bannière to Charenton as a
patient, and himself as an abbé.

While he mused, he examined the matter in all its
bearings. To request milder treatment for an incurable
was to run the risk of destroying his own hopes of influence at the very beginning; and he was anxious to show
himself at the outset a man of spirit as well as a good
Christian.

His aim was to utilize what power for good he possessed, and never to discredit his appointment. That was the leading principle in the Jesuit theory of conduct; and he had been required to govern himself by it from the time he was ordained.

However Champmeslé considered himself bound to show the qualities of a good apostle, even if thereby the qualities of a good Jesuit were held back for a while. Therefore he firmly resolved that if one single spark of sanity still lingered in Bannière's brain, he would fan that spark until it became a conflagration.

It must be said that Bannière's calm, reposeful, and resolute bearing aided him immensely in the task he had set himself.

In fact, as soon as Bannière espied him, he called out: "Ah, dear Abbé, dear Monsieur de Champmeslé, there you are! Come in quickly, and forgive me for having terrified you so yesterday."

"The fact is, my dear Bannière — " the abbé began.

"That you left me with the belief that I was mad; yes, I know," Bannière interposed.

"And I was so well disposed toward you, too, my poor boy!"

"Oh, never fear!" said Bannière; "I am resolved to win back your kindly disposition."

The abbé stared at him in surprise. "Oh, yes," continued Bannière, "you doubt it, because you saw me in something that resembled an attack of madness."

"Something that resembled it!" exclaimed Champmeslé: "you are quite right; it seemed to me that I saw you in an attack of downright madness."

"Oh, well, that's where you are wrong, dear Abbé; what you took for insanity was remorse."

"Remorse! you! One does not have remorse, my son,

except for crimes committed, and you had told me a moment before that God had willed that you should have nothing more than faults to reproach yourself withal."

"Alas, my father," said Bannière, raising his eyes heavenward, "one often commits a crime without suspecting it."

"In that case no guilt attaches."

"My dear Abbé, no one but you could allay my fears on that point; but in any event, criminal or not, I desire to die the death of a Christian."

"Ah, I 'm glad to hear it !" said Champmeslé; "that is something like."

"Under no circumstances will I return to the stage."

"Do you mean it ? " cried Champmeslé, joyfully.

"I will see Olympe no more."

"Have I your word ? "

"Why should I see her again," said Bannière, "since she no longer loves me ? "

"How do you know it ? "

"I have seen her."

"When ? "

"Yesterday."

"In a dream ? "

"No indeed, in the flesh."

"Nonsense! your mad fit is coming on again."

"Don't be alarmed; if you think I am wandering, just ask the keeper if a lady did not come here yesterday to see me."

"Indeed, as I was leaving the house, a woman came in."

"In a gray dress ? "

"Yes."

"With a pink cape ? "

"I think so."

"What! you think so?"

"I'm not sure; as I saw that it was a female, I lowered my eyes."

"What a pity! for you would have recognized her."

"She was not alone," Champmeslé ventured to suggest.

"Oh, I know that; she was with a very grand personage. Well, that woman was Olympe."

"And the visit?"

"The visit, Abbé, made me the most miserable of mortals."

"Why so?"

"Because it proved to me the cruel hardness of her heart."

"Did she know that you were here, pray?"

"She did not know it; at least I should judge so."

"Did she pass by without recognizing you?"

"On the contrary, she did recognize me."

"Indeed! and what did she say to you?"

"Nothing. I fainted; and she escaped, to avoid compromising herself."

The abbé shook his head.

"Ah!" said he, "if what you say is true — "

"It is the exact truth, Abbé."

"It was a cruel business, and it is justly said that woman is man's evil genius."

"You think it was outrageous, do you not?"

"It was beyond expression!"

"Very good!"

"Then you are cured of your passion?"

"Completely."

"You promise me that?"

"I swear it!"

"What proof will you give me of your cure?"

"Oh, Monsieur l'Abbé, remember that Jesus reproved Saint Thomas for his incredulity."

"Jesus was Jesus, and you are only Bannière."

"Alas!" said the poor fellow; "I too have been nailed to a very rough cross, and crowned with a crown of very sharp thorns."

"Never mind that! I must say that I should be very glad if you would give me some assurance against a relapse."

"Look at me, see how cool I am, feel my hand and the beating of my heart,— no more flying pulse, no more wild palpitation; everything is dead in me except for repentance and devotion."

"Very well, my friend," said Champmeslé, "you are now as I hoped to see you. So you have no longer any feeling for that woman?"

"Not the least."

"No further aspiration for that unhappy theatrical career which leads so many souls to perdition?"

"What I mean is that henceforth an order from the king would be necessary to induce me to go on the stage again."

"Good! better and better!"

"I will give you still another proof."

"What is that?"

"Oh, a convincing proof this time!"

"Well, what?"

Bannière drew from his pocket, from the lining of his coat, from his skin or from some hiding-place which heaven only can tell, a superb ring, so superb that Champmeslé exclaimed in wonder.

It was the ring which Monsieur de Mailly had given to Olympe, which he had sold, which the Abbé d'Hoirac had purchased and given to La Catalane, and which he

(Bannière) had torn from La Catalane's finger, as he threw a handful of gold in her face.

"Pray, where did you get such a jewel as that, my son?" Champmeslé asked.

"From her. It is the talisman which bound me to her; I now part with it."

"You part with it?"

"Yes; I beg you to keep it for me."

"You want me to keep it for you?"

"Certainly; but you must keep it on your finger, lest you lose it."

"A poor abbé can't wear such a ring as this on his finger."

"Why not?"

"Because it is worth more than two hundred pistoles."

"You can say that you are keeping it as a sacred trust."

"But —"

"I beg you to do it, my dear Abbé; I implore you!"

"Well," said the abbé, "since you will have it so —"

And he slipped the ring on his finger.

"There! now, dear Abbé, you will leave me to collect my thoughts, will you not?"

"For what purpose?"

"To prepare myself for a general confession."

"You desire to confess?" cried Champmeslé, transported with joy.

"I do."

"When?"

"As soon as possible."

"At once, then."

"No, this evening; I need at least twelve hours to prepare."

"But it is not customary to allow visits to be paid to the patients in the evening."

"Well, in the first place, I am not mad."

"True."

"And in the second place, you are the chaplain — "

"I will ask permission."

"Till this evening, then, my dear Abbé! "

"Is there anything you would like me to do between now and then? "

"Oh, yes, about my bread; they always give me too much crust, and not enough of the soft part."

"I will send you some of my own bread."

"Do you live in the house? "

"Yes."

"Thanks! I rely upon your promise."

"Never fear."

"The bread during the day? "

"The bread at once."

"And you? "

"And I this evening."

"Ah! I see that all hope is not lost."

"Prepare yourself, then."

"You may depend upon it."

"Till this evening? "

"Till this evening."

Ten minutes after the abbé left Bannière's cell, the keeper passed through the bars a loaf of fine white bread, which he had a very evident longing to keep for himself.

Any one who saw Bannière at his meal, after hearing him complain to the abbé that they gave him too much crust and not enough soft part, would have sought in vain to make his acts conform to his words, for he ate all the crust of the bread Champmeslé sent him, and saved the soft part.

Then he fell into so deep a fit of musing that any one

who knew his pious intentions for the evening would
have thought him engaged in searching his conscience.

Night came; and with the night Bannière became
more agitated. He stood at the door of his cell, observing
with much satisfaction that the court became more and
more deserted. At eight o'clock the doors were closed.
Once they were closed, the watchman made only two
rounds,— one at midnight, and another at six in the
morning.

Ten minutes after the closing of the door of the court
for the night, Bannière's door opened, and Champmeslé
entered.

Bannière's stool was carefully placed in the darkest
corner of the cell. He led Champmeslé there, and bade
him sit down. Then, kneeling before him, he began his
confession.

It was simply a circumstantial narrative of his flight,
his meeting with the marquis, and the incidents which
led to the game of cards; he told how, after his money
was gone, he had been informed by Marion that he had
been robbed; how he had fled with her, and how they
had parted. When he came to speak of the death of
the poor girl, he was not obliged to feign distress, for he
wept in good earnest.

Then Champmeslé understood why Bannière had so
savagely accused himself of being Marion's assassin,
since, without having dealt the blow, it was really he
who was responsible for her death by the hand of Della
Torra.

And yet Bannière was so blameless in intention that
Champmeslé did not hesitate to console him or to give
him absolution.

But although he had received absolution, Bannière
seemed determined to remain on his knees.

"Now, my dear Abbé," said he, still kneeling, "there is only one more point for us to settle."

"What might that be?"

"How I am to get away from here."

"Get away?"

"To be sure! I am very anxious to do proper penance, but not in a mad-house; I am very anxious to earn my salvation, but in some other place than Charenton. Charenton, I warn you, leads straight to hell, not to heaven."

"Yes, I admit that," said Champmeslé: "it's a hard case, and you would be much better off somewhere else than here; but how to get away, that's the question."

"Can't you sign a pass for me, my good Abbé?"

"Impossible, my dear boy."

"Why so?"

"Because I am not the manager of the institution."

"No; but you are the chaplain."

"A chaplain has charge of souls, that's all."

"A chaplain owes himself to his penitents, my dear Abbé; you are saving me from perdition, so you owe yourself to me."

"Up to a certain point."

"Up to the garden wall."

Champmeslé was so astonished at this suggestion that he made a movement as if to rise, but Bannière gently held him down upon his stool.

"The garden wall! you would escape! Why, you poor wretch, what becomes of the bars of your cell and the barred doors?"

"You can say that my attacks are becoming much less violent, and that I only need a walk in the fresh air to become perfectly calm."

"They will refuse."

"Then you can open my cell."

"Have I the key of your cell, pray?"

Bannière embraced the abbé's knees imploringly.

"No," said he; "but you have a file."

"A file!"

"Why, yes! a file is much better than a key; with a key you declare yourself my accomplice, while with a file I work by myself."

"But you know," said Champmeslé, whose resolution began to waver, — "you know that there is a steep roof to climb after you leave this court?"

"I have hands."

"And after that a second wall?"

"I have feet."

"And sentries?"

"I have feet and hands."

The abbé shook his head; it was so dark that Bannière guessed at the movement rather than saw it.

"Listen," said he, "either you are or are not my friend."

"I am your friend in anything but escaping."

"Then," said Bannière, "I will put the question to you in more concise form."

The abbé started in some alarm; for he detected in the determined, resonant tones of the prisoner something strange, — an indefinable threat, which was not reassuring.

But he maintained his courage.

"Strength will come to me from on high," said he.

"Will you or will you not assist me to get away from this place?" said Bannière.

"My conscience forbids me," replied Champmeslé.

Bannière thought a moment.

"I have it!" said he to himself.

He settled himself again upon his knees, and said in his most humble voice, —

"Now, my dear Abbé, since you deny me freedom, — that precious boon which you might confer upon me this evening with a wave of your hand, — give me at least a pretence of freedom, the shadow or the odor of it."

"Oh, that I will gladly do!" said Champmeslé.

"What is there outside my door?" Bannière asked.

"A corridor."

"Just see what a thing imagination is! I breathe more freely already. And after the corridor?"

"The keeper's wicket."

"Very good. And then?"

"The great staircase."

"Oh, yes, I remember! And next?"

"The little door by which I get to my apartments from the interior of the prison."

"To your apartments?"

"Yes, my parsonage, which is at one side of the entrance."

"Is it unguarded?"

"Entirely."

"Opening upon the street?"

"Only the windows."

"Are they barred?"

"No."

"Very good, my dear Abbé! I am greatly obliged to you."

As he uttered these words emphatically, Bannière threw himself upon Champmeslé, filling his mouth as he did so with all the soft part of the bread, which he then plastered over the abbé's lips with his handkerchief, making a sort of gag.

Then he bound the abbé to the bars with strips of his

bedclothes which he had torn in advance. He proceeded to despoil the poor chaplain of his clothes as dexterously as a monkey peels a green walnut, and emptied his pockets, taking therefrom two crowns which he put in his own, saying as he did so, —

"Never fear, Abbé; I will return your two crowns when I come to claim my ring and your assistance."

As he was fortunate enough to find in the abbé's pocket a pair of shears, he clipped off his hair and beard in the twinkling of an eye.

Then he put on the clerical garments and the clerical hat, and left the abbé half naked and wholly unrecognizable.

After which, without a word, and without further thought for the worthy Christian who endured this unworthy treatment without a sigh, he struck three hearty blows on the door, which the keeper opened, standing behind it, as his custom was, and bowing low as the abbé passed.

Bannière turned his back upon him, made for the corridor with long strides, passed through it and down the staircase, and disappeared through the little door, before poor Champmeslé, who had not made a very sturdy resistance, had made the slightest movement toward expelling the mouthful of bread which he was masticating with the most exemplary and complacent patience.

Champmeslé waited a long quarter of an hour, chewing away at his choke-pear, and thinking that if Bannière had not succeeded in making his escape in that length of time he must be a besotted fool, fit for nothing better than a cell; then he began to moan, and shake the bars, and pound on the flags with his feet.

These noises having failed to produce all imaginable

effect, Champmeslé adroitly uncovered one corner of his mouth so that he could use his voice.

The keeper hurried to open the door, and found the worthy chaplain bound like a calf and trussed like a pigeon.

He described the madman's violent attack, and concluded with the remark that perhaps the man who could conceive and carry out such a bold plan might not be so very mad after all.

The first emotion of the keepers and manager was utter stupefaction.

Their next impulse was to start in pursuit of the fugitive.

But they discovered that with the two crowns which he had borrowed from the good abbé, he had taken a fiacre a short distance from the house, and that the fiacre had gone off at a flying pace as soon as the pseudo-abbé had entered it.

The manager ordered horses to be saddled, and the fiacre was found near the barrier.

It was empty, however.

It seemed that Bannière, anticipating pursuit, had alighted on the way, and had crossed the river in a boat.

The boat was followed up, and they found that Bannière had taken another fiacre on the other side, and they could get no further trace of him.

The whole establishment was in an uproar until morning; and the story of the wonderful escape was told a hundred times over by the abbé, to whom every one came in quest of the details, and who was able to say with Æneas, —

"Et quorum pars magna fui."

The next day, at noon, a very elegant equipage drove into the courtyard of the Charenton institution.

A female alighted from it; it was Olympe again, this time unaccompanied.

She ran rather than walked to the manager's office, and requested speech of him.

As she walked across the courtyard, she was saluted most respectfully — in the first place for the sake of her beauty, and secondly in honor of her handsome carriage — by two officers of the prefecture, who came out holding in their hands papers similar to those which police officials always arm themselves with when about to make arrests.

Olympe paid little attention to the officers, in such haste was she to see the manager.

She was hardly within the door when she asked eagerly, —

"Monsieur, how is the prisoner whom I saw yesterday, — the madman ? "

" Is Madame interested in one of the madmen ? " said the manager.

" What, Monsieur ! " said Olympe; " have I not the honor of being recognized by you ? "

" Ah, yes! " said the manager, bowing; " Madame was here yesterday."

" With Monsieur le Duc de Pecquigny, yes, Monsieur."

" To see Number Seven," said the manager, bowing still lower at the name of the duke.

" Precisely."

" Well, Madame will not see him to-day, to my great regret."

" Why shall I not see him, Monsieur ? "

" Because it is altogether impossible, Madame."

Olympe supposed that she could not see the prisoner without permission; so she drew a paper from her pocket.

" An order from the king," said she.

"To what effect, Madame?"

"To set at liberty, immediately, Bannière, entered on the books of the institution as Number Seven in the stone gallery."

The manager turned pale.

"Well, Monsieur," said Olympe, "do you hesitate in the face of his Majesty's order?"

"No, Madame, I do not hesitate; but you know the proverb?"

"What proverb?"

"Where there is nothing, the king loses his rights."

"What do you mean by that?"

"Madame, the lunatic whom you claim under that order is no longer here."

"No longer here?"

"No; he escaped last evening, and we have been unable to recapture him."

Olympe uttered a cry, and let fall the useless paper.

"But pray, tell me, how did this come about?" said she.

The manager narrated the story of the escape, with all its details.

"And you say that no one knows what has become of him?" cried Olympe.

"Not in the least; but if you know any one connected with the man, warn that person that the day when he comes in collision with those whom he has a grudge against, there will be trouble."

Olympe shuddered.

"Very well," said she; "thanks, Monsieur."

She turned toward the door.

"You forget the order from the king, Madame," said the manager.

Olympe picked up the paper, and withdrew in consternation.

"Oh, *Mon Dieu!* she murmured, "is it written that everything shall turn out badly? So much labor and trouble expended in rescuing the poor fellow, so many wires pulled for the unfortunate madman, and his unlucky star defeats all my good intentions! Surely he was born to suffer and to make me suffer! Oh, poor Bannière! not even the consolation of proving to him that I am not a heartless creature! Not even the happiness of saying to him, 'You are free through my efforts!' Free! He is free by his own efforts, and it's much better so; for he will have the pleasure of being indebted to no one! Free! that wandering eye, that wild passion is free! All the fury accumulated during his captivity besets my path and threatens me. *Mon Dieu!* who knows what he may do to me if he meets me!"

Olympe shivered at the thought that Bannière might injure her.

"Must I make up my mind," she thought, "to watch every carriage, to peer into every dark corner, and to see in every cloaked figure an enemy, in every visitor a murderer? Must I report to the lieutenant of police that Monsieur de Mailly's life is in danger?"

As for her own life, Olympe was ready to make a generous sacrifice of that.

Furthermore, with a woman's heroic inclination to see the chivalrous side of every passion, she pictured to herself the superb tragic scene when poor, deluded Bannière should rush upon her, knife in hand.

She returned to the little house in Rue Grange-Batelière in a fever of terror and suspense, and yet she had the courage to smile upon Monsieur de Mailly when he questioned her about her pale cheeks and her nervous agitation.

The count, who had heard of Monsieur de Pecquigny's

visit, chose to attribute her restlessness to the duke, rather
than to seek for the real cause.

Moreover, he was not sorry to have another grievance
against Pecquigny, and he responded to Olympe's nervous
preoccupation with the sulks.

"All right!" said he to himself, "I am forewarned
now, and the first time that she goes out I will have her
followed."

Alas! Mailly was in no degree more perspicacious than
every other uneasy, jealous lover who ever lived; hot in
pursuit of an imaginary danger, he utterly failed to appreciate where the real danger lay.

Poor Olympe could not sleep at all from that time on;
her feverish, restless thoughts dwelt without ceasing upon
the only man she had ever really loved,— upon this
Bannière, whom for several months she had not dared
to remember, believing him to be false to her or altogether
out of conceit with love.

Now it seemed that the case was very different.

He was mad with love.

"Mad with love!" said Olympe. "Oh! one does n't go
mad with love for such as La Catalane!"

A hundred times a day she recalled the young man's
manly and awe-inspiring beauty, the wild spring he had
made when he heard and recognized her voice, the cry
which had accompanied it, the sorrowful yet loving
expression of his eyes, and last of all, his terrible fall, as
if stricken by lightning, upon the hard flags.

Then a voice would whisper in her ear and to her
heart,—

"He did it all for thee, Olympe; it is for thee that
the poor wretch, who has found no way to take a step
outside his cell since his arrest, found a way to escape as
soon as he saw thee."

And she would reply to the voice,—

"If Bannière is mad with love, it is for me; if he is mad with love of me, perhaps he will kill me! Very well! let him kill me; he will deliver me from the frightful torture of being loved by those whom I do not love."

From that moment Olympe awaited proudly, almost joyfully, the issue which God hid from her in the darkness.

God disposes.

XXIII.

"ALL GOES ILL; COME!"

WHILE the events we have been narrating were taking place at Charenton, the Duc de Pecquigny had not been wasting his time, and the Duc de Richelieu had been employing his to the best possible advantage, like a man who well knows its value.

At the review which the king witnessed, without taking the trouble to ascertain whether the commanding officer was Mailly or some other, Monsieur de Richelieu had taken care that the countess should be present, and so placed that every movement she might make would be directly under the eye of the young prince.

Poor countess! She was so beautiful, not alone in her natural beauty, but in the love and enthusiasm which inspired her; she cried, "Vive le Roi!" in such a tender, vibrating voice, — that more than once Louis stopped, or turned to look at her and smile upon her.

She returned home intoxicated with happiness and beaming with hope.

In her eyes the king was no longer a mere man; he was a god.

Richelieu, who had watched his Majesty's every movement with the utmost attention, and had now and then with due reserve made some suggestions, was more than moderately content with the day's work.

He was lying at his ease upon a sofa, wrapped in a dressing-gown of India silk, running over in his mind all the advantages, and counting upon his fingers the offices which would accrue to him as compensation for his skilfully conducted negotiations, when a perfumed billet in a strange handwriting was handed to him by Rafté, — the amphibious creature who served him as secretary and valet-de-chambre, and who possessed in his single brain as much cleverness as all the rest of the secretaries and valets in the world.

The duke unfolded the billet with his finger-tips, smoothed it out, and read these few words, —

" All goes ill; come! "

He turned the missive over and over; there was no signature.

Richelieu could hardly be said to detest mysteries; but he preferred that they should not take the form of insoluble enigmas or unintelligible logogriphs.

The duke crumpled the paper in his hands, bit his lips, and then read it again, —

"All goes ill; come! "

" Rafté ? " he called, raising his head.

" Here I am, Monseigneur, " said the secretary.

" Who brought this ? "

" A footman in gray livery. "

" A stranger ? "

" Absolutely. "

" Have you any ideas in your head ? "

" About what ? "

" This note; look at it. "

He handed it to Rafté, who read aloud in his turn, —

"All goes ill; come! "

" Well ? "

" Well ? "

" What is it that goes ill ? "

" I have n't an idea, Monseigneur. "

"What's the use, then, of your having more wit than I?"

"*Bon Dieu!* who said I had?" cried Rafté.

"There's an echo; 'come, come.'"

"It does say 'come,' does n't it?"

"'All goes ill!' that's embarrassing."

"Why, no, Monseigneur, that's not the embarrassing thing in my opinion."

"What do you mean?"

"Not many things go very well in this fine country of France; you may choose where you will."

"Ah, you villain, I have caught you at it!"

"At what, Monseigneur?"

"Speaking ill of Monsieur de Fleury."

"I!" cried Rafté; "I speak ill of Monsieur de Fleury?"

"*Pardieu!* you say that everything goes ill in France; and that's a slight reflection upon Monsieur de Fleury, I should say."

"Speaking of wit, Monseigneur, it is you who are showing it just now."

"'All goes ill; come!'" said the noble diplomat once more.

"It's from a woman," said Rafté.

"Ah, *pardieu!* a brave suggestion! But from what woman? There's the rub!"

"One moment," said Rafté; "if we name them all over, we shall come to the right one sooner or later. First, Madame de Mailly."

"I left her at five this afternoon, and everything was going well."

"Madame de Prie?"

"I have n't seen her for ages, and she is in the country."

" Mademoiselle de Charolais ? "

" She is lying in, and she is so used to it that she must be all right."

" Madame de — "

" No, a hundred times no ! " Richelieu interposed. " I tell you I don't know the writing."

" Then it is disguised," said Rafté.

" For that suggestion, I forgive you for not having guessed."

" An idea, Monseigneur."

" May it be a good one ! "

" Don't go where they tell you to."

" You simpleton, when they don't tell me where I must go ! "

" I am a double-distilled idiot, and Monseigneur robs me of half of my deserts in calling me nothing worse than a simpleton."

" Hold, Rafté, it 's my turn to have an idea now," said the duke, yawning.

" Better than mine, Monseigneur ? "

" I hope so. Let 's go to bed."

" I think that is much the best plan, Monseigneur, because this letter has to me all the appearance of a trap."

" I don't say that it has n't."

" Then, Monseigneur — "

" Get me to bed, I say."

" I think it is my duty to call Monseigneur's attention to the fact that it is hardly eleven o'clock."

" Look ! " said Richelieu, " speaking of eleven o'clock, there is a figure at the bottom of the note."

" Yes, there is a 4."

" What can a 4 mean ? "

" It must be the day of the month."

"Clown! it's the 25th."

"Then the letter must have been delayed *en route ;* or perhaps it came from a long distance, — China for example!"

"Do you know what that figure means?"

"No!"

"Well, it's the hour."

"Hurra! you've found it, Monseigneur; it's the hour."

"There's one thing to consider, Rafté; that if it was written at four o'clock, I am already seven hours late."

"That's very nice."

"What do you say to it?"

"Go to bed, Monseigneur."

"No, I will not; I have no desire to go to bed now, do you know; I am very remorseful."

"You, Monseigneur! impossible!"

"You see, Rafté, that it's no trap."

"Why not?"

"Because the writer would not have named the hour at which she set it."

"Then it must be from some close friend of Monseigneur, who believed that Monseigneur would guess her identity at sight."

"Very well! as I did not guess it, I shall not reply, and I am quit of her."

"Take care, Monseigneur; there is a firm character to the thick strokes, and daring in the upstrokes of this writing. This woman will begin again."

"Do you think so?"

"She who has written will write again."

The words were hardly out of Rafté's mouth when a footman entered and handed Richelieu a letter.

"Another!" exclaimed the duke.

"What did I tell you?" cried Rafté, triumphantly.

Richelieu broke the seal.

The handwriting was the same.

"You were right, on my word!" he exclaimed.

He read: —

"You did well not to come; it would have been imprudent."

"Hallo! how's that, Rafté!"

"Go on, Monseigneur."

"Instead of coming to see me at my hotel, come and speak to me. I am in a hired carriage at the corner of your street."

"Rafté, it's either a princess or a laundress."

"Monseigneur, the spelling is too good for a princess."

"My sword; I will go."

"It's unwise, Monseigneur."

"You are right; do you go. If it is a present, I will give it to you."

Rafté made a wry face.

"So be it," said he. "But consider, Monseigneur; if it is a princess, you are disgraced."

Thus they parleyed without coming to any decision.

"Rafté," said Richelieu, "if I am going, I must not keep her waiting; if I am not going, put me to bed."

But suddenly he started up.

"You were right!" he cried.

"Right in what?" said Rafté.

"It's she!"

"Good!"

"That is not a 4?"

"No?"

"It's an L."

"Ah! an L!"

"Yes, the first letter of her pet name: Laure. By the

powers, what a consummate ass I am, Rafté! My
sword! good; my hat! good; my cloak! good again.
Open the little door."

"Shall I accompany Monseigneur?"

"Be very careful that you do nothing of the kind. If
you put your nose to the door or the window, I will
discharge you."

With that he rushed into the courtyard, and thence
into the street.

Rafté shrugged his shoulders.

"Too much orthography," he muttered scornfully,
"altogether too much!"

Meanwhile Richelieu had reached the carriage, within
which a woman was waiting, lying back out of sight,
muffled up to the eyes, which glistened through the lace.

"Ah, Duke," she whispered, "you have made me
wait."

"Countess!" cried Richelieu, "I guessed as much.
Ah, Countess, I was very near not coming at all."

"Why?"

"I didn't know your writing, and the note was not
signed."

"Yes it was, with an initial."

"Ah, Countess, but your L is much like a 4; hereafter I shall know it, and not make any more mistakes.
But now let us hurry and make up for lost time. Do
you know that the vagueness of your note alarmed me?
'All goes ill,' you say. What is it that goes ill, in
heaven's name?"

"Duke, I am lost."

"How so, pray?"

"You know how kindly the king accosted me at the
review?"

"Yes, indeed."

"I thank you for it."

"That's all right! I congratulate you upon it in the first place, and myself in the second; that is not where the trouble is, I hope?"

"Duke, I must leave Paris to-morrow."

"Oh, nonsense!" cried Richelieu, jumping into the carriage.

"My husband came to me at half-past three to-day."

"Mailly?"

"In a furious rage. He was completely beside himself, and talked of killing the king."

"Oh, that was a joke, Countess."

"He also said that he would kill me."

"That is much more ominous; he has a sort of right to do that, without committing *lèse-majesté*; we must see that he does no harm in that direction, Countess."

"He said that they wished to take his property from him, but that he would defend it."

"The devil! Can Pecquigny have made more progress than we think?"

"Pecquigny?"

"Yes, I see what it means. How does he propose to defend his property? Did he confide that to you?"

"By sending me off to my estate in the country."

"Oh, we'll see about that."

"What can we do?"

"Have patience, Countess; this thing can't be decided by a turn of the hand."

"And meanwhile I must go away."

"What! you go away?"

"He has given his orders."

"Pshaw! you surely can obtain two days' delay."

"*Dame!* I'll do my best."

"Is he suspicious of me?"

"As if you were the plague."

"He is quite right.   And of Pecquigny ? "

"He perfectly loathes him."

"He makes no mistake there."

"But tell me what I shall do, Duke, if my husband insists ? "

"Why, you must insist, too, Countess."

"My whole family will join in the hue and cry against me."

"What do you expect ? "

"What defence have I against them ? "

"I will think it over."

"What authority can I invoke ? "

"Wait a moment ! "

"What is it ? "

"Wait ! "

"Well ? "

"I see my way, Countess."

"You see a way out of it ? "

"Yes."

"You will answer to me for myself ? "

"As for *my* self."

"Then I am saved ? "

"Yes, Countess, dear Countess, brightest and most fascinating of women."

"Do you give me your word of honor that I am saved ? "

"So entirely saved, Countess, that Mailly shall have occasion to say within a week that you are lost."

She hid her face in her hands, upon each of which Richelieu imprinted a kiss.

"I am working for the king," he said in an undertone, "and — I pay myself."

"Madman ! "

"No one is saner than I, Countess, and to prove it allow me to tell you that I was just on the point of going to bed."

"Well."

"And I am now about to do just the reverse, Countess. Can you imagine where I am going?"

"Who can divine all your wiles, Satanic tempter?"

"I am going to Issy."

"To Issy?"

"Yes, the country of lime-kilns. Good-night!"

He took his leave of her, hurried back to his own hotel, and entered his carriage a quarter of an hour later.

We, who know the ordinary result of family quarrels under Louis the Well-beloved, and who intend to be very careful not to describe any scenes which would jar upon our reader's feelings, will leave Madame de Mailly to return to her hotel and her bed.

It suits us better to see how Monsieur de Richelieu, when he had arrived at the lime-kiln region, succeeded in awaking the old minister.

XXIV.

"ALL GOES WELL; SLEEP!"

IF there ever was a visit which outraged every rule of propriety, but which was by way of compensation timely to the last degree, it was the visit which Monsieur de Richelieu was bold enough to venture upon at a few minutes before midnight.

On arriving at Issy, he began by arousing Master Barjac.

Master Barjac, to the honor of his conscience be it said, was sleeping the sleep of the just.

But this came to pass; to wit, that Monsieur Barjac at the outset did not look upon the affair with all the ardor which Monsieur de Richelieu brought to bear upon it.

He did not think best, he said, to disturb Monsieur de Fleury's rest on account of matters of small moment.

Monsieur de Richelieu tossed his head.

"Monsieur Barjac," said he, "when I interfere with my own enjoyment, or my own slumbers at midnight, you may be sure, believe me, that the game is worth the candle. But you, in your omniscient wisdom, do not so esteem it. Very good! that causes me to reflect; and as you are supposed to represent his Eminence's real thoughts more accurately even than he does himself, why, I conclude, Monsieur Barjac, that his Eminence looks upon these affairs as of no importance, as you say; and I will not amuse myself by embroiling myself with my own friends, who wish that the king should enjoy himself in their way, without regard to the ministers or cardinals or the nation. So then, Monsieur Barjac, I not only will not interfere to prevent the king's enjoying himself, but will advise him in my own way. With this, Monsieur de Barjac, good-evening, — good-morning I should say, for it is morning."

With his most magnificent air Monsieur de Richelieu turned upon his heel and left the room.

Whether Monsieur Barjac thought better of it, or whether he had been until then stupid with the effects of the sound sleep in which he had been wrapped a moment before, he suddenly came to his senses, and ran after Monsieur de Richelieu.

"Good-morning, good-morning," the latter repeated, with his hand on the door.

But Barjac stretched his sturdy legs; and the duke suddenly found him between himself and the door, with arms extended, and respectfully barring his progress.

"There, there!" he said; "pray pardon us, Monsieur le Duc! If you but knew what took place here last evening!"

"What was it, Monsieur Barjac?" said Richelieu, with arms akimbo.

"Ah, Monsieur le Duc, they were talking Jansenius and Molina all the evening; they criticised the great Nicole and Monsieur de Noailles; last of all, they read Fénelon! Monsieur le Duc, no saint could have stood it. I could sleep fifteen days after it, and this was my first hour."

"Oh, well! that's what I call a most excellent excuse, Monsieur Barjac," said Richelieu.

"Take a seat, then; I will go and try to wake Monseigneur."

" Do so."

Barjac took a step or two in the direction of the bedroom, then came back.

" Is it very serious? " said he.

" *Pardieu!* since you are awake, Monsieur Barjac, it must needs be more serious than Molina, Jansenius, Monsieur de Noailles, Fénelon, and the great Nicole, who put you to sleep. It is a matter much more important than efficacious grace or quietism."

" Does the little woman refuse? " queried Barjac.

" Wake up Monseigneur first, Monsieur Barjac."

Barjac went into the apartment of his master, whose reverberating snores, it must be said, though it derogate from the respect due to a cardinal and a minister of state, reminded one more of a night of Cardinal Dubois than of Cardinal Armand.

Barjac had risen, but Fleury did not leave his bed. Richelieu was ushered into his bedroom without ceremony.

" Well, Duke, what is there new? " was the old man's greeting.

" We have a husband, Monseigneur."

" A husband who bites? "

" Alas! yes."

" And upon whom it might be well to put a muzzle? "

" I have something better than a muzzle, Monseigneur, to divert the attention of my dogs when they want to bite me; I have bones."

" They cost more."

" Monseigneur, we must act or give up the ghost."

" Oho! has it come to that? "

" Alas! yes."

" Let us see the extent of the bite."

" It 's this. Monseiur de Mailly has been dreaming

of Montespan. He is furbishing up his sword and sharpening his tongue; he is going to make a scandal."

Fleury frowned.

" Under Louis XIV.," said he," there was the Bastille."

" It was the same under the regent," said Richelieu. " Ah! how all good things are done away with, Monsieur de Fleury! Can you not send Mailly to the Bastille?"

The prelate was musing.

" Is he violent?" he asked.

" Like Montespan."

" He has partisans too."

" And as the king is bashful, they will drive him off."

Fleury looked at Barjac.

" The king will fall into the hands of petticoat politicians," said Richelieu; " what a pity! while this one — "

" You were sure of her, were n't you, Duke?"

" I had her word."

Fleury heaved a tremendous sigh.

" Have you any suggestions to make, Duke?" he asked.

" A wretched one, of course."

" Pshaw! tell it; what matters it!"

" It is this."

" I am listening."

" You know that I am just from Vienna?"

" Do I know it! Your services there were too great for me to forget it."

Richelieu bowed.

" Vienna is a city where men with vivid imaginations cool down very quickly," he continued.

" Well?"

" Send Mailly to Vienna."

" Ah, Duke, he will at once divine the purpose of the stroke when he sees the hand that holds the weapon."

"Change the hand, Monseigneur."

"What do you mean by that?"

"Instead of ordering him to go to Vienna, arrange it so that he will ask for the appointment."

"Impossible! He's as stubborn as a mule."

"I don't deny that."

"He will refuse, I tell you, if it is offered to him, and will never ask for the place, if the matter is left to his free will."

"I have a way of making him."

"You are very fertile in expedients, Duke, apparently."

"What would you have; one is not a diplomatist for nothing; then too, while all hands were asleep at Issy, I was cogitating very deeply in my carriage, and by dint of much searching, one generally finds."

"*Quære et invenies*," said Barjac, who had at length arrived at the point where he could tack on a Latin phrase or two at the end of his master's speeches.

"Well?" said Monsieur de Fleury.

"Well, Monseigneur, to-morrow morning you must see the queen."

"For what purpose?"

"One moment; in the first place see the queen."

"I have some money to hand her, and I will take it to her myself."

"A splendid opportunity. But make a little sacrifice, Monseigneur; take my advice, and add an extra hundred louis."

The old fellow blushed, for he felt the stroke. Harpagon was not so weak with Frosine.

"Go then, Monseigneur, to see the queen, and tell her that a new ambassador is needed to the Germans, her friends and relations, because I have resigned."

"Ah! are you resigning, Duke?"

"Four years is long enough for one man to serve, I should say. Give some one else a chance."

"Then I will suggest Mailly."

"Exactly."

"The queen will refuse."

"No."

"I tell you she will refuse."

"Why?"

"Because Mailly does not speak German."

"Let him stay there four years, as I have, and he will learn. Besides, the queen is too devout a Christian to refuse to secure Mailly's salvation."

"His salvation!"

"*Pardieu!* what do you suppose he will do at Vienna? The time which one spends there is like years in the field; one year in Vienna is equal to two years in purgatory."

"But how shall I explain my request?"

"You will say — you will say that Mailly is ruining himself at Paris; that he has contracted all the bad garrison habits; that he is a gambler."

"*Dame!* his money is his own."

"You will say that he keeps mistresses, women from the theatre, and that this makes his wife unhappy."

"Very good, Duke! that is well thought of, and I can conscientiously say that."

"I should think so! Poor Madame de Mailly! she told me all the suffering her husband caused her, and wept as she told it, this very night; it was heart-rending."

"Oh! I really think the queen will be moved by such a complaint."

"Then you can suggest to her to ask for the Viennese mission for Mailly as a penance, and you can allow the promise of it to be extorted from you."

"Good, and then?"

"Then, Monseigneur?"

"Yes."

"Well, Madame de Mailly will tell you, if she chooses, what is lacking to complete her happiness; or if she shrinks from telling it to you, why, Monsieur Barjac here can do it for her — in Latin."

"Monsieur de Richelieu," said Fleury, "your advice is pure gold; I will follow it from point to point. To-morrow morning her Majesty will request me to give the Viennese mission to Monsieur de Mailly."

"And you will sign his commission?"

"I will consult the king," said Fleury, with a smile that was perhaps a trifle too diabolical for a Christian prelate.

"Will Monseigneur deign to notify me of the result, so that I may reassure poor Madame de Mailly?"

"By express, Monsieur le Duc."

"An excellent way, Monseigneur."

"This Monsieur de Richelieu," said Barjac, with a gracious inclination of his head, "seems a perfect Nestor to me."

"On account of my age, Monsieur Barjac?"

"No, Monsieur le Duc, because of the honey which flows from your lips."

"Or a Saint Jean-Chrysostome," added Fleury. "Ah! he was a Greek, Barjac; you can't meddle with him."

"Monsieur le Cardinal is wide awake," said the old valet, coldly; "that is evident from his keen wit."

Fleury began to laugh; he was caught by the flattery.

"Go on," said he to the duke.

Richelieu continued,—

"Monseigneur, I am poor Mailly's friend, his true friend."

"That's very plain," said the prelate, "from the way in which you interest yourself for him."

"In addition to that, I am very fond of his wife."

"Duke, Duke, are you so fond of her that the king could ever be jealous of your fondness?"

"Oh, Monseigneur, when I say that I am fond of her, I mean only contemplatively."

"I bow in honor of the adverb, which is superb."

"I therefore request, Monseigneur, that every favor which is to be granted to Mailly should reach him through me. Thus, for instance, his commission as ambassador, if signed —"

"Would get you into trouble with him, Duke."

"I will risk the trouble."

"Really?"

"I have my reasons."

"Vienna has made you very deep, my dear Duke."

"Oh, you see nothing of it, Monseigneur."

"Be careful! You alarm me."

"Oh, no, indeed! Monseigneur's vision is too clear for me ever to give him the vertigo. This commission —"

"I will send it to you as speedily as possible."

"Monseigneur, you overwhelm me."

"Just explain to me what advantage you expect to reap from all this."

"This, Monseigneur: I shall have a complete falling out with Mailly."

"Well! and then?"

"Then, being at odds with the husband, I can give good advice to the wife."

"*Optime!*" cried Barjac.

"Ah," said Richelieu, "you will see what resources we have; and when Mailly returns from Vienna, you will see what he amounts to."

Fleury and Barjac laughed heartily, with the silent merriment which priests affect.

As for Richelieu, he was so well content with himself for all the harm he was doing, that he laughed aloud as he entered his carriage, and kept it up a long while after he was seated in it, while the true master of France buried himself anew under the bedclothes after he and Barjac had slandered Richelieu to their heart's content.

Barjac, finding himself too thoroughly awake, set himself to thinking anew about Molinists and Quietists, and by that means, with the aid of a glass of orgeat syrup, resumed his interrupted dreams.

Richelieu made the journey home in three quarters of an hour, and before he retired he wrote to Madame de Mailly, —

"All goes well; sleep!"

XXV.

IN WHICH MAILLY IS READY TO GIVE IT UP.

MONSIEUR DE MAILLY, on making his appearance at the queen's card-party about nine o'clock in the evening following Richelieu's nocturnal visit to the cardinal, was greeted by Pecquigny, who approached him with a very sly expression.

"What's the matter, pray?" asked Mailly, who was less disposed than ever to be made sport of, especially by Pecquigny.

The fact was that Mailly had realized for some time that he was offering two handles to those who were inclined to make sport of him, and that nothing is so easy to take hold of as an object which has two handles.

"Nothing's the matter with me," said Pecquigny; "it's you who are out of sorts."

"Not in the least, I assure you."

"Oh, I understand," said Pecquigny, "you think that I am angry with you for the scenes which you inflict upon your mistress."

"Count, I do not speak of my mistress in the queen's presence. I am surprised that you don't understand that."

Pecquigny opened his mouth to say,—

"Why should not one speak of your mistress in the queen's apartments? There is enough talk about your wife in the king's!"

But he held his peace; whenever there is an honest sword-blade behind a poor joke, circumspection becomes obligatory.

And yet he could not restrain his tongue altogether; he broached the subject that was uppermost in his mind.

" Do you know," said he, " that the queen has been talking of you all day ? "

" Indeed! " said Mailly; " how do you know that ? "

" Oh, I have my informants at Versailles."

" Her Majesty does me great honor, my dear Duke."

"˜Yes, yes, yes! I can tell you more than that."

" What is it, pray ? "

" Several times the queen has asked if you were likely to be here this evening. Look! at this moment I 'll wager she is looking for you."

The queen did, in fact, seem to be absorbed by some preoccupation just as Pecquigny spoke: she was scanning all the different groups absently.

She was not looking for the king, for his entrance was always announced.

Mailly, despite his acute sensitiveness both as husband and as lover, was after all a courtier, like all the others, and in that capacity found food for reflection in Pecquigny's words. He thought that the queen might really have spoken of him; so he made his way toward the corner where she was sitting, to pay his respects to her and obtain a gracious word, if it so happened that her august glances were in search of him.

The courtier's estate is sublime in this, that it replaces for the moment all sentiment and emotion.

The actor, they say, is never conscious of physical suffering while he is on the stage.

The courtier knows no other emotion at court than that

produced by a favorable or cold reception from the sovereign. ·

The queen was playing cards, surrounded by a splendid circle.

Madame de Mailly had been admitted to the honor of a seat at her Majesty's table.

She held her cards in her hand.

Mailly, without looking directly at her, watched her face while he was watching the queen's.

He was waiting to notice the effect of the announcement of the king's arrival.

Courtier, lover, and jealous husband, does not his experience tend to make it easy to believe in the threefold functions of the divinities of mythology?

The queen's eyes at last met those of the count, who bowed as low as possible.

The queen gazed earnestly at him, as if to establish a connection between her present scrutiny, and the reports which had been made to her during the day.

Mailly found her prolonged observation of him very embarrassing. It certainly was no favor; so that if she had really been speaking of him, as Pecquigny had said, she could have had nothing good to say.

This seemed much more likely, as the queen's gaze, after several moments of stern observation of the count, passed on to the countess, and became much milder as it rested upon her.

" Oho ! " muttered Mailly, " what does this signify ? "

He waited for another glance, which was not long in coming, and when it came turned out to be as penetrating and severe and unpromising as the first.

Mailly continued to execute courtesies, which became more respectful in proportion as the queen's gaze increased in coldness and severity.

At last she condescended to reply with a motion of her head, and not till then did Mailly allow himself to breathe freely.

"Oh!" he thought, "there's something beneath all this, — an eel or a serpent."

Just as he was formulating this suspicion, we might better say this dread, in his mind, the king was announced.

Mailly looked earnestly at his wife, and Pecquigny looked at Mailly.

The queen rose, made a reverence, such as etiquette demanded, and resumed her seat.

Behind the king, at whose appearance Louise blushed under her rouge, came Richelieu, balancing himself now on one leg, now on the other, and vanquishing hearts with a look, a smile, a gesture, — for all the world like a Roman entering Rome in triumph.

The king saluted everybody, and immediately looked at the countess.

Richelieu keenly enjoyed the spectacle, which, though it lasted less than half a minute, contained a century of emotions for those who witnessed it.

The king walked through the rooms.

At that moment the queen interrupted her game, — which she was compelled to do when she began to lose, on account of the state of indigence, comparatively speaking, in which she was kept by Monsieur de Fleury, — and handed her cards to her neighbor.

It was the moment when each of the favored courtiers ordinarily endeavored to attract the attention of the young princess.

It was by no means a difficult task. Marie Leczinska was not in the least exacting; and when she addressed any person, congratulations upon her success or condolence for her losses were quite enough to lead to general conversation.

Mailly waited with beating heart.

The queen came straight toward him, and his heart began to leap.

She opened the attack.

"Monsieur," said she, "I am not altogether sure of your fidelity toward our sex, but I am sure of your fidelity toward your masters. It is through the latter quality that I have obtained for you what you wish."

Mailly, who was considerably bewildered, had no idea what the queen was talking about. The first words seemed to him to be the result of some complaint which Louise, as his wife, had laid before the judgment-seat of Marie Leczinska; while the conclusion took a strange turn, of which he could make nothing, anxious as he was to do so, however deeply he cogitated upon it.

However he bowed.

The queen seemed to accept the bow as a token of acquiescence. She passed to something else. Princes ordinarily do not use enough words to make their meaning clear; it is a defect which is commonly attributed to them, so that they may appear to possess some quality, even though it be a bad one.

Mailly, like a man lost in a wood, sought an answer to the riddle in the eyes of those who were near him, but to no purpose. He sought it especially in the eyes of his wife; but she, intent upon her cards, would have sacrificed both hands rather than turn her head or raise her eyes.

She felt that the king was looking at her, that Richelieu was watching her, and that Mailly was threatening her.

To which should she turn?

Mailly meanwhile was on the rack.

He sought out Pecquigny, who being on duty that day produced a stunning effect in his full-dress uniform.

"Well," said the duke, as Mailly approached him, "did the queen speak to you?"

"Yes."

"Then you are satisfied?"

"I confess that I did n't understand."

"Go on! you 're laughing at me; that 's not right."

"But if I swear—"

"Oh, don't trouble yourself, although I may be a little behindhand in learning what favor has been bestowed upon you, I have guessed it, nevertheless."

And with this half-impertinence the duke turned on his heel and sauntered away.

The count in despair looked around and saw Richelieu talking with the king.

He did not know which way to turn.

The cardinal came in. He was followed, as great ministers generally were, by a crowd almost as imposing as that which made Louis XIV. so jealous of Mazarin, and of which he used to say, —

"There 's the Grand Turk with his suite."

But Louis XV., gay and heedless young monarch, knew not the meaning of jealousy. When he had a grudge against any one, he took his revenge in satire; and very often, it must be said, his wit was so cutting that he was amply revenged.

Mailly was directly in Monsieur de Fleury's path; he stood aside to make room for his Eminence, stooping beneath the weight of his seventy-two years, and gracefully bent his knee before him.

The old minister's eye was keen; he saw and recognized Mailly at once. It may be that he also was looking for him. He motioned slightly to the count, who stepped at once to his side.

The old man was smiling, — a thing he was little accustomed to do, for he was stern by nature and necessity, as well as from old age.

"Aha!" thought Mailly, "there is an epidemic of good-humor this evening; everybody has a smile for me; I am like to be submerged under all these attentions. What does it all mean?"

"Monsieur le Comte," said the minister, "her Majesty the Queen begged so hard that you ought to be very grateful to her."

Mailly opened his eyes at this.

"Begged!" said he, "for what?"

"For you."

"For me?"

"Oh, that's what I said, and I have nothing to retract. You have warm friends, indeed."

"Do you mean the queen?" asked the count, with some emotion.

"Oh, you have friends! I tell you that fact, and congratulate you."

Mailly let his arms fall with an air of discouragement. He was no nearer comprehension than before.

He began to wonder if he were not the subject of some ridiculous wager, and if all these people were not amusing themselves at his expense.

Fleury passed on, and his procession with him. After paying his respects to the queen, he joined the young king, and talked with him a very long time.

"Upon my soul!" cried Mailly, "although I am not in the least inquisitive, I confess that I would give a good deal to know what it is that I am so successful in."

At that moment he noticed how confidentially the king was talking with Richelieu. Their two heads were as near together as respect would allow.

The young king was listening with all his ears. He smiled, and suddenly raising his head as if following out his thoughts, he looked first at the countess, then at Mailly.

Then he left Richelieu, and without affectation made straight for the count, saluting the ladies and saying a word or two to the men as he passed.

Pecquigny, meanwhile, was by no means the least attentive spectator of what was going on; and his features, wreathed with a conventional, meaningless smile, really expressed keenest disappointment.

Indeed it was more than disappointment, — it was downright chagrin.

"What," thought Mailly, "the king coming to speak to me! Verily, something extraordinary is going on here at court; the fairy who presided at my birth is making a bad use of her wand this evening."

The king stopped in front of him.

"Monsieur," said he, "I have signed. Believe that nothing could give me more pleasure."

It was not the moment to risk a question with him whom his subjects were not expected to question.

Mailly seemed overjoyed, and Louis passed on good-humoredly distributing smiles and nods among the hedge-rows of courtiers.

"By the gods," cried Mailly, "this is too much! The king has signed! Signed what? Nothing could give the king more pleasure than to sign! The devil fly away with me, but I must know what it is that the king has signed."

As he was working himself into a fever, he came into collision with Richelieu, who was coming toward him, rubbing his hands.

"At last!" he cried; "now I am going to find out something. Richelieu is too happy," he reflected, "not to have some bad news to tell me."

XXVI.

THE VIENNESE EMBASSY.

MAILLY summoned all his courage, and took a step toward Richelieu.

"Ah, my dear Duke," said he, "here you are!"

He must have been decidedly curious to allow himself to call Richelieu his "dear Duke."

"Good-evening, lucky mortal!" Richelieu began.

"Ah! you, too!" cried Mailly. "Well, I've got you now, and you shall not escape me like the others."

"God forbid!" rejoined the duke. "Pray tell me why I should want to escape from a man to whom I have naught but congratulations to offer?"

"Step aside a little," said the count.

"Very well."

Mailly drew his prey off to the end of the room.

"What is happening to me?" he demanded.

"It is happening to you to stir up tempests on all sides."

"On what ground?"

"*Parbleu!* they're jealous of you."

"Jealous of what?"

"Of your appointment."

"My appointment?"

"Come, don't pretend ignorance."

"On my life, Duke! on my honor, on my word as a gentleman, I haven't the slightest idea what it all means."

"Nonsense, impossible!" exclaimed the duke, feigning surprise.

"No. The queen hinted at something, Pecquigny teased me, Monsieur de Fleury pursed up his mouth at me, and everybody said the same thing. I guessed that they had some favor in mind; but what is it? That is what I don't know."

"What! You don't know what the queen asked in your behalf at Monsieur de Fleury's hands this morning?"

"I do not."

"And what Monsieur de Fleury at once asked at the king's hands?"

"I do not."

"And what the king actually put his name to for you?"

"I do not."

"Well, my dear Count," said Richelieu, with admirably assumed good-fellowship, "I am happy to be the first from whom you are to receive congratulations with knowledge of the cause."

"What are your congratulations for? There are some things for which they would not be appropriate."

"For your appointment."

"What appointment?"

"As ambassador."

"I, an ambassador?"

"Yes."

"To what court?"

"Vienna! an appointment which will make at least fifty persons burst with wrath."

"*Morbleu!*" exclaimed Mailly, "myself, first of all, if what you are telling me is not a joke, Duke."

"Come, come, Count, it is you who are joking."

"I am joking so little that I am almost suffocating."

" Upon my word, you 're as pale as a ghost."

" I can hardly contain myself."

" For joy ? "

" For rage."

" Pshaw ! "

" Oh, the mere idea of having this mystification put upon me drives me beside myself! What would be the effect if it were reality ? "

" Ah, Count, you must not try any of your tricks on me. Be reasonable! "

" I don't want it, I tell you! "

" But I have the commission in my pocket."

" My commission ? "

" Yes."

" As ambassador ? "

" Yes."

" At Vienna ? "

" Yes."

" To prove it," continued Richelieu, drawing a paper from his pocket, " here it is."

Mailly's head swam.

" You understand," said Richelieu, phlegmatically, " that I am too faithful a subject of his Majesty not to be deeply interested in you."

" Then it is to you that I owe this appointment ? "

" In great measure, yes, my dear Count."

" And by what right, I ask you, Monsieur le Duc, do you meddle in my affairs ? "

" I answer you thus: in the king's service, there is no indiscretion which I would not commit."

" Monsieur le Duc, this proceeding of yours is in the worst possible taste."

" Is it bad taste for me, having been intrusted with a mission as important as that to Vienna, to concern myself about my successor ? "

"Monsieur le Duc, this proceeding of yours is insulting."

"Is it insulting to a good friend of mine, to do my best to procure for him the succession to my own post, the most brilliant and important of all the great posts in the realm?"

"Oh, but whom shall I bring to book for it, then?" cried Mailly, violently.

"Be calm, my dear Count."

"Calm!"

"And begin by taking your commission."

"I would cut my hand off first."

"What! you decline such a favor as this? Why, are you mad, my dear Count?"

Richelieu uttered these last words with so much animation and in so loud a tone, considering the respectful silence which reigned in the room, that Mailly trembled at the thought of a scandal, and cooled down like a red-hot iron plunged in water.

The crafty courtier had trapped his man, and feeling that he had partly compromised him, he held out the commission to him again.

"Pray, take it, dear Count," said he.

"Never, I tell you! Never!"

"Then you decline! *Peste!* that's a serious matter! I must tell the cardinal without delay, so that he may govern himself accordingly."

"One moment, Monsieur," said Mailly, who would have aroused even his wife's pity, so apparent was his suffering; "one moment, spare me."

"Aha! you have changed your mind, have you?"

"No, Monsieur, no; but the king is the king, after all, and if I think best to decline the favor which he graciously offers, you will at least give me time, I suppose, to decline it in my own way."

"The devil, Monsieur!" cried Richelieu, "you will not be made ambassador against your will, never fear! Just say to him that you don't choose to go, and you will stay at home."

"Would you tell him so, Monsieur le Duc?" retorted Mailly, with flaming eyes.

"I, no; but you, a jealous man! yes."

This last blow struck home, and Mailly felt it in the very marrow of his bones.

"Monsieur le Duc," said he, "you have, for some reason unknown to me, inflicted upon me one of the greatest sorrows which man can inflict upon his fellow-man. Monsieur le Duc, God will not reward you for that."

"My dear Count, God has no part in all this business. You are wrong to lose your temper; I had an idea that I was doing you a good turn."

"Do you say such an infamous thing as that seriously, Monsieur le Duc?"

"Fine big words to use in the king's presence, Count, and within ten feet of the queen!"

"But you see that I am at my wits' end."

"Folly!"

"You stab me, and expect me not to cry out!"

"One moment, Count; do you choose, instead of losing your head, to talk with me quietly?"

"Yes, yes, yes, on condition that you pour balm on my wound, Duke, and not vinegar."

Richelieu shrugged his shoulders.

"Just remember, Count," he said, "that you will never have such another friend as I am."

"Oh, Duke, Duke, don't exasperate me!"

"I will prove it," continued Richelieu. "What is a friend's duty? This definition is not mine, but

Monsieur La Fontaine's, the great fable-writer.   He said, —

> ' Qu'un ami véritable est une douce chose!
> Il cherche nos besoins au fond de notre cœur.' [1]

Well, Mailly, I have sought at the bottom of your heart to find what you need; and as I could n't make it out very clearly, because of the whimsical construction of your mind — "

"Of my mind ? "

"Yes, it forks."

"My mind forks ? "

"*Parbleu!* yes, one path leads to Olympe, the mistress; another to Louise, the wife!   What is one to do with such a rocking-chair as that?   So I set about investigating the needs of your wife, and I found them; for, to do her justice, there is no fork in her mind."

"Oh, my God!" exclaimed Mailly, "give me patience, I pray!"

"'Madame de Mailly,' I said to myself, 'is madly in love with the king '"

Mailly groaned in anguish.

"Yes, madly! I must not hide the truth from you," continued Richelieu.

Mailly ground his teeth, and played with the hilt of his sword.

"Hide it from yourself, if you insist upon it, my dear fellow," Richelieu went pitilessly on; "but I warn you that the fable of the blind husband is played out.   Look, my friend, look; at this moment observe your wife's eye, draw a line from her lashes to those of the king, and tell me if it is n't a realization of what they teach at the

---

[1] " A real friend is a precious treasure; he searches our hearts to find what we need."

Jesuits' college: *Linea recta brevissima.* It is true as an axiom, on my word! an axiom, you know, does n't need to be proved."

Mailly sadly buried his head in his hands.

"Yes, yes, the head aches, and the forehead; we all know that, myself above all. I go on then."

"You are killing me, Duke!"

"My dear fellow, when one wants to cure a sick man, he must be treated without pity; now, you shall be cured this evening, or the devil can have me and welcome. So, then, I return to my subject; seeing that if Madame de Mailly should fall in love with the king, she would win his love in return (that is what we mean, you know, by saying that what woman wills, God wills); seeing that if this passion were interfered with, we should have to deal with Pecquigny, who would steal away your mistress, to gild the somewhat tarnished existence of our young monarch —

"CONSIDERING (that is the way they begin in Parliament, where we dukes and peers have the right to express our opinions), — considering that you care more for your mistress than for your wife — oh! don't shake your head, for I have guessed that, and guessed rightly too.

"Considering, I say, that he who takes Olympe from you cuts you to the heart, while he who takes your wife only rubs a little skin off your forehead, — for wounds in the head, you know, are the least serious of all, — this is the line of reasoning I followed.

"Mailly is in Paris.

"Mailly is jealous of his wife.

"His wife, who is madly in love with the king (I insist upon the word, you see) will seize his Majesty while he is at hand.

"Being jealous, he will make a row, and thereby will make himself ridiculous.

"If he is mystified, he will challenge somebody; and for violating the law against duels, he will be sent to the Bastille.

"In the Bastille he will make himself ridiculous again.

"Notice that the unfailing result of my logic is that you will make yourself ridiculous.

"Notice also that your wife will have taken possession of the king none the less.

"Notice also that your being present will quadruple the discomfort.

"Therefore I, Richelieu, your friend, have decided to send you off out of the way before anything is done."

Mailly made a movement.

"I swear, upon my honor," said Richelieu, "that nothing is yet done; but I also take the same oath that something will be done almost before your back is turned.

"You resist; observe the consequences, as I have set them forth. If you go, people will say: 'Mailly has gone away, Mailly is deceived. Ah! they did well to wait till he had gone; if he were here, things would have taken a very different turn!'

"See what a fine rampart I have arranged for you against the gossip of society, my dear friend.

"See what a fine specimen of an ogre, what a model man and husband, you will be in the world's eyes, thanks to me!

"You don't embrace me! you are an ungrateful fellow, Mailly! Such services as I am performing for you cannot be paid for. Try Pecquigny, and you will see if he does nearly as well by you as I have."

Mailly was overwhelmed and bewildered by this gushing stream of words, by this enunciation of a moral code which had never dared to raise its head and formulate itself since the time of Alcibiades.

"Here," Richelieu said in conclusion, "take your commission, and invite me to supper with Olympe."

Mailly stood some moments without speaking; then staggering like a drunken man, he made for the door.

"What! dumb?" said Richelieu.

"Adieu, Monsieur le Duc."

"The commission?"

"Thanks; keep it."

"Keep it! *Pardieu*, yes, I will keep it; for within a fortnight you will ask me for it."

"I?"

"Yes, you; and there is some chance yet that I may not refuse to give it to you."

Mailly made a despairing gesture, at which Richelieu disdainfully shrugged his shoulders.

"I am quite right," he muttered, "and I have not said a single word to this stubborn fool that is not gospel truth. But, *cordieu!* he must go to Vienna."

Then he turned about and continued his self-communing, —

"By Jove! how eagerly Pecquigny watched his exit! Let's see, how many days must we give the king to make up his mind that Mailly must go? A week? That's just the extent of his virtue. Faith, it seems a long while, I know, Madame la Comtesse, but it's the best I could do."

The duke returned to the king's side, skipping like one of those sanctimonious-looking crows who seem always to be sneering in one's face.

XXVII.

WHICH WILL ENABLE THE PENETRATING READER TO DIVINE BANNIÈRE'S PURPOSE IN ESCAPING.

WE think we have already said that they unbound the Abbé de Champmeslé, led him back to his own quarters, condoled with him, and made him tell his story over and over again.

As a matter of fact, the good abbé had not suffered much, and his martyrdom had been quite easy to bear. He at once caught Bannière's idea; it seemed to him amusing as the plot of a comedy, and very well done by the leading actor, so he had let things take their course, preferring a passive to an active complicity.

We know what had taken place.

Bannière entered Paris by Faubourg Saint-Marceau, which Voltaire stigmatized with the name of the hideous faubourg, — a truth which stands as one of the many great truths that great man wrote.

An abbé in Faubourg Saint-Marceau was not at all an uncommon sight, and Abbé Bannière did not attract attention.

But in order to preserve his useful incognito, it was essential that he should not wander too long about the streets; consequently he devoted himself to the necessary business of finding a lodging.

To find a lodging was not the simplest thing in the world for Bannière. He had no acquaintance with Paris, having passed but twelve hours there, and he had no idea of the customs prevailing there with regard to lodgings, having been accommodated at Charenton since the evening of his arrival.

Of the two crowns which he had borrowed from Champmeslé, two livres and ten sous had gone in payment of cab-hire, leaving him nine livres ten sous. It was an independent fortune compared with what he had possessed at the time of his first visit to the capital.

Thus he was not actually embarrassed for want of funds, since he had the wherewithal to lodge and board himself for four or five days, by hiring modest apartments and living soberly.

With that, to be sure, he could not afford to feed at wine-shops on oysters and chicken, watered by that delicious light wine which had proved so appetizing the day he found the crown in the pocket of the old linen coat; but he might have good white bread to eat and not lie in the street.

Compared with the king's hospitality to his guests at Charenton, it was a very perceptible improvement.

Bannière, with his nose in the air, devoted himself first to the important quest for a suitable hostelry. Priests at that epoch sometimes did as other travellers, when they arrived in Paris from the provinces without recommendation. It would of course have been much more consistent for Bannière to find shelter in some convent; but not only did he lack letters of introduction, — he thought on reflection that the Jesuits might have allies in the convent he should select, and Bannière was no whit more anxious to be buried in a Jesuit dungeon than in a madhouse.

On the other hand, it was urgent that he should find a place to lay his head, and that he should also barter his priestly garb for some other, since his description as

340 OLYMPE DE CLÈVES.

a fugitive dressed in that garb had undoubtedly been sent to the Parisian police.

Oh, how he then sighed for that affable old-clothes dealer, to whom he would with a good heart have returned the crown mentioned in an earlier chapter, on condition that she would give him a suit of any sort, even though there might be no crowns in the pockets!

However, Bannière was still at the age where one relies upon Providence, and he said to himself that he must find a hole to crawl into first of all, and the coat would come in its due time.

He fell in with what he needed in Rue des Fossés-Saint-Victor, — that is to say, a little chamber looking upon a courtyard, modestly furnished and neat.

He entered into possession, and began to reflect.

His reflections were divided into three parts: —

In the first place he thanked God.

In the second place he thought out a plan with reference to his costume.

Lastly his mind reverted to the good Abbé de Champmeslé, and he reflected upon what he had already done for him, and what he might still be expected to do.

This was his plan: —

He made a great noise on the stairs, pretended to have had a fall, which was extremely probable considering their steepness, and to have had the misfortune of tearing his coat as he fell.

Consequently a tailor was sent for.

When he was safely in the room, Bannière turned the key in the door behind him, and said, —

"My friend, I see it written in your face that you are a worthy fellow; I have escaped from a convent where they wanted to force me to take the vows. I am in hiding here; find me a suitable coat."

The tailor, luckily for Bannière, was a philosopher. He was delighted with the confidence reposed in him, for at that time there were many young men forced to adopt a religious life, and the story was quite credible. He shed a few tears, pressed Bannière's hand, carried away the clerical coat, and brought him a very good one, which he proposed to exchange for the other, which was quite new.

Bannière declined; the priestly garment did not belong to him, but to Champmeslé. However the honest fellow's proposition suggested a plan to him.

It was to leave the cloak in pledge for the coat; he would redeem it later.

It was really extremely considerate on Bannière's part; for in the tailor's shop, and representing a pledge, it would be much better taken care of than if it remained in the possession of Bannière, who had no servant.

Furthermore, if our readers will carry their minds back to the beginning of this veracious history, they will remember that on the day when Bannière began his dramatic career in the part of Hérode, Champmeslé had borrowed his cloak, as he had now borrowed Champmeslé's. Thus it was nothing more than an exchange of kind actions and cloaks between the two friends.

The tailor gave his address, and agreed to give up the cloak for six livres.

Bannière, very proud and happy to have a coat for the morrow, laid it out on a chair, went to bed, and slept long and soundly.

When he awoke the next morning, he heard the birds singing, a cat miauing, and pigeons cooing; he saw a piece of blue sky about the size of a handkerchief and fairly leaped for joy, as if he were the owner of half the globe.

He rose and wrote the following letter to Champmeslé : —

MONSIEUR AND DEAR BROTHER, — You will not have been
so uncharitable as to condemn me for what I did.

I trust that my harsh measures have left no bad impression
upon you, mental or physical.

I have left your cloak in a safe place.

If you care to take the trouble to walk in the main avenue
at the Tuileries to-morrow at two in the afternoon, I will
approach you and give you such satisfaction as I may.

You see, Monsieur and dear brother, whether I trust in your
loyalty and prudence ; but as the poet says : "One should be
an honest man under helmet or frock."

I should myself fail to be such an one, Monsieur, if I could
deem you anything else.

Your respectful servant and friend,

BANNIÈRE.

Well satisfied with this production, Bannière entrusted
it to the post, and waited for the morrow to come, keeping as close as he could. It is easy to see why that was
necessary.

His thoughts gave him enough occupation to prevent
time from hanging heavy on his hands.

Outraged by the thought that Olympe, after recognizing
him, had abandoned and denied him, that she had taken
her leave without witnessing the least atom of sympathy
for the poor lunatic, he asked himself whether she could
really have lost every spark of human feeling.

Was she right to act so ?

Was not her apparent callousness in itself a proof of
interest ?

Poor Bannière was still so deeply in love that he put
these questions to himself, and replied, "*Perhaps.*"

But after all, why need he anticipate, why torture

himself into a fever, when a speedy solution of his doubts
was at hand ?

The only question was, how was he to proceed ?

To seek out Olympe in hot haste was the best way to
terrify her and to invite his own arrest.

His plain course was to make sure of every step in
advance, and above all to make Olympe understand that
he was not mad.

Bannière felt that he was in love to such a point that
he would have started in a moment for the Indies, re-
gardless of time or distance, sure of winning back Olympe's
love when they had had leisure to calm down and look
each other in the eye.

Such selfish attachments as his have a power which
common men cannot conceive. They always succeed,
like everything else in the experience of mankind which
stands by itself.

The next day came at last.

Bannière in a neat green coat walked up and down
under the trees in the gardens of the Tuileries from ten in
the morning, holding a book in his hand to keep himself in countenance.

Of course he was not reading; he had many other
things to think about than the good or bad things which
were contained between the covers of the volume, which
he had borrowed from his landlord without even looking
at the title.

His heart was beating so fast as to endanger the green
coat. By noon the torture had become almost unbearable
to him.

At last, as two o'clock struck, he saw Champmeslé
turning into the main avenue.

Bannière immediately, without stopping to ascertain
whether the abbé was or was not an honorable man, or

whether he was bringing with him a gang of hirelings to
capture the escaped madman, rushed up to him, and
seized him effusively by both hands.

The abbé was very sober and cool; an imprudent smile
would make him Bannière's accomplice.

"Well!" exclaimed Bannière, "are you such a poor
Christian, Monsieur Champmeslé, that you can't forgive
those who have trespassed against you?"

"Yes, indeed," replied Champmeslé, "I forgive you
Monsieur Bannière, although you nearly suffocated me;
not only do I forgive you, but as you must be pretty
nearly at the end of your two crowns, I have brought you
two more; you can return the four together. I am not
rich, but, thank God! I am in need of nothing at this
moment."

"Not even of your cloak?" asked Bannière, with a
smile.

"Fortunately," was the naïve reply, "I bought a piece
large enough for two; so that I still have the one which
you see upon me."

"You shall have the other this evening, Monsieur de
Champmeslé," said Bannière.

"First tell me where it is, pray."

Bannière gave him the history of the garment.

"If the tailor is a dishonest man," said Champmeslé,
"it is gone before this, as you took no written acknowl-
edgment from him; if he is honest, he will return it in a
week as surely as to-day, and meanwhile you will have
the use of a crown, which may come in very handily."

"Upon my word," said Bannière, "you are my guardian angel, dear Monsieur Champmeslé; from the
first moment I saw you I have had no doubt of it, and
the more I see of you, the surer I am."

"Was it for no other purpose than to tell me that,

that you asked me to come here ? " asked Champmeslé, smiling.

" No; let us walk aside, I beg, for I have much to say to you."

" Are you afraid of the river-bank ? "

" Not in the least."

" Very well!   I noticed as I came along some men fishing with poles under the bridge.   We can pretend to be watching them, and can talk at our leisure meanwhile."

" Very good."

They left the garden, and went down under the bridge, as Champmeslé had suggested.

When they had arrived there, Champmeslé stopped, folded his arms, and said, looking fixedly at Bannière,—

" Monsieur Bannière, I have been asking myself since day before yesterday whether you are likely to become an honest man or a very clever scamp."

" Oh, Monsieur de Champmeslé," cried Bannière, " why, in heaven's name, should you suspect me of a tendency to become a scamp ? "

" Alas ! my brother," Champmeslé replied, " you are now fairly launched upon a stormy sea of violent passions. Ah, Monsieur Bannière, what a sea and what tempests! "

Bannière sighed.

" And what navigator," continued Champmeslé, raising his eyes devoutly toward heaven, " can answer for his safe arrival in port when he is thus assailed ? "

Bannière understood that Champmeslé was on the point of embarking upon a sermon. He saw why the abbé had taken him aside, and he shuddered at the risk he was running.

He resolved to cut it short.

" Dear Monsieur de Champmeslé, pray listen to me a moment," said he. " You are admirably fitted to adorn the pulpit, but I could never listen to you so attentively when you are speaking on moral subjects as I could if Olympe were your theme. Speak to me then of Olympe, dear Monsieur de Champmeslé, and you will see how I will hang upon your words."

"Lost! lost!" exclaimed Champmeslé, with deep sorrow.

"Come, dear Abbé," said Bannière, "be kind to me; don't forget that you were a man before you became a saint; remember that no human being was ever so unfortunate as I have been; and if there is still a living heart in your body since your sacrifice to the Church, allow that heart to be moved to pity for me, your neighbor. Don't bother now about God's business, dear Monsieur de Champmeslé. God is so strong and mighty, believe me, that he always arrives in time to look after it himself."

Bannière uttered this little speech with such vehemence, and even more conviction, that he saw that he had moved his hearer, and that the Jesuit was beginning to give way to the old actor.

"Well," said the abbé, "let us understand each other. You have what you want, have n't you?"

"What I want?"

"Why, yes; you wanted freedom, and you are free."

"True, but I am only the more unhappy."

"Oh, eternal instability of mankind!" cried Champmeslé.

"Monsieur de Champmeslé," said Bannière, clasping his hands, "are you willing to do me a service?"

"*Mon Dieu!* yes," cried Champmeslé, in the tone of a man who feels himself sliding down into an abyss; "I am very willing, provided you involve me in nothing which will endanger my chance of salvation."

" Oh, never fear, your salvation is quite safe with me, and I will be as careful of it as of my own."

" Then I shall be damned," said Champmeslé.

" Pray be reassured on that score."

" Say on, then. Well, why don't you speak ? "

" Oh, poor Bannière that I am ! "

" What 's the matter now ? "

" I am going to shock you, dear Monsieur de Champmeslé."

" You will find that rather difficult, after all that I have seen of you, Monsieur Bannière. I am quite prepared, — go on."

" No, I do not dare."

" Nonsense ! go on."

" Monsieur de Champmeslé —"

" Well, what is it ? "

" You told me day before yesterday that one of the Gentlemen of the Chamber was your friend ? "

" True, Monsieur le Duc de Pecquigny."

" Very well ! you can be my savior."

" Ah, I understand."

Bannière looked at Champmeslé, marvelling much at his precocious comprehension.

" Yes," continued Champmeslé, " you wish me to procure the erasure of your name from the records of Charenton; I may be able to do it."

" That, first of all, if you choose."

" What do you mean by ' that, first of all ' ? "

" Oh, I had not thought of that."

" What were you thinking of, then ? "

" Dear Monsieur de Champmeslé, Olympe made her début at the Comédie-Française."

" Yes, in the rôle of Julie, in which she seems to have been superb."

"Ah, so much the better!"

"*Parbleu!*" said the abbé, forgetting himself for the moment, "she has such great talent! Do you remember the way in which she used to say in her great scene with Britannicus — wait a moment, wait a moment — Oh, yes: —

'Combien de fois, hélas! puisqu'il faut vous le dire,
 Mon cœur de son désordre allait-il vous instruire!
 De combien de soupirs, interrompant le cours,
 Ai-je évité vos yeux que je cherchais toujours!
 Quel tourment de se taire en voyant ce qu'on aime!
 De l'entendre gémir, de l'affliger soi-même,
 Lorsque par un regard on peut le consoler!
 Mais quels pleurs ce regard aurait-il fait couler!
 Ah! dans ce souvenir, inquiète, troublée.
 Je ne me sentais pas assez dissimulée,
 De mon front effrayé je craignais la pâleur;
 Je trouvais mes regards trop pleins de ma douleur.
 Sans cesse il me semblait que Néron en colère
 Me venait reprocher trop de soin de vous plaire ;
 Je craignais mon amour vainement renfermé,
 Enfin j'aurais voulu n'avoir jamais aimé.'"

Champmeslé uttered the last few words with such expression that the fishermen turned to look, and Bannière clapped his hands.

"Bravo! bravo! my dear Abbé," cried the latter. "Ah! if you were not a Jesuit, what a teacher of acting you would make! Tell me, might there not even yet be a chance of your returning to the boards?"

"Wretch!" exclaimed the abbé, realizing that he had allowed himself to go a little too far in the direction of worldliness, — "wretch, you will not be content with destroying yourself, but must pull me down with you!"

"Dear Monsieur de Champmeslé!" said Bannière.

"Back, demon!" cried Champmeslé, acting as if he were about to flee.

But Bannière held him back.

"Messieurs," said one of the fishermen, with less forbearance than the others, "if you are going to keep up that row, just tell us so, and we will go elsewhere. Since you have been there we can't get a bite."

Champmeslé felt the justice of this complaint, and said to Bannière in a lower tone, —

"Well, tell me at once what you desire of me, and let me see if it is possible."

The two friends, — for in spite of all that had passed, perhaps because of all that had passed between them, we may give them that title, — the two friends stepped back a short distance; and Bannière, who seemed to have made up his mind, said, —

"Well, my father, it's nothing more nor less than a matter of asking Monsieur de Pecquigny for an order for a first appearance."

"For whom?" demanded Champmeslé.

"For myself," said Bannière.

"For you, Bannière!" cried Champmeslé; "ask Pecquigny for your everlasting damnation!"

"That's about it, dear Monsieur de Champmeslé."

"Ah, my good friend, no, enough of that! I will not make myself the instrument of your misfortune. Suffer for a time in this world, but don't burn forever in the other."

"Dear Monsieur de Champmeslé, when we get there we will see what we'll do; but meanwhile — "

"Yes, let us try to satisfy our animal, material nature, — the lusts of the flesh! I tell you *no!* "

"*Mon Dieu!* there is nothing to prevent our satisfying the spirit too. When one loves as I do, there is as much of the spirit as of the flesh in love, I swear to you, dear Abbé."

"No! you can kill me before you make me do such a thing. My mind is irrevocably made up."

"Kill you, dear, kind Abbé! Never! I hope you will go to heaven without suffering martyrdom at any one's hands; only put off going as long as you can, and until then assist me, I beseech you, with all your power."

"No."

"Dear Monsieur de Champmeslé."

"Never!"

"I implore you!"

"Never, never, I tell you!"

"Very well, then there is but one thing left for me to do."

"What can you do?"

"Go and see Monsieur de Pecquigny myself."

"Go! He will have you back at Charenton in the twinkling of an eye."

"So be it. Every day I will pray to the Lord to forgive the Abbé de Champmeslé for the terrible wrong he did me."

"All right! God will know what to think about it."

"'Oh, my God!' I will say, 'forgive dear Monsieur de Champmeslé, who was kind-hearted at bottom, the life of martyrdom, and the despairing, godless, blaspheming death, which, through him, are the fitting end of my long agony.'"

Champmeslé shuddered. With all his extravagance Bannière displayed a natural eloquence which was hard to resist.

Furthermore in the tones of his voice, which came from the very depths of his heart, there was a something which gave his words a truthful sound.

"But tell me," the abbé asked, despairing of finding any better reasons with which to meet Bannière's persistence, "why do you desire to resume the miserable profession of the stage, which I laid down with such delight? Why, you're a regular demoniac, my dear brother; you have two hobbies at once, and the maddest madmen have only one."

"But I have only one, dear Abbé."

"Bah! You can't get along away from the stage?"

"No."

"And you will die if you don't see Olympe again?"

"Very true."

"Well, there are your two hobbies."

"But don't you see that one of them naturally leads to the other?"

"How so?"

"Ah, dear Abbé, for a man who made his first appearance in — "

"Hush! never speak of that!"

"You are very hard of comprehension."

"In what?"

"Why, by procuring admission to the Comédie-Française, I shall find Olympe again."

"*Pardieu!* you have no need to go there for that; you can find Mademoiselle Olympe de Clèves wherever she is, if the devil still tempts you in that direction."

"No, indeed; there's where you are in error. In her own home Olympe will be guarded; there I shall find Monsieur de Mailly."

"But on the street or the Tuileries gardens, as you met me, for instance?"

"It would be by the merest chance if I should meet her."

"Pshaw! why was the post invented?"

Bannière shook his head.

"Ah! for an old actor, Abbé — "

"Well! what is it! what did I say that was so absurd, pray?"

"If I write to Olympe to meet me, wherever you please, there are two chances to one against me."

"How do you prove that?"

"In the first place my letter may be intercepted; many people find their profit in making themselves agreeable to Monsieur de Mailly, who is wealthy and powerful. If my letter is intercepted, Olympe does n't receive it. One chance against me."

"That will pass for one."

"Do you dispute it?"

"No. Now for the second."

"The second is that Olympe, who saw me at Charenton apparently mad, may still believe me to be mad, much more mad here in the Tuileries than in my cell. And then, you see, if it was fear that drove her away from Charenton, when she saw me safe behind bars and under lock and key in a cell, she will be much more anxious for her safety when she knows that I am free, without bolts or bars or keepers to restrain me."

"Aha!"

"In which case, not only will she not come to the rendezvous, but, out of consideration for my health, she will have me taken back to the hospital, just as Monsieur de Pecquigny would, so that the Abbé de Champmeslé's honest heart will still suffer the pangs of remorse, and will continually cry out to him that it is his cruelty which caused poor Bannière's death."

"Hum! hum! there's some truth in what you say," said the abbé.

"Are you then finally convinced? That's a good hearing!"

"Convinced that you need to see Mademoiselle de
Clèves again, but not to return to the stage."

"I need both equally, dear Abbé. You know very
well what the stage is, you who were an actor thirty
years."

"Alas!"

"Well, on the stage everything that is difficult elsewhere becomes easy of accomplishment. There I can
meet her, you see, without exciting anybody's jealousy;
and even if I should arouse that feeling, no one can prevent my seeing her, speaking to her, entering her dressing-room, closing the door behind me, and making her
understand that I was not mad, or if I have been, that it
was from despair at not seeing her."

"And when you have made her understand that?"

"When I have made her understand that, my vengeance will begin."

"You wish, then, to revenge yourself upon Olympe?"

"I have no other purpose!" cried Bannière, and his
eyes glistened at some thought which passed through his
mind.

"Well, upon my word! it needed only that," said the
abbé, disgusted at the last words; "he proposes to
commit a crime, and asks me to assist him!"

"No, no, indeed! Monsieur de Champmeslé, I have no
purpose of committing a crime; you exaggerate."

"You say that you want to be revenged?"

"Yes, but in Christian fashion."

"There is no such a thing as Christian vengeance."

"Abbé!"

"That sentiment is distinctly forbidden by the texts."

"Abbé, you don't do justice to your learning; this is
how I mean to be revenged —"

"No form of vengeance is permissible."

"Is it not permissible for me to make Olympe repent by proving to her that she has been less generous than I?"

"Ah, that's a different matter."

"You see that it is, don't you, Abbé?"

"But when you have proved to her that you have been the more generous, will she forgive you?"

"Perhaps."

"And then you will be reconciled?"

"I trust so."

"Very good! And I, a priest, shall have lent my aid to the commission of a deadly sin. That would be very fine!"

"Alas! Monsieur l'Abbé, we shall never be reconciled in all probability; but at least she will see that I am not mad, she will see that I have never deceived her, she will see that her pride was an evil counsellor against my ardent affection."

"If she sees all that, you will surely be reconciled. Impossible!"

"Oh, my poor friend! oh, my dear Abbé! for pity's sake, for God's sake, be the minister of his loving kindness, and not of his wrath!"

"Flatterer!"

"I see that you love me."

"I confess it."

"You have a heart of gold."

"I would it were of diamond."

"It would be worth no more."

"It would be harder."

"You consent then?"

"On one condition."

"Name it."

"It is this,— that the first offer you make to her shall be to join yourself to her in Christian wedlock."

"I ask nothing better, dear Abbé."

"Do you promise me?"

"I swear it, and I will promise you something more than that."

"What?"

"That if Olympe consents to this marriage, wherever we may be, you and no other shall join our hands."

Champmeslé's face fairly shone with pleasure. He had not yet performed the marriage ceremony.

"In consideration of this promise," said he, "I consent to do as you wish."

"Oh," cried Bannière, "let me embrace you!"

"Very well; but don't throw me into the water."

They had approached the river without noticing it.

"My angel, my good angel!" exclaimed Bannière.

"Messieurs," said the fisherman, testily, "can't you go somewhere else to embrace?"

"My friend," said Champmeslé, "you see that we are a terrible nuisance to this good fellow."

"Indeed you are," retorted the angler.

There is nothing in the world so savage as a man with a line in his hand, who has been sitting for an hour without a semblance of an excuse for taking it out of the water.

But Bannière was too happy to trouble himself about trifles.

"It is agreed, is it, dear Monsieur Champmeslé," said he, "that you will be my friend in this?"

"For the good of humanity, yes."

"You will ask Monsieur de Pecquigny for an order to make my début?"

"I will."

"And will you obtain it?"

"*Peste!* how fast you go!"

"Will you obtain it?"

"I can't answer for that."

"Why not?"

"Because the Duc de Pecquigny may not choose to commit himself without knowing you."

"Take me to him."

"Why, you forget that he saw you at Charenton, poor fellow!"

"I beg your pardon, I had a three weeks' growth of beard, and my hair was but ill cared for; besides, he only saw me an instant."

"That instant would be enough; your face is one not easily forgotten."

"I will not go then; you will do better alone."

"Suppose he should know your name?"

"Where could he have heard it?"

"At Charenton."

"You know very well that there are no names there, — nothing but numbers."

"But Monsieur de Pecquigny is not the whole world, and it may be that the manager — "

"In that case don't give my name."

"Then it will be necessary for me to lie."

"You will be lying only in obedience to your humane principles."

"I don't wish to lie at all. So listen! Suppose he asks me whom the order is for?"

"Well, tell him it is for the man who is fonder of you than anybody else in the world, for a man whom you care a little for yourself, for a man who will pay for the order with his everlasting gratitude, for a man, in short, who will give his life for you and the Duc de Pecquigny in return for what you will have done for him."

Champmeslé turned his head away; his eyes were wet with tears.

"This boy would have made a famous preacher," he said. "What a pity that he ever left the bosom of the Church!"

"Oh, come, come, my friend!" said Bannière.

"Yes, Monsieur, go," said the angler, beseechingly; "in that way you can please two people."

"What! you want me to start off at once?"

"Yes, Monsieur, at once," said the fisherman; "why can't you do it?"

"Come, come, my dear Abbé," persisted Bannière.

"But, after all, how—"

"Where is the duke?"

"At Versailles."

"I will go there with you."

"Come, then."

"Ah!" exclaimed the fisherman; "God be praised!"

Champmeslé ceased to exert his own will, and allowed himself to be carried away.

Such a love is quite as powerful as the vinegar with which Hannibal melted the Alpine cliffs, as we are informed by Livy with sober face; if it does not always succeed in uniting, it does always succeed in disuniting.

Bannière put the abbé's arm through his own, and they fairly flew in the direction of Versailles.

"We're not going to Versailles in this fashion, are we?" said Champmeslé.

"Yes, indeed."

"What! on foot?"

"No, in a cab; I will pay for it."

"Oh, yes, with the twenty livres you now have."

"Well, isn't that enough?"

"Yes, but what will you have left then?"

"Oh, as much as I need!"

Champmeslé shrugged his shoulders.

"Here," said he, "take these three louis too."

"Oh, no!" cried Bannière, in a burst of sublime self-sacrifice; "though you were to offer them to me a hundred times over, I would not take them."

Champmeslé, who was acquainted with the youth's past life, and knew what quantities of money had melted away in his fingers, was amazed to find such delicacy of feeling in the depths of a heart which most people would have believed to be withered.

"After all," he muttered, "all is not lost, and there is a soul for me to save. Love is as good a means as another, and the priest's crucifix does not make so many converts as the rose branch offered by an honest woman to him who loves her."

They took a carriage at the gateway of La Conférence, and made the four leagues and a half in three hours. To be sure the driver did his best, stimulated by the pourboire Bannière promised him.

When they reached the duke's hotel, Bannière undertook to wait in the carriage, but he soon alighted and sat upon a bench, and then began walking up and down; his impatience was too great to allow him to remain in any one place.

In a quarter of an hour Bannière offered up as many prayers in his mind as a bride on her way to the church, or a condemned wretch being dragged to the scaffold.

The abbé delayed, and Bannière was in despair. He was meeting with difficulty, perhaps; or it might be that they were listening to him attentively and he was just on the point of success.

A half-hour — a half-century rather — elapsed, during which Bannière invoked all the saints, of both sexes, in Paradise. He was more of a believer than Champmeslé thought.

At last the door opened, and Bannière darted toward it.

Champmeslé reappeared with a frown on his face.

" He refused! " cried Bannière, in despair.

" Look! " said Champmeslé, drawing a paper from his capacious pocket.

" Signed! signed! " cried Bannière. " Oh, may heaven's blessing rest upon you, Monsieur le Duc, and upon the good God too! "

The poor boy actually knelt in the street, and kissed the precious parchment.

Fortunately even in the time of Louis XV. the streets of Versailles were not crowded with passers-by, and the pavement was dry.

Bannière embraced Champmeslé a thousand times on the way back to Paris, and two thousand on the Place Saint-Antoine, where they parted, after they had been to the tailor's for the cloak.

But as Bannière must soon come to an end of his three louis, he accepted seven more from Champmeslé. Furthermore, at his request, as he no longer feared that it would be taken from him, Champmeslé returned the ring which he had received in trust.

Far more happy, certainly, than Louis XV. in his palace at Versailles, Bannière returned to his lodgings on Rue Saint-Victor, having given the abbé his promise to act prudently, and to keep him informed of everything.

XXVIII.

IN WHICH THE QUEEN SHIRKS HER DUTY.

LET us leave for a moment Bannière preparing exultantly for his début at the Comédie-Française, and return to that trinity whose members were the king, the queen, and Madame de Mailly,—a trinity which, it may be remarked, was very far from being a holy one, as it was from forming one single entity.

Let us begin with the queen.

She had listened with attention to what Monsieur de Fleury had said or caused to be said to her concerning Monsieur de Mailly.

The queen was not jealous.

Another in her place would have asked the explanation of Monsieur de Fleury's sudden interest in the count; another in her place would have investigated, would have tried to guess, would have ferreted out their designs upon Louis XV. and Madame de Mailly, and would naturally have refused to ask a favor which would eventually lead to her own shame.

But the queen happened to be the kind-hearted, virtuous, unemotional Marie Leczinska; she asked no questions, made no investigations, and suspected nothing, but she presented the commission to the king and explained the circumstances to him; and the king, who had at the bottom of his heart an instinctive feeling, which he could not explain, that he would like to have

Monsieur de Mailly as far away as possible, signed the document.

Poor queen! she was so far from suspecting that she had any reason to be jealous that she would have repelled very sternly anybody who might advise her to appear so, although be it said it would have been excellent advice.

As unfortunate as are most of the women who are virtuous to the last degree, and who, in that microcosm which is called a court, surrounded by adversaries with whom they ought to temporize, neglect to do so, and are forever at odds with their neighbors, and end by becoming accustomed to blows, the queen, whose most precious treasure the king really was, for she loved him very dearly,— the queen thought that his love for her would last forever. She reckoned without that deplorable masculine instinct of coquetry, without the impulsive and invincible ardor of Louis XIV. and the Duchesse de Bourgogne,— those many-sided tyrants, whom Hercules himself, the vanquisher of so many obstacles, and the hero of the twelve impossible "labors," could never have conquered.

Would Louis XV. have remained virtuous without Richelieu and without Fleury? It is for history to solve that problem, not for us. We content ourselves with the assertion that he might perhaps have remained virtuous, had it not been for his wife.

For at the age which he had attained, about eighteen years, Louis XV., the handsomest youth in his realm, regarded with eyes of admiration, we had almost said of desire, by all the women in his realm, had as yet had no eyes for any other woman than his wife, Marie Leczinska, who, as we have already said, whether because she was naturally cold or because she had confidence in her husband's virtue, was a long way from being as grateful to him for his fidelity as Marie-Thérèse would have been to Louis XIV.

But there was this difference between the two queens, — that Marie-Thérèse wearied Louis XIV. with her love, while Marie Leczinska wearied Louis XV. with her indifference.

And certain it is, that his wife's indifference must have been of the most aggravated description, to make of Louis XV., inordinately bashful by nature, the most dissolute rake in the monarchy.

But, at the time at which we have arrived, Louis was still a virtuous youth who had resisted all temptations; and so his pen was still wet after signing Monsieur de Mailly's commission, when, remembering what Richelieu had said to him of that gentleman's wife, as well as his personal souvenirs concerning her, he began to regret that he had opened for himself that door to seduction, by making Madame de Mailly half a widow.

It was not that he had promised himself that he would use the door, but he felt the temptation coming, and that was enough to frighten him.

Returning to his own apartments, he began to think about the queen, and his thoughts led him to the conclusion that she was the most lovable and lovely of women.

That was not the universal opinion, but it was the opinion of Louis XV. at eighteen.

He remembered that the queen belonged to him, and he said to himself that to seek pleasure elsewhere was to fly in the face of Providence.

He called Bachelier, and blushingly sent him to say to the queen that he proposed to call upon her.

While the worthy valet was absent upon his errand,

the king reviewed all the moral maxims which his preceptor, as well as the virtuous men among the courtiers, and the late king, had taught him; and as they fell in very well with the state of his heart that day, he found it very easy to put them in practice.

He was in such haste to see the queen that he had already laid aside his sword, which etiquette required that the valet-de-chambre should carry to the queen's apartments, when the valet aforesaid suddenly returned with features so expressive of dismay that the king, if he had been in the least degree suspicious, must have seen that he was putting most of it on.

Louis was all ready to go.

"What's the matter?" he asked, stopping on the threshold.

"Ah, Sire, stay where you are!" said Bachelier.

"Why so, pray?"

"Sire, the queen — "

"Is the queen ill?"

"No, Sire; at least her Majesty did not say so, and I don't think she is."

"Did you see her in person?"

"Yes, Sire, and her Majesty's coloring was superb; but — "

"But what?"

"Her Majesty sent word to the king that she desires to remain alone this evening."

Louis, in absolute stupefaction, fastened his great blue eyes upon his valet.

Several times the queen had allowed her dislike for her husband's nocturnal visits to appear, but thus far she had not refused to receive them.

Louis was so astounded that he remained dumb.

"It's surprising, Sire, is it not?" said Bachelier.

"Most surprising, indeed," rejoined the young king, blushing with chagrin and anger.

"So surprising," continued Bachelier, "that I took the liberty of making the queen repeat it, pretending that I did not understand."

"Did she repeat it?"

"In the same words."

"Bachelier," said Louis, "it must be that the queen is sick."

"No, Sire; but she has her own ideas, apparently."

"What do you call her ideas, Bachelier?"

"Will your Majesty allow me to tell you the truth, like the faithful and devoted subject that I am?'

"Go on, my good Bachelier, go on, especially as I know very well that her Majesty, who is moreover by nature and training cold, imagines that she displeases heaven by pleasing her husband. Isn't that what you mean to say, Bachelier?"

"Yes, Sire, it's partly that, I confess."

"It's very excusable, Bachelier. God before everything!"

"Oh, Sire!"

Bachelier accompanied this exclamation with a smile which was mocking enough to have satisfied Voltaire himself.

The king saw the smile, and was led to reflect thereby.

"Say on," said he.

"Sire, the first half of what your Majesty says is true, and the queen is very cold by nature. Oh, that must be so!"

"What! that must be so?" said the king, mistaking Bachelier's meaning.

"Yes, Sire, for if any other woman than the queen had for her husband the king such a king as you are, — that is to say, a beautiful young man, glowing with the exuberant vigor of youth — "

Again the king blushed, but it was with pleasure this time.

"But after all," he said with a sigh, "the queen is not that other woman you speak of. What would you, Bachelier? It's unfortunate, that's all."

And he sighed again.

Bachelier saw clearly what a void that night would make in the royal economy.

He determined to avail himself of the opportunity, and he persisted.

"No matter," said he; "the king is not happy, and I know of a petty officer in the guards who was very wrong to say, 'Happy as the king.'"

"Why so?" asked Louis.

"Because, returning from Porcherons or Saint-Mandé, he found two loving arms open to receive him."

Louis knit his brows.

"And then," Bachelier added, "you see, Sire, it's all time thrown away for confessors to preach that youth is youth,— that is to say, a season which is as brief for kings as for other men."

This truth was so self-evident that Louis, completely discouraged, threw himself into an easy-chair.

"What is your Majesty doing?" asked Bachelier, after a silence of some minutes.

"My Majesty is suffering with ennui," replied the king, in a doleful voice.

Then he rose to his feet again.

"But I will not suffer with it forever," said he; "I promise you that, Bachelier."

"Ah, Sire, that's a good hearing."

"So you are quite sure, are you, Bachelier, that the queen is not sick?"

"Oh, Sire, I thank God I can swear to that; further-more the physicians are there to set your Majesty's mind at rest, if you are anxious."

"Very well, Bachelier, since the queen shirks her duty,[1] from this day forth you will not carry any of my belongings to her apartments."

After he had assisted the king to retire, he hurried away, beaming with satisfaction, to carry the good news to Monsieur de Richelieu.

Thus did the caprice, slothfulness, and thoughtlessness of a queen whose one fault was too great virtue, change with a single word the course of a reign and the destiny of France.

---

[1] These (*puisque la reine refuse le devoir*) are the very words used by Louis XV.

XXIX.

IN WHICH THE KING DOES NOT DO HIS DUTY.

EARLY the next morning, after an uncomfortable night in his lonely bed, Louis XV. noticed Richelieu among the courtiers who were assembled at his bedside reception.

The king was cross.

Any private citizen is likely to be cross when he has slept badly, — *a fortiori*, a king.

He refused to hunt; he refused to listen to the regular morning concert, and went to Mass in a very absent frame of mind.

He ate little, and was very surly about it; but he made up for his lack of appetite by grumbling to his heart's content.

He visited his horses, which he thought in bad condition, and yet there were no finer horses in Europe. They were the get of some English stock which Dubois had brought from London when he was there to negotiate the treaty of the Quadruple Alliance.

When the king's ominous gloom was observed, every one trembled.

Was he about to have an attack of sickness? Was Monsieur le Duc d'Orléans coming back from the dead to poison him?

For every one knows that from 1715 on, every indisposition of the king, however slight, served to start the report that he had been poisoned by Monsieur le Regent.

The king ill,— what a blow was that !

He had not so much as opened his mouth before it was known from one end of Versailles to the other that he was ill.

Thereupon the courtiers all tried to copy his expression, and began to berate the physicians

Toward noon, however, the king concluded to take a ride, and Richelieu obtained leave to accompany him. They entered the small park, and rode toward the ponds.

His attitude was like Hippolyte's, with bent head, and he said never a word.

Richelieu rode up beside him.

" Sire," said he, " pray pardon my affectionate zeal; I may perhaps offend your Majesty, but my motive will be my excuse."

" Say what you please, Duke, without fear of displeasing me," said the king; " are you not of my friends ?"

" Sire, how generous! " said Richelieu, bowing to his horse's mane.

" I see that your Majesty is bored," he resumed.

" True, Duke," was the reply; " but how do you see it ?"

" Sire, a king of your age and your personal attractiveness, a powerful king, with a bearing like yours, ought not thus to bend his head, and ride with dull eyes turned upon the ground."

" Ah, Duke, one may have his reasons for sorrow, although he be king."

" Does your Majesty wish for consolation at my hands ?"

" How will you console me ?"

" Listen to my code of morality, Sire."

" Oh, indeed I will listen, especially if you propose to talk morality."

"Why if I talk morality rather than anything else?"

"Because I know what is commonly understood by those words: 'morality *à la* Richelieu.'"

"I have your Majesty's permission, then?"

"Yes, indeed, I command you; amuse me."

"Do you know, Sire, how a young man attains to the possession of a shining eye, a quivering lip, and a well-shaped leg?"

"Duke, it may be that I do not know, and you must teach me."

"Sire," replied Richelieu, "I am only a simple gentleman, but there is some good blood in my veins; and when I was of your Majesty's age, if I was not as beautiful as the day, — as beautiful as you are, in short, — I was, nevertheless, lucky enough not to displease the ladies."

"I know it, Duke; at least you have that reputation, and he to whom everything that has been said of you should be told, would learn some fine things."

"Well, Sire, I am not a fop, and I never had any occasion to be."

"A fop!"

"The truth, Sire; what they say of me is the truth."

"I congratulate you on it.   But how did you go about it, pray?"

"How did I go about it?"

"Yes.   Delightful love-affairs don't fall to everybody's lot."

"No, Sire, that's very true; only to the lot of those who seek them, and know how to find them."

"That is not suitable employment for a king."

"In that case, Sire, a king must be content with your present employment, — that is to say, digesting a large allowance of ennui.   I, a simple gentleman, who have

not the same reasons that a king may have for treating
ennui with respect, have always done my best to keep
clear of it. So it was a pleasure to see me, at your
Majesty's age, with my bright eye and red lip, light
and airy as a bird. After all, Sire, it must be admitted
that it 's hard to amuse one's self under other conditions."

"I shall never amuse myself, Duke, in that case."

"Why so, Sire ? "

"Tell me, what you would do in my place ? "

"Oh, I will tell you that in short order. In the first
place, you are the master, are you not ? "

"Why, yes," said Louis, trying to smile; "at least
they tell me so."

"I am not a sufficiently bitter enemy of myself to try
to convince your Majesty that my society is altogether
unattractive; but I think it would be possible for your
Majesty to find some one whose society would be much
more attractive than mine."

"*Mon Dieu !* where could I find such a one ? "

"What you say and your manner of saying it are
equally flattering to me, Sire. But your Majesty has
but to look, I don't say among the men, for I am certainly one of the least tiresome of them, but among the
women."

"Oh, Duke ! " exclaimed the king, blushing crimson.

"Ah, Sire," continued Richelieu, "you must agree
to one thing: it is that if we are much more agreeable
to the women than others of their own sex are, they,
reciprocally, are much the more agreeable for us men."

"Do you think so, Duke ? "

"Try it, Sire."

"Come, Duke," said the king, with an impatient
gesture which delighted the courtier, "you are forever
saying, ' Try it, try it.' But how would you have me

try it? Is it such a simple matter, pray, to annoy a woman and follow her about?"

"In the first place, Sire, when one is king, and has a face like yours," replied Richelieu, "one never annoys a woman, or, to speak more accurately, one annoys them all. I am going to speak to you according to my own temperament; but, be sure of this, Sire, that if I were king, all the women in my court would have been annoyed. It is the royal prerogative. I would reign over the women as well as the men, — indeed I would make them my especial care. But what are we to do now? Your Majesty avoids opportunities; your Majesty frightens off the ladies; your Majesty arouses sentiments which you refuse to reciprocate. Sire, your ancestor Henri IV. would have been more charitable."

"He was too much so, Duke."

"Who complained of it?"

"The people."

"Sire, listen to the popular *chansons;* in them is the true voice of the people, and, as they say, the voice of God as well."

"Well?"

"Well, you will see, then, whom they like the better, — the *Vert-Galant* (Henri IV.) or Louis le Chaste (Louis XIII.)."

The king sighed, bent his head, and doubtless began a mental comparison of the respective merits of his two ancestors.

At this moment he and Richelieu, with their suite, had reached the great pond in the forest of Sèvres.

On the left a female equestrian, followed by two servants, emerged from the woods, and passed out of sight at a slow canter. As she saw the king, she stopped for a moment and bowed very low.

"Who is that?" asked the king, absent-mindedly, accustomed to much saluting, and weary of the incessant ceremonial.

"I don't know at all," replied Richelieu, assuming a most absorbed expression like his master's. "But does not your Majesty see a calèche under the trees? It should have the arms on the door. Will your Majesty permit me to send and find out?"

"Oh, it's of no consequence!" said the king.

But Monsieur de Richelieu had had time to make a sign to Rafté the knowing, and Rafté understood.

He galloped away; and returning at the same gait, whispered in Richelieu's ear what they both knew perfectly well before.

"Sire," said Richelieu, "it is the Comtesse de Mailly."

The king made a movement which Richelieu caught on the wing.

"I was saying to your Majesty," he continued, without seeming to attach the slightest importance to the meeting, "that you have too much regard for the people, Sire, and not enough for yourself. Monsieur le Duc d'Orléans, the regent, who watched over your Majesty with such zeal and devotion, whatever we may all have said to the contrary, had mistresses in profusion, did he not? Well, Sire, as he did not enrich them at the expense of the state, they were never made a ground of complaint against him; and then, too, does one ever know what kings are about when they wish it to be unknown?"

"Oh, Duke, as for that last, it's always known; Monsieur de Fleury has told me so over and over again."

"What, Sire, do you still believe everything that Monsieur de Fleury told you when you were a child? Come now, although Monsieur de Fleury is a most excellent man and a good priest, would you not rely more on your own common-sense, where love is concerned, than on his?"

"Duke!"

"For instance, Sire, excuse me, but we are now in front of the pavilion, are n't we?"

"True."

"Perhaps your Majesty has never been inside the pavilion, although it is your own?"

"Never."

"It is very neat and attractive within. It makes a most delightful place to rest in while hunting. It is occupied by no one but a porter, and the good fellow is more than seventy years old. I will wager that he does not even know your Majesty."

"It 's quite possible."

"But he knows me perfectly well."

"What are you driving at, Duke?" asked the king, apprehensively.

"I am trying to prove to your Majesty that the people know nothing of what their king does, when he does not choose that it should be known, and more especially when he bestows the great honor of his confidence upon a friend like myself. To-day, for instance —"

Richelieu checked himself, and glanced at the king.

"Go on, Duke," said he.

"To-day, if the king were called François I., Henri IV., or Louis XIV. —"

"What then?"

"He would be taking his ride with Lautrec, Bellegarde, or Monsieur de Saint-Aignan."

"Well?"

"He would enter the pavilion to rest a moment; and if he should see there a pretty, fascinating woman —"

The king blushed.

"*Parbleu!* Sire," continued Richelieu, " your Majesty just met her yourself, — the woman I was describing — "

The king became purple.

Richelieu persisted: " For, only a moment ago, Madame de Mailly, who was unfortunate in not being recognized by your Majesty, passed a short distance from us."

" She did pass us, true," said the king; " but what good — "

" I was just saying, Sire, that if your Majesty had directed somebody to say to that fair creature that the king wished to speak with her a moment, and you had both rested for a while in this pavilion, no one, except the walls of the building and the two people inside, would have the least knowledge of the episode."

" Nonsense! " exclaimed the king, tremulously.

" No, indeed, Sire; it's as I say."

" But, Duke, you are talking folly."

" I was never more serious in my life. Is not the happiness of my king at stake? "

" But, Duke, unless I have been very badly brought up, a king ought never to approach a woman thus."

" Certainly not without some pretext; but in this case it seems to me that your Majesty has every conceivable pretext."

" To approach Madame de Mailly? not one! "

" Now your Majesty is joking."

" Not in the least, I promise you."

" I could find a thousand, were I in your place."

" You are very fortunate! "

" Why, just think, Sire, there's one all ready to your hand."

" What is that? "

"Your Majesty yesterday appointed Monsieur de Mailly ambassador at Vienna."

"I certainly did!"

"Very well; what could be more natural than his wife's gratitude? But in very truth, your Majesty is so shy that at the bare sight of her skirts we spurred away as if the devil were after us."

"I did not hurry, Duke; it was my horse."

"Let's go into the pavilion a moment, Sire; as Paillasse says, it costs nothing to see it."

"Very well," said the king.

Richelieu's heart leaped for joy; he hastened to have the doors thrown open. Rafté quickly led the horses away to the stable, and then started off into the forest alone.

"You are right, Duke; this is a lovely place," said the king, who was delighted because he had not seen a single soul, not even the porter.

Like the clever fellow he was, Richelieu had got everybody out of sight.

The king approached a window.

"How pleasant the solitude is!" said he, with a sigh.

"Just consider, Sire, just consider," said Richelieu, "what a pleasant hour you might have passed here if you had not been Louis le Chaste!"

"Tell me, pray, you who talk of opportunities, where are they?"

"Do you deny that they exist, Sire?"

"Yes, indeed, I do."

"Ah! how do you reason that out?"

"It's easy to see, I should say. We have the pavilion, to be sure."

"That's something."

"But we have not the company."

He had hardly finished speaking when two horses, cantering, appeared at the end of the avenue commanded by the window at which they were standing.

The duke uttered an exclamation as if surprised, and said to the king, pointing at the group, —

"Look, Sire!"

"What is it?" asked the king, anxiously.

"See that lady coming this way."

It was, in fact, Madame de Mailly, who came cantering up, as if by mere chance, with the graceful seat of an expert horsewoman, followed by her two servants.

She was striking the leaves of the trees with her whip, and her lovely hair was flying in the wind. From time to time her dress, rising to the stirrup, afforded a glance of a dainty foot shod in hunting-boots of blue satin.

The king left the window. The countess was approaching, and he went and stretched himself out, with wildly beating heart, upon a couch draped with silken hangings.

Richelieu had darted out of the room. The king heard the measured hoof-beats drawing nearer and nearer.

Five minutes passed, during which the king, believing the danger to be at an end, recovered his courage and his breath.

But the door suddenly opened, and Richelieu came in.

"Sire," said he, "will your Majesty deign to receive the visit of Madame la Comtesse de Mailly?"

"The countess!" cried Louis.

"Enter, Madame," said the duke.

The king drew back in terror into the darkest corner.

Louise, pale with excitement, with swimming eyes and heaving chest, appeared bright and fascinating in a ray of sunlight, which was excluded again when the duke, as he left the room, shut the door behind him.

She stood courtesying upon the threshold, completely abashed and with eyes cast down.

The king did not stir or open his mouth.

Madame de Mailly, after a moment which seemed a century, remembered that she was the subject, and Louis the king.   Therefore it was her place to approach him.

She took a step forward, courtesied again, and murmured in a trembling voice, —

" Your Majesty — "

There she stopped, waiting for the king to speak; but he remained dumb.

Louise then sought him with her eyes, and saw him standing in a corner, quite out of countenance and trying to muster a little self-assurance.

She made a mighty effort.

" Sire, " said she, " I come to thank your Majesty very humbly for the favor you have conferred upon me in honoring my family with this embassy; also for allowing me to come and offer you my thanks. "

The king moved his head slightly, but remained in his corner.

Louise felt that her heart was failing her.   One could have heard its beating in the absolute silence which prevailed.

She remained standing, and the king's pale and trembling lips never uttered a sound.

She stood there ten minutes, awaiting a word or an encouraging gesture on the king's part; but instead of moving toward her, he seemed to be trying to dig holes in the wall with his shoulders, so that he might get even farther away.

At last, frozen with shame and despair, unable to collect her thoughts, faint with excitement, Louise, whose pride began to assert itself, bowed a last time, and left the room with her face bathed in tears without having uttered another word.

She found the duke at the foot of the staircase, which she descended stumbling at every step.

He took her by the hand, and then in his arms with a satisfied expression.

"Countess," said he, "allow me to be the first to congratulate you."

"Duke, I am dishonored forever!" cried Madame de Mailly, in so strange a tone that Richelieu looked more closely at her and understood.

"Oh!" he cried, — "oh, Countess!"

In few words Madame de Mailly told him the terrible affront she had received.

"What would you have, Countess?" said the duke; "he is a veritable Joseph. *Mordieu!* I thought that you would have more spirit than Potiphar's wife, but you had less. The fool did at least tear his cloak; but you, Countess, did n't even put your hand upon it."

Madame de Mailly could listen to no more; she rushed away with her hands over her eyes to hide her tears.

XXX.

IN WHICH PECQUIGNY SEEMS TO HAVE A BETTER CHANCE OF SUCCESS IN HIS SCHEMES THAN MONSIEUR DE RICHELIEU.

RICHELIEU approached the king with a dissatisfied expression. On this occasion silence was the best possible lesson.

He did not dare to speak, fearing that the king would be so angry with himself that he would be very glad of an excuse to vent his displeasure on the devoted head of his confidential adviser.

Furthermore it was embarrassing to know just what to say to this young man, if solitude, love, and his twenty years had said nothing to him.

So Richelieu saluted the king as he entered the room, and waited, standing on the same spot that Louise de Mailly had just left.

The king was sitting down in his corner, and had his head in his hands.

" Ah! " said he, " you 're there, Duke, are you? "

" At your Majesty's service. "

" Well, let us go, if you are willing. "

Richelieu gave a signal through the window.

" Let us go, " continued the king, " and find the queen, who may be uneasy at having seen nothing of me this morning. "

These words proclaimed the master, jealous of his secret, and hard to attack. Richelieu realized that his purpose was to keep him in his place, and make that place as humble as possible.

He made way for the king to precede him, gave two louis to the porter, and mounted his horse.

He had not ridden twenty paces in Louis' wake, when the latter began to feel very ill at ease.

Richelieu's features still wore his little sneering smile, which helped to console him for not being able to speak his thoughts. The smile spoke at least a fourth part of them.

But Richelieu's triumph, such as it was, was of short duration. At the end of the avenue, near the pond, they encountered a picket-post of light cavalry, who were apparently patrolling the neighborhood to insure the king's safety, but who were really on the lookout for the benefit of a horseman lying in ambush under the trees.

This horseman was Pecquigny, who, jealous like all courtiers, and knowing that the Duc de Richelieu had had the privilege of riding out with Louis, desired at least to get some idea of the purpose of the expedition.

He had seen Madame de Mailly pass, almost mad with joy, on her way to meet the king.

He had seen her return, pale, sobbing, and smarting with bitter resentment at the rebuff she had received.

He understood what had taken place, and his delight was unbounded; he desired, however, to make perfectly sure of the accuracy of his diagnosis. At the head of his handful of guards he could without intrusion pass near the king and study his features.

The puckered eyebrows, tightly shut mouth, and long face of the king left him in no doubt as to the truth; and if any further confirmation were needed, Richelieu's dismay at his approach would have afforded it.

"You here, Duke?" the latter asked.

"On duty," replied Pecquigny.

"How convenient it is, this duty at Versailles, is n't it, Pecquigny?" sneered the poor countess's crafty patron.

"It is even more convenient to have no duty at all, my dear Duke."

These words, exchanged as they rode by each other, disclosed to each the fact that his purposes were divined by the other.

In the twinkling of an eye Pecquigny passed from absolute hopelessness to most exuberant hope.

The king would have none of Madame de Mailly, therefore he was in love with Olympe.

It was his business not to lose a moment, but to exhibit to Louis XV. the beloved object in all the splendor of her unsurpassed beauty.

"*Corbleu!*" thought Pecquigny, "I knew very well that the king had better taste than that, and that that little thin crow of a Madame de Mailly would never stand comparison with Olympe, the beautiful, to whom the Greeks would have given all the names of all their Venuses. There's a woman for you! It shall be myself who will provide the king with a mistress; it shall be myself who will make a queen, and govern as long as she governs."

Thereupon he drove his spurs into his horse, and returned to Paris like a ray of light. Richelieu, who saw him start off, suspected his object, and sighed because he could do nothing to interfere with it.

He arrived at Rue Grange-Batelière, just as Olympe was telling Mailly of her visit to Charenton, omitting, of course, all reference to Bannière.

It was one of those rare moments of perfect harmony:

Hercules spinning at Omphale's side, while she triumphantly pulls out her slave's hair, and beats him over
the fingers with the distaff.

Dinner was at an end, and the lovers were by themselves in the drawing-room, when Pecquigny entered
the house like a thunderbolt, and carried by storm all
the doors, that of the drawing-room included.

The first object he saw was Mailly. We should have
said the first person, if it were not for the fact that at
that moment Mailly was of no sort of account. He was
acting as prompter to Olympe, while she recited the
lines of "Agnès."

Peace had been purchased at that price.

As they saw Pecquigny, Mailly turned pale and
Olympe turned red.

"Good-morning," cried the duke by way of prelude,
"good-morning to the two turtle-doves."

Mailly rose ceremoniously, and Olympe courtesied.

"What can I do for you, Monsieur le Duc?" demanded Mailly; "for you must be in great need of something to burst upon us in this precipitate fashion."

It was less rude than to say "Begone;" but it
amounted to that.

Pecquigny, who knew whom he had to deal with and
his peculiarities, replied, —

"Monsieur le Comte, I am perfectly well aware that
you have forbidden my calling upon Madame; and between ourselves, it was wretchedly bad form on your
part."

"It is also bad form, Monsieur le Duc, to force your
way in."

"Monsieur!" interposed Olympe.

"Pray, Madame," said Pecquigny, "don't be at all
alarmed. You are at home, are you not? Very well!

As I do not come on my own behalf, I come when I choose, and I remain. Monsieur le Comte may roll his fine large eyes around as much as he pleases; he may, if he prefers, receive me inhospitably. I care but little for that, being received by you and sent by the king."

Pecquigny dwelt upon these last three syllables with an accent which would have made a whole army ground their arms.

Olympe rose at the name of the king; while Mailly, who had remained on his feet, sat down.

Pecquigny followed his example.

"I will take a seat, since you invite me to do so, fair lady," he said, "and proceed with my errand. But first, Madame, for mercy's sake, tell this poor Mailly that a man can be in love without making himself ridiculous. *Cordieu!* does he think I am going to fly away with you without so much as saying 'Beware'? Come, Mailly, let us talk like sensible Christians. The future will take care of itself."

Mailly found his tongue at last.

"Duke," said he, "you persist in calling me ridiculous because I love a certain person and choose to defend her; be more charitable, or more of a man, I beg you. You come here to take Olympe from me; I propose to prevent you, and it is my right."

"My friend, Madame is much more securely protected by herself than by your whole regiment."

"Pshaw! flowers of rhetoric, fine phrases, with which men are lulled to sleep!"

"Great heaven, Count, you would tire out a saint! What! when I have declared to you that you have nothing to fear from me, and that if you chose to cross swords with me I would accommodate you; when you know that in that case I should fight for the king and

you against him; when you hear me say that the king
sent me to Madame, — you still insist in your obstinacy.
Why, my dear man, since the late Monsieur de Navailles,
who was a very virtuous and winning gentleman, we
have seen nothing like you. What a success you will
make at Vienna! "

"The count going to Vienna!" cried Olympe.

"I decline, I have declined," Mailly made haste to say,
seeing the effect these words had produced upon Olympe.

"Oh, indeed, you have declined! It's all very well to
say that before Madame. But you know perfectly well
that one doesn't decline to go where one is sent by the
king."

"I will show the king and all the king's messengers
whether an honest gentleman is to be torn from his
family and his — "

"And his wife, you mean!" said Pecquigny.

"Demon!" cried Mailly, "you abuse — "

"Don't lose your head, for then you will be in the
wrong twice over. However I will stop tormenting you.
I desired to ask Madame if she still has any inclination
for the stage, in which case the king directed me, as his
gentleman of the chamber, to enroll her in his troupe — "

"Don't beat about the bush, Monsieur le Duc,"
Olympe interposed; "Monsieur le Comte de Mailly
knows all our plans. I have no secrets from him."

"Oh, then I have no more pity for you, as I had just
now, my dear fellow. Madame, this call has no other
end, as they say, than to beg you to play the new piece
as soon as possible. The king is bored to distraction, and
craves novelty. He is waiting; and that, you know, is
not the habit of his race."

"Monsieur," rejoined Olympe, "the king does me much
honor; and to reply according to my feeble ability, but

with all my zeal in his service, I will say that I am ready; I know my part."

"Is it possible!" exclaimed Pecquigny, with undisguised satisfaction.

"I know it, and will play it whenever you choose."

"To-morrow, Mademoiselle, to-morrow."

"To-morrow, so be it."

"There is to be a first appearance to-morrow of some friend of an old friend of mine, an actor, who asked me for the order; it was little Champmeslé, — you know him, I suppose."

"Ah! Monsieur Champmeslé?" exclaimed Olympe, who was reminded by that name of the first performance of "Hérode et Mariamne" at Avignon.

"Do you know Champmeslé, too?" the pitiless tormentor inquired of Mailly.

"No," was the ungracious reply.

"Is Champmeslé coming back to the stage, Monsieur le Duc?"

"Not he, I think; and yet it may be. I don't know who it is; all I know is that I signed the order for his début."

"In what play?"

"In — wait a moment! — oh pshaw! in that tragedy where the woman talks about a *bandeau*."

"Ah, 'Monime'!"

"'Monime'? No, it's a man's name."

"'Mithridate'?" asked Olympe, with a smile.

"You have named it. Well, then, to-morrow, first this début, and you next; a pleasant evening in prospect. Oh, Madame, Madame, be sure to be on hand."

"And I, too, shall I not?" said Mailly, gloomily.

"Bah! you are always whining. Madame, we are agreed upon to-morrow."

Olympe showed Pecquigny to the door in great state, and Mailly listened eagerly till they had said their last word on the threshold. We may be sure, however, that the duke was careful not to say a word too much, for he knew that Mailly was on the alert.

"After all," said the count to Olympe, when she rejoined him, "you must yourself agree that it is very strange that a duke and peer, who is also gentleman of the chamber, should bring stage-bulletins to an actress with his own hands. I never heard of such a thing."

"You are not courteous, Count," said Olympe, coldly.

"He is too forward."

"Is it my fault? Do you propose to pick a quarrel with me for such a trifle?"

Mailly ground his teeth, and gave vent to his despair in a long-drawn sigh.

Poor man! how he would have sighed had he known to what Richelieu, whom he did not load with curses, had exposed his fair fame that same morning!

"What a fine thing is ignorance!" said Pecquigny to himself as he rode away. "Here is this poor Mailly ready to tear my eyes out on Olympe's account, although the king has never laid a finger upon her; and to-morrow, when he has certain reasons for his fury, he will perhaps embrace me and ask my pardon. What infernal fools men are!"

The duke was so well satisfied to laugh at others that he did not pause to reflect upon the part he had undertaken to play in the affair.

XXXI.

THE PROLOGUE TO " MITHRIDATE."

THE morrow, hidden in the darkness of the future, and which was impatiently awaited by so many people, — the morrow which was to shine upon scenes more touching, more sombre, more ridiculous, and more laughable than those of the tragedy and comedy which were to be performed for the king's delectation, — the morrow finally dawned.

Betimes in the morning Bannière made his way to the theatre, where he exhibited his credentials, and attended to the preparation of his costume.

As for the rehearsals, he had said, to the unbounded satisfaction of the other artists who were to act with him in " Mithridate," that a single one would be sufficient.

He made an appointment to meet his comrades at the tavern an hour before the rehearsal, and by the expenditure of two louis for a passable luncheon, he became acquainted with them, and established his reputation as what was known as a " good fellow."

During the repast, as they felt no embarrassment because of the presence of a good fellow, they slandered Olympe; but as Bannière had declared that he knew her not, even by name, he was not called upon to contribute.   Much wine was drunk.   Bannière alone drank nothing.

After this luncheon and dinner in one, Bannière walked about for an hour to collect his thoughts and marshal his ideas, so that he might be in a position to reap all the advantage of perfect coolness in such an undertaking as lay before him.

Sure of himself at last, he entered the theatre, not, however, until he had looked cautiously about to see that no suspicious figure was lying in wait to pounce upon him as he passed.

He went first to his dressing-room, to assure himself that everything was in order; and before dressing, for he had abundance of time, he walked up and down in the lobby where the actors came in.

He knew Olympe's invariable custom when she was to act in any play for the first time. Like a true artist, she always went to her dressing-room three hours in advance, so that she might be sure of having that length of time to herself.

She appeared just as Bannière was making his second circuit. He was in a bright light, and she in the shade. He felt her presence, and she recognized him.

She uttered a cry, darted back, and flew to her dressing-room, as if she had seen a ghost.

Bannière had an hour to himself before he need dress. He rushed to Olympe's dressing-room, found the door open, and halted in front of the young woman, who had fallen, almost fainting upon a couch, and was sobbing as women do when an hysterical attack is imminent.

"It is I," said he, — "I, Bannière! I am not a shadow, but good flesh and blood."

Olympe gradually straightened up, galvanized into new life by the sound of his voice.

"Yes," she murmured, "it is he!"

"And overflowing with sanity, as I will prove to you," rejoined Bannière.

Whether she detected in these words something in the

nature of a threat, or suspected some hidden meaning, or understood them as a direct reproof, Olympe, as soon as they were uttered, put on the armor of indignation.

"If you are not mad," said she, "by what right do you intrude upon the privacy of my dressing-room?"

"Madame," retorted Bannière, with gleaming eye, "I have the honor to inform you that however desirous you may be to turn me out, you have no right to do it. I make my début to-day, and the theatre is as much mine as yours."

"Oh!" exclaimed Olympe, marvelling at and admiring such audacity and cleverness, and such perseverance as naught but madness or love could make possible for a mere mortal.

"If," continued Bannière, "you say that in your dressing-room you are on your own premises, which is quite true, by the way, and if you say that my presence is distasteful to you, I will not inflict myself upon you: I have no such purpose. I will never, by force or by permission, remain with one who was base enough to deny me when I was suffering, — yes, dying for her sake."

But the proud girl, instead of defending herself, curled her lip in a disdainful smile, and held her peace.

"Oh, yes," continued Bannière, — "oh, yes, I understand; you thought me mad. You never thought to say to yourself that if I was mad, it was with love. You felt disgusted, fair, perfumed lady, at my appearance, and ran away as far as possible without even a look behind. And I understand it all; far or near, my presence was a bitter reproach to you. Ah! whatever my faults, however deplorable they may be, there is not one, I vow, for which I do not consider that your outrageous conduct has fully absolved me."

Olympe maintained absolute silence.

"Furthermore," Bannière went on, gradually yielding to the emotion caused by the proximity of the beloved one, "my faults are open to denial, and I have brought you the proof. Here, Madame, is La Catalane's letter, wherein she declares that I never was her lover. Here, Madame, is your ring. Read, reflect, and repent; if you have a heart, repent of the base treachery of which you were guilty toward me."

He threw upon Olympe's dressing-table the letter in which La Catalane confessed her trick, and beside it he threw Mailly's ring, that precious bauble kept concealed with such difficulty from prying eyes during the remarkable series of mishaps which we have narrated.

Olympe raised her eyes, which seemed to grow larger than ever with wonder, and fixed them first on the letter, then on the ring.

"Madame," he added, "you may as well know the rest now. To keep that ring, I more than half starved myself; but I lived" (here he raised his eyes toward heaven) "because God so willed. I followed painfully upon your traces on foot, slept a fortnight in the fields, and passed another fortnight without sleep in the dungeons of Charenton. But not even yet have I suffered enough, for to-day I have the happiness of convincing you of my loyalty, and can teach you what a loyal, unbounded, ineffaceable passion is capable of. Adieu, Madame, adieu! Be happy: I have my revenge!"

Olympe had listened, devouring every word; already she had read La Catalane's letter, and knew it by heart; already she had taken the ring, and placed it on her finger.

As Bannière made a movement to leave the room, she made a spring like a tigress, and barred the way.

"Did you do all that?" said she.

"Indeed I did; and many other things beside."

"What did you do?"

"Reaching Paris the very day of your début, I tried to force my way into the theatre, for I had no money to buy a ticket, and did not want to pawn the ring; and then it was that I was arrested and beaten, and that I assaulted the archers; and as I kept repeating over and over, not your name,— for, fool that I was, I was afraid of compromising you,— then it was that, as I kept shouting 'Julie! Julie! Julie!' they took me for a lunatic, and carried me off to Charenton, whence I escaped a week ago, that is to say, the day after you came there and saw me."

"You did all that?" exclaimed Olympe.

"Indeed, yes."

"Why did you do it?"

"What care you? I did it,— that's all I have to tell you."

"Tell me why you did it,— tell me, I say!" repeated Olympe.

"Do you really want me to tell you?"

"Yes."

"Well, I did it to be revenged."

"No, it was not for that."

Bannière turned away; but Olympe seized his hands and compelled him to look her in the eye.

"I insist," said she, "that you tell me why you did all that. Pray tell me, my poor boy, so that I need doubt no more,— so that I may believe you."

"Very well! I did it all—"

"You did it all—"

"I did it because I loved you, because I love you now, because I shall love you forever; because I am a miserable coward, and grovel here in tears at your feet, begging for mercy, when I ought rather to curse you, for you will kill me! "

" Oh! " cried Olympe, raising him from the floor and pressing him to her heart; " you do well to love me, for I love you even more dearly! Come, Bannière, come! Give me your tears, that I may drink them; give me your lips, that I may there find my life renewed! Alas, alas! I have died, and you will never find again the Olympe whom you used to know! "

Bathed in tears, and quivering with the force of her pent-up passion given full sweep, her strength failed her, and she let herself fall into the waiting arms of Bannière.

But she was the first to collect her forces.

" Fools that we are! " she cried; " why these exclamations of joy, these kisses, and this warm clasp of the hand? Alas, alas! we are no longer anything to each other."

" Olympe," cried Bannière, " don't say that; you don't mean it! "

" What! " said she; " for what reason did I leave you? Because I was as unfaithful as I believed you to be. I was wrong, and accused you wrongfully; but I have myself, alas! been unfaithful in fact."

" You forgave me, Olympe; I forgive you."

" Oh, no, no! your forgiveness would not be sincere, Bannière. You would always be jealous at the bottom of your heart, and your jealousy and my repentance would be two vultures who would gnaw at the vitals of our happiness."

" Oh, what are you saying, Olympe? Do you think that I am a man like other men; that my love is like the love of other men? Do you think that whereas I am to-day madly, deliriously in love, I shall be cold and demure to-morrow? Oh, no, Olympe, you are to me as the half of every breath I draw; you are more than that, — you are my whole life; without you I could not live! Such as you are, I will take you; such as you might be at any future time, I would still take and cherish you. Do not hesitate, Olympe, do with me what you will; but not a moment's delay, — hasten to pronounce your decree. Choose between my joy and my despair, between my life and my death! Oh, I know what you will say, — that you are bound, that Monsieur de Mailly loves you, that to lose you will cost him his life. All those who see you love you, Olympe, and those who have loved you die. It is fate. So be it! let him die, let me die, let the heavens fall, but henceforth let no other stretch out his hand toward you! Let none but myself lay his lips upon your lips! Olympe, they say I was mad; but if you refuse me, if you say no, I will become something much worse than a madman; I will become an assassin!"

"What do you ask?"

"You."

"When?"

"Now."

"Your hand."

"Here it is."

"What oath do you wish me to take?"

"Swear by the faith of Olympe de Clèves, which is to say the most honorable woman in my eyes who ever lived; swear by the faith of my wife!"

"By the faith of Olympe, Bannière," said she, solemnly, "before God, no man, while I live, shall put forth his hand to me, no kiss except yours shall touch my brow or my lip."

"I thank you. Do you act this evening?"

"And you, too."

"After the performance will you speak to Monsieur de Mailly?"

"After the performance I will do better than that."

"What will you do?"

"What I have already done once: I will go away with you."

"You will go with me!" cried Bannière, beside himself with joy.

"Do you agree?"

"Oh, Olympe, God did not make my heart big enough. I am stifling with happiness!"

"The clock is striking, and you are to act this evening. Say adieu to Olympe, and go."

"To my wife, do I say it?"

"To your wife."

"Adieu, Olympe!"

"Adieu, Bannière!"

"Till the last scene of 'La Fausse Agnès,' is it not?"

"Yes."

"One more kiss."

"Take ten."

But it was not ten or twenty or a hundred that they exchanged, — it was one long delicious embrace, during which their two hearts met in one endless kiss.

At last they tore themselves asunder, each with a joyous cry, so acute that it was almost a cry of pain.

Such was the scene which preceded the first act of "Mithridate."

O Racine, marvellous poet! doubtless thy pen described in fitter terms the love of Monime; but I can assure thee of one thing, — that it was not really so priceless a treasure as the love of Olympe de Clèves!

XXXII.

IN WHICH OLYMPE ASSURES MONSIEUR DE MAILLY THAT SHE WILL NEVER BELONG TO THE KING.

WE are not sufficiently intent upon making of Bannière a hero endowed with all the talents, as the English novelists say, to claim here that he made his début on the occasion in question in such fashion as to take his audience by storm, or to win a place for himself among the great names of the profession at the first blow.

Bannière unfortunately is a real personage, whose misfortunes and defects are noted in history; therefore we will not attempt to make of him something which he was not, and which he never became.

He made his appearance with no flourish of trumpets at the beginning of the evening, before the arrival of the king, who indeed was expected only for the second piece.

He had, moreover, a difficult part, and one but little suited to his youth and personal beauty.

His appearance took place under the incalculable disadvantage of a sense of expectation which would have been enough to destroy the effect of a far better performance than his: the expectation of the arrival of the king, and of the appearance of a distinguished actress, who had been very successful at her début.

Bannière, applauded at first and barely tolerated toward the middle of the piece, was roundly hissed at the fall of the curtain.

We hasten to say, however, as becomes a conscientious historian, that poor Bannière had not the slightest idea what he was doing, because his joy and excitement had carried him entirely beyond himself.

He spoke his lines ill, and he knew less than half of them. His extraordinary memory, which was largely responsible for his success at Avignon, seemed to have filled up in the course of an hour with all sorts of things which were not in the play at all, and of which the gentle Racine never dreamed.

When it began to be remarked in the fourth act that he was saying something quite different from his lines, the surprise, which was unbounded at first, began to give place to indignation.

There was muttering in the hall; and poor Bannière was so confused by it that he made one line fifteen feet long, and then, to even matters, put in one of nine.

Then they hissed.

Olympe, all dressed for " La Fausse Agnès," had taken a seat in the wings, to feast her eyes with the sight, not of the actor, but the lover, — not of Mithridate, but of Bannière.

She got comfortably seated just in time for the culmi- nation of a broadside of hisses which much resembled in intensity the hissing of a shower of bullets.

Bannière had seen her, and at once lost what few brains he had left. The words either became unrecog- nizable as they left his mouth, or died altogether on his lips.

When it occurred to him to have recourse to the prompter, it was too late.

The habitués of the theatre, who had at first fidgeted about on their benches and easy-chairs, and had then begun to exchange meaning signs, and in some cases words, with the occupants of the boxes, rose and went out one by one, scornfully shrugging their shoulders.

Then Bannière was in the position of Pompey, who had the gods against him, but Cato on his side.

Bannière had the chairs and the boxes and the pit, all against him, but Olympe was on his side.

Olympe's smile brightened up the tumult, like a messenger from gentle Iris when the skies are blackest.

She put her fan upon her lips, and looked at Bannière with a smiling face so full of heartfelt love that the finishing touch was put to the poor débutant's fascination.

Meanwhile the curtain fell, and Bannière with it; or rather he had fallen first.

Olympe, while all others were turning their backs upon him, went to him, pressed his hand affectionately, and whispered these words, —

"Only a little while now."

"Yes," replied Bannière; "and I was in a great hurry to make my failure, and have it over with, so as to hasten the blessed moment."

He disappeared, swearing that he would never again set foot upon the ungrateful stage.

Meanwhile Olympe, calm amid the chaos, looked about for Monsieur de Mailly, whom she was much surprised not to see.

She was not altogether free from uneasiness, for it might be that he had met Bannière and recognized him. Such a meeting would have deprived her of all the credit of taking the initiative, and what she had to say to Mailly would become a simple explanation.

Pecquigny had been among the witnesses of Bannière's failure, and exclaimed after it was over, —

"Well, well; he's a fine fellow, this protégé of Champmeslé! Let no one ever tell me after this that actors are good judges of acting!"

Time flew, the violins tuned up, and the king arrived. Monsieur de Mailly, too, made his appearance at last, and took his seat upon the benches.

Bannière had been in his dressing-room more than ten minutes.

" La Fausse Agnès " began.

Olympe's experience was just the reverse of poor Bannière's; she was encouraged and stimulated to the highest point by her emotions. She gave both hands to Pecquigny, instead of the one which she meant to give him; she modestly received the compliments which were showered upon her, and intercepted Mailly's imploring smile; she knew in advance just what would be the effect of her every step, her every gesture, her every word.

She acted like the consummate artist she was; she won admiration by her ideal beauty, and aroused universal surprise by her distinguished carriage.

The king said a thousand pleasant things to Pecquigny, but in a tone, nevertheless, which left Richelieu very calm and almost hopeful as he stood behind his Majesty's easy-chair.

As for Monsieur de Mailly, it would be safe to say that his eyes never left the royal box, and that every impression felt by his Majesty was reproduced in his mind and cut him to the heart.

The play came to an end, as expansive modern critics would say, amid perfect thunders of applause, so much the warmer and more enthusiastic because of the complete failure made by Bannière.

The curtain fell. Olympe, for whom a brilliant future was predicted on all sides, was overwhelmed with congratulations and adulation.

Monsieur de Mailly, after he had kissed her hand,

hastened back into the hall to glean what he could of the king's opinion and other interesting news.

Olympe threw flowers and notes and compliments into a corner, and changed her costume as rapidly as possible.

Monsieur de Mailly entered her dressing-room just as she had removed her rouge, and had had her hair arranged. The hairdresser, as soon as she saw the count, left the room without giving him time to make a gesture of dismissal.

Indeed Monsieur de Mailly's features expressed such a world of serious thoughts that the stranger, with the well-known sagacity of theatrical folk, might well have guessed that her presence would be *de trop*.

Olympe, surprised and annoyed by his air of solemnity, buckled on her armor, for she divined that the impending interview would be a struggle.

The count looked all about, went to the door through which the hairdresser had vanished to make sure that it was closed, and said at last, returning to the young woman, who had followed his movements with her eyes, —

" Olympe, you are quite alone, are you not? And you can listen without being disturbed to what I have to say to you ? "

" Ah, " said Olympe to herself, " he is going to speak of Bannière; he has seen him, he knows all ! "

" I am listening, Monsieur le Comte, " she said aloud.

" And with favorable inclinations, dear Olympe ? "

" You should not doubt it, Monsieur. "

" Olympe, I left you a moment just now. Oh, I know you did not notice it, but I went to mingle with those who were about the king during the performance, and I bring back some ideas which are not exactly mirth-provoking. You can form your own opinion. "

Olympe moved uneasily; but Mailly, with a motion of his hand, asked her so imploringly to have a little patience that she waited.

"Allow me to tell you my sorrowful story," said Mailly. "You know, Olympe, that I am married."

"I know it," said Olympe, dryly, unable to understand why Mailly began the conversation with those words.

But he went on without seeming to notice the tone of her response.

"You know that Madame de Mailly is considered to have some claims to beauty."

"Yes, she is so considered," replied Olympe, more dryly than before.

"Very well! Olympe, the king has fallen in love with my wife, and some of my *friends* (one always has such friends) have undertaken to bring his inclination for her to a successful issue."

"Then Madame de Mailly no longer loves you, Monsieur?" rejoined Olympe, evidently perplexed by this preamble, and in haste to reach the dénouement.

"No," said Mailly, "she no longer loves me, Olympe, as you say; but she is my wife, and she bears my name."

"Well, what then?" Olympe asked with some uneasiness.

"Wait a moment, I beg you—"

"But—"

"You would prefer, perhaps, that an interview should take place at your own apartments? I should prefer it also, Olympe, but it cannot be postponed."

"Indeed!" said Olympe, returning to her first fear.

"I will say now what I have to say. Here is the king threatening my wife, and appointing me ambassador to Vienna, as Monsieur de Pecquigny said yesterday."

"And the purpose of that is to send you away from your wife, is it not?"

"Yes; but I have declined the appointment."

"Like a worthy husband."

"Don't be in a hurry to determine the cause of my declination, Olympe."

"Oh, *mon Dieu!* you declined, of course, on account of your conjugal sense of your duty to Madame de Mailly."

"No, Olympe. I declined on account of my love for you."

"Oh, Monsieur!"

"Be patient, Olympe, and I will give you sufficient proof that such is the fact; but first swear to me that you will answer my questions with absolute frankness."

"It is useless for me to swear it, Monsieur; it is not in my nature to answer in any other way. I have never deceived you."

"Very well. It is, I say, solely for love of you that I have declined the mission. It would take me away from you, Olympe; and in very truth, the king, not content with threatening my wife, threatens my mistress also."

Olympe shook her head.

"Oh, don't say no, Olympe! It is proved; I was told just now that the king thought you most beautiful, and desired to know you; and fresh schemes against my happiness and my honor are being concocted. Olympe, I appeal to your loyalty; alas! how much better I should like to say that I appeal to your love!"

"Go on, Monsieur," said Olympe, coldly.

"I am well aware that you have no great depth of affection for me, dear Olympe, and that it is naught but your spotless probity which has kept you faithful to me; but you know so well that I love you better than all the world, it has been proved to you so abundantly, that I will not weary you by reiterating it. It is now for you to decide my fate; you are to make or mar my whole life; for I confess that the separation from you which I took so little to heart a year ago, would be an impossibility for me to-day, and would surely be my death. Without you, Olympe, the whole world contains no joy for me. Swear to me, Olympe, that you will never yield to the king."

Olympe made a movement as if to speak.

"Swear this to me," Mailly went on, "and I will do that for you which man never did for his mistress, — I will cease to defend my wife against the king. Imitating the Arabs, laden with booty, who when pursued cast away the less valuable objects as a lure for their pursuers, who stop to pick them up, I will abandon my wife and my honor to the king, only too happy to rescue you if you are willing to help me a little. Two courses are open to me: if you will go away with me, I will accept the mission offered me; if you remain here, then I will decline it, and remain with you.

"In that case I shall, as you see, have lost what little favor I have at court, as well as my wife. The king, who would forgive me if I were to accept compensation, would wreak his vengeance upon me if I were to leave him alone in his dishonor. You have heard me, Olympe; take a little time to reflect, if your heart does not dictate an immediate response, and let me know what I am to expect at your hands."

There was so much true love and so much humble resignation in the count's words, his embarrassed demeanor betrayed so much nobility of soul and restrained emotion, that Mademoiselle de Clèves had a feeling akin to remorse.

She was too generous herself, however, to remain long irresolute at such a crisis.

"Monsieur le Comte," said she, "I shall never yield to the king."

"Oh!" cried Mailly, in ecstasy, "the mere word of such an honorable woman as you are, Olympe, is more sacred than an oath. You will never yield to the king; thank you for that. Then you will be mine alone! Oh, how good you are, Olympe! Shall I accept the embassy, and shall we leave for Vienna together? Oh, what bliss! Or do you cling to your Paris, dear love, and will you give me the joy of making my sacrifice complete by refusing the embassy, and submitting to disgrace here?"

"Monsieur le Comte," said Olympe, after a moment's hesitation, carefully weighing all her words, for she knew their importance, "do not accept the office; it is much the nobler course to remain and protect your wife who bears your name."

"But what about you?" cried Mailly, amazed at this reply,— "you, at whom all the king's attacks are aimed?"

"Oh, I shall be well protected," replied Olympe, boldly.

"Protected?"

"Yes, Monsieur de Mailly, the woman who loves is never conquered except by the object of her love."

Mailly changed color.

He knew Olympe well, and did not feel that her affection for him was great enough to permit her to say such pleasant things of him.

"Olympe, Olympe, there is some one whom you love!" said the count, looking in vain on her features for the smile which he tried to summon to his own.

"There is, Monsieur, and my word is given."

" Your word for what ? "

" To marry."

" When did this happen, for God's sake ? "

" Two hours ago."

" Olympe ! " cried Mailly, " what are you saying ? "

" I say that this evening, Count, I am to marry the man whom I love."

The count became deathly pale, and almost lost consciousness.   He was suffocating.

" Pray tell me who the man is whom you love without my knowledge, Olympe ? "

" You are mistaken, Monsieur, you do know that I love him."

" Why, so far as I know, Olympe, there is but one man ; and that is — "

The door of the dressing-room opening at this moment interrupted the count, and Bannière appeared on the threshold with beaming, transfigured face.

The count fell back as if he had seen a ghost.

XXXIII.

IN WHICH MAILLY DECIDES TO ACCEPT THE MISSION.

OLYMPE held out her hand to Bannière, who had stopped short on the threshold as he perceived Monsieur de Mailly.

"The man whom I love," said she, "is here before you, Monsieur le Comte; it is he whose name was on your lips,— Monsieur Bannière. I thought I had ceased to love him, for I believed he had deceived me. He did not deceive me, and I have the proof that he did not. I love him still; I ask your forgiveness, Monsieur le Comte."

The profound amazement of Bannière, the complete prostration of Mailly, and the proud and courageous bearing of Olympe combined to make a tableau which did not lack interest.

Olympe rose, took the count's hand, and said to him,—

"You are a brave and worthy gentleman, Monsieur le Comte, and one does not deceive men like you! God is my witness that I would rather suffer myself than cause you to suffer. But, alas! I am not the mistress of my feelings, nor of those which I cause in others. Fate has placed before me the cruel alternative of being either cowardly or barbarous in my dealings with you. You would prefer, I am sure, that I should choose the latter course, which is the only one consistent with loyalty. I throw myself upon your mercy, Monsieur le Comte, — my·

self and the man whom I love; you are powerful enough
to crush us both like reeds. Use your power as your
heart dictates; and if you do not force me to bless you,
be sure that I will never curse you, whatever may
happen."

The count did not raise his head.

Bannière, a shade paler even than the poor martyr,
because he knew what agony the count must be enduring
at that moment, effaced himself with true delicacy, and
admired from afar the awe-inspiring woman whose every
word held the means of life or death.

"You have made me wealthy, Monsieur le Comte,"
she continued. "Do not think I will, from any false
modesty, leave here the trinkets and the gold you have
given me; no, you are too great a nobleman to permit
me to pass from your house to indigence. Believe me
when I say that if I had not found Bannière again, my
thoughts would never have wandered away from you;
but the fate which guides all our footsteps had written
that it was to be. Command, and I obey; but first, I
humbly ask your forgiveness for the apparent cruelty of
my endeavor to be absolutely straightforward. Oh,
Monsieur le Comte, reflect that if I did not say to you
what I am saying to you at this moment, I should not
be worth the shadow of the grief which my words de-
pict upon your face."

The count rose. Passing an icy hand across his brow,
he said, —

"It is well, Mademoiselle; you are, indeed, an honest
woman, in every acceptation of the word, and I most
sincerely declare to you, while I do full justice to
the loyalty of your motives, that you have caused me
to-day the greatest anguish which my life has ever
known."

Turning to Bannière, who stood motionless with throbbing heart, for this marvellous generosity of which he felt himself incapable had moved him to the inmost depths of his soul, —

"I am too deeply afflicted," said he, "to congratulate Monsieur upon his good fortune. The only wish which I have the strength to form, Mademoiselle (and I doubt not, it is so sincere on my part, that it will be fulfilled by Providence), is that he will make you as happy as you deserve to be; as happy as I would have liked to make you, if he had not, unfortunately for me, been in the way to prevent it."

Having said this, Monsieur de Mailly saluted Olympe with the utmost respect, took several steps at random, as if vainly seeking the door, and at last went out, leaving the two lovers in the midst of their happiness plunged in the deepest sadness they had ever known.

Olympe hid her face in her hands, and the tears forced their way out between her fingers to fall upon the table on which her elbows were placed.

Bannière, motionless, dumb, and gloomy, did not try to comfort her; he realized the great depth of the love she had cast aside, — all the nobility of the heart which was ground to atoms without pity, to make the course of his true love a little more smooth.

Gradually the theatre became deserted, until the two lovers remained alone in the silence and darkness.

Monsieur de Mailly's step became firmer after he left the dressing-room. The catastrophe which had fallen upon him was so great and so complete that it imparted new vigor to all his physical faculties. Mentally he was a total wreck.

In the vestibule of the theatre the count espied a man seated upon a bench, leaning against a piece of statuary, and playing calmly and without the least sign of impatience with one of his legs, which he was dancing up and down on the other.

Twenty feet away from this man, whose hat was drawn over his eyes, two servants in the Richelieu livery were standing with uncovered heads.

Mailly took no precautions against being recognized, but passed at a rapid pace directly in front of the idler.

As he passed, the latter rose.

"Hallo there!" he cried; "Mailly!"

The count turned quickly, thinking that he recognized the voice.

"Monsieur de Richelieu!" he exclaimed.

"Good evening, Mailly."

"Good evening."

"How goes it?"

"Very well."

"I was waiting for you."

"For me?"

"Yes, of course; you see, don't you, that everybody else has gone, and that we two are alone *here*."

He emphasized the word "here" very significantly.

Mailly stopped, but made no reply.

"Well, my poor Mailly," said Richelieu, "I asked you how things were going with you."

"And I answered, 'Very well.'"

Richelieu shook his head.

"Yes, very well," Mailly repeated; "and I am especially delighted to meet you here."

"Nonsense!"

"You can do me a great service."

"Willingly, my dear friend."

"You can try to arrange that affair for me."

"What affair?"

"Yes, I know that it will be difficult. But as you were able to tie the knot once — "

"Well ?"

"You will probably be able to do it a second time."

"What knot are you talking about ? "

"Why, in that Vienna business."

"Ah, very good ! "

"You see what I mean."

"I was waiting for you for this express purpose."

"It is feasible, then ? "

"Entirely so."

"And the king ? "

"What king ? "

"King Louis XV."

"What about him ? "

"He is not too indignant ? "

"Indignant for what reason ? "

"Because of my refusal."

"The king does n't know that you refused."

"The king does n't know it ? "

"Why, you understand, my dear fellow, that I either am your friend or am not."

"Yes."

"Very well! if I am your friend, it is not for the purpose of disgracing you."

"Oh, how kind you are, Duke ! " said Mailly, with a smile, from which he tried in vain to extract the bitterness.

"Oh, don't laugh, Mailly; he is a better fellow than you think, this Duc de Richelieu, and it was no easy matter to keep your peace with the king."

"Pray believe that my gratitude is commensurate with the service done."

"Then it is very great, and sufficient for my purposes. So you have decided, have you ? "

"Yes, I desire to leave France."

"You are quite right."

"I would like to go to the end of the world."

"Stop at Vienna on the way, and be content with that; that is quite far enough, you will find."

"Oh, the grief I carry with me," said Mailly, pressing his hand upon his heart, "will not fail to follow me as far as that, Duke, never fear!"

"Grief? Oh, yes, grief gallops, I know, although I have never experienced anything more severe than disappointment, myself. Poor Mailly!"

"Pity me."

"Why not, if you are to be pitied?"

"Do you deny it?"

"Pshaw! you are not going to try to make me think that you regret your wife?"

"I regret nothing."

"Oh, yes; you regret Olympe. But what would you have, my dear Count; these infernal theatrical women, when they have once lowered themselves, are unmanageable. Ah! the woman who emancipates herself is worth ten men; but she has treated you badly, my poor friend."

"Ah! do you know of that?"

"Why, don't I know everything? But you can at least be revenged upon her."

"Be revenged on Olympe?"

"Well, if not on her, you can at least get even with the man."

"With the man?"

"Yes; did he not enlist in your dragoons at Lyons? Is he not a sort of deserter?"

"Oh!" cried Mailly, putting his hand to his head, "you remind me — The poor wretch! Come, speak quickly, Duke!" said he to Richelieu. "You were waiting for me, you said?"

"Yes, luckily for you."

"Why so? Come, let us make haste."

"Because after the disease, I bring you the cure."

"Explain yourself."

"You desire to start for Vienna?"

"Yes."

"You accept the mission?"

"Yes."

"Well, my dear fellow, here is your commission."

With that the duke drew from his pocket the same paper which he had previously offered the count, and which the count had refused to take.

"What!" said Mailly, in amazement, "you have kept it all this time?"

"I was so sure that you would come and ask me for it," said Richelieu, laughing, "that I have not been without it for a moment since the last time I saw you."

"Give it me, then."

"Here it is."

"Thanks! I am off at once."

"Faith! it's none too soon."

These words roused Mailly anew from the gloomy thoughts in which he was absorbed; but, as if he deemed it useless to invite the infliction of another blow, harder to bear, perhaps, than those that had gone before, he waved his hand to the duke, and left the theatre.

Richelieu, who had remained seated during the whole interview, now rose and stretched his arms and his well-shaped legs, clad in silken hose.

"*Parbleu!*" said he, "there's a very lucky man. At one blow he is freed from two terrible creatures. Henceforth the rascal will be a great favorite. How I pity the first woman he comes in contact with: he will drive her mad with love of him! It only shows," he added philosophically, "that the happiness of some always leads to the unhappiness of others, and *vice versa*."

Thereupon Richelieu called his servants, and ordered his carriage. As he was entering it, he saw Olympe leave the theatre by a side door, leaning on the arm of a young man.

It was half after twelve.

The duke followed them for a moment with his eyes, then said to himself, —

"*Parbleu!* I lost an opportunity there: I ought to have given Richelieu a trial against that creature. What a fine struggle that would have been! But it's too late now."

The servant approached the door.

"Well, what is it?" asked Richelieu.

"Monsieur le Duc gave no orders."

"True; drive home, — nowhere else."

But almost immediately he detained the man with a gesture.

"Oho!" he thought, "I should say I came very near making a fool of myself. Mailly is far enough gone this evening to ask his wife's pardon and take her off to Vienna with him, while Pecquigny is filling the king's head with Olympe. *Peste!* I should make a great mistake not to keep an eye on the dear countess."

"To the Hôtel de Mailly," said he, "and quickly!"

Monsieur de Richelieu's carriage always moved quickly without any special orders to that effect; the order having been given, they went off at a gallop.

Five minutes later he alighted at the door of the Hôtel de Mailly.

Richelieu was in error; Mailly was not thinking of carrying off his wife.

He was writing to Olympe.

XXXIV.

THE WEDDING.

OLYMPE, as we have said, had left the theatre on Bannière's arm, while Monsieur de Richelieu was talking with Mailly under the porch.

At the door both entered a fiacre which had been called for them by the hairdresser.

Bannière had taken the precaution to have it in readiness; this, among other things, he had attended to immediately upon the favorable ending of his explanation with Olympe. He was a lad who could at need guide the course of events or subdue wild horses.

The driver had received his instructions beforehand. He drove them straight to the Chapel of Notre-Dame de Lorette, near the office of the Porcherons.

There was a vast difference, however, between the Notre-Dame de Lorette of 1730 and that of 1851.

The little chapel, a branch of Saint-Eustache, fronted on a narrow square, formed by the junction of the Montmartre road, Rue des Porcherons, and Rue Notre-Dame de Lorette.

When the two lovers set out upon their pilgrimage, the night, already half spent, had shrouded in blackest darkness the cemetery of Saint-Eustache, which was but few steps from the chapel, and the vast meadows lying between the boulevard and Montmartre.

Rue Notre-Dame de Lorette, to-day one of the gayest little streets of the capital, was not built at this time, nor was the Montmartre road paved. More than that,

as the municipal authorities had not bestowed any street-
lanterns upon that quarter, it was as lonely as it was
dark.

Aside from the dripping of the muddy waters of the
great open sewer, and the rustling of the reeds and bul-
rushes in the marsh, no sound could be heard save the
straining of the fiacre up the rough slope.

A straggling ray of moonlight, slipping out now and
then between two clouds, silvered the little doorway of
the chapel, and cast a gleam of light, often obscured by
the rising mists, upon the front of two narrow wings,
one on each side of the chapel.

But the feeble light of a candle glimmered behind one
of the windows on the ground-floor of the parsonage, and
by its rays Olympe could distinguish the figure of a man
standing behind a curtain and waiting.

The fiacre stopped, and the door flew open.   Bannière
leaped out first, received Olympe in his arms, and
trembled in spite of himself, as he felt her warm, sweet
breath upon his face; drawing her after him, he went to
the little door of the wing in which the lighted window
was, and knocked.

The door was at once opened.

The man who was waiting was no other than Champmeslé.

He admitted the lovers, closed the door behind them,
and led them through a side entrance into the choir of
the little chapel, where they found themselves suddenly
in a brilliant light.

The altar was illuminated with six huge wax tapers,
and a profusion of flowers in all the vases imparted a
festal aspect to the chapel.

At a sign from Champmeslé, Bannière and Olympe
took their seats in front of the altar.

The former actor gazed for a moment without speaking at the lovely girl, pale and trembling to find herself in God's presence, and eager to make atonement for her errors with heartfelt repentance.

Champmeslé's strange personality was not lacking at that moment in solemn poetic sentiment.

Olympe and Bannière returned his gaze with a tender, respectful smile.

"Madame," he began, "this man" (and he pointed to Bannière) "loves you to the extent of being willing to sacrifice his body and soul for you at the same time. Alas! young as I am in my religious life, I know what ravages the tender passion is capable of working in the human heart. I know, too, how essential it is, even if it is not possible to preserve for God's service the whole heart and the whole mind, to preserve as much as may be of both. It is to make it possible for Bannière to live with due reverence to God, while following the dictates of his passion, that I am here, trying, like the dove of the Ark, to carry the olive branch from one of you to the other; so that he may have the right henceforth to pray for you and for himself in the same breath; so that every prayer that he utters may comprise an element of gratitude to me for having assisted him with all my power when he was anxious to find you again, and join his fortunes again with yours.

"Reflect, Madame, what an agitated life yours has been, brief though it be in years.

"Tell me what will become of that soul which is buffeted about by misfortune and passion, as a dismasted ship by the winds and waves? It is true, is it not, that you yourself cannot say? Seek a harbor, then, I beseech you; take refuge on the bosom of God, who will then bestow his blessing upon your love. Be a virtuous woman; bind yourself by a solemn oath to God, the only oaths which women in this world seem to have no right to violate."

Olympe rose with much dignity, and with even less color than usual.

"Monsieur," said she, in a voice so melodious and sweet that the arches of the chapel shivered, as when caressingly touched by the strains of a harp, — "Monsieur, you have done well to invoke God's law to recall me to myself. I was well aware that I was born to love, but I shall know hereafter that I must love none but Bannière, and my title of wife will be in my eyes a sacred barrier which I swear never to cross.

"But the service you are doing me is much greater in respect of other people than of myself. Other people, Monsieur, have seen in me a woman abandoned by men (I mean no reproach to any one) and abandoned utterly by God; and they have exercised over me that measure of authority which was due to their power and to my own weakness, the deplorable result of my pride. Henceforth, since I have an arm to lean upon, and am endowed with the title of legitimate wife, they will no longer be formidable to me, nor need I even look upon them as enemies.

"I thank you, therefore, Monsieur, and I pray God to receive my oath; I shall never be called upon to take one which will be more sweet to me, or more easy to keep."

With these words Olympe turned to Bannière, and with a glance of ineffable affection laid a cold trembling hand in his. All her blood poured back upon her heart.

Bannière, trembling beneath the precious burden, said not a word to good Champmeslé. He placed his lips upon Olympe's forehead, and stood for some moments mute and pale, as if his heart were overburdened.

Champmeslé left the chapel in quest of a young choir-boy, who was sleeping upon a bench, and began the service at the moment when a new day began, — as the clock was striking one in the morning.

Never was solemn function performed with deeper religious fervor. The two lovers shed tears of joy and love, and asked themselves why, when eternal union is so blissful a state, wretched mortals so often prefer that liberty which is the cause of untold woe.

Champmeslé was so profoundly moved that he could not refrain from kissing the bride, and saying to her as he performed that operation, —

"I can readily understand, Madame, that with your great talent and your peerless beauty it must cost you a pang to give up the stage; but it is a sacrifice which your salvation demands."

The two young people stared at the abbé in utter amazement.

"Why," Bannière timidly remonstrated, "you must not forget, my dear Abbé, that we are poor, my wife and I, and that, consequently, we cannot leave the stage out of our calculations."

"*Mon Dieu!*" cried Champmeslé; "is there no other means of livelihood in the world, pray?"

"Remember," said Olympe, with a smile, "that it is not open to him to turn abbé, as you have done."

"However, it seems to me that one may be an actor and an honorable man at the same time, Monsieur Champmeslé," ventured Bannière, "and you, thank God! are a living proof of my position."

"I do not say no to that," replied Champmeslé; "but listen to me carefully, my dear Bannière, and may the sanctity of the place where I stand be my justification for my profane words — for I am going to speak to you as a man — what do I say? — as an actor, and not as a priest."

"Say on, we are listening," said Bannière, with a smile.

"Very well! the stage, even if it is not a place of everlasting perdition for you in God's sight, will surely be your ruin, from the point of view of your worldly happiness."

"I don't understand you," said Bannière, who did, on the contrary, understand only too well; and the chord which the abbé was about to touch began to vibrate in anticipation.

"Yes, viewed in the light of your own happiness," continued Champmeslé; "for it will be bitter suffering for you to see your wife constantly flattered, worshipped, and courted for her charms and her talent."

Olympe made a movement as if to speak.

"*Mon Dieu!*" Champmeslé hastened to say, "I am far from hinting that all these wiles will not fall powerless before the virtue and love of Madame Bannière, who is a noble woman; but — "

"But what?" said Bannière, uneasily.

"Go on, finish, my dear Abbé," said Olympe.

"Oh, you understand me, Madame," said Champmeslé, "and it is useless for me to finish. You know very well that those wretches sometimes resort to force and treachery, when straightforward advances to actresses have failed of success."

"Yes, some great lord, you mean, dear Abbé, do you not?" said Bannière, knitting his brow.

"Monsieur," said Olympe, gently and with undisturbed serenity, "do not think ill of the absent."

"Alas!" said Bannière, "an evil impulse may, when pride has had a fall, lead the best men into sin."

"I am right, then," rejoined Champmeslé. "Very well! let me enter into your private affairs a moment, go over the figures with you, and prove — "

"Here?" queried Olympe, smilingly.

"No, let us leave the sanctuary," said Champmeslé, while Olympe pressed one of his hands, and Bannière the other; "let us go into the little parlor of the parsonage, and be grateful to the worthy man who consented to yield his place to me for the night, so that I might have the privilege of making you happy forever."

"Wait a moment," said Olympe. "Before I leave the chapel, allow me to put in the poor-box the modest sum which we in our happiness wish to bestow upon the poor."

"One moment!" cried Champmeslé, arresting the little hand, between whose fingers glistened a double louis.

"Why?" said she.

"Because there are poor and poor," said Champmeslé. "Come out into the parlor and let us talk it over."

He led them out of the chapel, dismissing the choir-boy with a piece of money which he slipped into his hand; and closing the door of communication, which separated them from the sanctuary, he gave each of them a seat upon an oaken stool polished by age, sat himself down before them, and took a hand of each.

"Now let us see," he began: "now that we are at home, — and take my word that I have excellent reasons for saying what I am about to say to you, — let us reckon up your wealth. This is addressed to you alone, Madame, for I am well acquainted with Bannière's resources."

"Yes, the ten crowns which I owe you," said our hero, with an affectionate smile.

"Therefore, as I said," rejoined Champmeslé, "I addressed myself to Mademoiselle de Clèves alone."

"Monsieur and dear friend," said Olympe, "I have almost a hundred louis in jewelry, and two hundred in dresses, linen, and furniture, which I can sell."

"Do you mean to sell them?"

"Most assuredly."

"Why so?"

"Because our intention — my husband's, that is, and mine — is to leave Paris; we should run too much risk here, and living is too expensive."

"Then you will go — "

"To Lyons, where my name is known; to Lyons, where I know what we may depend upon; to Lyons, where I can earn an honorable living in my profession, without being compelled to be an actress elsewhere than on the stage."

"In order to get to Lyons, you will have to spend ten louis each."

"Almost."

"That makes twenty louis, to begin with."

"Yes."

"And a big hole in your treasure. That is not all, either, as I will show you. After you reach Lyons you will be quite two months without an engagement, and during those two months you must live."

"Well, with two hundred livres a month, my dear Abbé," said Bannière, "we shall be all right."

"Oh, Madame could never live by herself on such a pittance as that," said Champmeslé. "I leave it to her to say."

"Olympe de Clèves could not," said the young woman,

"but Madame Bannière will do many things which Olympe de Clèves didn't do."

"And that is precisely what you must avoid," urged Champmeslé. "Madame de Bannière ought, on the other hand, to be happier than Olympe de Clèves ever was; otherwise, our purpose is defeated."

"Yes; but our purpose will be accomplished if we both act," said Bannière. "Olympe, with her great talent, can earn six thousand livres, and I can earn twelve or fifteen hundred. I know perfectly well that they will give them to me solely on her account, but that matters little, so long as I get them; and with that sum — that is to say, six thousand livres for her, and fifteen hundred for me, each spending what he earns, — we shall be perfectly happy."

"Marriage," said Olympe, "means equal division."

"Well, for all your reasoning, and despite your mutual love and devotion, I persist in imploring you not to return to the stage."

"In that case," said Olympe, "we should die of hunger, my friend; and allow me to suggest to you that it cannot be agreeable, in God's sight, that a husband and wife, who honor and glorify him by the purification of their love, should die of hunger, lose their life in this world, to assure their salvation in the other."

"No," replied the abbé. "And for the very reason that it cannot be agreeable in God's sight that such should die of hunger, take notice, dear friend, that God always sends succor, when succor is merited, and often when it is not."

"Oh!" exclaimed Bannière, with an incredulous shake of the head.

"God is very good," said Olympe, with much the same feeling; "but he said, 'Help yourself and Heaven will help you.'"

"But, after all," cried Champmeslé, whom one would have expected to be crushed by this quotation from Holy Writ, "would you not be very grateful to God, if he should supply you with the means of securing your immortal welfare and of living in happiness at the same time, — of living side by side, hand in hand as you are at this moment, until Bannière finds some honorable position, such as cannot fail to fall in the way of a man of his attainments, or until one of those events which change human destinies befalls you?"

"Dear Monsieur de Champmeslé," said Olympe, "we should indeed be very happy, we should indeed be very grateful to God; but where are these means? It will not be, my word for it, by holding our hands tightly clasped, while we dream of our love, as we are doing at the present moment, that we shall attain that happy existence which your question foreshadows."

"Who knows?" said Champmeslé.

"Oh, Monsieur de Champmeslé, there are, I am well aware, untold treasures in the love of God, but they are not temporal treasures, which are met with everywhere on earth. They find pearls in oysters, purses on the highway, a rich inheritance at the bottom of a notary's drawer; but beyond the borders of this world, Monsieur de Champmeslé, poor lovers can hardly expect to find the means of living corporeally, and just ask Bannière if he is not inclined to live in the flesh as long as possible."

"Faith, I am, indeed," said Bannière; "I am so happy!"

"Well, let us see," said Champmeslé; "suppose for a moment that the good God, moved by your earnest desire to do right, should vouchsafe to perform a miracle for you; suppose that you should find in your path one or the other of those temporal treasures which appear to be more to your taste than those which flow from the grace — "

" Let us not suppose that, dear Monsieur de Champmeslé," said Bannière; "for that is precisely the supposition which I built upon with more chance of success than I have at this moment."

" When was that ? "

" Every time that I took my dear Olympe's money to gamble with. 'If God would perform a miracle in my favor,' I would say, ' and I should win a fortune — ' "

" Well, what then ? "

" Why, I invariably lost, dear Abbé. What God did not do for me when I was helping myself, he will be less likely to do if I wait for fortune to come and seek me in my bed, in accordance with the advice of Monsieur de La Fontaine, your grandfather's collaborator. Oh, if I only had all the money I threw away so foolishly ! "

" You threw it away, my good friend," rejoined Champmeslé, evidently bent upon convincing Bannière; " you threw it away and lost it, because God does not approve of gambling."

" But," Bannière ventured to say, " those who won from me were also gambling."

" Perhaps, in winning, they lost much more than you did. But come, accept a supposition."

" If it 's one that can possibly be realized, I ask nothing better," said Bannière; " the hisses which greeted Mithridate, have made me forget the applause which Hérode won."

" Very well ! I will make it possible of realization, O man of little faith ! " said Champmeslé, smiling. " How much do you need to be happy, very happy, both of you, for one year ? "

" Three thousand six hundred livres," said Olympe,

with decision; "anybody can live on that sum, and I as well as the rest. We can live in modest out-of-the-way lodgings, receive no one, and abjure travelling."

"Indeed," said Bannière, looking fondly at Olympe, "we should be very happy."

"Well," continued Olympe, "we have that sum for just one year. A year has three hundred and sixty-five days for lovers as for other people. Do you desire us, in exchange for the service you have done us, to promise to wait three hundred and sixty-five days for God to perform a miracle for our benefit? We will wait; but on the three hundred and sixty-sixth we must —"

It was Champmeslé's turn to shake his head.

"You must not reason in any such way as that," said he; "it has heretofore led you, and will lead you again, into dissipation. An illness which survives treatment costs one dear, and lessens the duration of one's happiness."

"Yes, to be sure," said Olympe, "we ought to have two or three years assured; for then —"

She checked herself, smiling at a thought which came into her mind.

"That is my opinion, too," said Bannière, "but one has no more than one has. Once more, my friend, to the stage we must look to supply the lack of those treasures of the roadside we were speaking of just now; and that means of support will have the advantage of regularity."

"Promise me," rejoined Champmeslé, "that if you were certain of a livelihood for two or three years, you would not return to the stage."

"Oh, most certainly not!" cried Bannière; "we would not, would we, Olympe?"

"No," she replied. "I know of a little house at

Lyons, on the bank of the Saone. It has a wall on the roadside, and is hidden by trees from the river; the only noise to be heard there is that made by the horses toiling up the bank; it is a nest of verdure, fresh and sweet and calm. It would cost to hire, five hundred livres a year. We could furnish it in royal fashion with a fourth part of my furniture. That would leave three thousand livres a year for Bannière and myself. I shall have to spend nothing for my toilette, for I have dresses and lace enough for ten such lives as I shall lead. Bannière will need nothing but a velvet suit for winter, and two silk ones for summer, which, with washing and sewing, would cost five hundred livres, leaving two thousand five hundred. We should spend twelve hundred livres for the sustenance of master and mistress and cook, with the latter's wages, leaving thirteen hundred for pocket-money and unforeseen expenses."

"Oh, what bliss!" exclaimed Bannière. "Three years of such a life! One could afford to die then."

"But we would not die," said Olympe.

"Have you resources which you have not disclosed to us, dear Olympe?" Bannière asked.

"Yes," said Olympe; "I will tell you what they are when our three years are assured."

"Well," said Champmeslé, who seemed to be waiting only for a favorable opportunity to explain himself; "do you promise me to think a little more frequently of God?"

"As often as we think of our good fortune, dear Monsieur de Champmeslé," said Olympe.

"Very well, then," said Champmeslé, with a quiver in his voice, which explained all his dread and all his delay, "I have here in my pocket a purse and a little portfolio; they contain six thousand livres, which I intended to give to the poor upon taking the vows. I had promised myself the pleasure of distributing them on the first occasion, to which I looked forward with such eager longing, when I should say Mass. That occasion is to-day. That first Mass, which is the beginning of a career at the end of which I hope to find my salvation, I have now said. Poor people are lacking; indeed there are no poor people here but you. Do not interrupt me. You are really worthy poor, and I offer you my old louis and these two bank-notes."

"Oh," cried Bannière, "impossible!"

"Why impossible?" cried Champmeslé; "do you know what you are saying, have you ever thought what charity is, that you reply to me thus?"

"But you can make a thousand happy with six thousand livres."

"Yes, happy for a moment, and that's the end of it; while to you, on the other hand, I afford the means of perfect happiness for two years."

"Oh, but we will not accept it," said Bannière, wavering, and looking at Olympe, as if to find in her eyes the strength to accept or decline.

"You will not accept what I do in the service of God!" continued Champmeslé; "you will not allow me to save two souls!"

"Monsieur de Champmeslé," said Olympe, "I accept, for my part, because I realize all the meaning of your benefaction. With the money we shall both preserve our virtue, as you have truly said. Yes, I accept."

The good abbé's eyes shone with joy. He seized Olympe's hand, slipped the purse and portfolio into it, and kissed it with a gallant air, which recalled the man of the world, despite his pious enthusiasm.

Olympe smiled.

"And now," said she, "our worthy friend, I must reward you upon the spot; I must give to your generosity and your delicacy all the value which they really have. Without your six thousand livres, my dear Monsieur de Champmeslé, we should leave Paris, happy, to be sure, but without definite purpose. Now, nothing is lacking to our good fortune. With three thousand six hundred livres we should have difficulty in living one year; with nine thousand six hundred, we can live at least four, and at our age four years is an eternity. The things which I have not told you, Bannière, but which you perhaps know, are, first, that I am nobly born, and secondly, that although disowned and disinherited, I still have two or three old uncles who are quite capable of leaving me a hundred thousand livres each, on the day when I shall go to them, on my husband's arm and leading my child by the hand, and call them 'dear uncles.' To wait three years without asking them for anything will be a good deal, and with the fourth year we will begin our pilgrimage. Out of three it will be very hard if there is not one who will do for me what was done for the prodigal child,— who will throw his doors open to me, and kill the fatted calf."

"I was right then!" cried Champmeslé, "and I have found a good place for the money, which was so useless to me."

"But you must remember, dear Abbé," interposed Bannière, "that if we accept your six thousand livres, we only accept them as a loan, like the ten louis."

"Priests don't very often give money away, perhaps, my dear Bannière; but they should never lend."

"But you have a family, haven't you?" Olympe asked.

"None at all, and I wish for none save that of Jesus Christ."

"You will allow me, I trust, to say one thing to you," suggested Bannière, timidly; "and that is, that you are connected with the least desirable branch of the family of Jesus Christ. The Jesuits are grafts from a Catholic slip, to be sure, but one that has little of the Christian element."

"Come, come, don't say harsh things," said Champmeslé, with a smile, "because you would never have known me except for the Jesuits, and except for your acquaintance with me you would not have made your début in 'Hérode' at Avignon and in 'Mithridate' at Paris."

"You see, he will be right in everything to the end," said Olympe, with a charming smile; "but it is very late, I ought perhaps to say very early. We have despoiled him; and now that he has nothing more to give us, let us imitate the parasites of society and the birds of the field. Having crumbled and eaten the bread, let us fly away."

"Go!" said Champmeslé, "and do not forget the sacramental words of the marriage service."

"What ones do you mean?" Olympe asked.

"Crescite et multiplicemini."

"Which means?"

"It is Church Latin, Madame, and can be construed only by a husband."

With that these three worthy and happy mortals exchanged cordial embraces. Bannière was very anxious to give Champmeslé a seat in their fiacre, but he declined. He had a bed waiting for him at the house of the curate of the Chapel of Notre-Dame de Lorette.

He accompanied his protégés to their fiacre, and saw them off on their way to Olympe's quarters.

The good abbé, happy in the thought of the good work he had accomplished, returned to the parsonage, and slept the sleep of the just.

XXXV.

THE SILK COAT AND THE VELVET COAT.

AND now we beg leave to abandon for the time our excellent abbé, who need cause us no anxiety, warmly wrapped as he is between the bed-clothes of his friend the curate of Notre-Dame de Lorette, and to follow our newly made husband and wife, who are, as the reader has discovered long ere this, our heroes by choice.

Their twofold existence is henceforth merged in one. They are young and conscious of their own vigorous youth, they have the wherewithal to live for four years, and naught but a terrible, unlooked-for catastrophe can part them.

Alas! misfortune is, like death, invisible; we divine its presence only when we feel its touch to our sorrow.

They were driven straight to Rue Grange-Batelière; it was not far.

By Olympe's order, her maid had prepared all her clothes and linen; it made a pile which completely filled the bedroom.

Olympe had scarcely begun to reflect on the difficulty of travelling with such impedimenta, before Bannière's mind had evolved a scheme for circumventing it.

" We will pack all this stuff in a large chest," said he, " and forward it to Lyons; while we ourselves, free and unhampered, can go on ahead and get the house ready, and wait for the luggage to arrive."

" Come and help me pack," said Olympe, " for you are right."

Bannière at once set to work with her, filling the trunks with what constituted a large portion of the fortune of the establishment.

While they were thus occupied, working together gayly and hastily, the maid came running in with an important air, and made a sign to her mistress that she had something to say to her.

"Well, come here," said Olympe.

The maid approached and whispered something in her ear.

Olympe blushed; and Bannière, seeing it, blushed himself, and turned his eyes away.

Alas, poor Bannière! he thought he could already discern that his presence was an embarrassment to his wife.

Olympe reflected a moment.

"What is it, Olympe?" Bannière asked, still with more affection than jealousy in his tones.

"Something disagreeable has happened, my dear," said Olympe.

"What is it, in heaven's name?"

"Monsieur de Mailly has sent a messenger to me."

"Monsieur de Mailly!"

"Yes. He made up his mind to-night to go to Vienna; and before taking his departure — "

"He has written to you?"

"I think so."

"Indeed!" said Bannière.

He turned away, troubled in mind, unhappy and dismayed.

"Shall I receive him?" asked Olympe, in her natural manner.

"As you please, Olympe."

"That is no answer."

"You are the absolute mistress."

"You don't understand," said Olympe, somewhat piqued. "I did n't ask for your permission to receive the messenger; I simply asked whether it would be best for me to receive him."

"You have more tact and more experience in such matters than I, dear Olympe," said Bannière, whose heart was beating more rapidly than he wished, and whose voice, despite his efforts to control it, trembled with jealousy.

"Go and bring the messenger here," said Olympe to the maid.

She at once left the room with the delight which servants always feel when they have succeeded by some means or other in embarrassing their masters.

Five seconds later the messenger entered. He held in his hand a large square letter.

"For Mademoiselle Olympe de Clèves, from Monsieur le Comte de Mailly," said he.

Then, as his eye fell upon the young man standing and looking on with colorless cheeks, he added, —

"Or for Monsieur Bannière."

Whereupon, with a respectful obeisance, he turned upon his heel, without exhibiting the least embarrassment, although his visit had brought serious trouble into the new establishment.

Olympe had received the letter from him, and held it in her hand. She motioned the maid to withdraw, and she and Bannière were left alone. Then she held the letter out to her husband.

"This letter is yours," said she, "as all letters are which I receive henceforth."

"No," replied Bannière, half sad, half joyful; "no, it was handed to you, Olympe. Read it."

"Why will you not read it, my friend? Come, tell me why?"

"Because I know beforehand all that there is in it."

"You know?"

"Yes, I can guess."

"How so?"

"Why, it's not difficult, especially for me, to guess what a man who loves you and has lost you would be likely to write you."

"But didn't the messenger say the letter was for you as well as for me?"

"Yes; but I know equally well all that he can have to say to me."

Olympe took his hands.

"Come, Bannière," said she, affectionately, "must it be that in the very first hour of our married life you are to worry and fret about a letter which comes to me without my wish or expectation? Come, read it; perhaps it is not what you fancy."

"Do you suppose it contains a threat?" said Bannière, putting out his hand for the letter with a frown.

At that Olympe drew it back.

"No," said she, courageously; "the man who wrote that letter, believe me, Bannière, is incapable of an act of baseness."

"You know what there is in his heart, then," said Bannière, bitterly.

"Yes," said Olympe.

"Then you should know what there is in his letter, too; and it's useless to read it."

"True," said Olympe; "it is useless to read it, especially just at this moment. We will read it later, when he is at Vienna on the banks of the Danube, and we in our little palace at Lyons on the banks of the Saone."

Throwing an arm around her husband's neck, and putting her lips to his, Olympe slipped the letter, which he had obstinately refused to take, into the pocket of his coat.

His wife's kiss and smile and sacrifice completely disarmed Bannière, and restored peace to his heart.

"A plague on jealousy!" he cried; "I have the loveliest, the sweetest, and most virtuous of wives."

"And the most loving, too, my husband."

"But we must set about providing a secure haven for this wife of mine with all speed; and since I cannot read her letters, we must arrange it so that she will not receive any."

With increasing animation and high spirits, he cried:

"Now to the trunks! to the trunks!"

And he and Olympe began anew to pile the clothes into the great chest.

"How about the fiacre?" said Olympe, suddenly.

"The fiacre?"

"Yes; what has become of it?"

"It is waiting."

"So you kept it, did you?"

"To be sure."

"What for?"

"It will take us wherever we wish to go, until the horses can't stand."

"And then?"

"Then we shall be somewhere or other, and will make our plans. The essential thing just now for me, and for you too, Olympe, I hope, is to get away from here, to shake the dust of Paris from our feet."

"Very good! but for travelling at night, dear Bannière, you seem to me to be rather thinly clad."

"I was much worse off than this when I reached Paris in pursuit of you."

" Never mind that."

" Well, well," said Bannière, laughing, " here is the bride already turning up her nose at her husband's wedding coat."

" God forbid, my dear Bannière; on the contrary, my regard for it is so great that I wish to make a sacred relic of it."

She rang for her maid, and Mademoiselle Claire responded.

" Open the cedar chest," said Olympe, " and bring me the velvet coat you know of."

" A man's coat ? " queried Bannière.

" Yes, Monsieur, a man's coat," replied Olympe, with a smile.

Bannière's face clouded again.

" Olympe," said he, gloomily, " the time has passed when the Jesuit novice thought it a joke to wear Monsieur le Comte de Mailly's coats."

" Be silent, heart of clay ! " said Olympe, offering him the velvet coat; " look at this coat, recognize it, and blush for very shame."

Bannière took it to the light.

" Why," he cried joyfully, " I do indeed recognize it."

" It is the new velvet coat which you had just ordered, and which was brought home to you the day you were arrested at Lyons, at the instigation of the Jesuits; you never put it on except to try it. Bannière, I have kept it as a precious souvenir; I have looked at it every day, and kissed it every night. I have put the perfumes which I love in the pockets. Ah, that coat, with the memories it awakened, were almost all that remained to me of our days of love and happiness; it was like an embalmed souvenir of the time which was no more, and which spread its sweet perfume through my house and my heart ! "

Bannière uttered a joyful cry, tore off his silk coat, donned the velvet one, threw himself into Olympe's arms, and held her in a close embrace; while Mademoiselle Claire, with imperturbable phlegm, being very unsusceptible to sentimental scenes, folded the old coat very carefully, and laid it away amidst Olympe's possessions in the large chest.

When their emotions had subsided, the chest was full. Three o'clock was striking, and the horses attached to the fiacre were stamping and whinnying; they had been waiting at the door an hour and a half, and the driver was making as much noise as he could, thinking that they had forgotten him.

Olympe and Bannière took the keys of the chest, which was deposited on top of the fiacre, wrapped themselves in the same cloak, and were driven to a large wagon-office in Rue Montmartre.

Bannière left the chest there, paying the cost of transportation; then having made a bargain with the proprietor of the fiacre for two days at twelve livres each, the two happy lovers dismissed Mademoiselle Claire with an honorarium which seemed to satisfy her; and before daybreak they had passed the Fontainebleau barrier, breathing in, with exquisite pleasure, the cool vapors from the river, and from the valley of Gentilly, which was less muddy then than it is to-day, because much less of the washing of Parisian society was done there.

The driver, who went leisurely along at the rate of two short leagues an hour, singing upon his box in his joy at finding such good customers, was wondering why, with a little tact, he could not get the job of taking this newly wed pair to the end of the world at twelve livres per day.

XXXVI.

THE LITTLE HOUSE ON THE SAONE.

UNFORTUNATELY nothing is so uncertain as worldly calculations, even those which are made by drivers of fiacres sitting on their boxes.

Olympe had grown too economical over-night to assist the honest fellow in his calculations, which were based upon the actions of Bannière and herself.

While she was sitting in the fiacre by Bannière's side, she reflected that under those circumstances they would never make more than twelve leagues a day at an expense of twelve livres.

At that rate it would take them twelve days to reach Lyons, and meanwhile they would be obliged to provide some little refreshment for the horses, and a great deal for the driver.

Then the driver would consume twelve days more in the return journey, and would naturally expect to be paid for them at the same rate.

So when they reached Fontainebleau on the evening of the first day, Olympe communicated her reflections to Bannière; and the sequel of those reflections, with which Bannière fully coincided, was that the driver received his two days' pay and was dismissed.

Olympe then made an arrangement with a carrier who followed the Lyons coach to carry the luggage, and who had a little cabriolet in addition to his vans. This necessitated going very slowly; but the coach itself hardly went faster than a walk.

At that blissful period the post alone made good time; but Olympe and Bannière had become the most prudent couple on earth, — they did not consider themselves wealthy enough to travel post.

So they took the cabriolet and were content.

At five o'clock the next morning they took their places, and their journey began.

Sheltered behind leather curtains when it was cold or stormy, walking long distances when the weather was fine and the country beautiful, dining with good appetite, sleeping in neat and comfortable inns, they took ten days for the journey, and, aside from the fatigue, which Olympe battled bravely against with frequent baths and long nights of refreshing sleep, never was such a happy and delightful journey before.

Then, too, they had so much to tell each other of what had befallen them since their last parting. Love is so loquacious and so ready to listen too, Olympe's hand was so soft as it rested in that of Bannière, and the road they were travelling was so faithful an image of the long road which lay before them ere they reached the end of their youth and happiness!

And how they praised the worthy, the kind-hearted, the excellent Champmeslé! How affectionately did his two grateful debtors dilate upon his delicate nature and his generous heart! How heartily did they thank God for having placed in their path that pearl among men, whom they had had the good fortune to fall in with!

Champmeslé was quite right when he said that legitimate happiness adds something serene and noble to terrestrial joys. It is such a grateful aid to the conscience, which resumes its virgin purity, and when consulted unerringly and inflexibly separates right from wrong, just as a touchstone distinguishes between copper and gold: so that many opinions formed on false impressions are corrected; so that one begins to see mankind in a different light, and to distinguish more clearly the line, so often disregarded, which marks the separation between another's good and our own.

Their conversation, turning upon every conceivable subject, often turned upon Monsieur de Mailly. Bannière, like a man of sense and a man deeply in love, realized the necessity of having done once and for all with that incident of their past life.

Olympe, somewhat surprised at first, quickly understood what was going on in her husband's mind, and eagerly assisted him to cast out that unpleasant guest who goes by the name of jealousy.

It was easily done; she had only to let her heart speak.

She described her life with the count; she drew him as he was, weak but impulsive, and astray upon the dark road which divides honor as understood at court from human honor. She depicted his present unhappiness, and finally succeeded in arousing Bannière's compassion for the future of this man who lacked nothing to make him happy except happiness.

Bannière experienced the liveliest satisfaction which can fall to the lot of a lover, — the satisfaction due to the assurance of a decided preference for himself over a rival in many ways his superior.

Thanks to his wife's noble frankness, he felt inclined to pity Monsieur de Mailly, instead of envying him as he had done hitherto.

From that moment it seemed to him as if the winged monster with bloody claws and heavy body which sits upon lover's hearts, like a hideous, pitiless nightmare, — as if green-eyed jealousy had taken unto itself wings and flown away with doleful groans to seek some other victim.

This favorable disposition of his overcharged heart brought his mind back to Monsieur de Mailly's messenger.

"It is to be regretted, perhaps, that we didn't read what he wrote *us*," said he, "in the first hours of his despair at our union; it may be that he demanded that we return what he gave us. It would be a pity to keep his property."

"His property!" exclaimed Olympe. "Ah, let your mind rest easy on that score, my dear! Monsieur de Mailly, although generous by nature, had nothing which he could ask me to return. I spent for him the money which he gave me for myself. You know me, Bannière; I am not covetous, and I like better to give than to receive. Monsieur de Mailly's liberality has made me no richer than I was when we lived together on what we earned on the stage. Only, thanks to his liberality, I have not spent the money which I have earned; I have not been obliged to sell the furniture which I had at Lyons, and which is still there. That is why we have two hundred louis to-day."

"And the furniture of the house on Rue Grange-Batelière," said Bannière.

"Will remain in that house," replied Olympe. "The superb jewels in which Monsieur de Mailly wished me to array myself when I received his friends will remain in their boxes. I have looked upon it all as property, which is loaned, as it were, not given; of which the mistress in possession has the use, while the ownership remains in the master.

"All this Monsieur de Mailly knew very well; and my only fear is that he will insist upon giving them to

me, instead of asking me for them. You felt that letter; did it contain any package?"

"No, I felt nothing more than the thickness of an
ordinary letter."

"One may make a donation upon a single sheet.
Where is the letter?"

"*Mon Dieu!* I left it in my old coat," said Bannière.

"And Claire put the coat into the trunk with all the
other things," said Olympe.

"All right; let it stay there."

"At all events we shall find it with our other belongings at Lyons, and we will read the letter together,
won't we, dear?" said Olympe, gently. "If it contains
complimentary remarks, we will both claim them; if, as
I fear, it contains any sort of a gift, I will thank Monsieur de Mailly very humbly without wounding his self-
esteem. You shall see the letter in which I refuse to
accept it."

"You are an angel of virtue and cleverness, my
darling."

"I am just beginning to taste the pleasure of doing
my duty. Let us get to Lyons quickly."

"Yes, quickly; that is, if the cabriolet will permit,
dear Olympe."

The cabriolet refused to accelerate its pace; however,
by dint of going ahead it arrived at last.

But when Bannière's eye fell upon the heights of
Fourvières, and he saw Lyons, and all its houses with
smoke ascending, and those broad threads of pearl and
silver, the stream and the broad river, the Saone and
the Rhone, he heaved a tremendous sigh.

Olympe turned around in amazement.

"Pray, what's the matter?" she asked.

Bannière shrugged his shoulders slightly.

"Nothing."

"Yes, there is something. Your face is clouded, and it has come upon you all at once. Tell me what has happened."

"I don't like Lyons; I never liked that mass of black houses," replied Bannière.

"But you will like ours."

"We were so unhappy there."

"I don't mean that one; we will take nothing but the furniture from that one, and even the furniture we will sell if you prefer."

"Why did you select Lyons, dear Olympe, — Lyons, where I suffered so bitterly?"

"Because Lyons is large enough to hide in."

"Do we need to hide, pray?"

"Why, I thought we were agreed upon that. Why do you begin to hesitate now, after we agreed so thoroughly upon our plan?"

"I don't know; but my feet seem to have taken root on the spot where we are. I look at yonder city, and it seems to me a yawning chasm. Those streams which are so admired have to my eyes the appearance of longing to swallow up something or somebody. I don't like Lyons."

"Explain yourself."

"I do not like Lyons where La Catalane lived, and the Abbé d'Hoirac, and our enemy the hairdresser. I do not like Lyons, where there are dungeons and a magistrate and barracks, and I know not what besides. Look you, my darling, I think we should do well if we were to give up the idea of putting up at Lyons."

"Oho!" said Olympe, with a smile, "you bear a remarkable likeness to a superstitious man. Look at the beautiful sunlight, the green slopes, and the boats glid-

ing along through the blue waters! Just by the end of
that little islet, behind the houses, do you see a thick
growth of trees skirting a white road?"

"Yes."

"And the Saone in front of it?"

"Yes."

"Do you see what a quiet, tranquil spot it is?—a
fisherman on the bank, and children playing at the
water's edge?"

"True."

"Well, right there is the little house in which we will
live. See how far away it is from the noisy heart of the
city where we lived before! The uproar of the old days
will never disturb us there. That part of the city is
always asleep under the chestnuts and lindens. Imagine
that the winter has come, and the lonely region is
covered with a carpet of snow; imagine the little lamp
shining behind the curtains and the bare trees, like a
lucky star, as one approaches our home, and the bridge
which leads to the city gate. We have lovely walks
and a pure atmosphere; and now that you have considered all this, let us not go to Lyons, if you prefer
not."

"No, let us go, since you wish to," said Bannière,
stifling another sigh; "you can lead me to nothing
except joy and happiness."

Together they walked down toward the city.

Two hours later they had paid the carrier, freshened
up their clothes, and refreshed the inner man, and were
taking their ease at an inn, waiting until they should be
sufficiently rested to set out in quest of the house.

Olympe was too energetic to rest very long. The next
morning, while Bannière was still asleep, she left the
inn.

Twenty times, during her former stay at Lyons, when she had been driving alone, bewailing the misconduct or the neglect of Bannière, she had noticed the isolated house, and had always been much attracted by its charm- ing exterior, and the leafy bower in which it stood.

She had never seen anybody at the windows; in the summer she had concluded that the owners were in the country, in the winter she had said to herself that because of the cold and the fogs they kept themselves very closely housed.

So she went straight to the house to make inquiries, and if possible to induce the occupants to transfer their rights to her by offering them a bonus. She had learned to believe that nothing was impossible to a beautiful and amiable young woman who was willing to take the trouble of asking.

She feasted upon the pleasant prospect of returning to tell Bannière that the deed was done, and of taking his arm, and bringing him back with her to take up their abode in their new acquisition.

An hour of moderate walking brought her to the end of her journey.

She knocked somewhat excitedly at the little wicket in the wall which ran along the river bank.

For some time there was no response. She redoubled her blows, and soon' she heard steps coming along the gravel-walk of the little garden.

The wicket was not opened, however, and it seemed as if, with excessive precaution, some one was listening on the other side, or trying to see who had knocked.

But Olympe was wrong as to her first supposition. It was a very simple matter to ascertain who the intruder was, for the wicket was supplied with one of those little iron gratings, through which, in times of civil war and popular commotion, the good citizens in the provinces, and in Paris too, used to look to see whether the visitor was friend or foe.

Olympe saw a servant-girl's face at the grating.

"What is Madame's wish?" she was asked.

"My good girl, isn't this house to let?" said Olympe.

"No, Madame."

"Why, I thought I had heard that it was."

"Never."

And the girl prepared to close the aperture.

"Pardon me," said Olympe, "one more question, my child."

"Ask it, Madame."

"By whom is the house occupied?"

"Why," said the girl, "I don't know——"

"I have none but honest designs," said Olympe, slipping a crown through the grating to the servant, who at once became more favorably disposed toward her. "Listen! I am not watching or shadowing any one; I am very desirous to hire this house for myself, and it would be doing me a very great service to let me have it."

"But suppose, Madame, that the present occupant insists upon keeping it."

"Oh, I know all that you can say to me; but if it is possible for me to speak to the owner, I am sure I can find a way to convince him. I am a woman, and not at all dangerous. Is it not possible, I ask again, to allow me to come in and urge my reasons? If you will do what you can for me, my good girl, and I succeed in convincing your master, I will add a louis to the crown."

The dazzled servant smiled at the prospect of so rich a harvest.

"Madame," said she, "the owner of the house doesn't

occupy it. My master is only a tenant, and only comes
here now and then."

"Is he here at this moment?"

"Yes, luckily."

"Luckily? You have some hope then?"

"*Dame!* it's quite possible that he who is so fond of
bright eyes will allow himself to be persuaded by yours.
Allow me to speak to him; then he will come, and you
can talk together."

"Do so," said Olympe.

The girl ran off toward the house. Being herself a
woman, and young, she could not admit the impossibility
of a young woman's obtaining what she wanted.

In two or three minutes she returned, acting as guide
to a man who was chuckling to himself, and saying, —

"Is she really very pretty, Babette, this lady at whose
request you have disturbed me?"

Olympe started at the sound of that voice, and instinc-
tively turned to fly, but it was too late.

The face of the Abbé d'Hoirac was pressed against the
iron grating. He recognized her, and uttered a cry of
joyful surprise.

Olympe, terrified beyond measure, fled at her utmost
speed; while the abbé, cursing and swearing, was trying
to open the wicket, to capture the prey that had escaped
him again. But the servant had to go to the house for
the key; and Olympe meanwhile had disappeared, so that
the near-sighted abbé could find no trace of her when
the gate was at last opened.

XXXVII.

OLYMPE TAKES HER TURN AT HAVING PRESENTIMENTS.

OLYMPE, as we have said, fled shivering with terror at the sight of the Abbé d'Hoirac. When she stopped to take breath, she first began to realize how imprudently she had courted danger, despite Bannière's presentiments.

Alas! the lover had shown more keenness of perception than the wife.

Did Bannière love the more, that he had so clearly foreseen the dangers to which his love was to be exposed?

Olympe saw at a glance all the ideas which the knowledge of her presence in Lyons would be likely to arouse or renew in the Abbé d'Hoirac. That obstinate suitor, whom no rebuffs had availed to discourage, had incessantly laid siege to the mistress of Bannière, although he had perforce abandoned his pursuit of the mistress of the Comte de Mailly.

Would he show any more respect for the wife than he had for the mistress, particularly when the wife, by an evil chance which his self-conceit would certainly construe in his own favor, had herself come and knocked at his door.

Olympe began to run again; but after a hundred steps or thereabouts, she was again obliged to halt: the blood rushed to her head, and poured back into her heart till she was almost suffocated.

Her ears were ringing, too, and every sound seemed to say in an undertone, " D'Hoirac! D'Hoirac! "

Chance — for it was chance, of course; but how to make him believe that it was?

Was it chance, he would say, which led her to insist so upon being confronted with the master? Was it by chance that she gave money to the servant, and promised more?

How could an Abbé d'Hoirac fail to plume himself upon all those circumstances?

" Oh! " muttered Olympe, " I can hear him from here. He will say to himself, 'She knew where I lived, and hastened hither; and if she did fly when she saw me, she did it as Galatea did, — for the purpose of being followed. Now that she has notified me of her presence, she only wants me to seek and find her.' "

Oh! and Bannière?

Suppose Bannière to know of this episode, how would he reconcile himself to her visit to his ancient rival, or more accurately, his bitter foe? How could he be expected to believe in an accident in which she, its victim, hardly believed herself?

Did not everything combine to accuse a woman who was already the object of suspicion?

Above all, her haste to rise, to go out alone, and to visit an out-of-the-way spot! All that to end in meeting there unexpectedly — whom? — that scourge of Bannière's peace of mind, his second bugbear after Monsieur de Mailly, — the Abbé d'Hoirac.

Never, alas! in the face of such compromising appearances, does a woman find the courage to be perfectly frank, especially when she finds herself in Olympe's position. She was bending beneath the weight of a past which forbade her to be open. She hoped to atone for everything by maintaining silence, and that hope was terrified and shaken by the slightest echo from the evil days of long ago.

In the first place, then, she must have a secret, — a secret from the man whom she loved, yes, adored; from the man for whom she sacrificed a great nobleman, a king; from the man whom she had made up her mind to constitute the sole object of all her thoughts and the guide of all her acts.

She must do it, whatever the cost; she must hold her peace as to what had taken place, not for her own sake, but for his. For Bannière would never believe what was in truth very hard to believe. He might perhaps pretend to believe; but in that case he would be only the more wretched, because at the bottom of his heart it would be the merest pretence.

Thus forced back upon all the miseries of her former life, and with her mind made up to lie, Olympe returned to the inn, as uneasy at the thought of finding Bannière awake as she would have been anxious to find him in that condition and ready to receive her good news, if everything had fallen out according to her wishes.

As she turned into Rue des Vergettes, where their inn was located, she saw Bannière. He stood at the window waiting for her.

His face wore an anxious expression. His happiness was of too recent date for him to feel very confident of his grasp upon it. A new landowner does not fall at once into the comfortable enjoyment of his crops and his fruits. The first shot fired on his new property by the recent purchaser of a rabbit-warren always makes him turn his head to see whether the keeper who has his eye on him is about to draw up a report against him as hunting upon another's land.

Bannière had been waiting for a quarter of an hour.

Failing to find Olympe at his side when he awoke, the poor fellow had traversed step by step all the strata which extend from doubt to agony, from dawn to darkness; and the road which his imagination had thus gloomily traversed was lighted here and there by ominous flashes.

Had Olympe already thought better of her bargain? It was very soon. Had she got tired of seeing him asleep? Had she gone out to walk alone in Lyons? Had she been led to go out by some letter which she had concealed from him?

Such were the queries which Bannière propounded to himself, and to which he received no reply other than the more and more tumultous beating of his heart.

He spied Olympe, and leaped for joy. With the sight of her everything was almost forgotten already. He had feared he was not to see her again, and there she was before him.

He ran to the door, opened it, and received Olympe in his arms.

She was still pale and disconcerted.

After he had pressed her to his heart and kissed her, as Harpagon must have kissed his recovered casket, Bannière began to notice her pallor and her evident confusion.

Olympe was a great actress; but when a great actress's heart is enslaved, the great actress becomes nothing more than a poor, lovelorn woman.

"Where have you been?" Bannière asked; "where have you been, that you had to leave me while I was asleep, so that when I opened my eyes I looked in vain for you? Where have you been?"

"Inquisitive!"

"I would like to know," said Bannière, gently.

"And suppose I would not like to tell you?" rejoined Olympe, making a feeble attempt to be playful.

But they were not on the stage, and Bannière was not acting a part; he was living his own life, and expressing his own emotions.

"Aha! you don't want to tell me!" he exclaimed; "very well, then, I will guess."

"Do; and if you guess right, I will tell you so."

"You have been to find a house?"

"You have guessed."

"That little house?"

"What little house?"

Olympe blushed in spite of herself.

"Why, that little house on the bank of the Saone, you know; the one you pointed out to me yesterday from the hill."

Olympe made no reply.

"You know very well," continued Bannière, somewhat testily; "the one you spoke to me about, the one which has trees along the road; the pretty little house which made you long to own it, and which I am perfectly sure you have been now to hire, so as to give it to me, when I awoke, for a wedding present."

"Well, yes, that's it," faltered Olympe, driven into her retrenchments.

"And — "

"It is let."

"Let?"

"Yes."

"And *you* were satisfied with that reason, Olympe! You, Mademoiselle de Clèves, admitted the impossibility of obtaining what you wanted! Nonsense! I don't believe a word of it."

"You will have to believe me, nevertheless; the house is occupied."

"By whom?"

"How do I know? By somebody who does n't choose to dispose of his rights."

"Is there a man in the world so hard-hearted as to refuse my Olympe anything upon which her heart is set?"

"It would seem that such persons must exist, for they refused to listen to me. To be sure, it was not a man."

"Aha! a woman?"

"A servant-girl."

"And you did n't interview her master and mistress?"

"No," said Olympe, shortly, longing for the conversation to end before reaching a point where she would be obliged to lie, for thus far she had succeeded in avoiding direct falsehoods.

Bannière looked earnestly at her. If his gaze had been less loving, it would have killed the poor girl on the spot.

"So you have n't hired any house at all?" said he.

"No, we will go together, my dear, and have better luck, no doubt."

"Or else —"

"Or else what?"

"I have a little scheme of my own," said Bannière, laughing.

"What do you mean?"

"Nothing."

"My dear, what have you in your mind?"

"Oho! now whose turn is it to be inquisitive? I am thinking about going all by myself."

"All by yourself?" cried Olympe.

"Yes, I have an idea that I can succeed in doing for you what you were not able to do for me."

"What do you mean by that?"

"I mean that since you are so very desirous of that little house, why, you must have it, and you shall have it, or my name is not Bannière!"

Olympe shuddered. She pictured to herself her husband knocking at that door, recognizing D'Hoirac and drawing his own conclusions.

She was on the point of making a full avowal, but she had not the courage. She promised herself that she would not leave Bannière's side the whole day long, and would employ the day in persuading him to leave Lyons, — a task of no great difficulty, probably, in view of the repugnance he had expressed for the city.

Nevertheless she had argued so earnestly to conquer his apprehension that it was difficult for her to suggest the reversal of her plans of the preceding day, to which he had acceded.

"At all events," Bannière continued, as if following out some thought of his own, "that little house is probably not the only one in Lyons."

"I have looked everywhere, and found nothing," said Olympe.

"After all," said Bannière, "there are few houses which are just the thing for us in our present moderate circumstances; it was much easier for us to find suitable quarters when we were wealthy or when we were really poor."

"No, Lyons is certainly not the city of expedients that I imagined."

"I told you so yesterday, my darling."

"I know it; but when one sees it at close quarters — "

"One sees that one's husband was right."

" I confess it. "

" Meanwhile the husband in question always finds so much pleasure in doing what his wife desires, that since last evening Lyons seems to him the paradise of France."

" I suppose it's mere caprice," said Olympe; "but since last evening I have completely changed my opinion about Lyons."

" Really ? "

" Yes; I don't know why, but I dread some catastrophe. Your presentiments have infected me; your gloomy forebodings are forever in my thoughts, and terrify me."

" Nonsense! let us forget all that. You were the ray of sunlight which scattered the clouds; you smiled, and the sky became blue again."

" My dear Bannière, you may say what you will, — call me whimsical, fickle, if you choose, — but I do not want to stay at Lyons."

" Do you mean it ? "

" I am bored to death."

" Listen ! " said Bannière; " I do not care to seek for the reason of your sudden change of mind — "

" There is no other reason than those presentiments which you spoke of to me yesterday, and which have communicated themselves to me."

" The meaning of which is — "

" That we will leave Lyons, will we not ? "

" That shall be as you choose, my precious."

" And when I choose ? "

" This very minute."

Bannière rose laughingly to his feet.

" Look you, dear," continued Olympe, " I have thought it all over. I have reflected that it will cost twice as much to live in the city as in the country, and that we could hire two servants elsewhere for the sum it would

cost us here for one; that here we have no air except
the exhalations from the rivers, no foliage save that of the
black lindens in the paved streets, no blue sky save the
patches we can catch a glimpse of between the chimneys.
I said to myself that here we may meet an enemy or a
tormentor in every passer-by; if we have neighbors, they
may become spies. I thought of all this, and I admitted
to my own conscience that when my husband said the
self-same things to me yesterday, I ought at once to have
remembered that I was his wife, and consequently a
creature with no other duty than to obey his orders, even
though they were the merest whims."

"Very well!" said Bannière; "let us go, my adored
Olympe. Happiness, springtime, green leaves, blue sky,
life itself, are only where you are. Let us go, my darling, let us go."

"Yes, we will go. We will get the benefit of what
we have paid for our entertainment to-day; we will make
a bargain with another carrier, and to-night, — yes, to-
night, — like culprits, like thieves, we will steal away."

"Agreed."

A kiss sealed this new agreement of the young couple,
whose chief care thenceforth was to be to obey each
other.

They breakfasted together in high spirits; from time
to time their eyes met, and they smiled at the prospect
of leaving Lyons that day.

Olympe, however, seemed the more eager of the two;
it was her turn to be oppressed by presentiments of evil
to come.

XXXVIII.

OLYMPE'S PRESENTIMENTS AND BANNIÈRE'S ARE REALIZED.

THE rest of the day was employed by Olympe, like the clever woman she was, in preventing Bannière's thoughts from wandering in the direction of her secret.

But when evening came, and a hearty dinner had made them both feel the necessity of a walk, she could see no risk in going out with him; so she took his arm, and they walked toward the least crowded parts of the city.

The weather was beautiful; the sky was clear, and the pure air brought back to earth as many delicious odors as the earth wafted up to heaven.

The two promenaders, heedless of everything but their own unclouded felicity, reached the old gate, which we already know as the one near the barracks, where Bannière had passed two or three hours in his Majesty's uniform, by which he had been rescued from the hands of the Jesuits.

As they were admiring the architecture of the gate, and the long tree-lined avenue through which Bannière had galloped off, a heavy stage-coach arrived from Paris, emitting from its cavernous interior sounds of heavy snoring and the clatter of many tongues, which in public conveyances always form a hoarse accompaniment to the neighing of the horses and the oaths of the postilions.

A few passers-by collected in a group to watch the always diverting spectacle of travellers arriving or departing.

The coach stopped.

The door at once opened; a traveller had his trunk passed down from the roof of the vehicle, paid the guard, and fell upon the neck of his wife, who stood waiting for him with her two children, whimpering with joy.

"How is it with you, Monsieur l'Abbé ?" said the guard, speaking to an invisible passenger; "don't you get down here ? "

"Why here ? " a voice replied from within the vehicle.

"*Dame!* because it 's the nearest point to the establishment of the holy Jesuit fathers," said the guard.

"Ah, if that 's the case," said the same voice from the interior, " I will get down, I will get down! "

And a man in the costume of an abbé, with his cassock tucked into his girdle, alighted nimbly from the coach.

The guard, saluting him respectfully, handed him a slim portmanteau.

"You have been paid, have you not, my friend ? " asked the abbé.

"Yes, Monsieur, you owe me nothing."

"Except these thirty sous for pourboire. If I were richer, I would give you more."

"Ah, Monsieur l'Abbé," said the guard, resuming his place, "if everybody would only give as much! Hallo there! the horses! "

The coach continued its lumbering way into the city.

The churchman stood with his little bag in his hand, looking in some bewilderment to right and left, and apparently very uncertain as to the road he ought to take.

"How strange it is! " said Olympe; "since our dear Champmeslé brought us together again, married us, and

endowed us, I can't see a man of the cloth anywhere
without thinking of our kind friend."

"Well, well," said Bannière, following the direction
of Olympe's glance, "upon my word!"

"What?"

"It's he!"

"Who is he?"

"Why, Champmeslé."

"Champmeslé?"

"Champmeslé himself; you 'll see for yourself in a
moment."

"Champmeslé!" said he, raising his voice.

"Who is it?" said the abbé, turning round.

"There you see that it is he!"

"Monsieur de Champmeslé!" Olympe called.

"Why, my friends, my dear friends," cried the
worthy man, holding out his arms.

"Is it really possible that it's you?" said Bannière,
as he embraced him for the second time.

"Yes, yes, indeed it's I," replied Champmeslé,
joyfully.

"What lucky circumstance brings you to Lyons?"
asked Bannière.

"Were you running after us, I wonder?" said
Olympe.

"Ah, no! my friends, I was summoned back."

"Who summoned you?"

"Messieurs the holy fathers."

"And why?"

"Oh, because I am somewhat in disgrace, I fancy."

"You in disgrace?"

"Yes, I."

"Wait," said Olympe; "let us get away from these
groups of soldiers, who are watching us as if we were

strange animals, and then you can tell us of your new misfortune, if you have been unfortunate."

"Yes, let us move away," said Champmeslé. "Those soldiers really seem to be deeply interested in us."

"*Dame!*" said Bannière, "perhaps it struck them as singular to see a pretty woman kissing an abbé; for I beg leave to inform you, Monsieur de Champmeslé, that Olympe did kiss you."

"With all my heart, too," said Olympe. "But to return to your disgrace; what is it all about?"

"Well, I am accused of — of having helped Bannière to escape from Charenton, and of having connived at his return to the stage,"

"Who accuses you, pray?"

"Why, the inspectors of the order."

"The spies, you mean."

"They call them inspectors."

"Very good. It is on my account, then, dear friend, that you are harassed and persecuted?"

"It seems that I have done wrong."

"Why, no, I did my own escaping."

"True; but your escape was perhaps a little too cleverly planned for a madman."

"Because I was not a madman, or anything like it."

"True again; but it is very evident that some one found it expedient that you should be."

"Aha! yes, I understand."

"The fact is," continued Champmeslé, "that I have received something like a reprimand, and am ordered to return to my college as soon as possible."

"At Lyons?"

"No, at Avignon. The order is signed by Père Mordon with his own hand."

"Why did you stop here?"

"I must have my pay-check visaed."

"What! your pay-check?" said Olympe, laughing. "Are you a soldier travelling from one supply-depot to another?"

"The order is organized on military lines; we get our pay only by presenting the check for signature; otherwise," continued Champmeslé, thoughtlessly, "no money for travelling, and that would be hard."

"You have no money!" cried Bannière; "why, then, you must have given us all that you had!"

"No, no, indeed!" cried Champmeslé, ashamed to have been guilty of such a slip of the tongue. "I did n't say that I had no more money. Nonsense!" (He jingled some coins together in his pocket.) "Besides, that's not the question."

"Yes, indeed, it is the question!" said Bannière; "and as we have you in our clutches, you are coming to sup and pass the night with us."

"And then," added Olympe, "we will say to you, as the ogre said to the peasant, 'Warm yourself, warm yourself, my little man; it's your own wood.'"

"Oh, it's impossible!" said Champmeslé.

"Why so?"

"Because, if they were to find out at the college here in Lyons, that instead of going there to have my check visaed, I had passed the evening with —"

"With actors," laughed Bannière.

"No. Besides, you are actors no longer; you remember our contract. With friends."

"Well, what would they do to you?"

"What would they do to me?"

"That was my question."

"Perhaps when I reach Avignon they would put me in the Chamber of Meditation, which you once made the acquaintance of, or condemn me to some penance even worse than that. Let me embrace you once more, my friends; then I will go to the Jesuit college, pass the night in one of the dormitories there according to rule, and at daybreak be off for Avignon."

"My poor friend," said Bannière, "pray don't you see that these people bind you with heavier chains than a man who belongs to the Lord alone, ought to carry?"

"I see my salvation at the end of it all," said Champmeslé. "So farewell, my dear friends. Why, what a crowd of soldiers!"

"What a crowd, indeed!" said Olympe, as she noticed a number of uniforms coming out of the barracks, like ants out of an anthill, and walking back and forth with curious looks at her and her companions.

"I will leave you now," said Champmeslé. "Tell me where you are staying, so that I may come and say good-by to you once more in the morning, before the boat leaves."

"At the Coq-Noir, Rue des Vergettes," Olympe replied.

"Very well; I go now."

"Why, we shall not be there then," said Bannière, in an undertone to his wife.

"Oh, well! let us stay one night more," said Olympe, "so as to see the last of that noble man."

"We will stay," said Bannière; "you know that my wishes follow yours."

He turned again to Champmeslé, —

"Till to-morrow morning then, — so be it."

Champmeslé nodded, and took his leave.

Olympe and Bannière also moved away to get clear of the swarm of dragoons who were all about them.

"What a quantity of dragoons!" said Bannière.

"Look! Champmeslé has stopped; he is talking with some one."

Bannière tried to distinguish the abbé in the gathering darkness.

"With whom is he talking?" he asked.

"I can't make out," said Olympe, who had, however, made out only too plainly.

"One would say that it was an abbé like himself," continued Bannière.

"Yes, it is an abbé," said Olympe, with palpitating heart.

"They are turning this way."

"Do you think so?" said Olympe, stepping between her husband and the two ecclesiastics, for she thought that she recognized some of the Abbé d'Hoirac's peculiarities in the movements of the new-comer.

"Ah, now Champmeslé is leaving his brother in the Lord!" said Bannière.

"The Lord be praised for that!" muttered Olympe.

Taking her husband's arm, she drew him away toward the city.

She was not mistaken; Champmeslé had been accosted by the Abbé d'Hoirac.

The latter, who was accompanied by a woman whose face was covered by the hood of her cloak, but who seemed to see very clearly from beneath the hood, asked Champmeslé who the persons were of whom he had just taken leave.

Without the slightest suspicion he replied, —

"Monsieur and Madame Bannière, two dear friends of mine."

Whereupon he turned on his heel and left them.

"You see that I was not mistaken," said the hooded female to D'Hoirac. "Ah, you must understand that when I have dressed a person's hair, though only a single time — "

"All right, all right!" said D'Hoirac. "Here's a louis."

"Thanks," said the woman.

And while the Abbé d'Hoirac was also turning on his heel, but in the opposite direction to that taken by Champmeslé, she muttered to herself, —

"Ah, lovely Olympe, you turned me out of doors! Ah, Bannière, my fine fellow, you beat me! Oh, well, we shall see! Upon my word!" she continued, as she walked away, "it's a beautiful double louis; she must be a perfect idiot to prefer Bannière, who's as poor as a church rat, to this little duck of an abbé, who's as rich as a gold-mine; but we women, when we lose our hearts — "

She disappeared, still mumbling to herself, and shaking her head threateningly.

Meanwhile Bannière and his wife had moved away, as we have said; but they had scarcely taken fifty steps when they saw two men in the uniform of dragoons making straight for them. Other soldiers had been all about them, as has been said, but none had come so near as these two.

Bannière thought that they intended to insult Olympe by staring her out of countenance; so he proudly folded his arms, pulled his hat down over his eyes, and waited.

Olympe tried to drag him away; she begged him to go, fearing that a quarrel would ensue.

"Well, Messieurs," said Bannière, speaking first, "I would really be glad to know why you stare so at us?"

"We stare at you so as to see you; that's all," said one of the two.

"Impertinent scoundrel!"

And Bannière raised his hand.

"Very fine, Monsieur!" said the other dragoon, with a sneer.

Then he turned to his comrade.

"It is he, and no mistake," he said. "Did I not tell you that I recognized him myself, even before the abbé betrayed him?"

Olympe shuddered without knowing why.

"Look you!" said Bannière, "it's high time for you to explain your actions, Messieurs les soldats!"

"You are Monsieur Banniére, are you not?" the dragoon demanded.

"Yes, to be sure, I am Monsieur Bannière. What then?"

"Monsieur Bannière in person?" the other asked.

"*Parbleu!*" exclaimed Bannière, with a shrug of the shoulders; and he made a movement to push the fellow out of the way and pass on.

"Pardon me," said the latter, "but we have a certain major here who would be glad to say two words to you, Monsieur Banniére."

The major, however, had already come upon the scene with several officers; behind the officers was a handful of dragoons, and behind them a crowd of gaping on-lookers.

Olympe and her husband became in an instant the centre of a constantly narrowing circle.

"Well," said the major, "where is the man?"

"Here he is," said one of the dragoons, indicating Bannière.

"You are sure?"

"He admits it, my major; besides, you have his description: consult that."

"For heaven's sake, what is the matter?" cried Olympe; "Monsieur is my husband."

"Well, my little lady," replied the major, gallantly, "the matter is that your husband is a deserter; that's all."

"Oh!" cried Bannière, whose heart was pierced by the dreadful words.

The poor wretch had forgotten it all.

"Oh!" groaned Olympe, speechless with terror.

"Yes, yes, yes," the major continued, "this fine fellow stole from us a complete outfit of clothes, a sabre, and a horse with the equipments."

"*Mon Dieu ! mon Dieu !*" muttered Bannière.

"Further than that," continued the major, in the same tone, "he sold horse and sabre and uniform, which constitutes the most disgraceful of all offences in the eyes of a soldier who has the honor of serving in the king's army."

"Faith, we should have missed him but for the abbé," said one of the officers in the major's party. "The devil take me if I should have known him in that black coat! And yet it was I who gave him his riding-lesson."

"That devil of an abbè!" the major went on. "Ah, I should say that he is no friend of yours!"

"What abbé?" stammered Bannière, bewildered and overwhelmed.

"Alas!" cried Olympe; "lost! lost!"

"Come, Madame," said the major, "it is late; say good-by, and get it done with quickly."

"Good-by to whom?" asked Olympe.

"Why, to your husband, who is under arrest."

"Bannière under arrest!" cried Olympe, throwing her arms around the young man's neck.

"Ah! it's a long while that we have been on the lookout for him," said the major. "He passed himself off for a madman at Charenton, the rascal! Upon my word, you must indeed be mad, my friend, to come and burn yourself in this way at our fire."

"Poor fellow!" said one of the dragoons, touched by the spectacle of that living image of utter despair; "the little woman loves him dearly."

He gave vent to his emotion in a deep sigh; a feeling heart lay beneath that rough exterior.

Bannière felt heavy hands upon his shoulders. Olympe unlaced her arms from around his neck and fainted.

The prisoner was immediately taken into the barracks, while compassionate souls gathered around the poor senseless creature, in whom a merciful God suspended consciousness, thereby to interrupt her sorrow.

XXXIX.

THE JUDGMENT.

WHEN Olympe regained consciousness, it was late; everybody had disappeared save two women, who were watching over her, having laid her upon a bench beneath a tree, and were saying kind soothing words to her; for women alone understand misfortune, and know how to console the unfortunate.

She recalled what had happened, uttered a cry of pain, and asked where she was and what had been done with Bannière.

The women had no clear understanding of what had taken place; they told her that the dragoons, in obedience to their commanding officer, had dispersed the crowd, while some of their number were leading a man clad in black velvet into the barracks.

Olympe felt that a terrible drama was about to begin; that it was possible that Bannière would be deprived of his liberty; that they might deal harshly with the poor fellow to make an example to deter others, or to gratify some animosity.

She soon detected the perfidious hand of the Abbé d'Hoirac.

To whom should she apply? Where could she find the necessary support and influence to enable her to begin negotiations with the authorities?

What man was there in the city who would lend the strength of his arm uninfluenced by selfish designs to the poor girl?

Olympe did not hesitate a moment. She remembered what Champmeslé had said of his proposed visit to the Jesuits, and of passing the night there. In him she was sure to find a protector.

Rising to her feet, she thanked the charitable women a thousand times, and having inquired of them the way to the Jesuit establishment, was at once led there by them.

Champmeslé, after going through the formalities prescribed by the order, had received permission to eat his supper, and retire for the night in a little cell.

He was eating the meagre pittance which the Jesuits supplied to those members of the order who were not high in favor with the superiors, and was consoling himself for his hardships by thinking of the good he had done, when a ringing peal at the bell made him start.

His thoughts were so closely connected with those whom he had just left that he attributed the unusual noise to something connected with them without any transition.

He was informed that a woman desired to see him at any cost, in order to confess to him.

It was the expedient adopted by Olympe, with her customary forethought, to gain speech of Champmeslé.

Amazed to the utmost, he hastened to meet his visitor, and received Olympe, weeping bitterly and almost fainting, in his arms.

"Help! help!" she cried.

"What is it, dear Madame?"

"They have taken him away from me."

"Whom?"

"My husband."

"Who have taken him?"

"The dragoons."

"Is she mad?" Champmeslé asked himself; and in

the same breath, and upon that hypothesis, he coolly
asked Olympe if Bannière was not with her.

"Why, I tell you," she cried sorrowfully, "that they
have torn us apart. He enlisted by my advice to escape
the persecution of the Jesuits; Monsieur de Mailly took
him into his regiment; he made his escape; now they
have found him and arrested him."

"Oho!" said Champmeslé, with deep gravity; "this is
a serious matter."

"*Mon Dieu!*"

"Don't be over-frightened; the case is not hopeless,
perhaps."

"What must we do?"

"Indeed, I hardly know myself."

The good man lost his head. He had been an actor,
and he was a priest, but he had never been a soldier.

"Come," urged Olympe, "time is passing."

"True. But what to do? Tell me a few of the
details."

Olympe told him all that the reader has learned.

"Indeed," muttered Champmeslé, "that musk-scented
abbé accosted me with the question, 'Do you not know
that lady?'"

"And did you tell him my name?"

"I certainly did."

"Then I am lost! I alone am responsible for my
husband's destruction!"

"No, no, wait: I am inclined to ask the rector here
for advice in this strait."

"By no means! Bannière was once a novice; in that
capacity he must have left unpleasant memories in Jesuit
circles; they may bear him ill-will."

"Very well! let them be as ill-disposed toward him
as you please; at the worst, they will not kill him."

"What do you mean by that, in God's name?" cried Olympe, in deadly terror. "What word was that you used? They will not kill him! Then the others will kill him?"

"I did not say that."

"Explain yourself, in the name of heaven! What can they mean to do to Bannière?"

"Ah, my dear friend!" said Champmeslé, deeply grieved that he had spoken so thoughtlessly, "I don't know; but we can find out by going to the barracks."

"Let us go to the barracks, then; let us go."

She seized Champmeslé's arm, and pulled him toward the door like a madwoman.

"One moment, Madame," said he. "I am not free here; in order to go out, I must ask for my *exeat*."

"What's that?"

"A paper signed by the rector, a pass, anything you choose to call it, but which I must have before the porter will let me leave the house."

He had in truth to go and ask for his *exeat*, and to tell the circumstances to the rector, who, with the repellent coldness of despots of the third order, said to him, —

"Upon my word, my brother, you have very worldly connections; here you have been with us less than an hour, and now you are going out with a woman."

"In humanity's service, my father," said Champmeslé.

"Humanity, my brother, is not always a sufficient reason for breaking the rules."

"But time is flying."

"Go forth, if you will, my brother; but consider that we have cut loose from all family ties and all earthly friendships, for the precise object of not having to do the things which you propose to do this evening."

Champmeslé hardly listened to this admonition, he pounced upon the *exeat*, went out with Olympe, who was beginning to gnaw her hands in her impatience, and accompanied her to the barracks.

There they had to go through with other more difficult negotiations.

In order to leave the Jesuits it was necessary to supersede the regular order with an *exeat*; in order to enter the barracks, it was necessary to override the regular order with entreaties.

The sentry was immovable.

Olympe, while Champmeslé was parleying and berating the functionary with his logic, slipped under his carbine, and ran like a deer toward the buildings which she saw to be lighted up within.

There was a blaze of light in a lofty hall which was crowded with dragoons from the stairway to the doors.

But no one would let her pass; moreover the sentry had given the alarm, and they seized her and held her under arrest.

She wished to speak to the commander, and they told her that he was very much occupied.

She undertook to scream and struggle, and they told her that she would be choked or gagged, or turned out of the place.

The threats of brutal treatment alarmed her less than the fear of exclusion; so she rejoined Champmeslé, who had succeeded, by appealing from one officer to another, in working his way into the enclosure.

Suddenly Olympe had an inspiration. She remembered that several of the officers of the regiment had supped with her at Avignon on the night when Monsieur de Mailly set out for Paris before his marriage.

She asked for pen and ink, and with Champmeslé's

assistance wrote a touching letter to the commanding officer in which she told her whole story and avowed herself Monsieur de Mailly's mistress.

The letter had the result which she hoped. The officer at once came out to receive her.

At her first word he cried, —

"Ah, Madame, it is really you, — you whom I saw so happy! "

"I shall be happy again, Monsieur," said she, "if you give me back my husband."

"Your husband! Is Bannière really your husband? "

"Here, Monsieur, is the worthy priest by whom we were united."

"Ah! *Mon Dieu !* " muttered the officer, hiding his face in his hands.

"Monsieur, Monsieur! " said Olympe, "what is the matter, pray? What is it? Hide nothing from me, I implore you."

"Alas! "

"I am not a weak, silly girl; I love Banniére so dearly that uncertainty as to his fate would be a mortal blow, and ignorance of his situation would be like torture before death."

"You are brave," rejoined the officer, "but perhaps not brave enough to endure all the suffering which lies before you."

Olympe shuddered, and drew near Champmeslé, as if to seek in his strength the moral support which she was soon to need.

"Madame," continued the commandant, "take my advice; do not demand of Nature more resolution and firmness than she can supply. Accept the hand of Monsieur l'Abbé and leave us."

"Leave you! And Bannière? "

These words were pronounced in a tone which admitted of no reply or argument; the officer saw a light shining in her eyes which nothing could extinguish.

"Monsieur," she continued, emboldened and strengthened at the same time by the officer's silence, "remember one thing: that I am bound to Bannière for life, — for life, do you understand? Not until death arrives, have mortals the right to put asunder those whom God has joined. In the name of that God, who hears my words, I conjure you to restore my husband to me."

"Ask anything else of me, Madame; but as to that — "

"What! has Bannière committed a crime? Is he outside the pale of humanity?"

"Bannière, Madame, is a deserter."

"Well, what is done to deserters?"

"Ah, Madame — "

"Go on, speak — "

"No, Madame, no!"

"Ah!" shrieked Olympe, in a despairing state which bordered on delirium, "my husband! I want to see my husband!"

The officer was about to refuse again, but Champmeslé approached him.

"Monsieur," said he, "I know this poor creature's temperament; you will drive her to desperation. When she has once lost the control which she usually maintains over her reason, her violence will terrify you. Humor her by according her the favor that she asks."

The officer took Olympe's hand, and led her into the building.

They walked on for a minute or two, through various halls and up stairways, until they finally reached a large court, full of soldiers, — some full of business, others waiting.

The commandant, still holding Olympe's hand, spoke to one of these soldiers.

"Has the council assembled?"

"Yes, my commandant."

"Monsieur," said the commandant to Champmeslé, "I place Madame under your protection. I entrust these two persons to you," he added, designating three of the dragoons with his hand. "Take them to the room adjoining the council-chamber."

"Can I see my husband there?" asked Olympe.

"No, Madame, not at this moment; but you shall see him afterward."

"Afterward!" cried Olympe. "After what? Oh! these men terrify me with their ominous reticence. I want to see him at once — at once!"

"Oh, Monsieur!" said Champmeslé, imploringly, because he anticipated an hysterical paroxysm.

"Dragoons," said the commandant, "take these two people into the little gallery, and don't lose sight of them.

"Madame," he added, bowing to Olympe, "once more I say, it was you who would have it so. Please remember that I resisted. Remember that in gratifying your desire I have yielded to the fear that I might cause you more misery by my refusal than you will have to endure as the result of my consent."

He left them hastily; and the dragoons led Olympe, trembling and pallid and numb with apprehension, and Champmeslé, shivering from head to foot, into the council-hall itself.

Then began for these unfortunate creatures the saddest spectacle which loving hearts were ever called upon to witness in this world.

The hall, which was an ancient structure, with

pilasters of the Renaissance period, badly damaged by long use and wilful mutilation, contained twenty officers, more or less, clothed in red, who sat upon a platform in the feeble glimmer of a few torches held by dragoons.

The commandant took his place at the long table on the platform, presided over by the major, performing the functions of lieutenant-colonel or of the absent colonel.

The corners of the hall were shrouded in darkness, which seemed to fall in sheets from the smoky arches.

The major called the roll of officers, and wrote down the number present.

Then he said in a dismal voice, —

"Bring in the culprit."

A door opened at the left of the platform; two dragoons, sabre in hand, brought in Bannière, in his black suit, and pale as a graven image.

"Accused," said the major, "your name is Bannière?"

"Yes, Monsieur."

"Call me 'Major.' I am not 'Monsieur' to you; I am your major."

Bannière held his peace.

"Do you recognize your signature at the bottom of this voluntary enlistment?"

"I do."

"Do you admit that you received from two non-commissioned officers the following articles, to wit: first, a horse?"

"Yes."

"Second, a uniform?"

"Yes."

"Third, a sabre and pistols in the holsters?"

"I think so."

" Did you sell these articles ? "

" I exchanged them for civilian's clothes."

" Why did you run away ? "

" I never intended to be a soldier of the king. My enlistment was signed as a means of extricating me from jail, where I was held as an escaped Jesuit novice."

"That was an additional reason for respecting the provisions of your enlistment. However, be that as it may, you did run away. That fact is proved by your absence in the flesh."

Bannière made no reply.

"Messieurs," said the major, addressing the other officers, "is the proof satisfactory to you, and do you consider the identity established ? "

"Yes," the officers replied with one voice.

"Very well!" continued the major; "we sentence the deserter Bannière, dragoon in the Mailly regiment, to undergo the punishment provided in Article 6 of the royal ordinances, and we order that the punishment be inflicted at once."

With these words he rose, and the officers followed his example; all was confusion in the vast apartment, which seemed to swallow up officers, soldiers, and condemned in its gloomy shadows.

Champmeslé stood as if nailed to the rail against which he was leaning. Olympe, as rigid as if she had been already dead, asked in a sepulchral voice, —

" The punishment — the punishment — what punishment ? "

" *Pardieu !* " one of the dragoons began; but Champmeslé stepped upon his foot with such emphasis that he did not finish his sentence.

The commandant made his appearance at this juncture, and seeing Olympe still standing on the same spot, —

"Come, Madame," said he, kindly; "if you wish to say a few words to poor Bannière, come."

She followed; she flew after the officer, who escorted her to the small hall, adjoining the large one, where the condemned man, alone with a dragoon, was waiting with clasped hands and wandering eyes, like one in delirium, or a day-dreamer lost in reverie.

Olympe fell upon the beloved victim, enveloped him in her loving arms, and pressed him close to her heart.

"Ah, yes!" said he; "Olympe, dear Olympe! yes! yes!"

He did not emerge from his impassive, motionless lethargy, which was much worse to contemplate than violent grief.

She was herself terror-stricken.

"What!" said she, "where is our courage?"

"Courage — " he muttered; "why courage?"

"Am I not here?"

"For how long are you here?" said he.

"Why, forever. Oh, they will not separate us."

"That's a fine prospect," said the unfortunate wretch, whose words sounded as words from the lips of a marble statue might sound; "you will die with me, — what good fortune!"

He accompanied these lugubrious words with a strident, hysterical laugh.

"Die!" said she, "die! you and I, die?"

"Why, of course!"

She looked at Champmeslé, whose hands were resting upon Bannière's shoulders.

"Is death the penalty of desertion, Monsieur de Champmeslé?"

"*Pardieu!*" exclaimed Bannière, in much the same tone in which the dragoon had said it when Champmeslé stopped him.

Olympe passed her hand across her forehead, and made a superhuman effort to collect her ideas.

"Monsieur de Mailly will save you," said she; "is he not the colonel of this regiment? You are saved."

She knocked sharply on the door, which was opened at once. In the passage-way was her friend the commandant with several others; she had no need to approach him, for he ran to meet her.

"Monsieur," said she, "I know the worst now; let me speak to the major."

"Gladly, Madame; I have just told him your sad story; he is now dictating to the clerk the report of the proceedings. Walk in this way."

Olympe could see the major standing in his office, dictating. She fell at his knees so suddenly that the good man was surprised and troubled.

"Monsieur," said she, "tell me the truth! Where is Monsieur de Mailly? Is Monsieur de Mailly responsible for what you have done?"

"Madame," the major replied, "here is the letter which reached here yesterday from Monsieur le Comte de Mailly, our colonel."

He handed Olympe a paper written in a hand which she well knew. She read: —

MONSIEUR, — I am about to start for Vienna; my mission will last perhaps a year or two. Look after my regiment more carefully than ever, fill up the ranks, and receive the new officers whom I send you; be particularly careful that all deserters be apprehended and executed at once, according to the king's order. I shall hold you responsible for the slightest infraction of my orders, and for the least delay in putting them in execution.

Signed:

COMTE DE MAILLY.

"You see, Madame," said the major.

"Where is Monsieur le Comte?"

"On his way to Vienna."

"Oh, I know very well — "

She checked herself.

"You see, Madame, that anything you may ask is impossible."

Olympe said nothing.

"Monsieur de Mailly's letter is dated the 20th, and it is now the 31st; he is in Vienna at this moment."

"I will go to Vienna."

"Alas, Madame, you will not go to Vienna in two hours."

"No; but I will go in a week."

"We have only four hours to give you."

"Impossible!" she cried, "you will not murder Bannière without some little delay."

"Madame, here is our colonel's order in writing."

"In the name of humanity, Monsieur!"

"My orders, Madame."

"Monsieur, on my knees I implore you; see, I grovel at your feet."

"Madame, you rend my heart, because I am powerless to do as you desire."

"Give me time to speak to the king, Monsieur! time to write to the king, Monsieur!"

"Madame, we have but four hours," replied the major in a hollow voice, anxious to avoid a prolongation of the painful scene.

Olympe looked wildly about and beat her breast, as if hoping to force out some more persuasive accents.

The major bowed and left the room.

Olympe remained alone with the officer whose face was hidden in his hands.

"Quick!" said she, — "quick! take me to my husband."

And she turned away, murmuring to herself incoherent prayers, which God did not hear.

XL.

TWO BRAVE HEARTS. — TWO NOBLE HEARTS.

For an hour past, the existence of these two ill-fated beings had sped so swiftly that neither of them had been able to follow the headlong course of their woe.

So when they found themselves face to face, the one completely shattered by his arrest and summary judgment, the other utterly overwhelmed since she had learned the whole truth, they no longer had the strength to speak; they could not even think.

Champmeslé, standing between them, tried to arrange his own thoughts, and miserably failed.

" Well! " he said to Olympe at last.

"I don't know," said she.

" I was born under a fatal star," said Bannière; " all my life I have misused the happiness God has put in my hands."

" No, no, you are wrong, Bannière," rejoined Olympe, with terrifying *sang-froid.* " I am the unlucky star; I am your evil genius. Who was the cause of your first entering a theatre? I. Who implanted in you the taste for dissipation and extravagance? I. Who placed before you an evil, perverted example? I. Who made you enlist, thinking thereby to save you? I. Who forced you to come to Lyons when you would have shunned the place? I, I, I! always and forever I! If you do not curse me, Bannière, beware! God will never be able to invent sufficient punishment for me."

These words were uttered with a depth of conviction and feeling which sent a cold shiver over Champmeslé's body.

Bannière showed no sign of emotion.

He gazed at Olympe lovingly, sadly, earnestly.

" True," said he; " but the harm you have done me is blotted out by the bliss your love has brought me. Do not accuse yourself: I fall because it is my destiny.

" Come," he added, shaking his head, " I must be a man! Let us recover from our consternation, examine coolly our hopes of succor, if there are any, and look death in the face if it is inevitable."

Olympe raised her bowed head; his firm words awoke a noble echo in her heart.

" So far as the officers are concerned," she said, " there is no hope."

" Ah!" said Bannière.

" None."

" Reprieve?"

" He has refused it."

" Appeal to the colonel."

" The colonel is at Vienna."

" You can't obtain time to go to the king?"

" No."

" Then," said Bannière, sighing heavily, but finding a new source of strength in the certainty that his doom was inevitable, — " then, I see that it only remains for me to die; but we may postpone the moment for a few hours perhaps."

As he spoke, the door opened.

It was the officer, Olympe's friend.

" Excuse me, Monsieur Bannière," said he, " but I chanced to hear your last words. I bring the major's reprieve: you have until daybreak; it is now half-past ten, and he gives you until five o'clock."

Olympe started.

"Monsieur," said Bannière, "can I be permitted to say a word to the major?"

"Yes, certainly.   I will answer for him, and he will come here, if you wish."

"No, Monsieur, I don't ask that; I should be very sorry to disturb him.   Be kind enough to have me taken to him."

"At once," replied the officer.

He went out to order a detail of three men, who escorted Bannière to the major's office.

Olympe rose mechanically to follow her husband; but he motioned to her to remain, accompanying the motion with a sad smile, and she fell back upon her bench beside Champmeslé, placing her hand in that of the good priest.

The major was a worthy gentleman, an old soldier, instructed to maintain in the regiment the strict discipline and obedience to rules which Catinat and Turenne had introduced into the king's armies.

He loved life, and understood why a man should cling to it; he admitted but one case in which one might cease to regret it.   It was the case of an order or decree which provided that a living man should be put to death.

He supposed that Bannière had come to bewail his fate; and he waited for him to speak with eyes on the ground, eyebrows knit, and mustache bristling.

He was thoroughly determined not to be moved, on whatever side he was attacked.

"Monsieur," said Bannière, "permit me, I beg you, to explain my position to you.   I am a decent sort of fellow, of good family, passionately fond of my wife; it appears that I have merited death, although between ourselves I don't think so in the least; still such is the law."

"And the king's regulations, Monsieur."

"And the king's regulations, if you please," continued Bannière. "I bow therefore to the law and the regulations, and I swear to you, Monsieur, that I will cause you no embarrassment whatsoever."

The astonished major raised his head, and looked his interlocutor in the eye.

Bannière was pale, but calm, and magnificently handsome in his pallor and tranquillity.

He continued, —

"You have sent word to me, Monsieur le Major, that you consented to grant me a reprieve until five o'clock to-morrow morning; that is very little, I confess, and I come to you, not to discuss the main question, which seems to me irrevocably decided, but to haggle a little about terms."

"Ha, ha! that's very well put," exclaimed the major, smiling with the natural good-humor of a man who expected tears and remonstrances or weakness, and who found instead an unexpected firmness of resolution, that was almost playful besides. "You take it admirably."

"To tell you that I am highly elated over the prospect, Monsieur le Major, would not be true," replied Bannière; "and if I should tell you so, you surely would not believe a word of it. But I am sure that you are a brave and worthy gentleman. I look into your eyes, which are the mirror of an upright mind and a noble heart; so that I could never believe that you could take any pleasure in shedding my blood for mere sport. You don't drink blood; you prefer good champagne or Burgundy."

"That's as true as gospel, Monsieur Bannière. I am in despair at what has befallen you; but — "

"But there is no way of getting around the principal point?"

"On my conscience, no, Monsieur Bannière."

"Not the slightest possibility of being allowed to appeal to anybody?"

"To whom do you wish to appeal?"

"We have friends."

"That means delay. I leave you to judge how much discretion I have. Here is the colonel's letter."

He handed the letter to Bannière, who read it carefully, and returned it to him.

"And here is the king's regulation as to deserters."

Bannière took it.

"Read it, read it aloud; in order to carry it into effect, I need to hear its provisions read and re-read."

Bannière read what follows in expressive tones, while the major looked closely at him: —

"Every soldier of the land or naval forces, who without leave shall be absent three days consecutively from the regiment, corps, or ship's crew to which he belongs, shall be punished with death.

"Yes," said Bannière; "the article is very clear, that's sure."

He handed the regulation back to the major, as he had done with the colonel's letter.

"No, no," said the major, "read on; I propose to prove to you that my line of conduct is rigorously laid down for me, and that I am less harsh than the law requires me to be."

Bannière continued his reading: —

"The deserter when taken, recognized, his identity established, and the crime proved, shall be immediately shot, without any delay or reprieve, except such as may be necessary to enable him to receive religious consolation."

"Immediately," the major repeated.

"Yes, immediately."

"Without delay or reprieve."

"Permit me, Monsieur," said Bannière, with perfect courtesy; "it seems to me that after those words 'without delay or reprieve,' I see certain other words which are worth discussing."

"Which ones, Monsieur?"

"'Without delay or reprieve, *except such as may be necessary to enable him to receive religious consolation.*'"

He looked up at the major.

"Well?" queried the latter.

"Well, let us allow a little time for the arrival of this religious consolation."

"But, my dear Monsieur Bannière," retorted the major, "you have deprived yourself of that resource; you arrive here all cooked to a turn, and your wife has brought you a priest."

"The Abbé Champmeslé, — true," said Bannière. "The devil! the devil!"

"You see that you are within the rule on all points."

"Faith, I believe I am!"

"And your reprieve until five in the morning is a very particular favor."

"I am very grateful indeed to you. But, after all, what would happen were you to give me twenty-four hours instead of the six you have given me?"

"It would happen that I should be cashiered, which is nothing, I know, compared with a man's life, and I would gladly incur the risk of it did what you ask not constitute an infraction of rules, an act of disobedience, a subversion of discipline, of which I never have been and never will be guilty."

" My mouth is closed, Monsieur le Major."

" Believe that I pity you with all my soul, and that, if I were colonel of the regiment, instead of being major, things would wear a very different face."

" You are very kind. Well, then, since it is useless to urge that point — "

He stopped to afford the major an opportunity to reply.

" Quite useless," said he.

" I come to the trifling request which I wished to make of you."

" Let us hear it."

" All points save one are settled between us."

" What one is that ? "

" You grant me until five to-morrow morning ? "

" I have said it."

" But where ? "

" What do you mean by ' where ' ? "

" I mean just that."

" Why, here, I suppose."

" Here, in these barracks ? "

" Certainly."

" But that, if you will permit me to say so, is a little hard."

" Where the deuce do you suppose I am going to send you ? Into the fields ? "

" Have patience, Monsieur, and be kind enough to hear me to the end; you will then understand that I am not so bereft of reason as I seem to be."

" I am ready to listen to you."

" Monsieur le Major, I adore my wife, and am adored by her. Pardon my self-conceit," he added with his sad smile, " but one may say such things when one has but six hours to live. You know my wife, for you have seen her. To see her is to know her; you know her, therefore, I say again. She is beauty, intelligence, and refinement personified. I am in agony at the thought that I must pass the last hours of my life on a wooden bench beside that woman, who will suffer from cold and pipe-smoke and vulgar talk. She will not dare even to kiss me before the dragoons, and, stupefied with terror and embarrassment, she will see me pass from her lifeless arms to the death, uninviting enough at best, which the king and the law and you have decreed that I shall undergo to-morrow morning."

"Well?" said the major.

"I desired to ask you something else," continued Bannière. "You see that I am calm and resolute, that I can almost joke; but you must understand from my voice which trembles when I speak of Olympe, from my face which changes color when I think of her, that there are in that name a charm and an interest much more engrossing than those of my life. I shall die without ceasing to smile; but it is for you, Monsieur, to say whether my dying smile shall express an effusion of undying gratitude to my benefactor on this side of the grave, or the mere bravado of a stout-hearted fellow, who will force your dragoons to say, 'There died a brave man!' Will you do me this service, Monsieur le Major? Will you bestow upon me, in the last six hours of my mortal existence, the happiness of a whole lifetime? Will you, who will order me out to execution with no feeling of anger, be as kind to me as the musket-ball which will end my life painlessly to-morrow?"

"Go on!" said the major, deeply moved, and considerably overcome by the torrent of eloquence which poured from this loving heart.

"I ask your permission to return to my inn with my

wife, to that little room still filled with her favorite perfume and with the memory of our love; the flowering jasmine and clematis are climbing about our window to-night, as they were last night, when they breathed their gentle aroma upon me, and made me sleep until the sun was high. The room is easily guarded, — one window on the garden, another on the street, and a door leading to the stairway; station two dragoons beneath each window and one at the foot of the stairs; do better still, — take my word of honor and my wife's that we will make no attempt to escape. I will sign it with my blood, if necessary, Monsieur le Major. To-morrow morning at five I will be ready; but meanwhile be generous, like the brave, kind, loyal officer that you are; give me my wife for such time as remains to me to live."

The major felt as if his heart were coming up into his throat. He began to scratch his head, and winked his eyelashes, tormented by a tear which trembled at their extreme end. He coughed and walked to and fro in his office, trying to uproot the profound pity which the very audacity of the request had planted in his heart.

"Ah, Major," Bannière added gently, "if you refuse, put off your refusal as long as possible; I have so much time to suffer! If you grant my request, grant it quickly; I have so little time to be happy!"

The major emitted a vigorous "hum!" and tapped his spurred boot upon the floor.

The worthy man was fairly choking with emotion.

Suddenly he seemed to come to a decision, and stamped upon the floor.

At the signal a non-commissioned officer appeared.

"Let six men report for orders," said he, "and — "

"And a brigadier?"

"No, an officer."

Bannière understood that his request was granted. He fell on his knees and kissed the major's hand; his tears fell in rivers.

"Thunder!" growled the major; "let's have done with that, my fine fellow!"

Olympe must have been listening at the door, for at this moment she entered and threw herself on her husband's neck.

"Olympe," said Bannière, "thank Monsieur le Major; we are both to return until five o'clock to the little room at the inn."

Olympe said nothing, but she moved her head and lips sadly.

"Before we go," said Bannière, "give to Monsieur le Major, to whom we owe this good fortune, your word, as one nobly born, that you will do nothing to assist me to escape the fate which is in store for me."

"Nothing," said she; "I give my word."

"And I add mine to hers, Monsieur le Major," said Bannière; "in any event there is nothing to prevent your taking all needful precautions. Thanks; and to-morrow, if I have the honor of seeing you again, expect to receive the most sincere and earnest expressions of gratitude which human heart ever uttered in return for a benefaction."

The major pressed Bannière's hand, and gave his orders to the officer who was to watch the inn.

Olympe and Bannière walked ahead with Champmeslé along the avenue which led to their abiding-place.

Only the officer walked beside them; the squad followed a short distance in the rear.

Champmeslé, when they reached the little room at the inn, gave Bannière his blessing, tearfully embraced the two unfortunates, and whispered in Bannière's ear, —

" At what hour in the morning shall I come and arouse you, in the name of God ? "

" At four, my dearest Abbé, " was Bannière's reply.

As they closed the door behind him, eleven o'clock was striking on a church tower near by. Olympe fell, sobbing bitterly. upon the couch which her husband placed beside her.

XLI.

SUPREME JOY. — SUPREME GRIEF.

THE jasmine and the clematis were climbing along the wall, as Bannière had said, and formed, with their dark green foliage and white flowers, a frame of verdure for the window, through which the pure air and the rays of the moon stole silently in.

The dragoons established themselves in the garden, in the street, and upon the staircase, as Bannière had suggested.

The lovers were left to each other, with naught to hinder the free exchange of kisses, mingled with tears, which Bannière's pride and Olympe's prudence and despair had hitherto held in check.

A fearful night it was, when every sigh, every caress, every word brought them one step nearer the end.

The stars were shining in heaven, — the same stars which Olympe might gaze upon to-morrow at the same hour, from the same window, while the eyes of Bannière, her dearly beloved Bannière, would be forever closed to everything save the black darkness of the tomb!

Bannière bestirred himself, tried to shake off his dismal thoughts, and exerted all the force of his passion in showering new proofs of it upon the desolate, forsaken creature, who would seek in vain on the morrow for any vestige of the life that was in him now.

Olympe, white and cold as a dead body, did not remove her lips for an instant from those of her husband.   In four long hours she said not a single word, that she might not lose the time for a kiss.

Naturally impulsive and headstrong in his passion, Bannière at last succeeded in galvanizing the statue into life with the last powerful currents of the existence which was so near its end. It was an alliance between matter rebelling against its impending annihilation, and the spirit which realizes that its earthly joys cannot endure beyond the last breath, — an alliance which enables man to rise above himself, and in a burst of pride or it may be of despair, emboldens Titans to storm the gates of Heaven.

On the threshold of death the lovers forgot their woes in the ecstasy of living.

Dawn was beginning to break along the horizon. A pale line appeared between earth and sky, and the rivers began to stand out from the darkness, like threatening swords drawn from their scabbards by angels of death.

The fresh dewy air of morning entered the chamber of despair, and sent a slight shiver through the delicate limbs of Olympe, who emerged from her ecstasy with a sob.

Shiver and sob alike were absorbed by Bannière in a long and ardent kiss.

The birds began to sing in the garden, and the voice of a soldier was heard in the street at the same moment.

Four o'clock rang out on the same church-bell which impassively had rung for the beginning of their fatal happiness the night before.

With the same impassibility it now marked its close.

There was a slight scratching noise at the door, like that which courtiers make at the door of their master. It was Champmeslé, who had passed the night in prayer in an adjoining room, and who, faithful to his promise, had come to speak to his friend of the providence of God.

What a priceless favor did God in his providence bestow upon these unhappy mortals! The priest who came to prepare Bannière to meet his doom was a loving friend, with mild features and caressing glance, a friend full of tact and compassion, a veritable angel of light, who, instead of closing the doors of life with gloomy words, opened to him the doors of heaven with an ineffable smile of pity.

He sat down in front of Bannière and Olympe, who were sitting with clasped hands on the edge of their bed.

"Speak for us, my friend," said Olympe.

"Oh, I have nothing to say to you, for you are more eloquent than I. I know your heart to a sigh, almost to a word. God has forgiven you; he has given you his blessing, and will make up to you in the other life for all that he has made you suffer in this."

"You think, do you not, my friend," said Bannière, "that God is inflicting bitter suffering upon us?"

"Yes, since he parts you from each other."

"Oh, no," said Olympe, with a smile which revealed the origin and the explanation of her tranquillity, "God will not part us, my father. At least," she added in a lower tone, and glancing upward, "I hope he will not."

"What do you mean by that?" asked Champmeslé, in surprise.

"I say that God is great and good, my father, and that he inflicts sorrow upon us in proportion to our strength; that 's what I say."

Bannière understood, and folded her in his arms.

Electrified by his warm embrace, Olympe felt her courage renewed, and nothing seemed impossible to her.

She kissed Bannière, and pulled into the middle of the floor the great chest which the luggage-van had brought to them from Paris the night before.

" What are you looking for, my child ? " asked Bannière.

" I am looking for some clean embroidered linen for my love," she replied, " so that he may go to meet his death, not like a poor soldier, but like a gentleman."

" Ah, I shall be glad of that! " said Bannière.

Champmeslé shook his head.

" It 's a suggestion of your pride, my daughter," he said to Olympe; " why divert his mind from his God and his salvation in these last moments by vain thoughts of his toilet ? "

But Olympe paid no heed to her friend's mild remonstrance; she was pulling linen and laces out of the chest pell-mell, and scattering the floor with things for which she had no use.

Then she dressed Bannière to her satisfaction, so that he was fresh and clean when the officer knocked at the door with his sword-hilt at quarter after four.

" Come in, " said Bannière.

He added playfully: " You see how prompt we are, my dear Monsieur. "

The officer bowed respectfully before the heroic courage which lay beneath the pallid features of the young husband and wife.

" If you are ready," said he, " be good enough to follow me. "

Olympe threw a cape over her shoulders, and was ready before her husband.

The officer looked at her in astonishment.

" Let us go! " said she.

" Where, Madame ? " said he, placing a detaining hand upon her arm.

"Why, where my husband goes, Monsieur."

"It is not possible," cried the officer, "that you propose to accompany your husband, Madame!"

"Why not, I pray to know?" demanded Olympe, tossing her head.

"Because the very idea is repellent, Madame; my soldiers are not executioners, and not a dragoon of them all would fire upon a man in his wife's presence."

"Oh, so much the more reason for my going, then!" she cried.

"Come, be reasonable," said the officer, struggling not to give way to his own feelings. "I have my orders, and they are precise."

"Pardon me, Monsieur," said Bannière, joining in the discussion; "but ought not a wife to be permitted to give her arm to her husband at least as far as —"

"By no means, Monsieur," replied the officer; "and I depend upon you to persuade Madame not to insist upon putting herself in such a situation."

"Never!" exclaimed Olympe. "I will obey neither you nor him in this matter; where he goes, I will go."

"Madame," said the officer, "you force me to adopt harsh measures."

"Monsieur!" cried Olympe.

"It is not my fault."

He turned toward the door.

"Dragoons!" said he.

Ten men appeared, a reinforcement having been sent from the barracks.

"Six men for escort to the prisoner," said the officer; "four to keep Madame in sight in this room! — Come, Monsieur l'Abbé," he said to Champmeslé, "help us, in heaven's name!"

Champmeslé, in obedience to his own sense of what

was best, even more than to this authoritative appeal,
exerted himself to soothe Olympe, whose grief and rage
burst forth in full fury, having been hitherto held in
leash by bonds which had broken at last, giving full
play to the tempests surging in her heart.

Even Bannière himself, with his prayers and entreaties, was powerless to calm his wife. Champmeslé, torn
by conflicting emotions, began to lose his courage simul-
taneously with his power of decision.

To which of the two, the dying man or the desperate woman, should he attempt to speak of God, — man's
only refuge in death and despair?

The officer put an end to the painful scene, to the
shrieks and tears, with the inflexible decision of a soldier
devoted to his duty.

The six dragoons led Bannière away, while the other
four stood around Olympe in a circle which she could not
break; and in their midst, at the end of her strength,
with dry, staring eyes, she fell back in a sitting posture
upon the open chest, still overflowing with all the beloved objects which Bannière had touched.

Champmeslé, holding the victim's arm, weeping copi-
ously, embracing him and making him kiss the crucifix,
stirred to their lowest depths the hearts of the troopers;
and more than one faltered in his gait under the weight
of his pity and his sorrow.

In due course they reached the enclosure adjoining the
barracks where the execution was to take place.

By a ghastly fatality the enclosure was so situated that
the group, with weapons loaded, in attendance upon Bannière, could see with perfect distinctness the clematis and
jasmine-embowered window, on the other side of which
had taken place the awful scene of separation which we
have not dared to narrate in all its grewsome detail.

When Olympe recovered consciousness, her excitement had given place to the most complete torpor.

She raised her eyes, looked about her, and discovered the four dragoons, each of whom had retired to a corner of the room, whence they followed all her movements with a sort of dread.

The wild expression of her eyes, her trembling hands, and the tremulous movement of her whole body indicated that the crisis had passed.

Yet no one of the four dared to address a word, a single word, to the poor girl.

One of them approached his comrade, and nudged him with his shoulder.

"Really," he said, "we ought not to leave the little woman here."

"Why not?" asked the man addressed.

"Look there; but do it without seeming to have any purpose in looking."

With the butt of his carbine he pointed to the garden window. Through the branches of the little garden and two or three others, they could see the enclosure where mounted dragoons and the reserve force were awaiting, with their officers, the arrival of the dismal procession.

To reach the place Bannière and his escort had to make quite a long detour; and then, too, they marched very slowly.

A few curious spectators — very few they were, because of the early hour, and the general ignorance of what was going on — were beginning to climb the walls and the trees, and to line the streets.

The dragoon to whom his comrade pointed out all this felt very ill at ease.

"True," he said in a low voice; "in this room she will hear it all, poor soul! Let us try to get her away."

" Or to close the window at least."

" She will hear them all the same."

This dialogue did not arouse Olympe from the bottomless pit of despondency into which she had fallen.

Her hand, moving mechanically about, came in contact with the laces and linen and other articles which had fallen from the chest, — sweet relics, cherished mementoes, as the Latin poet says; souvenirs of a past which had been all love.

While her hands were thus occupied, her eyes resumed their office; and as if the absent Bannière on his journey to eternity had wished to recall himself to his wife's thoughts, the first object upon which Olympe's eyes fell was the coat in which Bannière had been married in the little church of Notre-Dame de Lorette.

Carefully folded and packed away by the maid-servant, this coat, impregnated with subtle perfume by the scarfs and gloves which lay near it in the chest, evoked a bitter groan from Olympe de Clèves.

Alas! she had no more thought for what she was doing, than the daughter of Jairus had for her life when she came to herself on the brink of the grave; but she felt a pang of grief and a thrill of pleasure at the same time. The grief was for the wretched present; the pleasure, in the awakened memories of the past.

Olympe slowly unfolded the coat in which it seemed to her as if she must find Bannière. Her fingers were roughened by the soft material of the lining; and the weight of the garment, slight as it was, wearied her aching arm. With the same slow, measured, almost automatic movement, she raised the coat to her lips, hid her face in the soft stuff, burst into tears, and sobbed so bitterly that all the contents of the little room — flowers, furniture, and curtains, — waved and trembled, even to the hearts of the four soldiers.

These heart rending paroxysms, which made sad inroads upon her peerless beauty, became at last intolerable to one of the dragoons, who left the room, preferring to run the risk of being punished rather than be compelled to gaze upon such an agonizing spectacle.

One of his comrades followed his example, but Olympe paid no heed to their movements.

" I can stand imprisonment, stripes, anything you please," said one of the men to the other; " but I do not propose to be there presently when the smoke from that volley blows in upon her face."

And the dragoon crouched upon the stairs, holding his hands over his ears.

Olympe sobbed on, kissing Bannière's wedding-coat the while.

Suddenly one of the soldiers, who, despite the sobs and tears which tore his heart, had remained at his post, approached Olympe, with a forlorn hope of checking the tide of her grief, and not knowing just how to begin to implore her to take pity on herself, he said:

" Pardon, my little woman, but you are losing something."

With that he picked up from the floor a square envelope which had fallen from the coat, and handed it to Olympe.

The cool paper and the sharp corner which hurt her hand aroused the young woman, who looked up at her interlocutor.

She took the envelope absently, and recognized it as the letter from Monsieur de Mailly which each of them had declined, from motives of delicacy, to read on their wedding-night; it had been left in the pocket of Bannière's wedding-coat, and had been thrown into the chest with the coat by the femme-de-chambre.

The thought of Monsieur de Mailly awoke neither love nor anger nor hate in Olympe's breast.

Yet he was the real author of this calamity; yet he had written to the major to give him those severe and precise instructions, in obedience to which poor Bannière had been denied pardon or reprieve. Monsieur de Mailly, therefore, was the cause of this innocent's death.

Olympe mechanically broke the seal, simply that she might be busied with something which Bannière had touched.

The envelope fell to the floor, leaving the letter in the hands of Olympe, whose eyes fell upon the following lines, —

MADAME, — Since you are about to wed, I ought to make you a wedding-present, and I do not think I can offer you a more precious one than your husband's liberty.

Monsieur Bannière enlisted in my dragoons; they are looking for him, hunting him as a deserter, and if they capture him, they will take him from you; for, as I am on the point of setting out for Vienna, I shall not be there to defend him. I have given extremely severe orders for the punishment of offences of this nature among my troops, and the king's regulations are precise and unmistakable.

You will find in this cover a leave of absence, antedated. I have dated it on the day following that on which he was released from prison, that is to say, on the very day of his flight from the barracks.

By these means he is free from all danger of annoyance, and will belong to you absolutely. If I have been able to help make your happiness complete, which has been the constant object of my wishes ever since I have known you, I shall consider myself once more your obliged and fortunate servant,

COMTE DE MAILLY

Olympe leaped to her feet with a piercing shriek which brought the dragoons who had left the room back to her side in short order.

She held in one hand the count's letter, and in the other a paper on which were written these three lines: —

Good for unlimited leave of absence granted by me, Colonel of the Mailly regiment, to the dragoon Bannière, voluntary recruit.

LYONS, 28th March, 1729.

"Why, then," cried Olympe, gasping for breath. and waving the paper in the faces of the dragoons, who thought she had gone mad, —" why — why, then he is saved!"

"Saved, do you say — who?"

"Bannière. my husband!"

The dragoons glanced at one another, shrugging their shoulders at the sight of the poor woman's mad joy.

She realized what was passing in their minds, and, burning with impatience to make them understand what had happened, she cried, —

"Just read, read! It's his leave of absence, his leave of absence! He had leave of absence signed by his colonel! Let me pass, let me pass, I say!"

The dragoons barred her passage.

"Oh, read it! pray, pray read it!" shrieked Olympe, in despair.

God willed that one of them knew how to read.

"Why, it's true, it's true!" he exclaimed; "here's the poor fellow's leave of absence signed by our colonel!"

"Well, quickly, quickly, then!" cried the others; "come, come, poor girl!"

"Do you go," said one of them; "run ahead, run, run!"

"Oh, *mon Dieu!* oh, *mon Dieu!*" cried Olympe, following the soldier at a distance, and rushing along the boulevard.

But Bannière was already far away; he had a lead of a quarter of an hour over those who were running after him.

Olympe called God and his angels to assist her; she longed for wings for the good soldier who had preceded her, tearing along as if Satan were at his heels.

At last she arrived at the entrance to the enclosure, crying "Pardon!" and waving above her head the precious leave of absence.

She saw the dragoons drawn up in line, and shouting in response to her cries; she rushed into the ranks, pushing the crowd aside, still crying "Pardon!" and still waving her hand.

Suddenly, just as she espied Bannière standing by himself against a wall, the horrible, death-dealing explosion rent the air, and the body which her eyes had just seen standing proudly erect upon its legs, wavered and fell upon the sand, half hidden by a cloud of smoke.

A thousand cries of grief swallowed up Olympe's agonized scream.

She fell into Champmeslé's arms, surrounded by a score of compassionate officers.

Cold, speechless, terrible in her agony, she held out to them the paper which, a second sooner, would have saved her husband's life.

A deep wave of grief and regret overwhelmed the little troop, and the officers themselves were bowed with the weight of the innocent blood which fell in fiery drops upon their heads.

The shock was so great that the dead man was completely forgotten in the outburst of sympathy for the widow.

Bannière, stretched upon the ground, was bleeding to death from five fatal wounds, all in the chest.

A sixth bullet had broken his arm.

The messengers of death had spared his face, which was more noble and beautiful in the death agony than it had ever been in the happiest days of his life.

Olympe went to where he lay, kneeled beside him, leaned over his trembling frame, and called him by his name.

He opened his eyes, already dimmed by the shadow of death; and as he recognized his wife, his face was lighted up with a last glad smile.

He tried to hold out his arms to her, but could raise but one from the ground; the other had, as we have said, been shattered.

Olympe placed her lips upon her husband's, fixed her eyes intently upon his, and slowly drained the cup of life in that supreme last embrace.

She uttered a feeble cry. Her heart had broken.

At once her strength failed her; her head swam; she lost her balance, and fell by the side of her beloved, in the warm crimson flood in which Bannière's life was ebbing away.

Bannière, whom God had vouchsafed to let live to enjoy this last embrace, cast a grateful glance toward heaven; then letting his eyes rest lovingly upon the noble creature who, though stricken after him, had gone before him, he murmured, —

"Oh, my God, I thank thee! She will be wholly mine in the other world, as in this."

And he died.

Champmeslé kneeled beside the two martyrs, and did not leave them until they were laid side by side in the same tomb.

Over them he had said his first marriage Mass, and over them he said his first Mass for the dead.

EPILOGUE.

At almost the same hour which witnessed the deaths of Olympe and Bannière at Lyons, a door of the *petits appartemens* at Versailles was opened stealthily, and a lovely woman, enveloped in a cloak which but partially hid her disordered attire, stole secretly out of the closet which adjoined the bedroom of Louis XV.

She seemed to be looking for some one whom she did not find.

Two men, however, were waiting at the foot of the stairs.

One was the Duc de Pecquigny, who was regularly on duty for that day, and the other Monsieur le Duc de Richelieu, who was doing voluntary duty.

The last-named was detaining the other with a smile, although Pecquigny seemed to think that they might find a more convenient place than a staircase to converse at five o'clock in the morning.

" What in the devil's name makes you keep me here, when I want to go somewhere else ? " he asked.

" Stay just a few seconds more."

" What for ? "

" Because I want to show you something."

" Very well! tell me what it is that you want to show me."

" Look there," said Richelieu, pointing to the female form descending the stairs.

" Madame de Mailly coming out of the king's closet so early in the morning ! " cried Pecquigny.

" Say so late, rather. "

" Why so ? "

" Because she went in there last evening. "

Pecquigny looked a second time at the countess, who approached them triumphantly with glistening eyes.

" Ah ! " he exclaimed, bewildered by the apparition which his rival had so cunningly forced upon him.

" Well, Countess ? " asked Richelieu ; for he saw that on this occasion it would be safe to ask questions.

The countess opened her cloak with a shamelessness worthy of the courtesans of old, and uttered these few words which lighted the fires of joy in Richelieu's heart, and pulverized Pecquigny's hopes, —

" *Oh, Duke, for mercy's sake, see how that rascal has treated me !* " [1]

Thereupon, with an indescribable smile, she disappeared.

" Well, " said Richelieu to Pecquigny, " I fancy they will not accuse the king of being a child any longer. Vive Henri IV. !

" Now, " he continued, turning on his heel, " if you want to go, we will go ; I have nothing else to learn here or to teach you, for I presume that you know now as much as I do. "

" Ah, upon my word ! " said Pecquigny. " It was just as well that Olympe did not care to go on with the

---

[1] " At last Madame de Mailly emerged in a sort of amorous deshabille from the room in which she had been alone with the king, and passing before those who were interested in knowing the result of her venture, she said to them only these very significant words : ' See for mercy's sake, how that rascal has treated me ! ' " — BOISJOURDAIN, *Mémoires historiques et anecdotiques*, vol. ii. p. 208.

experiment, and that she has gone to play the shepherdess in the provinces; she would have been beaten. It is pretty clear that actresses have no chance beside duchesses! "

Poor Olympe!

TO THE READER.

A MELANCHOLY story is it not, which I have told, — the more so as the vice which it contains is almost as sad as the tears.

It is not the fact that I did not hesitate to let Bannière die, because of the terrible accident of a letter lying forgotten in a coat-pocket, but inexorable history was at my elbow; history forbade me to show any mercy, and I obeyed its commands.

For it is real history which I have been narrating, and not a romance: that poor heart whose beating you have seen cease did once actually beat; that chest which you have seen heaving with emotion and bathed in blood was really pierced by bullets.

You search your memory, and the name of Bannière suggests nothing to you. No, his was an obscure life and an obscure death; and the whim one day seized me to let a little light in upon the almost unknown facts concerning them.

Do you doubt what I say! Look, then; cast your eye over this notice which I borrow from the biography of dramatic artists, — from Lemazurier.

BANNIÈRE.

Few first appearances have resulted in so varied an assortment of extraordinary occurrences as that of the actor in question; the reception accorded him by the public at his first attempt would have been sufficient to discourage twenty of the most intrepid beginners of ordinary mould. But Bannière was a Gascon, and the natives of the fortunate regions watered by the Garonne are no more lacking in self-assurance than in wit.

Born at Toulouse about the beginning of the eighteenth century, of one of the best families of that great city, Bannière received a very good education.   Destined to enter the ecclesiastical profession, he passed some years in an orthodox seminary, where he studied hard and faithfully. He devoted himself with especial diligence to those studies which were essential for the profession which his parents wished him to adopt, and the success which he met with aroused strong hopes that he would shine in the pulpit. However, he did not pursue the career in which he had made so auspicious a beginning, but, thinking that greater prizes were to be won at the bar, he exchanged his little frock for the gown of an advocate. He did not wear it for long. Yielding to the fickleness of his character, he ceased to be attracted by the study of jurisprudence, and plunged headlong into geometry, in which he made rapid progress.

After having quitted the society of theologians for that of jurists, and the latter for geometricians, one might have thought that he was fixed for life ; but he was nothing of the sort. Carried away by an eager longing for a military career quite natural in a young man, he abandoned mathematics for the profession of arms, and enlisted in a dragoon regiment, in which he served for some time.

The leisure afforded by garrison life made it easy for him to cultivate a growing taste for literature. He wrote a tragedy entitled "La Mort de Jules César," produced it at Toulouse, and took the leading part himself. Having had the good fortune to give the lie to the familiar proverb, and to be a prophet in his own country, the applause which was showered upon him as author and as actor turned his head, and awoke in him the desire to devote himself to the representation of dramatic works ; and a dispute which he had with a professional actor, who claimed that his talents were superior to Bannière's, turned the scale finally.

Without previous connection with any provincial company

and with no experience beyond an occasional appearance in amateur performances in the bourgeois circles of Toulouse, he did not hesitate to present himself to the gentlemen of the chamber. Marvelling at his assurance, they granted him an order to appear at the Comédie, by virtue of which he made his bow for the first time on Thursday, the 9th June, 1729, in the rôle of Mithridates.

Faithful to the historical characteristics of the Gascon, he sent for the prompter some time before the rising of the curtain, and said to him, with a degree of self-conceit which could be equalled by no other people on earth : "I tell you beforehand, Monsieur, that I shall not need your services. I am perfectly sure of my memory, so I beg you not to prompt me, even if I should seem to forget my lines."

The prompter promised to obey his instructions, and the curtain rose. Bannière had not forgotten his studies of the old days when he aspired to success as an orator; he walked to the front of the stage, nerved himself for a great rhetorical effort, and addressed to the pit a very well-rounded little speech, in which he solicited such indulgence as he might need, skilfully bringing in a compliment to Baron, whom he said he had always in mind as the model to be copied. This adroit proceeding was loudly applauded, and put the audience in a favorable disposition. But the debutant had not spoken ten lines of his part, when, absolutely overlooking the necessity for moderation and discretion in gesture and declamation, he threw into both, beyond the ordinary vivacity of his race, so much ranting, furious passion, little suited to the majestic tone of the tragedy, that the spectators, instead of being moved or inspired with awe, could not refrain from shouts of laughter throughout the whole performance.

Bannière was not in the least disconcerted, but continued to act his part on the same lines to the last word, without allowing himself to be discouraged. When the play was at an end, he harangued the audience a second time.

"Messieurs," said he, "though the lesson I have learned from my first appearance is deeply humiliating, I invite you to come again on Saturday to see if I have profited by it."

These words, uttered boldly and confidently, caused renewed laughter and considerable applause, some of which, no
doubt, was ironical; they made it plain that although the
young man's acting bristled with extraordinary faults, he was
at least a youth of pluck and resolution.

The report of what had taken place on this memorable
occasion, the speeches and ranting, and the unblushing assurance of the Toulousan actor, quickly spread all over Paris.
Bannière was the principal topic of conversation in all social
circles, and there was a tremendous rush for seats on Saturday
the 11th, when according to his promise he played Agamemnon in "Iphigénie en Aulide."

Those of the audience who had seen him on Thursday, as
well as those who had heard the story of his inordinate ranting, expected to laugh at him, and to have as much sport as at
the most amusing of farces. They were all deceived alike.
Bannière had taken his previous lesson so well to heart that
he had succeeded in changing his style of acting completely,
in moderating it, and confining it within proper limits; instead of evoking peals of laughter, he was rewarded with
universal applause, and the most exacting judges agreed that
it was fairly earned.

He seemed a little youthful for the line of parts in which
he made his early appearances, and indeed one can hardly
expect to produce a complete illusion in the parts of Mithridates and Agamemnon, at twenty-eight or nine, which was
Bannière's age in 1729; but he was found to possess many
excellent qualifications for such parts, and they were fully
appreciated. He was tall, well-made, with a manly cast of
countenance, black hair, fine limbs, and a noble expression.
On the side of moral fitness for the profession, he was found
to be clever and quick-witted, and to have an admirable voice
with plenty of power behind it.

He subsequently played the Gascon Marquis in "Mé-
nechmes" in most original fashion, and made a great hit in it,
as he did in the rôles of Pyrrhus in "Andromache," Joad in
"Athalie," and Cinna, in which he appeared one after the
other.

Thus far everything went well with him. He displayed genuine talent, and it seemed probable that he would become a member of the king's company. A terrible incident put an end to his acting and his life.

We have said that he had enlisted in the dragoons. The colonel of his regiment learned that he was acting at Paris instead of doing guard duty in garrison. He had him arrested and brought before a court-martial, which sentenced him to be shot. Many people, notably the members of the Comédie troupe, begged that he might be pardoned; but nothing availed to save him, or to mitigate the severity of martial law, which then provided that deserters should be put to death. But Bannière was not really a deserter; he had left the regiment by virtue of a leave of absence which had not expired, but he had the misfortune to lose it, and paid for his carelessness with his life.

Now you know what is written in history, and you can compare it with the work of the poet.

History created Bannière, and I have created Olympe.

If I did wrong to bring her into the world to be our hero's ruin, I have at least a respectable precedent to fall back upon, — that of God taking from Adam's side the woman who was destined to lead not one man only but all mankind to perdition.

As for Madame de Mailly, I have confined myself strictly to the truth in regard to her. Forced upon Louis XV. by Fleury and Richelieu, she reigned over him for ten years without attempting to rule over France. It is true that she was a woman of expedients; one of those which she employed was to give to the king her two sisters. Her two sisters, did I say? I should have said her *three* sisters, — Madame de Lauraguais, Madame de Vintimille, and Madame de la Tournelle, who became Madame de Châteauroux.

Unfortunately for poor Madame de Mailly, Madame

de Châteauroux, less complaisant than herself, preferred undivided power, and demanded that the king should discard her rival.

Precipitated from the pinnacle of favor and influence, Madame de Mailly withdrew from the world, to all intent; like another La Vallière, she sought consolation in religion. This woman, who used to be seen at court richly and handsomely clad, absorbed in dissipation and the pursuit of pleasure, was noticeable after her fall, says the chronicler of the eighteenth century, only for her extreme modesty, her gentle ways, and her humble piety.

It was said that she went one day to hear Père Renaud preach, and arrived after he was in the pulpit and the sermon had begun. In making her way to her seat, although she was as careful as possible, she could not avoid causing some confusion and disturbance.

"Well," said a man, as she passed him, "that's a good deal of noise for a harlot to make."

"Since you recognize her," said Madame de Mailly, "pray to God for her soul!"

This is the last word which history has noted from the lips of the ex-favorite. Must we not agree that it is sublime in its spirit of humility and penitence?

THE END.